The
HOUSE
for
LOST CHILDREN

BOOKS BY MARTY WINGATE

The HOUSE for LOST CHILDREN

MARTY WINGATE

bookouture

Published by Bookouture in 2025

An imprint of Storyfire Ltd.
Carmelite House
50 Victoria Embankment
London EC4Y 0DZ

www.bookouture.com

The authorised representative in the EEA is Hachette Ireland
8 Castlecourt Centre
Dublin 15 D15 XTP3
Ireland
(email: info@hbgi.ie)

ISBN: 978-1-80550-212-8
eBook ISBN: 978-1-80550-211-1

To Leighton

PROLOGUE

SUFFOLK

Lone Survivor of Indiscriminate Bombing Raid

Entire Terrace Demolished in Bold Daylight Attack
Children Mourn Their Mothers' Deaths

Workers digging through the rubble of a terrace in Poplar that was destroyed by a Nazi raid carried out three days ago, which killed the mothers of children at local Hazel End Charity School, were shocked to find a survivor among the destruction. A girl, age 6, had been buried alive, but was found unharmed and is being looked after as the charity school makes plans to evacuate.

Louisa's heart raced. She laid a hand on the newspaper and felt the terror of the bomb strike – the screams of the women, the explosion, the bricks flying everywhere. Then, for that small child, silence. Silence that felt like an eternity.

She heard footsteps and took a sharp breath to clear her

head, then climbed the ladder and returned to what she should've been doing – repairing the blackout curtain.

'Lady Brightford?'

Louisa glanced down to see the cook, Iris Darnley, neat as ever. She stood with her hands behind her back as if she were about to recite a poem at school.

'There's no need for the "Lady Brightford" business,' Louisa said as she returned to fussing with the curtain. 'It's just the two of us.'

'Can I help?' Iris asked.

Earlier that morning, Louisa had whipped the blackout curtain open with such vigour that the corner had come loose. She certainly didn't need a fine from the Air Raid Precautions warden in the village for showing a speck of light. She couldn't afford the two pounds – but also she would never let Oxburrow give any advantage to the enemy.

'No, thank you, I've sorted it now.'

'The post arrived,' Iris said.

Louisa began hurrying down the ladder. 'Is there a letter from David?'

Where was Louisa's son at that moment – chasing down a German bomber over the Channel? Mothers weren't allowed to know details, and that made Louisa feel sometimes better and sometimes worse. David had joined up to fight for God and Country, but mostly to gain his father's approval. He was twenty years old, but there were moments when Louisa could only think of him as the light-hearted boy who loved books and a ramble through the wood. Surely that boy hadn't disappeared altogether when he became an RAF pilot?

'No, nothing from David,' Iris said, and added, 'Careful coming down.'

It was her reply and not the warning that slowed Louisa's last few steps. Standing on the floor once again, she brushed off her dust-coat and pushed her hair off her face with the back of a hand. 'I hope it isn't all bills,' she said.

Iris didn't answer, but presented the stack of letters to Louisa. The one at the top caused her to catch her breath – a crisp, cream-coloured envelope addressed to her with 'Bates, Lowrey and Lowrey' written in the corner.

Louisa snatched the envelope and clutched it to her breast. Not bothering with a letter opener and with her hands trembling, she tore it open, mumbling as she read. 'The marriage of... The Lord Brightford... Louisa, Lady Brightford... judge having decreed... divorce absolute...'

She gasped as it hit her like a blow.

'I'm free, Iris.' Louisa looked up with shining eyes. 'Free.' The word was sweet liquid in her mouth.

Iris whooped and did a jig where she stood while Louisa danced round the library, whirling as if she were the ballerina she'd wanted to be as a girl, instead of the gangly woman she'd grown into. Until she stubbed her toe on the corner of the chesterfield sofa.

'Ouch!'

They both collapsed on the sofa, laughing. Panting slightly, Louisa took off her shoe and rubbed her toe. 'Let's have a tot of something to celebrate.'

Iris poured two sherries from the drinks cabinet and perched on the low table across from Louisa, who ran her fingers through her hair, pulling out hairpins.

'Damn. Where do hairpins go?' she asked. 'I remember having handfuls of them and now I'm down to three.'

'You'd better hold on to what you've got,' Iris said. 'You won't find hairpins in the shops now. They've most likely gone for the war.'

'Hairpins and servants,' Louisa said.

The small household at Oxburrow had shrunk once war had been declared the previous September. The young men signed up and the young women left to become typists and secretaries or to work in a munitions factory.

'We've still got old Figg in the garden,' Louisa pointed out. 'And we can bring in a girl from the village if need be.'

'And pay her from what?' Iris asked. 'Hasn't the household account been cut in half?'

Louisa didn't see the need to answer. It had been part of the arrangement with Max. He received his freedom – a divorce due to desertion, a category that had been made legal only the year before. He was free to be with his companion, a wealthy widow who remained a shadowy figure in Louisa's mind. In return, Louisa received Oxburrow on a ninety-nine-year lease.

'The household account doesn't matter,' Louisa said. 'What matters is that I'm free and we have more important things to attend to.'

'What's that supposed to mean?' Iris asked. When Louisa didn't answer, Iris shook a finger at her. 'What have you been up to? You aren't thinking of taking in paying guests, are you? It would never work – there's a war on. Who can manage a holiday in the country these days?'

'Yes, there's a war on,' Louisa repeated, 'and we need to do our part. There are children to be saved.'

She had so wanted David to have brothers and sisters. That was no longer possible, but this was.

'Children?' Iris echoed. She shook her head. 'Louisa, you can't!'

'I can!' Louisa said with vehemence. '*We* can. We can make a difference, Iris. We'll take in children from London, orphans and evacuees. They'll be safe here – we're in the middle of nowhere.'

'You'd take in half of London if they'd let you.' Iris clicked her tongue. 'Who have you spoken to?'

'I'll ring William Lowrey. He'll know what to do.' Louisa took the newspaper she'd been reading and held it out to Iris. 'I want us to take in these children, from Hazel End Charity School.'

Iris read the item with a sigh of resignation. Louisa ignored it. Her heart and mind were set and she would not be moved. Already she could hear the children. Their laughter echoed down the corridors, their feet slapped on the stone floors and their shouts rang out as they ran outdoors into the golden autumn light of the Suffolk fields and hedgerows.

CHAPTER 1

My darling mum,

Is it damson time? I'm sorry I can't be clawing my way through the hedgerows and climbing up trees for you – mainly I'm sorry to miss the jam! I hope you and Iris are keeping each other company at Oxburrow. Quiet moments are precious these days, and I'm taking a few to write as we wait for word to scramble. I'll hand this letter off to be posted now.

Much love,

David

Louisa had wasted no time in ringing Bates, Lowrey and Lowrey. She had a chat with William, who promised to do what he could for her in regards to the children from Hazel End Charity School. But he warned her that it was entirely possible they had already found another home. Wouldn't the Women's Voluntary Service help her find suitable evacuees?

True, she could've contacted the local organiser for the

WVS. But going through William – the firm had been solicitors for the Brightford estate for generations – was the most direct route. 'I'll leave you to sort it out,' she said.

Children were children, and Louisa would take any who needed refuge, but the schoolchildren from the bombed terrace were different. Without knowing why, she already considered them hers.

The next day, a clerk from the solicitor's office rang with a message from Mr Lowrey, who was in court. The children and two teachers from Hazel End school would arrive Saturday. The clerk added that Mr Lowrey had said the 'stars aligned'.

'Saturday!' Louisa exclaimed as she and Iris walked into the Debden Ash village hall, where the WVS carried out their war work. 'Saturday, Saturday!'

'You'll wear that word out,' Iris teased. 'But look here, it's Tuesday – shouldn't we have stayed back and got to work?'

'We'll start first thing tomorrow,' Louisa replied. 'I'll ask Minns to help. You've mentioned the divorce to Mrs Byers, and it would look odd if we didn't turn up today. We always come on Tuesdays, and I want to get it over with.'

Iris carried a bundle of worn bedsheets – good enough to be cut into strips – and Louisa toted a collection of old sweaters from Max's wardrobe. They'd be turned into blankets for injured servicemen. Just not David – please, not David.

'She'll have told the others,' Iris said. 'Mrs Byers.'

'What will they say about a divorced woman among their group?' Louisa wondered.

'You can't worry about what others say,' Iris replied.

'Right then,' Louisa said and set off at a brisk pace.

Their steps slowed as they neared the village hall. Louisa listened to the buzz of activity within, then pushed open the door. Conversation ceased and there was an uneasy quiet.

'Hello, all,' Louisa said with a knot in her throat. 'We've

only a few bits and bobs today. Shall I take them into the knit-ting room?'

The women avoided her gaze.

'I'll take them,' Barbara Byers offered. 'Your donations are always welcome. Come on, everyone, back to work.'

A sturdy young woman with her black hair in plaits pinned over her head hurried up to Louisa, breathless, as if she'd run a mile. 'It's so kind of you to come, Lady Brightford, when you are... are...' She faltered, searching for words. 'Are you still Lady Brightford? I mean...'

'Hush, Minns,' someone whispered.

Louisa smiled. 'Yes, Minns, I am still Lady Brightford – divorce or not. Who knows – maybe there'll be another Lady Brightford someday. I hope we don't receive each other's post!'

Barbara sniggered, Minns giggled, and a collective sigh of relief spread through the room.

'Just Louisa will do,' she said. 'For all of you.'

She didn't think that would fly with many of the women, but she wanted to make the offer.

'Have you brought a cake for tea, Iris?' one of the women asked.

Louisa sighed inwardly. *There, that's done with.* And everyone returned to their sewing and knitting.

Later, Mrs Byers set out four jars of raspberry jam, and a small bidding war erupted. When it ended, two shillings sixpence had been raised for the Red Cross parcel fund.

'I hear children are coming,' Mrs Byers said to Louisa while they had tea.

'Yes, Saturday. Arranged swiftly by our solicitor.'

'Remember that we have a room of children's clothes ready. Come back when you know what you need.'

At the end of the afternoon, Louisa said her goodbyes and walked out to wait for Iris. Mrs Greet, who lived in the old rectory, approached her, her tone confidential.

'This is a trying time,' she said.

'Yes,' Louisa said, unsure how else to reply.

'In these situations, there's always the expectation of a guilty party, isn't there?' Mrs Greet said softly. 'People look to see who is at fault.'

Louisa's jaw dropped and she was just about to tell Mrs Greet to mind her own business when Iris came out. Good thing, too. Better to part on polite terms.

On their way back to Oxburrow, Louisa confided in Iris.

'"There's always a guilty party," she said to me. Implying I was the one. Ha! I live like a nun while Max swans round London with his wealthy widow. Not that I envy her,' Louisa added.

Next morning, Louisa fetched the post from under a stone at the door. The postman had become accustomed to doing this as the house staff shrank. Louisa had thought she might cut a hole in the old oak door so that the post could be put through. It was how she had grown up – proper letter box, milk delivered to the front door and, if you needed a fresh loaf you walked to the shops. People had always known Lady Brightford to be a bit different – but did she want them thinking she'd truly gone round the bend?

She sorted the mail, setting aside bills, then noticed a plain brown envelope with a typewritten address. She slid her finger under the flap and opened it.

Dear Lady Brightford,

This is to inform you that the War Office has requisitioned Oxburrow Manor for use by His Majesty's Territorial Army for the training of fresh units. You and any others in the house must vacate before 29 September.

Sincerely,

Harold Courtwright, Second Undersecretary

'The beast!' Louisa shouted, rushing to the back stairs and down to the kitchen, bursting in on Iris as she poured the tea. 'Look at this' – she thrust the letter at her – 'will you look at what Max has done!'

Because she knew it was Max behind it. He worked at the War Office.

Iris took the letter, her brow furrowing as she read.

Louisa paced, fury bubbling. 'He planned this,' she whispered. 'He got his divorce, but he can't leave it alone. He wants to raze Oxburrow, sell the land. He's using the army to drive me out.'

'Don't jump to conclusions,' Iris warned.

'The army requisitioned Oldbury Park near Colchester. Within six months it had *burned to the ground*! Once Oxburrow is destroyed, I'll have nothing and Max will still have the land. He's holding a grudge,' Louisa said darkly. 'He thinks I'll give up. Not a chance.'

She snatched the letter from Iris and stalked to the telephone room beside the entrance hall. Her fingers trembled as she dialled.

'Bates, Lowrey and Lowrey,' a smooth voice answered.

'Good afternoon. Lady Brightford here – may I speak to Mr Lowrey?'

'One moment, my lady,' the voice replied.

She pleaded her case to William – her hope that the army wouldn't take Oxburrow and her determination to keep the children safe.

'I do appreciate the faith you have in me,' William Lowrey said in his usual calm fashion. 'But you may want to consider that your compensation from the army would be higher than the fifty pounds you'll get for the children.'

'The money doesn't matter,' Louisa said. The money did matter – she was now poor as the proverbial church mouse – but the children and thwarting Max mattered more. In that order.

She restated her case and ended with, 'I had no one else to turn to.'

'Yes, all right. I will see what I can do,' Lowrey said.

'Thank you. Thank you so much,' Louisa said, tears welling up. 'We will be ready for the children on Saturday.'

'We've got Minns to work for the day and Figg is coming up from the garden,' Louisa said, returning to the kitchen. 'We'll need to move the servants' beds from the attic into the second-floor bedrooms, and rearrange the furniture to make space.'

Iris shot her a sceptical look as she put a beef bone on to simmer for the morning. 'Your pie-in-the-sky attitude can take us only so far. You can't magic the army away if they come rumbling up the drive in their lorries. They're bigger than the both of us.'

Louisa ignored her pessimistic attitude. Even in school, they had been like two squabbling spinster sisters – pragmatic Iris and dreamer Louisa, fiercely devoted to each other.

She tied on her apron, trying to feel hopeful despite the uncertainty. 'Let the army act like Goliath – I'll keep my spirits up if you've got your slingshot ready.'

Iris grinned. 'Then let's get to it.'

Minns arrived eager and ready. Her sole occupation in life, apart from her work with the WVS, was taking care of her grandad and great-uncle, and so she looked for any opportunity to get out of the house.

Old Figg came up from his cottage beyond the kitchen garden, fit for duty. Surprisingly, by the end of the day they had managed to move wardrobes, washstands and beds from the servants' quarters in the attic down into the new dormitories. Minns left with a jar of pickled eggs and a shilling, while Figg enjoyed a hearty supper before heading off to the pub with sixpence.

On Thursday, Louisa and Iris washed mountains of bedlinens, ran them through the mangle, then hung them outside, where they flapped and snapped in the wind under clear Suffolk skies. Finally, at sunset, they sank into chairs at the kitchen worktable with cups of tea, exhausted but satisfied.

Oxburrow still looked much the same – peeling wallpaper in the library corner, the roof still leaky – but after two hard days of work Louisa's pride burned brighter than her fatigue.

'We did it,' she said. 'And we have another entire day before the children arrive on Saturday.'

'Did we bring enough beds down?' Iris asked.

'If not, we'll take yours up,' Louisa replied with a straight face.

'Ha ha.'

Iris's quarters were down the hall in the basement – once the butler's, then the housekeeper's, and now her own, since the housekeeper had gone years ago.

'Will the children go to the village school?' Iris asked.

Debden Ash's school had only two teachers – one old and one young – and limited space. Louisa shook her head. 'It doesn't seem like it. Our children have their own teachers coming with them.'

'Where will they have lessons? And how will they get here from London – the station's miles away.'

'It'll all work out,' said Louisa, rising. 'We'd best finish bringing in the laundry.'

'Today, we must deal with the damsons,' Iris said first thing on Friday morning. 'They won't last long.'

They set to work after breakfast, cooking down the fruit with the sugar rations they'd been saving. It was a bumper crop, and only in the late afternoon did they finally finish. Louisa stood in the kitchen, hands on her hips, admiring the rows of jars lined up on the long table.

Louisa had worn her oldest apron and tied her hair back with a worn tea towel, which was now splattered purple. She paused, pushed a sticky lock of hair from her face, then licked her finger.

'They won't go without jam, will they?' She grabbed a bucket of scraps. 'I'll take this to the chickens, and after that I'm having a long, hot bath.'

Louisa stepped into the yard and made her way down to the chicken run. The hens gathered along the fence chattering *tuck-tuck-tuck* as she neared, with the cockerels strutting behind. But then they turned away from her as one and stared up the rise towards the drive.

Louisa looked, too, shading her eyes against the late sun. A stand of scrubby hollies obscured her view of the drive, but she heard the rumble of an engine – and her stomach clenched. Had the army arrived?

She hurried up the rise, bucket in hand, and paused, staring at the place where the drive emerged from the spinney into the wide forecourt. What could she do? How could she turn the army away?

The engine roared louder, and with it came boisterous singing – 'We're Going to Hang Out the Washing on the

Siegfried Line'. But it wasn't soldiers. Suddenly, out of the woods, a charabanc appeared.

Louisa gasped at the sight of the open-topped coach, with its fluttering canvas roof. Could she be really seeing this? Who went on holiday in wartime?

Bang, went the coach's exhaust, and a squeal rang out. Louisa peered at the travellers and then froze.

The children had arrived.

The charabanc stopped and the children cheered, leapt from their seats and spilled out onto the forecourt.

'Sit down!'

The command came from a woman older than Louisa. Her grey hair was scraped and stowed under a small saucer hat, and she wore a grey wool suit. She stood at the front of the row, her steely tone demanding silence and obedience. The children climbed back into their seats.

'Mr Barrie,' she continued, 'please keep them under control.'

Mr Barrie, in the last row of seats, stood and removed his hat. He ruffled his thick russet hair, which stood up like a stook of hay. He surveyed the scene with a serious expression – forecourt, house, landscape. He was like a soldier on reconnaissance. Finally, his eyes settled on Louisa. She looked away.

The children waited, and the woman stepped down and glanced about until her eyes fell on Louisa.

'You there,' she called, 'I am Mrs Harrison and this is Mr Barrie. Please tell Lady Brightford the children from Hazel End have arrived.'

Louisa opened her mouth to speak, but shouts erupted and Mrs Harrison turned her attention to the children.

Two boys in the middle row scuffled. One was clutching a rucksack and crying for help, while the other struggled to wrench it free.

They fought until Mr Barrie's voice – quiet but clear – cut through. 'Johnno, listen!'

Silence fell, and in the stillness came the roar of engines. It was a sound becoming commonplace in the Suffolk skies, but to Louisa no less ominous.

Everyone looked up as five aeroplanes sliced through the single cloud. 'Hurricanes!' Johnno called out.

'Where are they headed, Alf?' Mr Barrie asked.

The smaller boy, who had kept hold of his rucksack, watched the planes pass overhead. 'South, south-east, sir.'

With a nod, Mr Barrie said, 'Right then, out you come.'

The children spilled out, tumbling onto the gravel like fledglings leaving the nest. They giggled and scrambled to explore. Mr Barrie kept an eye on them as he spoke to the driver, then began unloading cases.

Louisa's gaze returned to the sky, lost in thoughts of David, until Mrs Harrison barked, 'Didn't you hear me? Go and find Lady Brightford and tell her we've arrived.'

'But—' Louisa started.

'I don't care if you are a scullery maid,' Mrs Harrison said, voice rising above the din. 'Find someone who will tell her.'

Louisa took a deep breath, then shouted, 'I am Lady Brightford!' Her voice carried, silencing the children. She added in a quieter tone, 'And you are a day early.'

Mrs Harrison looked flustered. 'I'm terribly sorry, my lady. The opportunity came to depart today instead of tomorrow. Even leaving this morning we were delayed – all the road signs are gone and we became quite lost.'

Louisa's good humour returned. 'It's not just the signs. The village is tucked into a fold in the landscape and easy to overlook. It's a pity your journey took so long. If you'd arrived earlier – I might've put you to work making jam.' She addressed the children. 'You are very welcome to Oxburrow. I hope you'll consider it your home for as long as you need.'

The children looked at her warily. One girl, thin with nearly white hair, asked, 'What have you got there?'

Louisa looked down, and realised that she still held the bucket. 'Just some bits of damsons for the chickens.' At once self-conscious, she pulled off her tea towel, letting her hair fall to her shoulders.

'Chickens?' Johnno asked.

'Yes,' Louisa said, pointing down the rise. 'They're down behind those trees. Want to see?'

A surge of children rushed down the slope as if a starting pistol had gone off.

Mr Barrie ignored the chaos, while Mrs Harrison shouted, 'Children!' reaching out to catch them, but only managing to grab one girl by the collar of her coat. She looked about eight, with brown skin and dark curls that framed her face, and the rest of her hair tied high in a band.

'Athena—' Mrs Harrison began.

'But Lady Lightfoot said we could see chickens,' Athena protested, trying to wriggle free.

Louisa laughed. 'Not "Lightfoot", Athena. My name starts with B. I'm Lady B—'

'Lady Bee?' Athena asked. 'Can we call you Lady Bee?'

'Don't be impertinent,' Mrs Harrison scolded. 'You'll address her ladyship properly.'

'Lady Bee?' Louisa repeated. 'I like it. Yes, you may call me Lady Bee.'

A few other children had lingered – one small boy and two girls.

'Who are your friends, Athena?' Louisa asked.

'I'm Priscilla.' The girl with white hair curtseyed.

'She's Priss,' Athena added. 'Should we curtsey to you?'

Louisa smiled. 'No need. You can save that for the king.'

'I'm George,' mumbled a boy in an Eeyore-like fashion. 'Pleased to meet you, Lady Bee.'

'Hello, Priss,' Louisa said. 'Hello, George.'

The other girl stood apart, as if in her own world. Smaller than Athena and Priss, she wore a soft grey-brown coat too large for her. She had a round face and small dark eyes. Her chestnut hair was cut across her forehead in a blunt fringe and hung straight at the sides. It framed a severe expression – a frown on her brow and her mouth set in a hard straight line. Her arms hung at her sides, fists clenched, as if the world was her enemy.

'Hello,' Louisa said softly. 'What's your name?'

The girl gazed at her but remained silent.

'She's Gracie,' Athena said. 'She doesn't talk.'

'Athena,' Mrs Harrison reproved her.

Louisa's heart gave an extra thump as she knelt to be eye-to-eye with Gracie. She offered a gentle smile. 'It's all right. You don't have to talk. Do you want to see the chickens? Take my hand, and we'll go together.'

She held out her hand. Gracie stared at it, then started to tremble violently. Louisa reached out instinctively, fearing she might be having a fit, but Gracie leapt back, fists clenched, eyes wide with fear.

'I'm sorry, love,' Louisa whispered, her voice shaking. She looked to Mrs Harrison, who sighed impatiently, then to Mr Barrie.

'Athena,' he said calmly, 'take Priss and Gracie down to the others. George, you go, too.'

'Yes, sir,' Athena said. 'C'mon, Gracie.' The girl, fists still clenched, followed in silence.

Louisa pressed her hand to her chest. 'I didn't mean to frighten her. I'm sorry.'

'Everything frightens Gracie these days,' Mrs Harrison replied.

'Was it the bombing?'

'It took its toll,' Mrs Harrison said, watching Mr Barrie sort out the luggage. 'The school governors are searching for relatives, but with little hope. The children's lives are upside down, and it shows in their behaviour – happy one minute, terrors the next.'

'Gracie isn't happy,' Louisa said quietly.

'It was different for her,' Mr Barrie said. 'She stayed home that day.'

Louisa caught her breath. 'She's the one who was buried in the rubble?'

Mr Barrie met her gaze, giving her a hard look.

She looked away down the hill toward the chicken run. She imagined the children gathered around, watching the hens, while Gracie stood apart – fists clenched, at war with the world. Something about that little girl touched her deeply, and she fought a rising sob.

'The doctor said she might recover or not,' Mrs Harrison said. 'We're not to interfere. No provoking emotions.'

Louisa's head snapped back. 'He what?'

'He said leave her be.'

'The child's in pain from the greatest loss imaginable. She needs love. Leave her be?' Louisa's voice was sharp. She looked again down the hill. 'Not bloody likely,' she muttered.

She turned back to the teachers. Mrs Harrison busied herself with her handbag, while Mr Barrie continued to watch Louisa with a sceptical expression. His face was weathered, rugged – more like a seasoned farmer than a schoolteacher. Maybe he doubted Louisa could handle this. But he would learn. The teachers had brought the children out of London; now they needed to understand that they were safe at Oxburrow Manor.

CHAPTER 3

A cacophony of squawks arose from the other side of the scrubby hollies, followed by squeals and then a boy shouting, 'Let go! Let go! Let go!'

Louisa lifted her chin and stuffed the tea towel in one pocket. She scooped up her hair, twisting and rolling it, and secured it with the three hairpins from her other pocket. She retrieved the pail of wormy damsons and smiled at the teachers. 'Well, I'll just go and see what this is about, shall I?'

She marched down the hill and, when she got within view of the chicken run, she paused. Johnno and Alf were at it again over the rucksack while the others watched – all except Gracie. She was looking up the rise at Louisa.

'Boys!' Louisa called, approaching.

Johnno stepped back. 'He wasn't supposed to bring it,' he said, pointing at the rucksack. 'Mrs Harrison said not to.'

Alf shot Louisa a fearful look, clutching the bag close to his chest – gently, as if protecting a treasure. Who could begrudge the boy a keepsake from home?

'Have you got something special in there, Alf?' Louisa asked softly, moving closer. As she approached, she saw the rucksack wriggle and heard a faint whine.

'See,' Johnno said, triumphant.

'I couldn't leave her,' Alf said in a teary whisper. 'She's got no one else.'

'May I have a look?' Louisa asked gently.

Alf looked at Johnno, then at the other children, and gently set the rucksack on the ground. He opened it, and a tiny, shivering dog blinked up at them. It had long, matted slate-grey fur and one forepaw wrapped in a dirty rag.

'It's a dog!' Athena exclaimed.

'What's her name?' Louisa asked.

'She's called Lulu,' the boy said, hope flickering. 'She's injured – probably shrapnel. She was my mum's dog, ma'am – I mean, your ladyship.'

Louisa smiled. 'You call me Lady Bee. Now, give me Lulu.'

Alf hurriedly closed the rucksack.

'No, it's all right,' Louisa said gently. 'I'd say Lulu would like her tea and then perhaps a bath. We can do that in the kitchen. Look, Mrs Darnley's here to help.'

Iris had come out, and stood watching the scene.

'So,' she said, 'you've arrived.'

'Mrs Darnley is our cook and housekeeper,' Louisa explained, then gestured to the teachers, who'd followed her. 'This is Mrs Harrison and Mr Barrie. And here are the children – Athena, Priss and... I haven't met all of you yet.'

'That's Dolly and Gloria,' Athena said. 'They're sisters.'

'I'm older,' Gloria said.

'Sisters Dolly and Gloria,' Louisa continued. 'And Johnno, Alf, George and...' She looked to Athena.

'Sydney,' the girl said.

Louisa extended her hand toward Gracie, who stood several feet away. The girl flinched at the gesture. 'This is Gracie.'

'Pleased to meet you all,' Iris said with a nod.

Mrs Harrison gave the little dog a wary look, but then turned to Iris. 'Mrs Darnley, could I have a word about housekeeping?'

'Of course,' Iris replied.

'But first, Iris,' Louisa said, handing her the dog, 'could you see to Lulu? We'll gather the luggage, then I'll take everyone inside.'

Iris headed back with Lulu in her arms, Alf watching them go. Louisa dumped the damsons into the run – the hens set upon them at once – and led the group back up the rise to the forecourt. She glanced back to see Gracie – the girl's eyes fixed on Louisa – bringing up the rear.

'I told him to leave the dog,' Mrs Harrison said sharply. 'It's enough caring for children, you shouldn't be burdened with animals, too.'

'But isn't it a lovely way to teach kindness?' Louisa replied. 'When my son David was five, a farmer was about to put down his old herding dog. David fussed so much the farmer said, "Take her, then." And he did. That old dog lived three more years. Animals teach us a lot.'

Mrs Harrison sniffed. Mr Barrie said nothing.

On the forecourt, two large suitcases sat apart – one with steel-capped corners, the other well-worn leather. Louisa suspected Mrs Harrison would claim the first, Mr Barrie the second. The rest were a jumble – small bags, some cardboard, tied with twine or bootlaces. Shipping tags dangled from the handles, each bearing a child's name. Nearby was a heap of small cardboard boxes with straps – gas masks. Louisa and Iris's hung nearly forgotten in the boot room. Now, others would share the space.

'Lady Brightford,' Mrs Harrison said, 'the children can carry their own cases.'

'I don't mind helping,' Louisa said and lifted the one marked *Gracie*. It was very light. Was there anything inside?

The children had followed them to the drive and now Mr Barrie handed out their cases.

'There was little left for the children to bring with them,' Mrs Harrison said. 'They've been sleeping at the school until the arrangements came through.'

'We'll find them new togs,' Louisa assured her. 'We have a whole room of children's clothes at the WVS – dresses, trousers, sweaters, vests and pants. Nightwear, too. Leave it to me – I'll get what they need.'

Louisa held Gracie's case out to her. She stared at it for a moment and then took it carefully without touching Louisa's hand.

'Ready, children?' Louisa asked in a cheery voice. 'Off we go!'

As Louisa turned towards the house and the children followed her, she tried to look at Oxburrow with the eye of a stranger. Built in the 1830s in what Max described as the Gothic Revival style, it was of deep red brick with decorative stonework at the windows and portico.

Architectural style mattered little to Louisa, but she had loved Oxburrow at first sight. Her devotion had only deepened as she'd settled in, had a son and watched him grow. Suffolk, with its vast skies and open fields stretching wide around her, was a world apart from her childhood home of Sheffield, nestled in the foothills of the Pennines. Oxburrow, David, Iris and the village – they were her true home now. Max had been a part of it for years, of course, but now their lives were truly separate. Starting today, the old house would have a new life.

It was a challenge to lead the children through the entrance hall – everything amazed them: tiled floors, portraits, a bust of Aristotle on a Doric column.

Finally, they climbed the grand staircase to the broad first-floor landing. There, Louisa asked Mr Barrie to wait with the boys and she led the girls up the left-hand staircase and along the corridor.

'Here you are,' she said, opening the door of a second-floor bedroom. Darkness greeted them. 'Hang on,' she said, crossing the room. She threw back the blackout curtains. 'That's better.'

Four narrow beds lined one wall, with two more opposite, on either side of the fireplace. Louisa and Iris had cobbled together trunks, cabinets and chests and placed them at the end of each bed. There had been plenty of room for everything once they had dismantled the four-poster and dragged it into the next room.

The girls, wide-eyed, crowded the doorway, with Mrs Harrison behind them.

'Which bed's mine?' Athena asked, sounding both hesitant and eager.

'You can choose whichever you like,' Louisa said. 'Come in!'

Dolly and Gloria dashed to the beds near the fireplace, shouting, 'Mine!' Athena and Priss claimed beds by the window. Mrs Harrison and Gracie waited in the hall, Gracie clutching her case.

'Gracie,' Athena called, 'you can have the bed next to mine. Mrs Harrison can have the last one.'

Mrs Harrison's face went pale. Louisa stifled a laugh and then coughed.

'It's all right, Athena,' Louisa said. 'Mrs Harrison has her own room and bathroom at the end of the corridor. Girls, your bathroom is just there. Once you're settled, you're free to look around—'

'Thank you, Lady Brightford,' Mrs Harrison said briskly. 'Girls, put away your things. Wash your hands and faces, then rest. As we are a day early, my lady, we don't expect an evening meal.'

Athena looked up from her open case. 'But I'm hungry!'

The others, except for Gracie, voiced agreement until Mrs Harrison silenced them with a sharp, 'Girls!'

'Of course we will have an evening meal,' Louisa assured them, although she herself had wondered what that might consist of. 'We'll have all the proper meals – breakfast, dinner, tea and a light supper. I'll ask Mrs Darnley about pudding too – we mustn't forget pudding.'

As the girls looked round the room, peered out of the window and chatted, Gracie opened her case just far enough to draw out a soft toy that looked as if it had been sewn from a sock. It had legs, feet, ears and a tail attached. It was singed and dirty, but Louisa could see stitched-on whiskers and round eyes. When Gracie saw Louisa watching, the girl stuffed it under her pillow.

Louisa approached, but cautiously. 'I hope you'll like your room,' she said softly, 'and I hope you'll welcome Mrs Moffatt when she comes to say hello. She's my son David's cat – black with a white bib and four stocking feet. You'll look out for her?'

Gracie stared at the bed, frowning.

'Don't dawdle, girls,' Mrs Harrison said.

Oh, let them dawdle, Louisa thought. She drew Mrs Harrison out into the corridor and said, 'I hope you'll find your own room comfortable.'

A roar of laughter came from below. Louisa excused herself and hurried down to the landing where she'd left the boys.

One of them sat on a step retying the twine on his case. Alf was racing up the stairs backwards. George stood in the middle of the landing writing in a small notebook and Johnno was arguing with Mr Barrie.

'But they sting!' the boy said. He saw Louisa and said, 'Those are beehives I saw, aren't they?'

'They are,' Louisa said. 'The kitchen garden is inside those high brick walls you saw and beyond it are the hives. We have a local beekeeper who has hives all around the village. His bees give us honey.'

'They sting,' Johnno said darkly. 'It hurts.'

'Well then, you know to keep clear of them, don't you?' Louisa said.

Mr Barrie shot her a stern look and seemed about to comment when Alf called out, 'Mr Barrie says they found a Saxon chieftain's grave in Suffolk.'

'Mr Barrie says we can make a giant map of Suffolk,' Sydney said.

'Mr Barrie says,' George added, 'that you have a library.'

Leaning against the banister, Mr Barrie said nothing, leaving Louisa wondering where this apparently loquacious version of her guest was hiding.

'Mr Barrie is right, we do have a library. You'll see it soon enough.'

She led them upstairs. The blackout curtains were open and the boys ran in and around the room like a swarm of the bees Johnno had complained about. Then, they each flopped onto a bed without discussion.

'Bathroom's down the corridor,' Louisa told them. She looked at the four boys and the six beds and said to Mr Barrie, 'We put in extra just in case.'

'Is one of those mine?' Mr Barrie asked.

Louisa had made light of Mrs Harrison's stuffiness, but with Mr Barrie it was different. Was this a jest or did she sense a bit of the resentment of privilege in his voice? Was he determined to rub her the wrong way? Perhaps he thought Oxburrow was not up to his standards.

She stalked out, and he followed. Turning, she said, 'You may be surprised to learn you'll have your own room and bathroom, Mr Barrie. Oxburrow's a comfortable house, and we'll do all we can to make it a home for you, Mrs Harrison, and the children. I know other schools have decamped to places like

Blenheim or Castle Howard. I realise we're not as grand as that, but I wanted to do what I could. Maybe you think we're not worthy.'

His eyes widened – brown, but sparking like flint striking steel. 'Is that what you think?'

'Is it what *you* think?' Louisa challenged.

Suddenly a loud metallic clang echoed from inside the boys' dormitory. Louisa remembered the medieval copper pot on a stand in the corner.

Alf's head appeared at the door. 'S'all right,' he said. 'It bounced.'

Louisa left the boys to their antics and headed down to the kitchen, which was empty except for a small dog occupying Mrs Moffatt's bed near the oven. It was Lulu, transformed. Her well-groomed fur was long silky grey with streaks of bronze. It shimmered in the light. Nearby sat a dish that had been licked clean.

'Feeling better, Lulu?' Louisa asked softly. The dog opened her eyes, pricked her pointed ears, then snuffled and went back to sleep. Louisa hoped the children would recover as swiftly.

Iris had left a note on the worktable to say she'd gone to the village, and the potatoes needed peeling. Louisa set to work on the mountain of spuds, and an hour later they were simmering on the hob.

When she went to the door to the yard with the peelings, she saw Iris climb down from the grocer's horse and cart, driven by young Colin. The boy had taken on all sorts of jobs around the village since the men had gone to war. Colin handed Iris five bottles of milk, nodded to Louisa and clicked his tongue at the horse – and they were gone.

'Mrs Harrison gave me the children's ration books,' Iris said, patting her coat pocket. 'I've got them registered.'

'You see, Iris,' Louisa said, taking two of the bottles, 'it's all going to work out.'

Iris made a noncommittal sound.

When they'd set the bottles on the table, she looked Louisa up and down. 'Didn't you say something about a bath?'

She had, yes – before the children arrived. Louisa hurried off to her own room on the first floor, below the girls' dormitory. At the landing a movement caught her eye, and she glanced up the staircase to the second floor, but no one was there.

Getting dressed for dinner was simple for Louisa – she threw on a clean frock in reasonable condition and topped it with a jumper or cardigan to ward off the indoor chill. Once ready, she stepped onto the landing and paused to look in the large gold-framed mirror. A purple damson stain still lingered along her jawline, and she resigned herself to letting it wear off. She scooped up her hair, twisted and rolled it and secured it with her three precious pins, and then turned, to see Mr Barrie standing at the top of the stairs leading to the boys' dormitory.

'Ah,' she said. 'Were you looking for me?'

'No,' he said a bit too quickly. 'Just... er... admiring the house.'

'Yes, well,' she said, slightly thrown. Where had his stern attitude gone? 'I'm happy to give you a tour any time – you and Mrs Harrison – but, as you've probably already seen, Oxburrow is neither fish nor fowl. Certainly not a grand place like Chatsworth.' She looked at the stair runner, worn through to the webbing from a century of use. 'Oxburrow's a home and I feel as if it's been waiting for this – to be filled with children.'

She had forgotten herself for a moment. She stole a glance at Mr Barrie, who'd settled on the top step of the boys' staircase, elbows on his knees, as he listened.

Louisa cleared her throat and checked her wristwatch. 'I

was just coming to say we'll eat downstairs in the old servants' dining room. Another twenty minutes or so? You'll find the stairs at the back.' She noticed how quiet the house was. Ordinarily, that would not alarm her. She lifted her eyebrows, making light of her question. 'You haven't kept the children penned up, have you? They can wander as they like.'

Mr Barrie chewed his cheek before answering. 'The children are not penned up, Lady Brightford. And, before you ask, we don't lock them in at night either.'

Was he being serious, or just returning her jest? He certainly looked serious enough. Flummoxed, Louisa was saved by one of the children. 'Look, here's George.'

The boy stood at the bottom of the stairs, notebook in hand.

'I'm counting steps, Lady Bee,' he said. 'From our dormitory to the stairs and the stairs to the outside.'

'George is concerned about everyone getting out safely if there should be a bomb,' Mr Barrie said.

'If it's dark and we can't see,' George said, 'we could count. I didn't count the steps at home. I wasn't prepared.'

'Oh George,' Louisa said, her throat tightening. 'Nearly time for your tea. Will you help Mr Barrie tell everyone? I'll see you downstairs.'

She stopped in the library first. Shelves in the far corner held David's favourite books – *Just William*, *Winnie-the-Pooh*, *Swallows and Amazons*, *Treasure Island*, *The Swiss Family Robinson* and Jules Verne. She pulled them down and spread them out on the table in front of a squishy sofa where her son had spent many a happy hour. He would be glad to know others would do the same.

While moving the books, she noticed Gracie slip into the library, stopping behind a wingback chair. Louisa paid her no mind, instead softly calling, 'Mrs Moffatt? Mrs Moffatt? Here puss-puss-puss.'

Mrs Moffatt sat on a shelf in the shadows, regal as an

Egyptian goddess. When her name was called, her golden eyes opened and she yawned. Louisa heard a small gasp behind her.

'What do you have to say for yourself, Puss?' Louisa asked, picking up the cat. Mrs Moffatt had been treated like a sack of potatoes since David had first brought her home five years earlier, the runt of a barn cat's litter.

He'd nursed her to health, and Louisa had told him, 'You could be a vet.'

'I could be a vet,' the fifteen-year-old David had agreed. Would that have satisfied his father? Louisa had thought at the time. Unlikely, she'd decided.

She set the cat on the table. 'Mrs Moffatt, this is Gracie.'

The cat ignored them and began washing her face.

'Would you like to pet her?' Louisa asked.

The thunderous look on Gracie's face faltered, but quickly reasserted itself. She kept her eyes on the cat, fists clenched.

'Maybe later. Now, it's time to eat,' Louisa said. 'We don't want to keep Mrs Darnley waiting.'

She left the library, glancing back to see the cat following her, and Gracie following the cat.

Dear David,

The children have arrived! Four boys and five girls, plus teachers – Mrs Harrison, she's in charge, make no mistake – and Mr Barrie – though a bit rude to grown-ups, the children like him well enough. One little girl, Gracie, hasn't spoken since the bomb fell two weeks ago. I can see the pain in her eyes. She's already taken a piece of my heart in her tiny hands – the part you left behind. I only hope I can help her find her voice again. The house is full of hope even though the war is practically on our doorstep. Be safe, dear boy. The storm is coming, and we must all be ready.

All my love,

Your old mum

CHAPTER 4

When Louisa reached the basement, she heard Mrs Harrison, across the hall in the servants' dining room, instructing the children. But that was almost drowned out by the joyful chaos in the kitchen – Alf and Lulu's reunion. The dog yipped and pranced on her short legs, barely favouring her injury, while Alf giggled uncontrollably.

Mrs Moffatt sauntered into the kitchen, then froze. Louisa felt an electric current in the air.

Lulu yipped, Mrs Moffatt growled and the chase was on – cat pursuing dog. Out of the kitchen they skittered and into the dining room across the hall, from where came a burst of laughter and the clatter of chairs. Then back they came into the kitchen, Lulu heading for a straw-filled cushion on one side of the cooker and Mrs Moffatt retreating to her own bed. They plopped down and sighed.

Iris took up an enormous cottage pie, which consisted of a thin layer of mince under a thick slab of potato and carrot mash, topped with the suggestion of cheese. Louisa followed her into the dining room with a bowl of peas and a platter of squash, thinly sliced and fried in a judicious amount of bacon fat.

'Don't expect this every night,' Iris said. 'Supper is usually bits and bobs. You'll get your dinner in the middle of the day, as it should be. But God knows when you last had a proper meal, so I've put on the dog for this first supper.'

'Not Lulu!' Alf exclaimed and giggles rippled round the table.

The children and teachers sat with girls on one side and boys on the other. Louisa took the head and Iris stood at the other end and stuck the serving spoon into the pie.

'We are accustomed to blessing the food first,' Mrs Harrison said.

Iris left the spoon where it was and bowed her head, but not so low she couldn't throw Louisa a look.

As the meal began, Louisa tried to chat with Athena, who glanced at Mrs Harrison.

'We prefer the children not to talk at table,' the teacher said. 'It can lead to disruption.'

It can lead to enjoying mealtimes, Louisa thought, but decided it would be better to bide her time.

The children ate eagerly, leaving not a speck of food – even Gracie opened her fist long enough to hold on to a spoon handle.

'We've no proper pudding this evening,' Louisa explained, 'but we do have bread and butter and two kinds of jam. Athena,' she began, 'would you like damson or strawberry?'

'Strawberry!' Athena shouted and then her gaze flew to Mrs Harrison. 'Please, Lady Bee, thank you.'

Round the table Louisa went, asking each child. Strawberry was the overwhelming favourite. When she reached Gracie, she asked the question again. 'Damson or strawberry?'

Gracie frowned at her buttered bread in silence.

'Well,' Louisa said easily, 'let's try damson – see if you like it.'

The girl made no complaint and ate her bread, as did the

other children. Once all had finished, Mrs Harrison announced that it was time for bed. Louisa thought she wouldn't mind an early night herself.

As the children trooped up the stairs, the teachers hung back.

'Lady Brightford,' Mrs Harrison said, 'I do hope we'll have time to talk once the children have settled.'

'Yes, of course,' Louisa said. 'Why don't you and Mr Barrie come to the library when you're ready. Would you like a sherry, Mrs Harrison?'

'No thank you, my lady. I am teetotal.'

'Oh, I see,' Louisa said. 'Ovaltine perhaps?'

Mrs Harrison offered her first small smile.

'Yes, thank you.'

'Ovaltine, Mr Barrie?' Louisa asked.

It might have been a bit of the devil in her – she could've offered him whisky. Regardless, he twitched nary an eyebrow at her.

'Yes, thank you.'

After they had washed up, Iris prepared a vat of porridge for breakfast, put the kettle on and spooned Ovaltine into mugs. Louisa left her to it. Upstairs, she found the teachers waiting for her in the library – Mrs Harrison standing with her notebook in the crook of her arm and Mr Barrie studying the books Louisa had laid out for the children.

'Shall we begin?' Louisa asked and gestured to a square table.

They took their chairs and Mrs Harrison set a notebook and fountain pen on the table. 'Lady Brightford,' she said in an officious manner, as if conducting a parish council meeting, 'once again we thank you for taking us in under such circumstances.'

'We're pleased to have you here,' Louisa said, 'but I'm afraid I know little about your school.'

'It's a small enterprise,' Mrs Harrison said, 'which began from charitable contributions and a dedicated board of governors.'

'And are there other teachers?'

'Not at present. I teach maths and science,' Mrs Harrison said. 'Mr Barrie is fond of reading.'

At that moment, Iris came in with the Ovaltine and Mrs Harrison turned and asked her about breakfast matters.

Louisa inclined her head toward Mr Barrie and, in a low voice, said, 'Fond of reading? She says it as if it's a curse.'

She saw that spark in his eyes, then he put on a frown, which she didn't entirely believe. She nodded toward the table of books.

'Did you see one of your own favourites?'

'I'm partial to *Just William*,' he said with all seriousness, causing Louisa to snigger.

'Now,' Mrs Harrison said when Iris had gone, 'will you and Lord Brightford remain in the house while the children are here?'

'I will remain here. I'm eager to help with the children in any way I can.' She paused, then plunged forward. 'Lord Brightford lives in London. We are divorced.'

Mrs Harrison blinked. 'I beg your pardon? Divorced?' She said the word as if it were in a foreign language, frowning and pursing her lips. 'Divorced? No one told me...'

'It has only recently become final,' Louisa said.

'Divorce is against the law.'

'It's perfectly legal,' Louisa said, tensing.

'It is against God's law and the Church's law,' Mrs Harrison said, her face sprouting red blotches. 'This won't do. No, this will never do. How can we have the children living under such conditions? We would be complicit in the arrangement. What sort of an example would we present?'

Louisa's face stung as if she'd been slapped. She groped for a reply, but before she could speak Mrs Harrison had reloaded.

'The school governors must not have known of your circumstances, else they would never have allowed the children to be sent here.'

Not even the vicar had treated Louisa this way when she'd told him.

'No, no, I'm sorry. We cannot stay here.'

Bang! Mr Barrie slammed his hand on the table and Louisa and Mrs Harrison jumped.

'What a load of rubbish!' he snapped. '"Would never have allowed"? Have you forgotten under what conditions the children were living? They've been in the schoolhouse sleeping on pallets, and eating whatever could be patched together.' His weathered face had taken on heat and he jabbed his finger on the table. 'They have no parents and no homes to go to. And now, Lady Brightford opens her home, gives them beds and fills their bellies, and you'll turn your nose up at her?'

'Mr Barrie!' Mrs Harrison whispered harshly.

'Get off your high horse,' he retorted.

Louisa, reeling, said nothing.

'The children are my utmost priority,' Mrs Harrison said with quiet fury. 'Warm and well fed is all well and good, but what of their spiritual needs? I'm sorry, Lady Brightford. Of course, I don't know your circumstances... but it is clear that I must inform the school governors. I see no way round that. It is my duty.'

'I'd say that Lady Brightford sees her duty a bit clearer than you do,' Mr Barrie shot back.

Mrs Harrison continued as if she hadn't heard. 'It has been such a difficult time – keeping the children together, securing transportation.' She frowned as if sensing she was straying from the topic at hand, but continued regardless. 'Mr Barrie found the man with the charabanc, and he was available only today. The journey was interminable...'

Finally Louisa found her voice. 'I hope you will stay, Mrs Harrison. Of course, I have no wish to infect the children with my wickedness' – Mr Barrie coughed – 'I agree with you that we must think of the children. I believe that remaining at Oxburrow would be best for them, but I will not move out.'

'We are of course grateful for your generosity, Lady Brightford.' Mrs Harrison's words sounded as if they were a set-up for another volley, but then she paused and looked puzzled. 'Forgive me, but are you still...?'

'Yes.' Louisa bit off the word. 'I am still Lady Brightford. Now, about school' – proceeding as if the matter was settled – 'will the children have lessons here?'

'Yes, we've arranged for desks to be brought out,' Mr Barrie said. 'They should arrive tomorrow along with books, blackboards, notebooks, pencils, rulers and the like.'

'Are they coming by rail?' Louisa said as, in her mind, she searched Oxburrow for a schoolroom. 'We've a young man with a horse cart who could go to the station.'

'No, a fellow with a coal lorry will bring them out,' Mr Barrie said. 'Things might need a bit of cleaning.'

'However did you find enough petrol coupons for all this coming and going?' Louisa asked him.

'The school governors provided,' Mrs Harrison said.

Louisa nodded. 'Of course, you're welcome to have lessons here in the library, but as for the desks and such we'll use the formal dining room. All we need to do is shift a few things.'

The long dining table, the chairs, the displays of eighteenth-century porcelain vases, the bowls and platters, the sets of crystal glasses, goblets, snifters... It didn't matter. Once the schoolroom had been set up, surely Mrs Harrison would see that she couldn't move the children out. Louisa stood to leave and Mr Barrie rose, too.

Mrs Harrison remained seated, looking at the notebook in front of her as if wondering what to write.

Louisa turned to Mr Barrie. 'We'll begin first thing tomorrow.'

Louisa slipped into bed and stared at the ceiling as her thoughts raced. The children had only just arrived, but already she couldn't bear the thought of them leaving. They carried wounds – inside, but real – and needed time to heal. Gracie especially. She would fight Mrs Harrison for them. She'd stand her ground with the school governors.

She repeated her convictions over and over and the repetition relaxed her. Just as her eyelids grew heavy and she hovered on the edge of sleep, a piercing shriek shattered the silence.

CHAPTER 5

Louisa shot upright in bed, heart pounding, adrenaline flooding her veins. Was it an air raid? Were the Germans on their way – or perhaps already in the village, as some had feared? Then she realised the sound was coming from inside the house – above her on the second floor, where Mrs Harrison and the girls were sleeping. Louisa leapt from bed, slid into her shoes, and threw on her dressing gown as she ran toward the noise.

By the time she reached the girls' dormitory, the shriek had stopped and had come again twice more, each time shorter. The door was open, and the lamp in the corner cast a dim light. Gloria and Dolly were sitting up in bed, whimpering. Priss and Athena had pulled the covers over their heads. Mrs Harrison stood at the bottom of Gracie's bed observing the girl, who lay with eyes squeezed shut and fists clutched under her chin.

Gracie's cry pierced the silence again – a short, sharp scream. Louisa hurried towards her just as the girl quieted.

'Don't interfere,' Mrs Harrison said, reaching out to stop Louisa. 'It'll only make it worse.'

'Nonsense,' Louisa whispered and gently placed her hand on Gracie's arm. But as soon as she touched her the girl began to flail, pulling away and crying out. Louisa quickly withdrew her hand.

'She'll settle on her own,' Mrs Harrison said, slipping her hands into her dressing gown pockets. Her long gray hair was braided over her shoulder. The lamplight threw shifting shadows on her face – one moment stern, the next haggard.

Louisa struggled to keep from touching Gracie – she stretched out a hand, then jerked it back again. 'I'm sorry. It's just she must miss her mother terribly, and long to feel comforting arms around her.'

'The doctor says she should work through this on her own. I don't know if he's right, but I do know she is worse when we try to intervene.'

Louisa looked around. Gloria and Dolly had already settled back into their beds; and Priss and Athena, whether they were awake or asleep, hadn't stirred. Her heart ached for all of them, but especially for Gracie – haunted as she was by the memory of being buried alive. She would do anything to help her.

'I'm sorry we disturbed you, Lady Brightford,' Mrs Harrison said.

'Not at all,' Louisa said. Now the nightmare had passed, she dared to pull the blanket up to Gracie's chin. The girl sighed peacefully.

Louisa left and Mrs Harrison followed, switching off the lamp on her way. Further down the corridor, Louisa saw a light spill out from the teacher's doorway.

'It's quite dark in the country,' Mrs Harrison commented. 'London's dark, of course, as is necessary, but even with the blackout curtains it seems brighter.' She shook her head. 'That makes no sense.'

Louisa, having grown up in Sheffield, understood. Darkness – blackout curtains or no – was different in the country. Would the teacher add that to her list of complaints to the school governors? 'Not only is our hostess full of sin, we can't see where we're going.'

An awkward silence grew. Before Mrs Harrison could think of another objection to raise, Louisa said simply, 'Good night' and left.

When she reached the staircase's centre landing she saw Mr Barrie standing at the top of the boys' side, wearing his jacket over his pyjamas.

'The poor girl,' she said. 'At first, I thought I was hearing the air-raid siren from the village – we haven't had to use it, but they do test it now and then. Is it every night?'

'It has been,' Mr Barrie replied, descending to sit on the bottom step. 'The boys have been sleeping in the junior room and the girls in the infants room on pallets. Gracie's nightmares started out frightening everyone, but now they unsettle some more than others. They're good lads, though – they haven't said a word about it. They seem to understand what she's going through.'

Louisa sank down on the step across the landing from him.

'To think she survived and her mother died,' she said. 'Had they become separated?'

'No, Gracie stayed with her mother.' He watched Louisa for a moment as if getting the measure of her, and then continued. 'The entire terrace collapsed. We started in immediately, digging, but they weren't found for two days – her mother dead, Gracie alive.'

'My God,' Louisa whispered.

They sat in silence in the dark for a moment. Louisa imagined the scene – the destruction, the death – and one life. She closed her eyes and rested her head against a stair rail. She was gaining new respect for what the teachers had gone through for the children. Despite air raids and loss, they had gathered their flock and kept them safe. An image floated through Louisa's mind of the children covered in curly wool, huddled together.

She caught herself just before she fell asleep, and sat up. Mr Barrie was still there.

'So,' he said quietly. 'Lord Brightford has given you Oxburrow as a part of the divorce arrangement?'

'Yes,' Louisa replied. 'The house at least, but not the land. Max hopes Oxburrow will fall into ruin so he can wash his hands of me. He even tried to give it to the army to hurry its destruction.'

A sharp pang of fear struck her as she realised there were two enemies trying to take the children away: the army and Mrs Harrison.

'Thank you for what you said earlier about me,' she said. 'About the divorce. I hadn't looked too far ahead, I suppose, to consider what others would say or think. Or, I knew but didn't want to admit it.'

'What anyone else thinks doesn't matter,' Mr Barrie said softly. 'It's what you believe that counts.'

'But could she move you out?' Louisa pressed. 'You must know the school governors – can't you put in a good word?'

'I've only met a few in passing. Mrs Harrison is in charge, and she can be blinkered. But if she demands the children be moved, she'll have a fight on her hands.'

Louisa blushed with gratitude, but didn't know quite how to respond. She let her gaze fall to her feet, which brought her attention to her attire – outdoor shoes and an old pair of David's plaid flannel pyjamas, patched so often that little of the original fabric remained. Over them, she'd thrown on a kingfisher-blue silk dressing gown with a Chinese motif that had been part of her trousseau twenty-two years ago, but she'd forgotten to tie its belt.

'Oh dear!' Mortified, she leapt up, pulling her gown closed under her chin. Then with a parting 'Good night, Mr Barrie', she hurried away.

· · ·

On Saturday morning after breakfast, Louisa was standing at the kitchen sink eating the scrapings out of the porridge pot when she heard the quiet clearing of a throat behind her. She turned, pot in hand, wooden spoon halfway to her mouth, and saw Mrs Harrison in the doorway. She closed her mouth.

'Lady Brightford, might I use your telephone?'

'Certainly,' Louisa replied. 'It's just next to the boot room off the entrance hall.'

'I will be telephoning the school governors to inform them of our situation,' Mrs Harrison said calmly. Louisa felt her hackles rising. 'I don't wish to go behind your back,' she continued, 'so I am telling you this now. If you'd prefer I make the call elsewhere, I will do so.'

For a moment, Louisa didn't speak. She could feel her grip on the wooden spoon tightening, but when she spoke her voice, too, was calm and even.

'You are welcome to use the telephone here,' she said.

'Please understand, I am not calling your personal integrity into question. It's a matter of—'

'Of course you're calling my integrity into question,' Louisa snapped, her face hot, her eyes pricking with tears she refused to let fall. 'How else will it look?' She wondered if she could get hold of William Lowrey on a Saturday morning. But then, what power would he have to stop the evacuees from being evacuated? She clenched her jaw.

Iris appeared behind Mrs Harrison, carrying a tray with the last of the breakfast dishes. The teacher stepped back into the corridor and disappeared.

'What's that about?' Iris asked.

Louisa threw the spoon into the empty pot. 'Nothing. Iris, do you have the children's ration books handy? I want to copy their names into my accounts ledger so we have a permanent record.'

'In there,' Iris said, nodding to a drawer in the Welsh

dresser. 'By the way,' she added in an offhand manner, 'the post arrived. I've put it in the morning room.'

Joy washed over Louisa, sweeping her black mood away. Post left on the table in the entrance hall was humdrum – or worse, overdue bills – but post left in the morning room meant a letter from David. She dropped the pot into the sink with a *clang* and hurried away.

The morning room lay on the east side of the house and had good light once the blackout curtains were thrown back, which Louisa found Iris had already done.

Apart from her desk, the room held little furniture – a red Victorian chaise longue, perfect for an occasional nap, a few tables and a grouping of chairs round the tiled fireplace. Even with the scent of old coal fires clinging to upholstery and wallpaper, the atmosphere of the morning room was light and airy and comfortable – the antithesis of Max's dark, stuffy study on the opposite side of the house. Louisa rarely saw any reason to go in there and, nowadays, it was little more than a lumber room.

Louisa pulled the door to behind her and went to the desk in front of the windows. David's letter lay next to a photo of him at seventeen, wearing his cricket whites and leaning on his bat in a jaunty manner that matched his slightly crooked smile. Louisa smiled back at that image, then sat and gazed at the letter. His flowing cursive had always looked like a piece of art to her. She laid her hand on it for a moment before opening it.

Louisa had read the letter through twice – rushing the first time and more leisurely the second – when there was a soft tap at the door. She looked up to see Mr Barrie.

'Good morning,' she said cheerfully. 'The school desks haven't arrived yet, have they? I've had a letter from my son today.' She waved it in the air. 'He's a pilot at a base in Somerset. Flies Spitfires. He won't tell me details, but every time I see one I think it might be him looking down on us. I don't quite know how they can find their way round, these boys in the sky. He wishes for one of Iris's Dundee cakes. He loves all her cakes, but Dundee has always been his favourite. Oh, do come in and sit down. Did you want something?'

Mr Barrie entered and perched on the back of the chaise longue. 'Good morning.'

Louisa chuckled. 'Sorry for rabbiting on. It's strange how a letter can lift the worry, even if just for a moment. Do you have children of your own, Mr Barrie?'

'A son,' Mr Barrie said. 'He lives in Canada with his grandmother.'

'Oh,' Louisa said waiting for more, trying to find a way to ask about his wife without seeming to pry. But she didn't need to.

'My wife died when he was a year old,' he said. 'I wasn't good for much in the years after the war and so it was best that his gran took him.'

Louisa imagined the story went much deeper than that, but who was she to pry?

'I'm sorry for your loss,' she said. 'Canada is awfully far away. Are you in touch?'

'We exchange letters,' he said with a slight shrug. 'His are cordial but very much the write-your-father-a-letter sort.'

'How old is he?'

'Nearly eighteen.'

'Will he sign up?'

'I hope to God he doesn't.' Mr Barrie's reply was heated, and then he caught himself. 'Sorry.'

She set the letter on the desk. Outside the window, a cloud scuttered across the sun. 'I never thought David would go into the RAF, but he had a friend signing on and thought that if he were a pilot he could prove to his father he was...'

Louisa's voice petered out and Mr Barrie didn't press her. They sat quietly for a moment until he cleared his throat and began, 'Lady Brightford.'

'Can we dispense with the title?' Louisa asked. 'It isn't necessary.'

'Mrs Harrison may have trouble with that.'

'Mrs Harrison.'

Louisa said the name as an epithet, but didn't explain, because through the closed window drifted far-off shouting – calls of victory, cries of anguish and a few squeals of pain.

She could see nothing out of the window, and so, without a word, Louisa ran, with Mr Barrie just behind her. They took the stairs to the basement and ran out of the door into the yard, pausing for a moment to listen. To the melange of sounds had been added the full bass tones of Figg shouting, 'Out with all of you – do you hear? Out!'

Ah, the kitchen garden. Louisa and Mr Barrie took off again and, as they reached the gate in the brick wall, a potato flew past, nearly hitting Louisa in the head.

'Oi!' she shouted. 'What's all this?'

Figg had come in the opposite gate, and stood like a referee while on one side two boys – Johnno and Alf – froze, with ammunition still in their hands. On the other side, Gloria held stock-still but Priss let loose one last volley.

In response, Alf raised his hand, and Louisa pointed at him. 'Don't you dare.' Alf dropped his potato.

The other children had gathered to watch the battle, but now backed off to make it clear they had no part in it. Gracie stood behind the raspberry bushes on the east wall, peeking through.

Figg stormed over to Louisa, wiping his hands on the old tweed jacket he wore over a holey sleeveless jumper. He took his flat cap off and slapped it on his thigh. 'I won't have them in here, my lady, I won't, not if it means ruining a crop.'

'Indeed, Mr Figg,' Louisa said. She picked up a spud that was at her feet, tossed it in the air and caught it. 'These last late potatoes are vital and if the children spoil the garden there will be nothing for any of us to eat, will there?' She aimed the question at the four participants in the melee. 'Come here.'

Johnno and Alf, Priss and Gloria lined up in front of Louisa. They hung their heads in appropriate fashion, looking terribly sorry for themselves.

'And so, what are we to do, Mr Barrie, about this wanton disregard for someone else's hard work?' Louisa asked.

Mr Barrie studied the children as he thought. The children's gazes flew from one grown-up face to the other.

'Punishment should fit the crime, I'd say.'

'Yes,' Louisa said, 'I see what you mean. We'll put Mr Figg in charge.' The children glanced nervously over their shoulders at the gardener. 'Mr Figg, they are yours to do with what you will.'

'Aye, aye, my lady.' Figg had been a midshipman during the Great War and often fell back on his training.

'Right, the rest of you,' Mr Barrie said, 'off you go.'

The children ambled off toward the house, except for Gracie, who remained behind the raspberries. Louisa held the potato out to her.

'Will you carry that up to Iris for me?' she asked.

Gracie eyed the spud and then Louisa. She came out from behind the raspberries and took it carefully – it was a small potato, but a handful for the girl. She set off toward the kitchen yard in as near a skip as Louisa could hope for.

'Did I step on your toes there, Mr Barrie?' Louisa asked as they walked back to the house. 'Perhaps you should've taken them in hand.'

'You managed quite well.'

'I've never seen the point of punishment for punishment's sake,' Louisa said, 'and I've been called a "soft touch" for that belief. Well, never mind. Figg may be a bit rough on the outside, but he has a good heart really. You wait and see, he'll turn them into gardeners.'

When they reached the kitchen yard, they heard the sound of engines in the air, growing louder. They stopped and looked up as three planes passed over, silhouetted against the blue sky.

'Spitfires,' Louisa said. 'That's right, isn't it?'

'It is.'

'It could be David.' She squinted up at the planes.

The tooting of a horn came drifting toward them from the drive and sheep in the nearby field answered with matching bleats. Louisa and Mr Barrie climbed the slope and reached the top just as a lorry rattled to a stop in the forecourt of the house. It was piled high with school desks and boxes, as if it was about to split its wooden sides. The fellow behind the wheel stuck his head out of the open window. He wore a frayed flat cap pulled down so far that his ears stuck out.

'Well done, Jack,' he said to Mr Barrie as he pulled a grimy handkerchief out and wiped his bulbous nose. 'You've landed in a place even 'itler couldn't find.'

CHAPTER 6

My darling mum,

Briefly lost my way returning from a chase across the North Sea and remembered when I was seven or eight and tried hiking out to the lake on my own. You and Iris nearly called in Scotland Yard for the search, but I came back to you by nightfall, although a bit worse for wear. Learned a thing or two from that.

Love you,

D

'Looks like you did all right,' Mr Barrie replied. 'Chuff, this is Lady Brightford.'

Chuff stuffed the handkerchief back into a pocket and tugged at his flat cap. 'How do, your ladyship,' he said, 'pleased to meet you, I'm sure.'

Louisa's attention had been taken by hearing Mr Barrie's Christian name – Jack – but now she turned back to Chuff.

'You're welcome to Oxburrow.' She looked round and saw Iris had come out. 'This is Mrs Darnley.'

Chuff nodded and Iris stuck her hands in her apron pockets.

The children had appeared, and they stood together, admiring the lorry.

'Have you met the children?' Louisa asked.

'Well, in a manner of speaking,' Chuff said. 'Not formally, like.'

Louisa carried out the introductions, ending with, 'and that's Gracie at the very back. Give Mr Chuff a wave, Gracie, so he sees you.'

Against all odds, Gracie lifted a hand – still holding the potato – and offered a weak wave. Mr Barrie caught Louisa's gaze and gave her a nod.

'Hello, children,' Chuff said. Then something caught his eye – Mrs Harrison had come out and was standing under the portico. 'Cor,' Chuff muttered as he opened the door and slid out of the lorry.

'Mr Chuffleigh,' Mrs Harrison said in a heavy tone.

'Mrs 'arrison, ma'am,' Chuff said, pulling his cap off and holding it over his heart. 'I swept the back out, I did.' He sniffed, took out his handkerchief again and wiped his nose. Mrs Harrison averted her eyes. 'Not a bit of coal dust left, ma'am, I can promise you that. Now, we'd best get everything unloaded – I've promised myself to two dear ladies who need a load of chimney bricks delivered. You just say the word, Mrs 'arrison, and we'll get to it.'

Mrs Harrison stood still, as if assessing the situation. Chuff wiped his nose again. Louisa put her hands on her hips.

'Well, Mrs Harrison,' she said, 'what did the governors have to say?'

'The governors?' Mr Barrie asked with a flash of anger. 'You actually spoke to them?'

'What was their verdict?' Louisa demanded. 'Has Mr Chuffleigh wasted all that petrol bringing out the school furniture only to turn round and take it back again?'

'Here now,' Chuff complained, 'I'm not taking this lot back. I didn't drive out here on a lark, Jack.'

'No, Chuff,' Mr Barrie said with his eyes on Mrs Harrison, 'it's no lark. The furniture stays, if I have to have a word with the governors myself.'

Mrs Harrison gave him a hard look, which was followed by a flash of weariness. Then she drew herself up in an officious manner. 'There will be no need for that, Mr Barrie. The furniture stays.' A brief pause, then she added, 'For the present.'

What had the school governors told Mrs Harrison when she telephoned them that morning? Perhaps she was to await further orders. Perhaps she hadn't accounted for Chuff's appointed delivery. Louisa knew that the school furniture arriving didn't mean she'd won, but, until a battle plan could be sorted out, she'd be happy to claim victory in this skirmish. There was a war on, even at Oxburrow.

'Well then,' she said, 'let's get started.'

'Set the furniture out on the drive, Mr Chuffleigh,' Mrs Harrison said, taking control once more. 'We'll wipe everything down before we take it in.'

Chuff grumbled under his breath as he let the gate down on the back of the lorry. He and Mr Barrie began unloading. Louisa joined them, along with Iris and the children – even the little ones lent a hand.

When the lorry was empty, a motley collection of furniture, blackboards and crates lay strewn on the drive.

'Mr Chuffleigh, I count only five desks,' Mrs Harrison said.

'There's a reason for that, Mrs 'arrison, ma'am,' Chuff said, 'and that reason is that the other four were in such bad shape that when I picked them up they nearly fell to bits.'

'They were well used when they came to us,' Mr Barrie said.

'You just leave them with me, Jack,' Chuff said. 'I'll have them right as rain and bring them out to you as soon as I can.' He took out his grimy handkerchief and dusted off a desk or two.

'That will do, Mr Chuffleigh,' Mrs Harrison said, her face wrinkled in distaste. 'You may go.'

Chuff crammed the handkerchief back into his pocket and turned. Louisa – hoping she wasn't doing it just to spite Mrs Harrison – put a hand out.

'We're having our dinner at noon, Mr Chuffleigh. Would you like to stay?' She saw his eyes brighten. 'Unless you must be on your way to collect those chimney bricks.'

'Well,' Chuff said in a reasonable tone, 'it isn't as if my ladies are waiting with trowels in hand.' He wheezed a laugh.

'Lovely,' Louisa said. 'First, you can help us turn the formal dining room into the schoolroom, then we'll move all this indoors and—'

'Hang on, Jack's not paying me for a full day's work, are you, boy?'

Iris appeared with a handful of clean rags. 'Iris, what are we having for dinner today?' Louisa called. 'Isn't it mutton stew?'

'Mutton stew?' Chuff gave Iris a wistful smile. 'You wouldn't believe it, but I've been dreaming of mutton stew.'

'We'd best get to it, then,' Louisa said.

The children set about wiping off any coal dust that had the audacity to remain where Mrs Harrison didn't want it, while Louisa surveyed the industrious group.

'Where's Gracie?' she asked.

'She's in our room,' Athena said.

'She prefers to be left alone,' Mrs Harrison said.

There's alone and there's abandoned, Louisa thought.

They headed indoors, where she gave instructions about

how to clear space in the formal dining room, then went off and opened Max's study. It was in worse shape than she remembered. Chairs in need of repair were stacked against the bookshelves, paintings – one, a frightful depiction of a foxhunt – leaned haphazardly against the wall and a century's worth of estate ledgers gathered dust in the corner. Still, with a bit of shifting, they were able to fit five porcelain urns as tall as George, gilded plaster busts of Bach, Beethoven and Mozart and a hastily packed crate of blue-and-white Chinese plates.

'Could you use these?' Louisa asked, pointing to two spindly-legged tables. 'To fill in until the other desks arrive?'

Chuff put his hand on one of the tables and gave it a shake. It held firm. 'That's a fine piece of work, that is. Solid.'

As the teachers discussed the arrangement of the new schoolroom and Chuff and the children awaited directions, Louisa slipped out and up the stairs.

The girls' dormitory was empty. The beds had been neatly made with hospital corners – had Mrs Harrison been a nurse? – and each pillow was adorned with a doll in some form or other. On Gracie's pillow was the little cat made from a sock. Oh yes, Louisa thought. A cat.

She went to the library. It, too, appeared uninhabited at first glance, but the sofa in the far back corner couldn't be seen from the door, not with the map table and the wingback chairs in the way. Louisa approached, humming as she went to announce her arrival.

When she got closer, she saw her guess had been right. Gracie had snuggled into the corner of the sofa with an open book – *The Tale of Tom Kitten* – under the supervision of Mrs Moffatt, who sat on the back of the sofa as if reading over her shoulder.

Gracie looked up at Louisa and, for the briefest of moments, her face held no pain or defiance or fear. She could have been any little girl reading a book. Then it was gone, and the pain and anguish came rushing back. A curtain dropped behind her eyes and the happy little girl was hidden away.

'There you are, Gracie!' Athena called as she ran in. 'Lady Bee, Mrs Harrison says mice have eaten half a lace doily and Mrs Darnley says she's adding more potatoes to the stew and Mr Barrie says... oh, well, Mr Barrie didn't say anything.'

'... and so we hid it in the stove,' Chuff said to Johnno, next to him, 'and it was fine until Teacher lit the first fire of the season. Then the place stank to high heaven!'

Snorts of laughter flew round the table. All propriety had gone out of the window with the inclusion of Chuff at dinner. He had no reason to take notice of the dark looks Mrs Harrison threw him every time he began a raucous story about his schooldays.

After dinner, Chuff left and the children began arranging the schoolroom. All except Alf, who offered to stay in the kitchen and help Iris – he credited her with saving Lulu's life. Lulu, dozing peacefully beside the cooker, seemed to have forgotten her trauma.

'You'll be up for sainthood before we know it,' Louisa said.

'There'll be statues of me with little dogs at my feet,' Iris replied. 'Here, Alf, there's a stool in the corner. Bring it over so you can reach the sink and dry for me.'

Louisa went to the boot room, put on her red boiled-wool jacket, tucked David's letter in the pocket and set off to church. Crossing the drive, she looked back, and saw Gracie watching from the window at the top of the stairs. Louisa thought to return and ask her along, but the little girl vanished. *Too soon,* Louisa told herself and went on her way.

The church, St Gregory's, was at the village edge, a short walk down the footpath through oak and beech woods. The wood held only the suggestion that autumn was upon them –

the leaves on the occasional birch had begun to turn buttery yellow and there was an earthy smell underfoot. Maples in the hedgerows had begun to drop their leaves and a breeze stirred them into an eddy that curled round Louisa's legs and made her shiver. She'd given up wearing stockings. They weren't rationed – at least, not yet – but they were becoming both hard to find and expensive.

Louisa thought of the wood as the transition between Oxburrow – now hidden from view – and the church and village, still to come. In truth, hiding Oxburrow wasn't a difficult task. It wasn't an impressive manor on the hill or one of those grand Georgian houses built on the foundations of a medieval feast hall that had taken the place of a Roman villa. Oxburrow was its own self – a rather oversized and, these days, shabby but beloved Victorian family home. And now it had quite a family within, Louisa thought with a smile.

When she came out of the wood and to the lychgate next to an ancient ash tree, she was met with the chords of 'Eternal Father, Strong to Save' being played on the harmonium. Louisa paused. Barbara Byers and several other women in the WVS had sons in the navy. Already one had been lost, and Louisa hoped there hadn't been further bad news.

In the church porch, the usual notices about the parish council meeting and the flower schedule were now nearly crowded out with war posters – *Clear Your Plate, Keep Scraps for the Hens* and *Freedom is in Peril*. There was a call from the RAF for more pilots – *Mightier Yet* that showed Spitfires flying in front of fluffy white clouds.

Louisa pushed open the thick oak door of the church and the music grew louder. There at the harmonium sat Hugo Oldham. He caught her entrance out of the corner of his eye and lifted his chin in greeting, but kept playing. She didn't go all the way up to the Brightford pew, but instead took a seat in the third row back and listened, breathing in the chilly air, fragrant with sweet olive from vases set in the deep windowsills.

St Gregory's wasn't grand enough for a pipe organ – the harmonium was a modest-sized instrument for a modest-sized village church. Louisa watched as Hugo worked the pedals, pulled the stops and played the keys. He was a young man, not yet thirty, but his red hair was already receding. He wore round, tortoiseshell glasses and had an impish grin, which he now flashed at Louisa over his shoulder, and then ended the hymn with an improvised fanfare, which sounded too light-hearted for a funeral.

'No bad news, then?' she asked. 'Not one of our Debden Ash boys?'

'No, only prayers for their well-being and safe return.' Hugo scooted round on the bench and added, 'Sea, land and air.'

He pulled a letter out of the pocket of his cassock and held it up. Louisa held hers up, too, and they adjourned to the vestry, where Hugo lit the spirit lamp and set the kettle on it.

They met up each Saturday afternoon and shared David's letters, comparing the stories he told, imagining aloud what his life was like. Other men wrote home to their mothers and their sweethearts – David wrote to his mother and to Hugo.

Louisa had learned about her son's preferences when he was sixteen. He had taken a lovely girl to the school Christmas dance – the daughter of a marchioness over near Ely – and had come home late that evening and said, 'Mum, I want to tell you something.'

It hadn't shocked her, but rather answered questions she'd never asked. Her reaction to his confession was an overwhelming love. He trusted her with this, even though others – especially his father – wouldn't understand. She was delighted when he and Hugo met, but couldn't deny that it hurt her that David's life would be hard. But whose wasn't in one fashion or another?

Hugo wasn't fit for duty in the services because of his eyesight, but he wouldn't have had to join up anyway. Not because he was the organist, an air-raid warden and fire watcher, but because he was the vicar, a reserved occupation.

Louisa doubted the village could ever do without him. Beside his assigned duties, Hugo helped anyone at any time – sewing blackout curtains, digging in allotments or going off on a wild goose chase when elderly Mrs Chalmers thought she saw a German at the bottom of her garden. That had turned out to be an actual goose.

Louisa and Hugo settled with tea and biscuits, and pored over David's letters. When they could squeeze nothing else out of them, Hugo sat back and said, 'No word about leave.'

'No,' Louisa said. 'But surely he'll have time soon. It was April the last time we saw him.'

'You wait now,' Hugo said with a smile, 'you'll open the door and there he'll be as a surprise.'

Louisa's generous smile sprang onto her face. 'He would do that, wouldn't he?'

'Will you bring the children to church tomorrow?'

'Of course I will,' Louisa said. 'They're a part of Oxburrow and I want them to be a part of the village, too, even if they do have their own school.' The more they were a part of Oxburrow, the less likely it would be that the school governors would remove them – surely even Mrs Harrison would understand that.

Louisa left St Gregory's feeling renewed and planning for David's visit. As she reached the forecourt, she saw Mr Barrie striding quickly from the house.

She stopped and put a hand to her chest. A war will do that to you – you are always half expecting terrible news, but never fully prepared, so that when it comes it seems out of the blue, hitting you before you have time to brace yourself.

'What is it?' she asked, her heart pounding.

He frowned and took her hand. It was warm and dry and she held on.

'It's nothing,' he said, but too earnestly. 'We need to learn how to keep an eye on the children and yet give them freedom. That's all.'

That wasn't all. 'Who is it?'

'Gracie has—'

'Gracie is gone?'

CHAPTER 7

'We'll find her,' Mr Barrie said. 'It's just that at the moment we don't know where she is.' He was the picture of calm and, although she longed to keep hold of him, she pulled her hand away.

'Have you searched all the rooms?' she managed, her heart in her throat so that she could barely get the words out.

'Yes.'

She hurried across the drive with Mr Barrie at her side.

'She's gone off before,' he told her. 'Twice since the terrace bombing. She was making for home – or what was left of it.'

'Did you look in the library?' Louisa asked, but she knew they had. 'When did you see her last?'

'It's been more than an hour.'

Louisa stopped at the portico. 'I saw her,' she said.

Mr Barrie spun round. 'When?'

'As I was leaving,' Louisa said. 'I looked up at the house' – she pointed upward – 'and saw her in the window. But then she was gone.'

It sounded like the start of a Victorian ghost story and it

made Louisa sick with worry. She shook the silly notion out of her head. Gracie had been watching her since her arrival the day before – Louisa had sensed it. Had she followed her out of the door?

'I'm going back to the church,' Louisa said.

Mr Barrie caught on to the idea immediately. 'I'll go and tell the others and come after you.'

'It's down the footpath – about fifteen minutes,' Louisa called as she ran.

Running helped because, although she stumbled on tree roots and sunken places in the path, she had to take deep gulps of air, and it's difficult to cry when you're out of breath. She burst from the woods and saw the church ahead. By the time she reached the lychgate, she had slowed considerably and was breathing heavily.

She wrenched open the oak door and ran inside, her footsteps echoing in the empty sanctuary. She dashed over to the vestry, but the door was locked. Then she spun round – Hugo would be in the vicarage, his cottage on the village side of the church, and he would help. She ran out, a cold chill seizing her as she wondered how far they would need to search.

'Louisa!'

She heard her name but at first couldn't see who called. Then she saw Minns waving to her from the far end of the church, on the path that led round to the back and the church-yard. Louisa ran to her, and when she stopped – would she ever be able to catch her breath? – Minns nodded toward an ornate grave that sat in pride of place on a small knoll among other burial plots. A sarcophagus with a stone effigy of some long-ago prominent man, surrounded by a railing.

Louisa crept closer and there, huddled against the railing with her knees tucked under her chin and her arms wrapped round her legs, was Gracie. She looked up at Louisa with her usual severity, but Louisa also saw relief.

'Oh, Gracie,' she said softly, sinking down beside the girl and feeling her own flood of relief. 'Minns, how did you find her?'

'I wanted to add a few Michaelmas daisies to the church flowers,' Minns said. 'There's a patch growing on my mum's grave in the back there, and I came out and here was this wee thing. She was a bit skittish and wouldn't say her name, but Reverend Oldham thought she might be one of your children.'

'She is indeed,' Louisa said. She looked at Gracie and smiled. Small dark eyes looked back.

What to do – chastise Gracie for running off? Quiz her on her motivation? Both seemed useless.

'I'm so happy to see you,' Louisa said, 'but you shouldn't...' *No, now was not the time.* 'We'd best get back to Oxburrow. Athena has probably been looking for you.'

Gracie stood, shivering.

'Here, put this on.' Louisa took off her jacket and held it out. Gracie obeyed, sticking her small, fisted hands into the sleeves. She was good at taking direction. Do this, do that – obeying required no emotion. But Louisa felt certain what this girl needed was a cuddle and a good cry. *Let me in,* she thought. *Please let me in.*

Hugo came round the corner of the church in a rush, then stopped at the sight of them, his pinched, worried face breaking out in a smile. 'Well, here's a jolly reunion. Everything all right?'

'Everything's fine,' Louisa said. 'This is Gracie, who is one of the children staying at Oxburrow.'

'Yes, Gracie,' Hugo said. 'I rang when Minns came to tell me. Iris sounded quite relieved.'

'I imagine she was. Well, ready to go?' Louisa asked Gracie, who didn't reply. 'Thank you, Minns. Thank you, Hugo.'

'Bye-bye, Gracie,' Minns said, opening and closing her hand in a wave. 'Take care now.'

Louisa and Gracie had barely made it through the lychgate when Mr Barrie came running out of the wood. He stopped when he saw them and bent over to put his hands on his knees, coughing and panting.

'Good, good,' he said between gasps. 'I'm more of a long-distance runner than a sprinter.'

Louisa laughed and Mr Barrie looked up and then he laughed, too. It startled Louisa – and pleased her. His smile transformed his world-weary face with genuine good humour, hidden until that moment.

'Gracie followed me when I came to see Hugo – Reverend Oldham,' Louisa explained. 'He's already telephoned and told Iris.'

'And she has, I hope, called off the hunt,' Mr Barrie said.

'Let's go and find out.'

'Here.' Mr Barrie took off his jacket. 'Yours is in use and it's chilly in the wood. I've already warmed up.'

He held it for her and, as she slipped into the jacket, his hands rested briefly on her shoulders – perhaps a moment longer than necessary. She felt his warmth through the fabric and it comforted her, but her emotions were running high and she had to blink away tears before whispering, 'Thank you.'

They walked back with Gracie between them.

'It's a peaceful countryside,' Mr Barrie said as they walked through the dappled shade of the woods. 'Are you from Suffolk?'

'No, I come from Sheffield. But I've been here more than twenty years, so it's home to me.'

On the other side of the woods, a single plane – loud and lumbering – flew overhead quite low. They both stopped to watch.

'A Wellington,' Mr Barrie said. 'Bomber.'

When Louisa looked down, she saw that Gracie had vanished.

'Gracie?' she called, looking round.

This time, the girl hadn't gone far. She had stopped a few steps back, and was standing near the grey trunk of a beech.

'It's all right,' Louisa said. 'Come along now.'

When the plane disappeared from view, Gracie stepped out, and they continued on their way.

'Mr Barrie,' Louisa said, 'if Mrs Harrison permits, I would like to deal with this.'

'I wish you would,' he replied.

They reached the forecourt to see Mrs Harrison standing like a stone figure beneath the portico watching their approach, her hands clasped at her waist.

'Well, Gracie,' she said when they reached the door, her voice dropping into an ominous tone.

Iris emerged from behind Mrs Harrison, her hands in her apron pockets. 'Well, she was lost and now she's found.' It was an offhand remark, but Louisa detected the relief in Iris's voice.

'Where is everyone?' Louisa asked.

'Downstairs, getting ready for tea,' Iris said.

'Why don't you all go ahead,' Louisa said. 'Gracie and I will follow in a few minutes.'

Mrs Harrison didn't move, and neither did Iris, nor Mr Barrie.

'Lady Brightford,' Mrs Harrison said, 'you do not need to mete out punishment for one of our students. I am quite capable of handling it myself.'

'If you don't mind, I would like to.'

'Gracie is our responsibility,' Mrs Harrison said. The

unspoken message was clear – why should it matter to Louisa when the children wouldn't be there long?

'But *I* was the reason Gracie left Oxburrow,' Louisa said. '*I* was the one she followed.'

She wasn't sure who would win the stand-off until Iris stepped in.

'Mrs Harrison,' she said, 'before you sit down with your cuppa, I have a question about the children's ration books. Sorting out the food budget is such a chore these days. May I have a word?'

Well played, Iris. Louisa had already seen that practical, concrete issues were right up Mrs Harrison's street, and Iris had seen it too. Sounding only mildly reluctant, the woman said, 'Yes, certainly, Mrs Darnley,' and allowed Iris to chivvy her downstairs. Mr Barrie gave Louisa a nod and followed them.

'Right, Gracie,' Louisa said, holding out her hand. 'Come with me. We need to have a talk.'

Gracie looked first at the hand, then at Louisa. Here was her choice – would Gracie insist on remaining untouchable or would she respond as a child facing up to her misbehaviour? The determined straight line of Gracie's mouth took a decided downturn at the corners. She put her hand in Louisa's and off they went to the morning room.

Louisa dared not squeeze the little hand she held – this was serious business. Still, a thrill ran through her at this small victory in breaking through Gracie's defences.

They went to the morning room and sat facing each other in front of the cold fireplace. Gracie's brow furrowed. Her eyes were wary and her hands clenched tightly in her lap.

'We were worried about you this afternoon,' Louisa said gently. 'I was afraid something had happened to you. I was frightened.' She saw a flicker in the girl's eyes. 'Perhaps you lost sight of me, and you were frightened, too. Gracie, you are welcome to come with me on errands, but you must not slip away when no one's looking. You must tell me you want to go.'

Gracie watched and listened.

'I'm so happy you've come to live at Oxburrow,' Louisa said. 'I want you to feel safe here, but you are not a grown-up and you cannot go off on your own.'

She looked at the girl, and in that glance thought she saw a softening.

'That's enough of that,' Louisa said, rising. 'Now, we're late for tea. Will it be damson or strawberry jam for your bread?'

Gracie said nothing, of course, and so damson it would be. Louisa had made progress, but not that much.

When they entered the dining room, the children cheered, only to be silenced by Mrs Harrison's sharp look.

'Gracie, we looked everywhere for you!' Athena said. 'Were you walking back to London?'

'Gracie had gone along with me to the church,' Louisa said, 'it's only that I didn't realise it. You'll see the church tomorrow and meet Reverend Hugo. Won't they, Mrs Harrison?'

'They will indeed,' she replied. 'And that means baths tonight.'

Mrs Harrison silenced the groans with a raised eyebrow. Louisa couldn't fault her on this account – they could every one of them well do with a bath.

Tea ended and the children, allowed free time, scattered – except for Alf. Without being asked, he carried a stack of plates to the kitchen, and Louisa followed him with glasses and platters. Both stopped in the doorway to watch Mrs Moffatt and Lulu in a playful chase, weaving around the legs of the worktable until it was impossible to distinguish the chaser from the chasee.

'Oi, you two,' Iris called from the sink, and the animals

abruptly stopped. Lulu retreated to her bed by the cooker, but Mrs Moffatt yawned nonchalantly and sauntered out of the door.

'That's better,' Iris said. 'All right there, Alf? Put those down and go out for a run around why don't you.'

'Yes, Mrs Darnley,' Alf said.

When the dishes were finished, Louisa took the damp tea towels outdoors to hang them to dry, and found Mr Barrie sitting on the ground with his back against the low stone wall that curved round the drying shed. He had a book in his hand, but was watching the horizon. When he noticed her, he stood.

'Stay where you are,' she said. She pegged the cloths on the line and then went over and sat on the wall. 'Enjoying the scenery?'

He lifted his eyebrows. 'I feel a bit as if I'm skiving off – as if I'm taking a holiday from the war.'

'Nonsense,' Louisa said. 'You've got a great responsibility as a teacher – what would the country be if every teacher signed up to fight? And besides—'

'I'm too old to sign up,' Mr Barrie said with a half-grin. 'Yes, there's that.'

They sat quietly. The bleating of sheep, the complaining of jackdaws in the treetops and the voices of children nearby created a glorious symphony. Louisa thought she would hold on to it with all her strength.

'Was that a black mark against me?' she asked. 'Losing Gracie. Will Mrs Harrison keep track of my failures?'

Before he could respond, terrified shouts came from down the slope beyond the chicken run. Without another word, they both took off. Louisa ran through the kitchen garden and out of the far gate. Off to one side, she saw old Figg was hurrying up from his cottage. On the other, Johnno wielded a stick like a weapon and kicked at one of the wooden beehives – so forcefully that it toppled over. The lid slid off and the frames spilled out.

Bees – a mass of small brown dots – rose in the air and swarmed around Johnno and their broken hive. His screams grew frantic as he waved his arms and ran in circles.

'Johnno!' Mr Barrie shouted. 'Come away.'

'Slowly,' Louisa said, approaching the boy and ignoring the bees. 'Don't wave your arms. Come over here.'

They coaxed him, speaking calmly and firmly. Then they took his hands and led him into the garden. Louisa closed the gate. The few bees that had followed swarmed upward and vanished over the top of the brick wall.

'They'll follow me!' Johnno cried. 'They'll come over the wall and attack!'

'They'll leave you alone,' Louisa said in a soothing voice. 'You're safe here. The bees have other things to worry about at the moment. Sit down on this bench.'

Johnno sat, then screwed up his face and burst into tears.

Louisa knelt before him. 'Are you stung?' she asked, but he only sobbed, so she looked up and down his bare arms. Mr Barrie followed suit and examined the boy's face, neck and his bare legs.

'Here,' Louisa said, and nodded at a red spot on the inside of Johnno's elbow. She held on to the boy's wrists gently but firmly. 'Look at me, Johnno. Stay still, now. I'm going to get the stinger out. Watch how I do it.'

Johnno snivelled, but his sobs subsided as he watched Louisa pick at the red spot with a fingernail.

'There now,' she said, showing them both the small stinger removed with its venom pouch intact. 'We got the stinger out without damaging it, so you'll only be a bit sore.'

They made him take off his shirt, but found only two more stings – one on his neck and one on the back of a knee.

'Iris will put witch hazel on those stings,' Louisa said. 'How do you feel?'

Johnno sniffed and nodded.

Mr Barrie handed over his handkerchief. 'Now, what happened?'

'I only wanted to see them up close,' Johnno said, defiant but trembling. 'I took a stick so I could lift the lid off the box. And they flew out at me.'

'The hive is their home, Johnno,' Louisa said, gently. 'They thought you were attacking them. None of us likes our home attacked, do we?'

His eyes welled up again, and he sobbed even harder.

Figg appeared at Louisa's elbow. 'I went up to the house, my lady, and rang Mr Gedge.'

'Thank you, Figg. Mr Gedge is the beekeeper, Johnno. He'll come round and see to the damage.'

'Am I in trouble?' Johnno asked. 'Will the police come?'

'It isn't a matter for the police,' Mr Barrie said and gave Louisa an enquiring look. She nodded. 'It's between you and Mr Gedge. And I'll be there, too.'

'Put your shirt on,' Louisa said.

As the three of them walked up to the kitchen yard, Louisa thought that the children's trauma of losing family and home was emerging in different ways. Johnno's burst out as anger and George wanted to impose order on his world. Gracie withdrew entirely, or so it seemed. They each needed attention in their own particular way.

She thought back to how she and Mr Barrie had handled Gracie's running off and now Johnno's bee incident – how their ideas for dealing with the children seemed to complement each other like different strands of linen yarn being woven into one piece of fabric. She frowned, feeling her face grow hot. She glanced over at him, but he didn't seem to notice.

Before their supper, the children had free time. Alf made

for the kitchen – something about rolling out pastry for Iris – with Lulu at his heels. Johnno disappeared upstairs and the other boys shot out of the door with great purpose.

The girls stayed indoors and set up a hopscotch game in the tiled entrance hall, just in front of the bust of Aristotle. They used small stones that Priss produced from her pocket, as if always at the ready. Only when Louisa looked closer did she realise that the stones were actually pieces of broken brick. Tiny mementos of home.

'Gracie, want to play?' Athena called out.

Gracie shook her head. The game went on. While Gracie watched the other girls from the corner of the entrance hall, Mrs Moffatt, sitting between two rails on the landing above, watched Gracie.

When Mr Gedge arrived and went to the hives, Louisa went to tell Mr Barrie and Johnno in the boys' dormitory.

'You must tell the truth and apologise,' Mr Barrie was saying when she looked in. 'The thing is, Johnno, the younger boys look up to you, so you've got to pull your socks up and set a good example. Show them how best to handle a bad situation.'

Iris had soothed the boy's stings with witch hazel, but the incident had drained Johnno of his usual bravado. He now stood before his teacher looking pale and a bit twitchy.

'He won't beat me, will he?' he asked.

'He won't beat you,' Louisa said from the doorway. 'I promise that. Mr Gedge is a Quaker.'

Whether the boy understood what a Quaker was or not, her words seemed to calm him. Louisa followed the two as far as the landing, where George lingered near the Chinese palm.

'Lady Bee,' he said quietly, sidling up to her, 'when we were looking for Gracie, I found something. I think it might be important.'

'What did you find?' Louisa asked.

'I went to the library to look for her,' George said. He was obviously a boy who liked to tell a story in proper order. 'I looked in all the chairs and the sofa and behind the blackout curtains just in case.'

'It's a good idea to be thorough,' Louisa said, wondering what stupendous item George could've found worthy of this buildup.

'Mrs Darnley said, "Leave no stone unturned" and so I was looking under the table and there it was.'

'There what was?'

He held out his hand and opened it to reveal a true treasure.

'A hairpin!' Louisa exclaimed. 'Well done, George.' She took it, twisted a loose lock of hair and had it pinned up in a flash.

George looked both proud and a bit let down. 'I thought it might be part of a bomb.'

'Yes, well, let's hope we never find bits of a bomb inside the library.'

Iris came up from the kitchen as Mrs Harrison emerged from the direction of the schoolroom.

'Supper,' she announced to the hopscotchers. 'Although first, we'll need to get the blackout curtains pulled shut. Tell those boys out there.'

Athena shot out of the door to deliver the message. The others headed to the dining room for their meal, but Louisa noticed that Gracie was not among them. And where was the cat?

She went straight to the library. Gracie lay on the sofa, sound asleep, with Mrs Moffatt snuggled up against her tummy. Louisa closed the blackout curtains, then switched on a nearby lamp. She leaned over and gazed at the girl, whose hair had fallen into her face. The frown had been smoothed away from her forehead and her fingers loosened from their usual fists.

'Gracie, love,' Louisa said quietly. She gently pushed hair off the girl's cheek.

Gracie stirred. 'Mama,' she said.

Tears pricked Louisa's eyes. 'Gracie, love,' she said again, her voice nearly failing her. 'Time for supper.'

Gracie opened her eyes and stared at Louisa. Her thoughts were unreadable, but at least she didn't pull away. Instead, the girl heaved a great sigh as if taking up a burden she'd set aside for all too brief a time. She sat up. Louisa dared not offer a hand, and so the two of them walked not touching, but side by side together to their supper.

CHAPTER 8

Supper, marking the end of their first full day at Oxburrow, began quietly. School furniture had been delivered. Gracie had been lost and found. Johnno had gone to war against the bees – Mr Gedge told him they would wait a few days to see if the bees settled, then discuss reparations.

As the children ate, Louisa put an elbow on the table and her chin in her hand, and watched them. Surely after this the days would be easier. When Mrs Harrison looked askance at Louisa's elbow, she removed it.

Dolly and Gloria began a discussion about whether the oatmeal sausages on their plates contained any actual sausage. Mrs Harrison – her face pale with exhaustion – reminded them they were not to talk at the table.

Louisa could've settled their debate – yes, there was sausage, although very little – but she decided there was no reason to point this out because, with the aroma of seasoning and a bit of fat to fry them in, it hardly mattered. They were tasty and quickly devoured.

There was little conversation over the meal – even the grown-ups, who were allowed to talk, attended mostly to their food. When one spoke, it was about neither bees nor war, but neutral subjects, such as which winter crops grew best in Suffolk.

Eyes lit up when Iris brought out the pudding – a syrup tart. They all tucked in and it vanished quickly. Louisa watched as Gracie chased the last piece of pastry around her plate with her spoon. Finally, she picked it up with her fingers and popped it in her mouth. When she looked up, Louisa caught her eye and gave her a wink. For a fleeting moment, Gracie paused in her chewing.

The day ended in the chaos of bath time. There were tears from the young ones – both boys and girls – along with squeals, shouts and a great deal of accidental and intentional splashing, as each child took their turn. They went by age, and so the oldest had the cleanest water and the youngest – well, at least they didn't seem to mind.

Louisa lit fires in both dormitories to help the children dry off before bed, and then helped Iris mop up the bathroom floors – they couldn't decide which was in the bigger mess at the end, girls' or boys'. She wished everyone good night, offered Ovaltine to Mrs Harrison – who accepted – and to Mr Barrie, who declined. Iris volunteered to deliver the Ovaltine and so Louisa went to bed.

But she did not sleep – at least, not at first. Instead, she lay awake listening and waiting, more prepared this second night. She wore better pyjamas and had already tied on a long wool dressing gown. But it was only after she had drifted off that the shrieking started. She awoke with her heart pounding and dashed to the girls' dormitory.

The lamp in the corner of the room was lit and dying embers in the fireplace gave off a faint glow. Mrs Harrison stood at the foot of Gracie's bed. The other girls remained still.

When Louisa approached, Mrs Harrison raised her chin.

'Thank you, Lady Brightford, for your concern as to Gracie's well-being.'

It sounded to Louisa as if the woman was giving her the push.

'But it's unnecessary,' Mrs Harrison continued, 'for you to be here for every episode Gracie has. I will see it through.'

Another shriek started, keeping Louisa from replying that she'd bloody well come to the girl's bedside if she wanted to. By the time the scream had subsided, Louisa had got hold of her manners.

'Mrs Harrison,' she said in a low voice, 'I believe I can help Gracie by showing that she's still loved even though her mother is gone.'

'She cannot go chasing after you every time you walk out of the door,' Mrs Harrison whispered harshly.

'Oxburrow is the children's home and they should have the freedom to learn about the countryside and the community.'

'There's no point in getting their hopes up,' Mrs Harrison replied.

'You'd rather move back to London and have another bomb fall?' It slipped out before Louisa could stop it.

Mrs Harrison turned red as a beetroot and Louisa felt ashamed.

'I understand you care for the children,' she said. 'Can you not see that I do, too?'

Gracie fretted in her sleep as if working her way up to another shriek.

'Gracie love,' Louisa said softly, going to the side of the bed. 'You're safe. It's all right, you're safe.'

And that was the core of the problem – Gracie might be safe, but her mother wasn't. She had left her mother behind.

Louisa spotted Gracie's sock kitty on the floor by the bedpost. She retrieved it and gently brushed it against the girl's cheek. Gracie's hands closed round the soft toy. She squeezed it and tucked it under her chin, and her fretfulness ceased. Louisa gently smoothed out her covers, said good night to Mrs Harrison and left.

Mr Barrie, still dressed, waited on the boys' side of the landing.

'Mr Barrie, would you care for a drink?'

They went to the library, where she directed him to the drinks cabinet while she switched on the wireless. When it had warmed up, the music of an orchestra floated out. Louisa imagined the London clubs where they seemed to dance the night away regardless of bombs falling. Mr Barrie held their glasses of whisky while Louisa turned off the lamp, parted the blackout curtains and opened the French windows out onto the stone terrace. A few flagstone steps led down to the lawn. It was, she thought, the perfect vantage point to view the countryside.

They sat in deckchairs and Louisa was glad for her wool dressing gown in the chill night air. The orchestra struck up 'The Way You Look Tonight'. It had been such a long time since she'd been to a dance. She swayed to the music and sighed, then remembered she was not alone.

'It's the only way I can sleep some nights,' she said. 'Sitting out here and listening to music. I love Suffolk at night – the blackness of the sky meeting the flat landscape and how after a few minutes you can see even though all you have is starlight.'

A soft breeze rustled down at the bottom of the garden hedge. Louisa sipped her whisky.

'It must've been terrible in London,' she said.

Their eyes met and, as when telling her Gracie's story, it was as if he were considering how much to say – or whether to say anything at all. Then he looked away, out into the darkness.

'Once the bombing started,' he said, 'it seemed as if it didn't stop, and you couldn't breathe for the brick dust and smoke. The air-raid warning sounded every night. We'd go down to the shelter – there's a warehouse a few streets in from the docks with a good solid undercroft and it's been kitted out. Every morning we'd come up to more destruction. The docks were on fire for two nights.'

'But it was a day attack that hit the terrace?' Louisa asked.

He nodded. 'When the air-raid siren sounded, the children lined up and off we went – one bit of order in the chaos. We were in the shelter two hours.'

'Did you hear it?' Louisa asked. 'The bomb.'

'Heard and felt,' Mr Barrie said. 'They've attached a whistle to their bombs, so you hear it coming down, and when it hits it's as if the earth herself jumps.'

Louisa heard a blackbird calling in the night and, further off, a fox cried out.

'When the all-clear sounded,' he said, 'we came up, and found the school had damage to the roof. Otherwise, it was fine. Then someone came running round the corner, shouting I don't know what. Ambulance and the fire brigade came racing up, clanging their bells and heading towards the terrace. The children broke away and ran for home and we ran after them and when we all turned the corner, we stopped – because there was nothing there. The entire terrace, just a heap.'

'How many died?'

'Fourteen all told, when the count could be made.'

'At first you thought Gracie was among the dead?'

'We did,' he said with a bitter tone. 'For two days. It wasn't as if we weren't working at digging out the bodies – we worked as long as we could see. And at last, there she was, the wee mite, at the very bottom of it all.'

His voice was thick and Louisa's chest hurt as if someone squeezed her heart in a vice. 'Was she conscious?'

'Yes. And unharmed physically except for a few cuts and

bruises. She was covered in dust and debris and holding on to her mother's hand for all she was worth. She blinked at us and a shout went up that she was alive. "Don't cry," they told her. "Don't cry." She never cried, but when we pulled her out she screamed and fought us every inch of the way. We had to pry her fingers off her mother's hand.'

Louisa took a ragged breath. 'What's Gracie like, really?'

His brows lifted and his voice became lighter. 'She's a happy, talkative girl who likes books and cats.'

A sob escaped and Louisa wiped her face with the cuff of her dressing gown.

'And you and Mrs Harrison have been living with the children in the school?'

He nodded. 'I lived in the terrace, too – a two-room flat, I didn't have much to lose. Mrs Harrison gave up her lodging in Finsbury to stay with the children. The school governors promised they would find a home for us as quickly as they could.'

'And they have,' Louisa said with fervour. She silently blessed William Lowrey for making it happen. 'You're safe now – all of you are safe. Why does Mrs Harrison want to cut off her nose to spite her face? What good will it do to move the children?'

'I am a mere teacher. Mrs Harrison is head and she is – at least to me – an enigma. If you solve the puzzle, please let me know.'

'She's a widow?' Louisa asked.

'Apparently, but I've never heard a mention of Mr Harrison.' He frowned, and followed it with a chagrined smile. 'We aren't quite what you expected, are we? We're a peculiar lot.'

Louisa didn't argue the point. 'I don't mind – we live in peculiar times. Look at what the children have been through. What you all have been through. And you arrived only yesterday. We need time to settle in together.'

They were quiet for a moment as Louisa's mind drifted. Mrs Harrison may be an enigma, but surely she could learn more about Mr Barrie. 'Have you always been a teacher?' she asked.

'I trained to be a teacher,' Mr Barrie replied, 'but only took it up three years ago.'

'What happened?'

'The war – the last one – threw a spanner in the works, as it did for many of us. I rather lost my way for a while.'

He'd been so talkative a moment ago, she waited in case he wanted to say more. But instead he turned the tables on her.

'If you're from Sheffield, how is it you came to Oxburrow?' he asked.

She thought for a moment and then said, 'Doing a favour for my dad.'

He seemed to be waiting on the chance that she would elaborate. Perhaps another time she would. Perhaps he would, too.

'Right, well.' He downed his whisky and rose. 'Thank you for the drink.'

'You're welcome,' she said. 'Good night, Jack.'

He paused and then gave her a half-smile. 'Good night, Louisa.'

On Sunday morning, the children were instructed to gather in the entrance hall, ready for church. They had clean faces and clean clothes – the latter thanks entirely to Iris, who had mended, washed and ironed dresses, trousers, shirts and such. 'They've barely more than the clothes on their backs,' she had told Louisa.

Not everyone had come down yet, and, when Louisa realised she'd forgotten her gloves, she thought she would have time to dash up and get them. But at the landing, she heard wails of anguish coming from the girls' dormitory above. Which girl? Instead of counting those already gathered below, she ran up to the second floor, down the corridor and into the room. Mrs Harrison stood with her hands behind her back and a stern look on her face before a weeping Athena.

The girl wailed, 'I want my ha-a-a-a-at!' but the words came out only half-formed between hiccups and sobs. Tears streamed down her face.

'Athena,' Mrs Harrison said, 'you cannot wear such a thing in church. It would be disrespectful.'

Athena noticed Louisa and ran to her, clasping her hands in supplication. 'Please, Lady Bee, please I want to wear it. It's my mum's hat and... and I found it and I want to wear it.'

'Why can't she wear her mother's hat?' Louisa asked.

The teacher drew from behind her a handful of yellow felt streaked with black soot and dirt. Not until Louisa took it could she see that it was a hat – an old-fashioned cloche with a strip of veil hanging in shreds.

'May I wear it, Lady Bee? Pleeeze,' Athena begged.

'This was your mother's?'

'I found it where our house was,' Athena said as she wiped her face. 'They wouldn't let us go back, but Priss and I did and she found a little box that her mum kept a ring in and I found my mum's hat.'

'I didn't know she had it until this moment,' Mrs Harrison said.

Louisa could barely speak at the thought of the girls picking through the rubble where their mothers had died.

'It's a lovely hat,' she said at last. 'Perhaps later Mrs Darnley can help you with a few repairs, but in the meantime I don't see any reason why you can't wear it to church.'

She looked at Mrs Harrison, who pulled in her chin. 'Well, if Lady Brightford gives permission, then of course you may, even though I'd hoped the children would leave behind a better impression.'

With that threat, Mrs Harrison walked out. Athena took the shapeless felt, pulled it onto her head and ran over to the mirror. It was a poor excuse for a hat, but the girl's smile made it look like haute couture.

They organised themselves in the forecourt with the children in twos behind Louisa and Iris. Jack and Mrs Harrison brought up the rear. Louisa caught Gracie's eye – Mrs Harrison had lined them up by age and the girl was at the back – and gave her a smile. Gracie had come downstairs wearing Louisa's red boiled-wool jacket. Louisa had put it on her in the churchyard the afternoon before and Gracie had not returned it. The jacket looked like an oversized coat on Gracie and the sleeves were too long. Louisa would shorten them for her.

Mrs Harrison had put up a protest about Gracie 'appropri-ating' Lady Brightford's clothing until Louisa said she'd given her the jacket. Mrs Harrison, with no more ammunition, had retreated.

Louisa and Iris led the way down the footpath and, before they reached the oak and beech wood, Gracie had made her way to the front.

'You know the way, don't you?' Louisa asked her. Gracie looked up, her scowl in danger of disappearing altogether.

There was a chill in the air, but the day was clear, with banks of clouds on the horizon like woolly sheep in a field. The children needed to get out in the countryside – Louisa filed that thought away for the future, but then worried about how long that future would be. A few days before they were snatched away?

She glanced back at Mrs Harrison, who was explaining to George that not every person's step was the same length, and perhaps he should measure and compare. She was helping George deal with his trauma by channelling it into a school lesson. She cares about the children, Louisa thought with exasperation. Can't she see I do, too?

The people standing outside the church when they arrived watched the parade. Minns saw them and called out 'Good morning, Gracie!' and the girl spun round to see who this was who knew her. She blinked at Minns. Louisa interpreted this as a return greeting.

The Brightford pew hadn't been full in decades, if ever, but now the contingent from Oxburrow crowded in and then filled the next pew as well. This bumped Mrs Greet, who usually sat in the second pew, into the third. Louisa insinuated herself between Gracie and Priss, looked back at the woman and smiled. Mrs Greet, wearing a brave, albeit put-upon, face, nodded in return.

Hugo filled the service with words of kindness and acceptance – probably going completely off the rails from the Church's usual lectionary, bless him. He began by welcoming the children and teachers from Hazel End Charity School to St Gregory's and the village. He then carried through the theme with scripture – 'Suffer the little children to come unto me' and hymns including 'All Things Bright and Beautiful'. He kept quite busy during the service as he moved from pulpit to harmonium and back again.

Louisa had never heard the small church so full of singing. Several of the children joined in, with full voice albeit with a few muddled words. Jack – at the end of the pew – sang out in a strong baritone while, at the same time, helping George find the right page.

When it came time for the sermon, the children found other interests. Sydney kicked the pew in front of him where Dolly sat, and she turned round and stuck her tongue out at him. Athena took off her hat and put it back on again several times. She dropped it once and slid off her seat to crawl over and retrieve it from under the kneeling rail. Alf fell asleep, and yelped when Johnno gave him a sharp elbow.

The quietest in the group were George, who paged through the *Book of Common Prayer*, and Gracie, who kept her hands in her lap and watched Hugo with a faraway look in her eyes.

After the service, the congregation spilled out of the church porch and stood along the walk lined with red and orange chrysanthemums. The village children and Oxburrow children eyed each other cautiously across an imaginary boundary line until the sound of engines was heard and everyone outside the church looked up.

The planes hadn't come into sight yet when Johnno called out, 'Spitfires!' and the collective sigh of relief might've been heard all the way to Oxburrow and back again. Others returned to conversations that had been interrupted, but Louisa put a hand up to shield her eyes and counted the planes. Five of them. She sent a silent message to David, just in case he was piloting one.

Johnno and one of the village boys began discussing aeroplane identification and Priss volunteered the detail that Alf was as good as a compass and could tell which way the planes were going.

'South, south-east,' Alf said with a shrug as if it were nothing.

A general discussion ensued among the older children about how many different aeroplanes they knew on sight, until Johnno made the comment that it was a Stuka that had bombed their terrace. The group fell silent. Word had spread, Louisa thought, about the reason for the Oxburrow children's sudden arrival.

Minns intervened.

'Here now, why don't we all say our names – no point in staying strangers, eh?'

Introductions under way, Louisa shifted her attention to

Mrs Harrison and Mrs Greet. The two women appeared to be exchanging pleasantries, but Louisa, remembering Mrs Greet's comments at the WVS the day everyone had heard about the Brightford divorce, worried they might instead be forming an alliance.

Gracie trailed after Louisa as she walked over to Minns's grandad – Mr Grainger – and her great-uncle, known to everyone as Uncle. The former leaned on a walking stick and the latter sat in a wheelchair. They were bidding another parishioner good day – a lively and loud conversation due to all three of them being a bit hard of hearing.

'Good morning, my lady,' Mr Grainger said.

'Any word from your son?' Uncle asked.

'Yes,' Louisa said, 'he's doing well.' It worried her to say the words too loud in case she jinxed David; and, besides, Mrs Waite stood nearby and, just the week before, her son, fighting in North Africa, had been reported missing.

Minns joined them. 'Will we see you at WVS tomorrow, Louisa?' she asked.

Mr Grainger shook his head and muttered that his granddaughter should know her place, or words to that effect. But Louisa had asked Minns to use her Christian name, so the two women took no notice.

'Yes, of course you will,' Louisa said. 'The children will start lessons tomorrow, won't you, Gracie?'

Gracie looked up at her mildly.

'And so I'll be on the mending table as usual.'

'Well, Minns, we'd best be off,' Mr Grainger said and sighed. 'Can't say as I wouldn't like to be going home to a Sunday joint of beef. Gone are those days.'

'For now,' Uncle said as Minns got behind his wheelchair and pushed. 'For now.'

Their discussion continued as they made their way down the road.

'Gracie!' Athena called. 'Come and look at the bird's nest Mr Barrie found.'

Gracie hurried off to the children crowded round Jack. He had pulled down a branch of a yew and was pointing within. As Louisa watched, Hugo approached.

'Thank you for the lovely service,' Louisa said to him. 'I hope this isn't both their first and last Sunday here.'

'They've only just arrived,' Hugo said. 'They're not leaving, surely?'

'Not if I can help it,' Louisa said. 'But Mrs Harrison has her own ideas. She believes this place is a bad influence on the children. Morally.'

'This place?' Hugo glanced at the villagers as they dispersed. 'Who has been filling her ears?'

Louisa gave a sad laugh. 'I have. I confessed to being divorced, you see, and that makes me a fallen woman and a bad example.'

'Dear God,' Hugo said, and meant it.

'I want the children to know that Oxburrow is their home, Hugo,' Louisa said. 'If they are entrenched in life here, the school governors couldn't move them. They need to heal' – she glanced over at Gracie – 'and I will do everything I can to help them. The trouble is, as soon as Mrs Harrison learned about the divorce, she rang the school governors. I've no idea what she'll do next. I feel as if we are in a race against each other.'

When they returned from church, Iris took off her coat and as she went down to the kitchen said, 'I wouldn't mind a few peas for dinner.'

'Righto,' Louisa said, 'I'll get them.'

'Are you going to the shop?' Dolly asked.

'No, the garden,' Louisa said. 'Come with me and I'll show you.'

'I like the garden,' Dolly said. 'Mr Figg says there are worms in the garden. Some are good and some are bad.'

'Alf, what about you?'

If it was a favour for Mrs Darnley, Alf was in.

The rest of the children had drifted upstairs, but Gracie had stayed behind and was standing by the newel.

'Gracie, want to come along?' Louisa asked as if she expected an answer. 'We might find a worm.'

Gracie wrinkled her nose and then, as if catching herself in the act of being a little girl, scowled, but only slightly.

Louisa nodded out the door. 'Let's go, you three.'

Alf led the way, Lulu prancing at his heels. Gracie walked on one side of Louisa and Dolly on the other. As they went, Dolly told a long story about her gran who had grown a marrow vine that wound itself round and round and round the outdoor lav until 'you had to crawl underneath the thing to get in and do your business!'

'Fortunately,' Louisa said, 'Mr Figg keeps our marrows well under control.' Inside the gate of the walled garden, she took an empty basket from a peg on the doorpost and went over to a long row of vines that climbed up a string trellis as tall as herself.

'Our instructions from Mrs Darnley are to pick as many peas as we can for our dinner.'

The children glanced about them with puzzled expressions. Finally, Alf asked, 'Where are they?'

'The peas?' Louisa asked. 'They're hanging right in front of you.'

Alf wrinkled his nose. 'They don't look like any peas I've ever seen. Peas come in tins.'

'Before they're put in a tin, they grow in pods on a vine.' Louisa plucked a pod and split it open to reveal five fat peas. Alf gasped.

'There they are!' he exclaimed.

Louisa ran her thumb down the inside of the pod and the little green orbs popped out into her hand. 'Here, try one.'

Dolly picked up a pea between thumb and forefinger and studied it for a moment. She took the tiniest of nibbles. 'It tastes like a pea. Gracie, you eat one.'

Gracie followed Dolly's instruction.

Alf followed suit and Louisa ate one, too. 'There's one left,' she said. 'Who wants it?'

'May Lulu have it?' Alf asked.

The dog sat at Louisa's feet, ears at attention.

'Yes, all right.' She tossed it up and Lulu snapped it out of the air. 'Now, let's get picking.'

They worked to fill the basket with pods, Gracie quietly and diligently, Alf distracted by Lulu and Dolly continuing to tell stories of her gran's two china dogs that she and Gloria had played with.

Hugo came to Sunday dinner, having given Iris his bacon ration for that week. He worked his way round the parish that way, eating dinners as a guest in different homes, but without being a burden.

'Shall I give thanks for our meal?' he asked.

During his blessing, their dinner – a ham and potato casserole straight out of the oven – bubbled and hissed like a steam engine.

'Amen.'

Iris was reaching for the serving spoon before Hugo spoke his last word. She dished up the plates and passed them down the table. To accompany the casserole, they ate potato and cabbage croquettes, carrots, leek pudding and a steaming bowl of peas, for which Dolly and Alf claimed responsibility. 'Gracie, too,' Dolly said.

Gracie looked up from pushing her peas into the casserole to keep them from rolling around her plate.

Also, there was a bowl of chutney – last year's. The cooking apples had started coming in, and counting the windfalls alone they already had nearly a crateful.

'Thank you, Iris,' Louisa said, 'for this delicious food.'

In truth, there weren't great amounts of anything, but Iris had a knack for making their plates look full by providing an array of dishes.

'Your voices added a richness to our service this morning,' Hugo said. 'All of you – although I heard Sydney and Mr Barrie in particular.' Sydney paused with his fork halfway to his mouth. 'We don't have enough for a weekly choir at St Gregory's,' Hugo continued, 'but I can wheedle a few parishioners on special occasions. I hope you two and any others of you might join us.'

Sydney's face glowed. 'May I, Lady Bee?'

'I think it's a fine idea,' Louisa said, then expansively added, 'I'm sure Mrs Harrison and Mr Barrie would agree.'

Mrs Harrison conceded with a nod. 'Thank you, Reverend Oldham. I'm sure Sydney will do his best if the occasion arises.'

Louisa heard what Mrs Harrison meant – '*If the occasion arises before I abscond with the children.*'

'What about you, Mr Barrie?' Hugo asked. 'You wouldn't have a drop of Welsh blood, would you? Yours was the other voice that stood out.'

'Mr Barrie taught us to sing "We're Going to Hang Out the Washing on the Siegfried Line",' Athena said. 'Would you like to hear it?'

'Athena!' Mrs Harrison admonished. 'We don't sing at the table.'

'Yes, ma'am,' Athena said.

'I will hear it before I leave,' Hugo told the girl.

'Gracie,' Hugo said, and she looked up from her plate. 'You

seem to be a great observer of the world round you. I don't suppose you've ever seen a dragon, have you?'

Although she didn't speak, her scowl vanished and, as the other children peppered Hugo with questions, Gracie listened with the widest eyes Louisa had ever seen on her. Over pudding – stewed mixed fruit and custard – he told them about the dragon that had lived down near Bures.

'The Bures Worm, they called it,' he said.

'The Bee-yor-ess Worm?' Athena repeated.

'That's the one,' Hugo replied.

Questions flew – what did the worm eat, could it fly and did it live underground or in a cave? All the while, Gracie squirmed in her chair as if she had a question, too, and it was fighting to burst out of her. What would loosen that tongue, Louisa wondered. And when?

'Maybe it's a worm like the one Mr Figg says eats the cauliflower,' Dolly said and giggled.

'Thank you for that interesting story, Reverend Oldham,' Mrs Harrison said, dousing their fun. 'Now children, if you have cleaned your plate, you are excused from the table.'

Iris led the children out and, when they'd gone, Hugo said, 'You must feel grateful and relieved, Mrs Harrison. That you and Mr Barrie and especially these tender children whose very souls have been beaten and bruised have landed safe and protected and cared for here at Oxburrow.'

Tears pricked Louisa's eyes at the fierce love in Hugo's voice. He was an easy-going, generous and kind man, but Louisa knew he could stand up for a cause. He'd talked the village round to acceptance when the Gedges' son refused to fight on religious grounds.

Hugo persisted in his praise. 'I can see Gracie healing before my very eyes – from yesterday to today. And of course, I'm sure we can all agree that's down to Louisa and her loving spirit. And I'm sure you've realised she won't give up' – a slight pause, as if to catch his breath – 'helping the children heal.'

Mrs Harrison sputtered at Hugo's declaration, managing nothing more than 'I... yes... no, I mean... that is...'

'We are more than grateful,' Jack said, his eyes on Louisa. 'It's something of a miracle.'

Mrs Harrison – her face beetroot red – sprang from her seat.

'Will you excuse me, please,' she said. 'I must—' and, without finishing, she hurried from the room.

CHAPTER 9

The woolly-sheep clouds on the horizon had darkened and spread across the sky as Hugo, Louisa and Jack stood out on the forecourt.

'What is it that's making her blind to what's before her?' Hugo asked. 'And does she really have the power to take the children from you?'

'It would seem the decision lies with the school governors,' Jack said with a frown as if annoyed at his own words. 'I am very much subordinate in this outfit.'

Louisa smiled. 'But you want them to stay and you've already stood up to Mrs Harrison. Don't underestimate yourself.'

Hugo's gaze darted from Louisa's generous smile to Jack and back. He lifted his brows slightly.

From indoors came the strains of 'We're Going to Hang Out the Washing on the Siegfried Line' from a few of the children – a repeat performance. Now, Louisa could recognise Sydney's voice above the others.

Hugo cocked his head to listen, too. 'Louisa,' he said, 'you do remember we have the harvest festival coming up on Saturday?'

'Of course,' Louisa said. 'I'm awarding ribbons. Iris will have chutney on the judging table. We'll take the children, of course.'

'You could do better than take the children,' Hugo said with a sly smile. 'You could get them to sing.'

Louisa gripped Hugo's arm. 'Yes! Commit them to an event at church – Mrs Harrison couldn't take them away before that.' Then she took hold of Jack's arm, too. 'Will you lead them?'

'I'll give it a go,' Jack said. 'What shall we sing?'

'How about "We Gather Together"?' Hugo offered.

Jack nodded. Brushing her hands off, Louisa said, 'Then job done. At least it gives us a week to change Mrs Harrison's mind.' Although she wasn't certain what she'd do about the army if they came calling.

Louisa and Jack watched Hugo walk across the drive and down the path, and they remained where they were without speaking after he'd disappeared into the wood. A sense of well-being and nostalgia settled on Louisa. She was reminded of standing in the same spot and watching David set off for school when he was a boy.

Max had raged at her insistence that David should go to the village school, but she would not be moved and he had relented at last, with the compromise that their son would go to a boarding school in Cambridge when he turned eleven. Louisa had thought the idea of a boarding school in Cambridge, which was just up the road, a bit silly. Still, David had done all right at both schools, ending up with good marks and a wealth of friends.

She turned now to find Jack watching her, and she had just started to tell him her thoughts when a fat drop of rain fell *splat* right on her nose. She gave a little cry as there came another and another, landing on their shoulders and bouncing off the chippings. They ran indoors and stood in the tiled entrance, laughing as the rain beat on the windows. There was a crack of thunder, but even louder than the rain was the noise the boys and Priss made as they came flying out of the library and circled the entrance hall with arms outstretched and voices rumbling like engines.

Jack herded them back the way they had come and Louisa headed upstairs. On the landing, she met Gracie coming down from the girls' dormitory. She was wearing Louisa's red boiled-wool jacket.

'You weren't thinking of going out, were you?' Louisa asked.

Gracie blinked. *Was that an answer?*

'Let me turn up your cuffs,' Louisa said. Gracie stuck her arms out and Louisa turned them up twice, then said, 'That's better, isn't it?'

The girl put a hand in one of the jacket pockets, drew out Louisa's letter from David and held it up.

'Oh, look,' Louisa said. She hadn't forgotten where she'd left the letter, but didn't want to take possession of the jacket if Gracie felt comfortable in it. 'This is a letter from my son, David. He's a pilot. Sit down with me and I'll read it to you.'

She sat on a step and, after a slight pause, Gracie sat, too. For a moment, Louisa thought she might speak – ask how old is David or when is supper or where is Mrs Moffatt – but, of course, she said nothing.

Dear darling Mum,

The children should've arrived by now, and I hope they know their great fortune being at Oxburrow, and, more importantly, being with you. I consider myself an expert in the matter, as you can imagine. It sounds as if they've had a dreadful time and now they need all the love you have to give – and that is an unending amount.

Show them a good time and take them on country outings. I'll go, too, next time I visit.

Please ask Mrs Moffatt to do her best to make them feel at home.

Mrs Moffatt had joined them and was sitting on the other side of Gracie, and at these last words the girl took hold of the cat and gave her a hug. Mrs Moffatt did not resist, and, when Gracie let go of her, the cat stayed put and began washing her face.

'Come down to the morning room,' Louisa said to Gracie, 'and I'll show you a photo of David.'

Gracie studied David's photo and looked all round the morning room while Louisa finished a letter to her son she'd started earlier. When it was ready for the post, she and Gracie and the cat went to the library, where the children were looking mournfully out of the French windows at the deluge.

'Now would be the perfect time to organise our lesson books for the morning,' Mrs Harrison said in a voice raised above the clamour of the rain. She seemed to have fully recovered from earlier, when she'd fled from the dining room after Hugo's resounding praise for Oxburrow Manor. She gave Louisa a nod of greeting before continuing. 'We'll begin with maths.'

Jack looked up from an open atlas on the map table, where he'd been pointing something out to George.

Louisa thought organising lesson books a dreary task for a Sunday afternoon, rain or no, and countered with 'Anyone want to play Happy Families?'

This was met with more enthusiasm and Mrs Harrison was forced to concede. Louisa dug out three different decks of cards as Jack arranged the children into two tables. Gracie watched the activity.

'Would you like to play?' Louisa asked the girl.

Gracie gave the slightest shake of her head and retreated to the sofa in the corner, where a stack of books awaited. And the cat.

'I will find a way in,' Louisa said to Jack as she paced the library that night. 'She's separated from her emotions – keeping them at bay – and that can't be good for her. The longer it goes on, the more difficult it will be. She needs to be a little girl again.'

Jack leaned against the map table, whisky in hand, watching and listening. They had met on the stairs after Gracie's nightmare – blessedly brief – as if it were already a standing arrangement. The rain had continued, and so they stayed indoors instead of opening the French windows to the terrace. Louisa had turned the wireless on low, and the orchestra carried on as usual.

'Hugo's right,' Jack said. 'You're making a difference even if you don't see it. She's watching you.'

That heartened Louisa, but it also prompted a question that had been niggling her. One she feared to ask.

She took a swig of her whisky and out it came. 'Do I look like her mother – is that why she's drawn to me?'

Jack sputtered and seemed at a loss for words, but finally managed to speak. 'Irene loved her daughter very much. She would've done anything for her. That love gave Gracie comfort and a safe place even in bad times, which were more common than not. Life was a struggle for Irene. She had no other family that we know of. She was older than most mothers with a young daughter. Not a sign of Gracie's father.' He looked down into his glass. 'The easy answer is that you look nothing like Irene.

What you have in common with her is your love for Gracie. That's what the girl feels.'

Louisa acknowledged the statement with a nod, which she hoped covered up her quivering chin. 'As much as I want Gracie to break out of her shell, I don't want to push her over the edge. I don't want to hurt her more than she's already been hurt.'

She plopped down on a footstool, causing a hairpin to drop into her lap and a curl of hair to fall onto her shoulder. She twisted and rolled it and stuck the pin back and, as if that had changed the subject, said, 'Well, so. Tomorrow is the first day of school at Oxburrow for the children from Hazel End.'

Jack spun the globe that stood next to the map table. 'It's all right to have lessons in here, too? Geography and history – your library is well equipped.'

'Of course – consider the library a part of the schoolhouse,' Louisa said. 'So, you do more than read books? I knew Mrs Harrison was missing something.'

Jack grinned. 'I was reading *Treasure Island* aloud in the evenings this past fortnight as we camped out in the school – just to keep the children's minds off their situation. Mrs Harrison thought it a bit frivolous.'

'They deserve to be frivolous,' Louisa said. 'Why don't we have story time in the afternoon when they've finished their lessons? I would listen.'

Jack turned pink. 'I don't know…'

'Oh now, don't be modest,' Louisa said in a cajoling tone. 'I'll bet you do a fine rendition of… what's the parrot's name?'

'Captain Flint,' he said, laughing. 'And flattery will get you nowhere.'

Monday morning – the first day of school at Oxburrow. Louisa and Iris were in the kitchen seeing to breakfast as the children filed into the dining room. Mrs Harrison and Jack were upstairs readying the lessons. There was a quiet mood over the proceedings, a sort of 'getting back to business' feel in the air. Louisa liked it – it spoke to her of a permanence.

'Morning post arrived,' Iris said, giving the vat of porridge a last stir. 'I've put it on the hall stand. A stack of brown envelopes.'

'Bills then,' Louisa said as she set bowls on a tray. 'I'll see to them this morning.'

'But can they be paid?' Iris asked as she poured the tea.

'Of course they can. That was promised – fifty pounds in the post office account to start off. I'm going into the WVS this morning and while I'm in the village I'll check with Mrs Nethergate to be certain.'

Louisa lingered outside the door of the formal dining room long enough to hear Mrs Harrison begin to drill the older children on their times tables. Then she stood outside the library as Mr Barrie worked with the younger ones on counting by twos, before she took herself off to the morning room.

She left the door open in hopes that some warm air would come in or cold go out. It was a pleasant room, although without a fire it could be a bit chilly. It seemed extravagant to heat a room used so little. Instead she buttoned up her cardigan and threw the blanket from the chaise longue over her shoulders. At least she had the sun on her back. She settled in with a stack of brown envelopes and the accounts ledger.

It wasn't a pretty sight, how much was owed. Max's allowance for the household budget had never been overly generous even when he had been a part of the household. After he'd decamped to London he had tightened his grip on his money, but Louisa and Iris had got on all right. Now, after the divorce, they would have even less. It was a bonus, the money from the Ministry for taking in the children, although Louisa would've found a way regardless.

After an hour on the accounts, she closed the ledger and turned her mind to other things. She went to the kitchen and looked in on Iris, who was putting up the first batch of chutney.

'I'm off to the WVS,' Louisa said. 'You all right here?'

'Mmm,' Iris replied, eyeing a mountain of chopped apples on the worktable. 'I'll save you the washing up.'

The village hall was already abuzz when Louisa arrived – women were greeting each other and exchanging news before they went about their work knitting blankets and coverlets from a stockpile of left-over yarn or sewing new garments from old. A bit of creative stitchery could make men's shirts out of worn bedsheets.

Minns called out, 'Good morning, Louisa,' lifting her chin, as her hands were busy rolling bandages. Others spoke, too, and Louisa made her way to the back of the hall exchanging greetings until she reached Mrs Byers, doling out yarn at the knitting table.

'Good morning,' she said. 'I hope you don't mind if I beg off mending today. I need to find clothes for the children.'

'So, they're staying?' Mrs Byers asked.

'Staying?' Louisa echoed as the ground beneath her feet seemed to shift. 'Why do you ask?'

Mrs Byers dismissed the topic with a shake of her head. 'It's nothing, only Charlotte Greet mentioned it might not be a permanent move.'

Louisa had noticed Mrs Greet and Mrs Harrison chatting outside the church yesterday, and now she knew what the topic had been.

'Mrs Greet must've misunderstood,' she said, realising it wouldn't do to point the finger at Mrs Harrison, the source of the problem. 'The children aren't leaving. We've transformed the dining room into their schoolroom and they've started lessons just this morning. We're quite settled.'

'I'm very glad to hear that.'

They went back to the children's clothing room together.

'Take whatever you think they need,' Mrs Byers said. 'If what we've gathered isn't for your orphan school, I can't imagine who it would be for.'

Louisa dug in, going through neat stacks of clothes and picking out what she thought might fit each child, particularly keeping an eye out for suitable cold-weather items. Autumn could be quite brisk and in Suffolk they were no strangers to winter snow. Searching through the boys' clothes, she came across quite a few of David's things. She had given them up because there had been no need to save them, and yet here she was pulling them out to take them back to Oxburrow. It was a funny old world.

She'd packed up two large, heavy boxes that included night-dresses and pyjamas, and had just realised she would need Colin and his horse and cart to take them back for her when Minns peeked round the door.

'Here you are,' she said. 'Iris rang.'

Louisa's blood ran cold. Why would Iris ring except with bad news? And what news was so bad she couldn't wait until Louisa had returned?

She couldn't move – it was as if all her muscles had seized up.

The words finally came out. 'Is it a telegram?'

Because that would be the worst news.

'No,' Minns said in a rush, understanding without being told. 'Not a telegram. But, she wanted you to know that a Captain Wentworth rang. From the army.'

CHAPTER 10

Louisa flew back to Oxburrow, pausing once to lean against a beech tree, her chest searing with pain. She started up again, and was gasping for breath by the time she broke out of the wood expecting to see the army's lorries nose to tail on the forecourt. It was empty, but that didn't settle the turmoil in her tummy.

She dashed round to the yard and went in search of Iris, who stood over a cold pot of boiled beef bone, skimming the fat off to use later. Louisa burst in, gasping. 'I don't believe it!'

The room began to spin and she grabbed a chair to steady herself.

'Sit down now,' Iris said, 'before you fall down.' She left off the beef fat and took hold of Louisa and guided her into the chair. 'I didn't say they were knocking down the door, did I?'

Louisa's legs ached and, now that she was breathing regularly again, she felt quite cross.

'I wouldn't put it past him,' she said.

'Captain Wentworth?' Iris said.

'Max.'

'Why don't you ring him – this Captain Wentworth, I

mean. He didn't say what he wanted, only that it wasn't an emergency, but he'd like to speak with you. It may be nothing about the army moving in.'

'Fat chance,' Louisa said. 'It's Max behind this. Pulling strings, bullying people. He knows that William Lowrey made the arrangements and that the children are here. I won't let him turf them out.'

'And so, Captain Wentworth?'

'Oh, Captain Wentworth will hear from me,' Louisa said. 'Make no mistake about that.'

A bit of bravado there. Could Louisa talk the army out of taking Oxburrow? She decided to wait until her mind was clear before dealing with Captain Wentworth, and so she set him aside. For the moment.

Louisa calmed down sufficiently to enjoy Iris's dinner – a pie chock-full of roasted parsnips, carrots and potatoes and held together with a few eggs, making it rather like a savoury baked custard. Iris had already learned that anything involving pastry was a hit with the children.

Afternoon lessons had yet to begin when Louisa came up from the kitchen and heard Mrs Harrison and Jack talking just inside the library.

'We can't abandon their penmanship, but I don't know what else we can do,' Mrs Harrison said. 'They can have lessons aloud this afternoon.' At the sudden burst of loud laughter from upstairs, she added, 'Now, I'll go and see that they're washing their hands.'

Mrs Harrison took the stairs, and Louisa looked in.

'Is there a problem?' she asked Jack.

'We're out of lesson books,' he said. 'Supplies were short and we brought what we could, but we'll have to appeal to the school governors to see to it.'

'You can't let lessons stop for want of paper,' Louisa said. 'The newsagent in the village sells stationery. I'm going in and I'll buy enough notebooks to tide you over.'

'We're indebted to you enough,' Jack said.

'Nonsense,' Louisa replied. 'It'll all come out of the money from the War Office, won't it? Who do you have this afternoon?'

'I've got the young ones.'

'Why don't you read them a story?' Louisa asked with a mischievous smile. 'You've got an entire library at your fingertips.'

She went to fetch her coat and then remembered her letter to David, so she dashed off to the morning room, and when she returned Gracie was standing outside the library door with the red boiled-wool jacket on.

'What have you got up your sleeve?' Louisa asked her.

Instantly, Gracie raised her wrist and peered inside and then looked up at Louisa, who laughed.

'Hang on.' Louisa glanced inside the library and motioned to Jack. 'May I take Gracie with me this afternoon into the village?'

Jack nodded. 'That's a fine idea. The children will need to know about the village and Gracie can give a report when you return.'

Gracie looked at the floor.

'We'll be practising our song for the harvest festival this afternoon,' Jack said, 'so be back in time for that.'

Louisa smiled at this. Jack had caught on to the way she was treating Gracie, as if the girl were about to say something in the next moment.

She introduced Gracie to the people they met in the village, and no one seemed to mind the girl not answering questions. 'Dreadful place, London, isn't it?' the butcher asked. 'Aren't you glad to be away to the country?' a mother with her baby in a pram enquired. They chalked her silence up to her being shy and went on their way.

'And here is Mrs Nethergate's,' Louisa said. 'She has the post office window inside her sundries shop, and I must stop and have a chat.'

They stood for a moment in front of the display window crowded with an enormous jar of sweets, a selection of shoelaces, a pyramid of tins of tomato soup, a notice about the availability of blackout material and a poster encouraging the women of Britain to *Come Into the Factories!* It was a busy display, but Louisa could see Gracie's gaze resting on the most important item – the jar of sweets.

Inside, after introductions, Gracie wandered around with her hands behind her back, examining the fare, while Louisa explained about the money in her post office account.

'No, my lady,' Mrs Nethergate said, 'I've not seen a penny come into your account, but I'm sure these things can take the government days, you know.'

'Yes, of course,' Louisa said. It had been nearly a week since they'd had word of the children coming, but there was a war on, after all.

Now Oxburrow Manor was behind with the grocer, electricity and the telephone and Louisa had just ordered coal. Still, she stopped in at the newsagent, bought nine notebooks and put them on account.

Louisa and Gracie walked back to Oxburrow in silence as Louisa worried. Did this have something to do with Captain Wentworth? Had he telephoned to tell her that permission for the children had been withdrawn? She had told Iris she would ring him back, but had put it off hoping he would go away of his own accord. She huffed in irritation, then saw that Gracie was watching her with a slight scowl as if she'd picked up Louisa's mood.

Enough of that. 'I'm looking forward to tea, aren't you?' she asked the girl brightly. 'A slice of bread and butter. With jam. Can't beat a spoonful of... I don't know. It might be raspberry.'

Gracie said nothing, but at least the scowl had vanished.

Immediately upon their return home, Louisa sent Gracie back to her lessons in the library and went into the telephone room. But instead of telephoning Captain Wentworth she rang Bates, Lowrey and Lowrey. Louisa had persuaded William Lowrey to send her the orphans from Hazel End Charity School and he had done just as she'd hoped. She'd rung again when the letter about the army came, asking him to plead her case to the War Office, and he'd taken that in hand, too. Or so she'd thought.

She was told that William Lowrey was in court in London, and unavailable until midweek and would she like to leave a message for him? For a moment Louisa dithered, but then she plunged ahead. Yes, there were two items she would like to discuss with him – compensation for the children, and the army. She hoped she didn't sound greedy, and started to explain, but got no further than 'You see, it's only that—' before she cut herself off. William would understand.

The children's lessons came to an early end when Colin arrived on his horse cart with the boxes of clothes from the WVS – Minns had arranged it. Colin toted the cartons to their respective dormitories and wouldn't take a sixpence for his troubles. 'It's for those little ones,' he said even though at sixteen, he was barely five years older than the oldest. Instead of a coin, Louisa took him to the kitchen, where Iris sat him down and gave him bread and cheese and a bottle of ginger beer.

Louisa went to the girls' dormitory to find them standing in a row from tallest to smallest – from Priss to Gracie – wearing nothing but their vests, pants and socks. They looked a chilly lot.

'Now girls,' Mrs Harrison was saying, 'We will do this in an orderly fashion. I will lay out the clothes on the extra bed and we will select something suitable for each of you.'

'May I help?' Louisa asked. 'I chose the clothes and packed the boxes, so I already know what's in them. It could save you a bit of trouble.'

'Yes, of course,' Mrs Harrison said reluctantly.

Louisa dived in, pulling out a frock for Priss, a skirt and blouse for Athena and pinafore dresses for Dolly and Gloria to wear over their jumpers. Gracie had edged over to the carton and was peering inside as the other girls were handed their pieces.

'Do you like flowers?' Louisa asked Gracie, who immediately straightened and scowled. Louisa held up a blue collared dress in a flower print. 'Here now, arms up. Buttons go in the back, so I'll do them up for you.'

Gracie stuck her arms in the air and Louisa, all business so as not to alarm the girl, set to it with the buttons. 'It's a bit loose on you,' she said, 'but that'll soon be sorted with Iris's cooking, won't it? And all that damson jam for tea? Or would you prefer strawberry?'

The girl threw her a look and Louisa nearly laughed.

It was a gay party as Mrs Harrison dutifully buttoned and unbuttoned, pulled on and off and gave directions. 'Tuck in that blouse, Gloria.' 'Athena, you missed a button.' But Louisa thought she said those things in a kind manner and might even have been entering into the fun. Did Mrs Harrison have fun?

Louisa discovered doll clothes tucked into one corner of the box. It didn't surprise her – one of Minns's favourite occupations at the WVS was collecting any scraps of fabric not used for blankets or proper clothes and fashioning them into soft toys or dolls' clothes to give away to those who wanted them. It was a kind and comforting thing to do.

'Look here,' Louisa said to the girls. She held up a doll's dress to her own chest and asked, 'Do you think this will fit me?'

The girls squealed with laughter.

'Well then, who could it be for?'

Priss held up her doll. 'It might fit my Winnie!'

'There you are, Priss. The rest of you come over and see what Minns sent.'

Gracie surveyed the offerings from a distance.

Louisa picked out a small blue pinafore and held it up. 'Your kitty would look like Mittens or Moppet in Tom Kitten's story wearing this.'

'Gracie's kitty is named Agnes,' Athena called over. 'Just like her real kitty.' She threw Gracie a look and then added, 'Mrs Harrison said Agnes ran away.'

Another loss. 'Agnes is a lovely name,' Louisa said. She held out the little frock. 'What do you think?'

Gracie studied the pinafore for a moment and then took it from Louisa, sat on the edge of her bed and carefully dressed her sock kitty.

'Thank you for your assistance, Lady Brightford,' Mrs Harrison said.

Louisa was well able to take the hint of dismissal. 'You're welcome. I'll just go and look in on the boys.'

She left as Mrs Harrison began instructing the girls in how to fold their clothes.

Louisa could hear the sounds of squabbling from behind the door of the boys' dormitory as she approached. She gave a knock and called out, 'May I come in?'

'Yes,' Jack replied, the single word filled with an ocean of relief. 'Yes, please do.'

When she opened the door, the boys fell silent. They were standing here and there in various stages of undress. Sydney –

wearing a shirt that reached his knees – and George, wearing only socks, pants and vests, were in a tug-of-war over a jacket. Alf's head and one arm stuck out of the neck of a jumper too small for him. Johnno hadn't yet removed a stitch.

'All right, boys?' Louisa asked and was peppered with answers.

'Alf took the jumper I wanted!'

'Lady Bee, whose trousers are these?'

'George laughed at my shirt!'

'Sydney won't put on a clean vest!'

Jack sighed with exasperation. 'We're having a bit of trouble.'

'Do tell,' Louisa said and gave him a quick smile as she strode directly to where the contents of the box had been strewn across two beds. 'Right, boys, let's start at the beginning. Sydney, off with that shirt. Alf, let's get you out of that.' She tugged on the sweater, trying to get it over the boy's head, but the boy came with it. After a shake or two and a yank, the jumper seemed to give up, and flew through the air on its release.

She gathered up the clothes and put them in order – silently acknowledging that occasionally Mrs Harrison's organisational skills were useful – then handed out pieces to be tried. When she reached Johnno, who Louisa suspected of being around eleven years old, she looked him up and down. 'Johnno, would you like to wear long trousers?'

Johnno's face lit up at this offer of moving out of boyhood. 'Mr Barrie, is that all right?' he asked.

Jack nodded. 'If Lady Bee says it's all right, then it is.'

Louisa held up a sturdy pair of brown serge trousers. 'Try these on. We'll see if they need turning up.'

'Lady Bee,' George said, 'I found a bear in the box. Two bears and a fox.'

'And a horse,' Sydney said. 'Or maybe it's a goat.'

Minns at work again. She knew it wasn't only girls who needed the comfort of a soft toy now and then. But it was tricky with boys these days – one never knew if they wanted a bear or if they thought that having a soft toy was too childish.

'Those are from Minns,' she said. 'Perhaps she thought you might have left your own animals behind and would like something on your pillow.'

'May I have the horse?' George asked. 'To keep my bear company?'

'It isn't a horse, it's a goat,' Sydney said.

'I don't need one of those,' Johnno said, sticking his chest out with a show of bravado.

'Because you already have a bear,' Alf said.

'I do not!'

'Do you know,' Louisa interrupted, 'my son, who flies Spitfires, took his bear with him when he went off to training.'

'Oh,' Johnno said. He frowned and shrugged one shoulder. 'Well, I might have brought an old bear along.'

'Perhaps he would like a friend,' Louisa said. She brushed off her hands. 'Well, Mr Barrie, that's got them started at least. See you at supper, boys.'

Jack followed her into the corridor.

'You shouldn't have to manage the children all on your own,' Louisa said. 'You or Mrs Harrison. I want to be a part of their lives.'

'They already know that,' Jack said. 'I can see it in how they are with you.'

'But it's easier for some than others. Gracie has the farthest to go.'

'You'll get her to talk,' Jack said. 'You got me to talk, didn't you?'

Louisa laughed. 'True, you were a bit... taciturn when you arrived on Friday. I thought you weren't terribly happy to be here.'

'I only needed a bit of country air.'

She knew it was more than that – it wasn't only the children who needed to recover from horrors. What had the grown-ups seen as the terrace rubble had been searched for bodies?

Laughter erupted from within the room and Louisa looked in to see Sydney wearing a pair of underpants on his head like a hat.

'Right,' she said to Jack. 'I'll let you take it from here.'

That evening when the children had just gone to bed, Louisa went down to help set up for breakfast. Iris stood over a pan on the stove.

'Mrs Harrison's Ovaltine,' Iris explained. 'You wouldn't like to deliver it to her, would you?'

Not particularly, but she wouldn't make Iris walk all over the house just because Louisa considered herself finished with Mrs Harrison for the day.

'Am I allowed to set it outside her door, knock and make a run for it?' Louisa asked.

Iris barked a laugh. '"You children are nothing but a gang of hooligans!"' she shouted in a high, creaky voice – a fine imitation of a grumpy old woman who had lived in the next street over in Sheffield. When Louisa and Iris were about seven years old, they had goaded the woman mercilessly by knocking on her door and running off. The prank lasted several days – until Louisa's mother caught them at it.

As the milky water heated, they laid out bowls and spoons and cups for breakfast, and Louisa told Iris about the baby steps she'd made in edging closer to Gracie.

'You're making her feel safe,' Iris said. 'Like a mother would.' She gave Louisa a quick glance. 'Is that what you want?'

Yes was the overwhelming answer, but what would her wants and wishes matter if Gracie were taken away from her?

CHAPTER 11

Dear David,

The children are really feeling at home now – Oxburrow is full of squabbles and laughter and the sounds of running in the corridors – it's glorious. Hugo has asked them to sing on Saturday at the harvest festival. Do you remember the year you won a blue ribbon for best decorated marrow that you'd stuck with countless little twigs and turned into a hedgehog? I doubt we have any spare veg this year, but the singing will do the children good. Except for Gracie – I told you about her. I wish you were here to help her – she needs an older brother to lean on.

Love always,

Your old mum

When the house had quietened, Louisa went to bed wearing her wool dressing gown, prepared to rise at a moment's notice. But when she awoke it was to silence, and when she checked the time it was morning. She threw back the blackout curtains and squinted at the sun.

She had slept the night through and it both comforted and worried her. Had Gracie had a peaceful night or had she called out and Louisa had slept through it? She dressed and hurried down to the first floor, where she met Mrs Harrison.

'A quiet night?' Louisa asked hopefully. 'That's good. It's progress, don't you think?'

'It has happened twice before since the bombing,' Mrs Harrison replied. 'Nothing else has changed.'

But Louisa would not let the woman burst her bubble.

'Good morning, girls!' she called out. The girls, criss-crossing the corridor between bathroom and dormitory, called back their greetings. Gracie looked out from the bedroom, still in her dressing gown, her thick brown hair matted from sleep and her fringe standing straight up. Louisa gave her a small wave.

She got as far as the landing and there was Jack.

'Good morning,' she said. 'I slept straight through the night.' She felt as if she owed him an explanation.

'You deserve that,' Jack replied.

'Yes, but then I missed our chat.' She frowned. Perhaps he didn't look at it as a standing appointment. She would feel ridiculous in that case. 'You could've had a drink on your own.'

'It wasn't the drink I missed,' Jack said.

At that moment, a shout came from the boys' corridor.

'Come back here!'

Lulu came racing down the stairs with a sock in her mouth. In one swift move, Jack bent over and scooped the wriggling dog up.

'See you at breakfast,' Louisa said.

·   ·   ·

She continued to the kitchen, but she hadn't been there long before Alf came rushing in with both socks on and Lulu at his heels. They brought with them a chill air from outdoors.

'Mrs Darnley, may I chop the carrots for soup before breakfast?' Alf asked.

'Good lord, Iris,' Louisa said, 'Alf isn't a kitchen maid.'

'But I like to do it, Lady Bee,' Alf said. 'And I like to stir things together and see how the pot comes to a boil and I want to know why carrots take longer to cook than peas. Peas come from a pod,' he added as if to point out that he had retained this bit of new knowledge.

'The boy's a scientist,' Iris said. 'And a scientist needs a laboratory, doesn't he, Alf?'

'Right, but porridge first, Mr Scientist,' Louisa said. 'Come along.'

While Iris turned her hands purple chopping beetroot to pickle, Louisa poured all her energy into chutney that morning – going out to the orchard and picking up more windfall apples, peeling and cutting out the wormy bits. It was all she could think to do with Oxburrow affairs so unsettled. She couldn't talk to William Lowrey, and was reluctant to ring this Captain Wentworth until she had. She couldn't confront Max about his underhanded ways in case that landed her with the army for certain. Even Mrs Harrison's threat of taking the children away had taken a back seat in her mind.

Iris set a heaping bowl of the fresh chutney on the table at their midday dinner, but Louisa, her head and nose still full of pickling, didn't think she could face it and so passed it on. When she noticed Gracie doing the same, she changed her tune.

'Oh, look at me,' she said, 'I've forgotten the chutney.' She took it back and gave herself a generous spoonful, then set the bowl down across the table near Gracie, who then also took a serving.

'On Saturday,' Louisa said, 'Mrs Darnley's chutney will be judged at the harvest festival. I imagine she'll win her usual blue ribbon, because it's really the best.'

'And speaking of the harvest festival,' Jack said, 'we'll practise our song just as soon as afternoon lessons end.'

Mrs Harrison hadn't been best pleased when she had learned that they – Louisa and Jack – had promised Hugo that the children would sing on Saturday. Jack had attempted to take full blame, but Louisa would have none of it. The saving grace was that it was for church and a hymn. Or was it that the teacher was really just humouring her and didn't believe the children would last that long at Oxburrow?

Later in the afternoon, Louisa sat at her desk in the morning room and started a letter to David, even though she'd sent one off only the day before.

Movement outside the window caught her eye. She could see, beyond the terrace, that the children had finished their lessons and were on the lawn playing football – both boys and girls, and in mixed teams. Only Gracie stood apart – she was easy to spot as she wore Louisa's red jacket. Alf let loose an impressive kick that nearly made it past Priss as goalie, but she leapt sideways at the last moment and caught it.

Louisa, indoors and out of earshot, cheered and clapped, dislodging a hairpin, which she caught in her hand as a heavy lock fell loose. She took out the other pins and stuck them between her lips, combed her fingers through her hair, then began the process of sweeping it up, rolling and twisting, and then securing it one by one with her hairpins. When she had finished, she turned, to see that Jack had come halfway into the room.

'Were you watching the match?' she asked, nodding out of the window.

'No, I was watching you pin up your hair,' he said.

It caught her by surprise – his look, the way she went weak in the knees, how warm the room had become.

She exhaled in a breathless laugh. 'Oh, now, Mr Barrie—'

His brows shot up.

'Jack,' she corrected herself. 'I don't know, Jack,' she said, shaking her head and filled with longing and apprehension in equal measure. 'I don't know.'

He didn't reply, but walked over, stood behind her and looked out of the window.

'They played girls against boys once,' he said, 'and the girls won. You should see Athena kick. The boys cried foul, so now they play mixed and everyone's happy.'

The subject had changed, but only on the surface, and so, when Iris gave a single knock and put her head in the door, they both started.

'Mr Gedge is here about Johnno.'

'Right, I'll go and get him,' Jack said.

After he'd left, Iris leaned against the doorpost and looked at Louisa.

'What?' Louisa asked.

Iris didn't answer.

Louisa crossed her arms in front of her. 'You think you interrupted something, but you didn't. There was nothing to interrupt.'

'Is that so?' Iris asked.

'And there won't be,' Louisa said. 'It isn't a good idea.'

'It's the best idea you've had in ages.'

Louisa laughed. 'Come on,' she said, 'I'll help you with tea.'

·　·　·

Later, when Louisa went out to the hives, Mr Gedge had gone and had left behind him a convert to beekeeping.

'And then Mr Gedge said the queen was all right and so the bees didn't leave,' Johnno said to Louisa and Jack.

The boy talked as he bounced sideways in a scissor-step fashion as the three of them walked up from the kitchen garden. Johnno wore what he described as his bee uniform – a sort of pith helmet entirely covered in heavy netting, which was tucked into the neck of his shirt along with a duster-like coat, slightly too big for him, that had seen better days.

'We repaired the hive,' he continued, 'and added a new frame and Mr Gedge says I can help when he goes to check his other hives if it's all right. Is it all right, Mr Barrie?'

'If you're interested and Mr Gedge is willing,' Jack said, 'I don't see why not.'

'Will you ask Mrs Harrison for me?'

'I will.'

'And we'll see if Mrs Darnley can patch those holes in your coat,' Louisa said.

Johnno looked down at the coat in admiration. 'Mr Gedge said this was his son's coat and it was all right if I wore it.'

The boy's enthusiasm continued undimmed as he sat down to tea, still dressed in full regalia until Jack pointed out he wouldn't be able to eat if he didn't take it off.

It heartened Louisa to see the difference between the angry boy who had arrived and the one who sat at table now. He was healing, as they all were. She looked across the table at Gracie. There had been nary a scowl from the girl all day.

'It was kind of Mr Gedge to give you a jar of honey and kind of you to share it with us,' Louisa said. 'Shall I give everyone a spoonful or would you like to serve?'

Johnno considered the open jar in front of him. 'No, Lady Bee – you can do it.'

Louisa stood by Johnno, dug the spoon into the jar and

twirled it, then lifted it high over the slice of buttered bread in front of him. It fell in a thin stream and landed in a golden-brown puddle that oozed its way to the crust edge.

There were *oohs* round the table and Johnno beamed proudly. Louisa continued round the table, doing the same for each child, remembering that David had never grown tired of watching his mother's performance.

'Now children, eat carefully and do not get sticky,' Mrs Harrison said.

An impossible command that went completely unheeded. By the time they'd finished, stickiness abounded – fingers, mouths, chins – and it wasn't limited to the children. A small pool had drizzled over the edge of Louisa's bread onto the plate and, when Mrs Harrison wasn't looking, she quickly scooped it up with a finger and stuck her finger in her mouth. Across the table, Gracie watched her. Louisa wiggled her eyebrows at the girl.

Afterwards, the children queued up at the kitchen sink and washed the stickiness away. Mrs Harrison joined the queue, before leading them upstairs to the library and reminding them that they would need to give oral reports on the books they'd chosen from the Oxburrow library.

Louisa hummed, 'We Gather Together' to herself as she and Iris washed up.

'Gracie might talk about Tom Kitten,' Louisa said as she drew a dripping plate out of the sink.

Iris took the plate from her and dried it. 'That's pie in the sky.'

'She's this far from talking' – Louisa held her thumb and forefinger not an inch apart – 'I know she is. There was no nightmare last night and there'll be none tonight, I'll wager. Care for a flutter?'

'I've always lost any wager against you,' Iris replied. 'So, no thank you.'

'You're a wise woman, Iris Darnley,' Louisa said, wagging a wooden spoon at her. 'Now, what do you need from the garden?'

Late that evening, Louisa waited in the library. There had been not a peep or shriek from Gracie. Fat drops of rain splattered outside on the terrace, and so Louisa left the blackout curtains closed and instead turned on a lamp in the corner and switched on the wireless. When it had warmed up, out floated the strains of the orchestra. She imagined the scene at the London club – ladies gliding across the floor in sparkling dresses and men sporting waxed moustaches. She remembered her father had a pot of wax for his. Did men still use it?

A light tap at the door and Jack looked in.

'I've left you a ten-bob note in the morning room,' he said. 'For the notebooks yesterday.'

'That wasn't necessary,' Louisa said. It also hadn't been necessary for him to come to the library this late and tell her.

Neither had it been necessary for Louisa to still be dressed instead of wearing her woollen dressing gown.

The orchestra struck up 'A-Tisket, A-Tasket'. Louisa's foot started tapping and, against her better judgement, she held out her hand. 'Dance?' she asked.

He didn't hesitate, but took her hand and pulled her up and to him. For a brief moment they stood close, Jack's hand flat on her back and Louisa's on his shoulder. It was all she could do to keep from reaching up and running her fingers through that unmanageable hair of his, but she caught herself and covered by breathing an embarrassed laugh. They waited through a measure of music and began as one.

They managed to stay off each other's toes – just – and Louisa even twirled once, but that ended badly and they both laughed. Jack hummed along as they danced and Louisa, for a moment, imagined them at the club in London, but then decided that dancing at Oxburrow was infinitely better. When the song came to a finish, they dropped their arms but stayed where they were, fingertips barely touching and neither looking at the other. If another lively number came up, Louisa told herself, that would be all right.

But it was 'Cheek to Cheek', and Louisa thought that a bit too... cheeky. She stepped back, but Jack took hold of her hand and she allowed him to take her in his arms again and they danced, just as the song said. His end-of-the-day beard was scratchy and it was all Louisa could do to keep from rubbing her face against it.

The song ended too soon and another number began, but they remained standing still for the longest time. Or was it only a moment? Louisa couldn't tell. Jack leaned back slightly and looked at her.

'I'm no Fred Astaire,' he said.

'Just as well,' she said. 'I'm no Ginger Rogers.'

The roar of engines seemed to come from nowhere. Louisa held her breath. The windows rattled as the aeroplanes passed overhead. The rumble faded, but the spell had been broken and she suddenly felt foolish.

'It's late,' she said. She stepped away and switched off the wireless, annoyed by her own actions. Why did she have to be a wet blanket?

'Yes, it is late,' Jack said. 'And we need to have our wits about us for the new day. This morning, Alf went down early, sneaked the dog up to the dormitory and hid her under his blanket before I even knew he was awake.'

'And you let Lulu stay.'

'Well,' Jack said, 'it wasn't long until breakfast.'

She grinned at him. 'You're a good egg, Jack Barrie.' She had meant to walk straight past him on her way out, but instead stopped long enough to kiss him on the cheek. 'Good night.'

. . .

'Are you drawing pictures in your new lesson book?' Mrs Harrison asked.

'It's a chicken,' Athena said.

Louisa had been passing by the schoolroom as lessons began and hadn't intended to interrupt, but couldn't understand why Mrs Harrison sounded so annoyed. She went back to the doorway and looked in to see the teacher standing over Athena, who sat at one of the spindly-legged tables.

'Is it one of our hens?' Louisa asked. 'May I see?'

Athena held up the notebook. 'It's the black-and-white one with spots,' she said.

'That's lovely,' Louisa said of the drawing. It was, at least, most certainly a chicken. She looked up at the teacher. 'Don't you think?'

Mrs Harrison pursed her lips. *At me?* Louisa thought. But it wasn't as if she had disturbed a morning lecture. The children were copying out times table problems from the chalkboard, and she saw that Athena had already finished and had drawn the chicken beside her maths work.

'The children shouldn't spoil their lesson books,' Mrs Harrison explained.

'She's loads of room still,' Louisa said. 'And it's a lovely bit of decoration. It's rather like the medieval monks decorating the pages of the scripture they copied out.'

Mrs Harrison's raised eyebrows made it clear that she thought Athena's chicken had no relation to medieval monks.

Alf sidled over to Louisa and held up his lesson book. 'I drew a Spitfire.'

'Well done, Alf,' Louisa said. 'Wouldn't it be lovely to put that against a blue sky?'

'We only have our pencils,' Athena pointed out.

'So I see,' Louisa murmured. She looked up brightly. 'I'm so sorry to disturb, Mrs Harrison. Back to maths, children.'

Louisa had an idea, but she would ask Jack what he thought first. He had the younger children in the library, and Louisa stopped outside the door and peeked in. Dolly, Gloria and Gracie were sitting on an upholstered bench under the shelves of ancient history and the boys – Sydney and George – perched on the edges of chairs pulled over from the fireplace. Jack stood beside a blackboard.

'In what country do we live?' he asked.

'England!' came the answer from everyone except Gracie, who at least looked attentive.

'Yes, England. And our nation?'

'Britain!' called out Dolly.

'What county are we in?'

There was a brief pause, then George answered. 'Suffolk.'

'And what is the name of the village?'

There was an even longer silence.

'Oxburrow?' Gloria offered in a tentative voice.

'Oxburrow is the name of our house,' George said. 'Lady Bee's house.'

'Your house, too,' Louisa said, stepping inside. 'I hope I'm not disturbing the lesson.'

'You're most welcome,' Jack said. 'You can answer the question for us.'

'Our village is called Debden Ash,' Louisa said.

The children tried out the words for themselves.

'Who lives in Debden Ash?' Jack asked.

'Lady Bee,' Gloria said.

The others chimed in with, 'Mrs Darnley!' 'The Reverend!' 'Minns!' 'Farmers!' and – from Sydney – 'Sheep!'

'Right,' Jack said and handed a piece of chalk to Dolly. 'Put all of those names up there and add anyone else you can think of who lives in the village. You can leave off the sheep.'

'What if we don't know the spelling?' Sydney asked.

'George will spell them for you.'

The children got busy and Jack and Louisa stood near the door.

'Do the children enjoy drawing and painting?' she asked. 'I've seen Athena draw, and Alf, too.'

'I believe they would, but they've had little chance to try.'

'Well, I have an idea to give them the opportunity. You see, David loves to paint and he's quite good. I love to paint and I'm rubbish but that doesn't matter. Every Christmas for many years, we gave each other watercolour sets. There's something wonderfully fresh about using a new set. We kept the leftovers, of course, and they're packed away in the attic. I'll go and see what I can turn up and you can explain it to Mrs Harrison.'

Jack looked at her with a sceptical eye.

Up to the second floor Louisa flew and down to the end of the corridor, where she opened a door and took the winding stairs up to the top. Half of the attic had been servants' quarters, but the other half held more than a hundred years of Brightford paraphernalia. Louisa stood in the middle of it all and turned slowly, looking for the right trunk. There was an Edwardian rocking horse that wouldn't rock and a long-case clock that had ceased working probably before Prince Albert died – along with more recent furniture and belongings that no longer had a place below. But where were the watercolour sets?

'Aha!' She spotted the green ribbon tied through the latch of the trunk, marking it as full of David's childhood toys. Inside, among wooden trains and building blocks, lay an ageing and slightly misshapen cardboard box. She pulled it out and took off the lid, and found her treasure – a heap of small, coloured paint tiles that were the remnants of all the watercolour sets combined. Lying on top were two handfuls of brushes.

'Let's get this sorted,' she said aloud. She set the cardboard box atop a dusty table and, as she did so, noticed under the table the old wind-up gramophone that had been still in use when she arrived at Oxburrow. She dragged it out along with the box of records and selected 'When My Baby Smiles at Me.' She gave the handle a long crank, then dropped the needle.

Memories flooded through her. She and Max had danced to this song. Louisa seldom let her mind slip back to those happy, early days. She would never want to go back there again, but still it made her sad that their marriage had disintegrated and angry that Max had never stopped blaming her.

She took the record off and looked through the others. Then, out of the corner of her eye, she saw a shadow at the top of the stairs. Gracie had followed her. Louisa smiled at her and, without speaking, took the record she'd just spotted – Tchaikovsky's *Swan Lake* – and put it on the turntable. It was an old favourite and she knew just where to drop the needle. The waltz.

As the music swelled, Louisa stood, held her arms out at her sides, and swayed in time, then danced her way over to the girl. Gracie's eyes grew wide and bright. At last close enough, Louisa held out a hand to her.

'Louisa!'

Iris's voice cut through the music and both she and Gracie jumped.

'Yes?' Louisa called down. 'Hang on.' She switched off the gramophone and went to the door. Iris had come halfway up the stairs.

'What is it?' Louisa asked.

'You'd better come down.'

Instinctively, Louisa backed away. 'Why?'

'The school governors are here.'

CHAPTER 12

Louisa, fearful that Iris had come to say a telegram had arrived, laughed with relief – but then the words sank in. The school governors – Mrs Harrison had made good on her threat. A wave of anger swept over her. The woman had given no indication that morning that this was afoot. She was doing her best to catch Louisa out.

'Gracie, love.' She turned to the girl and saw the magic moment had disappeared – the light had gone from her eyes and her hands were clasped in fists.

Iris came to the top of the stairs. 'I've put them in the drawing room,' she said, in an even tone, but Louisa saw a fiery fury in her eyes. 'Mrs Harrison has sent the children to their rooms. She's told me to stay with the girls.'

Did she want to hide them away? Was she frightened that the children would look too happy, too well fed?

'Go with Iris,' Louisa said lightly to Gracie. 'I'll see you soon.'

Gracie obeyed and Louisa dashed to her own room, threw off her cardigan and put on the smartest jacket she had. She pulled the pins from her hair in such a frenzy that she dropped them and had to scramble around under her dressing table. By the time she had her hair in some semblance of order and had made it to the landing, she was in such a state she had to hold on to the newel with both hands. Jack stood waiting for her.

'Oh, Jack, she's going to take them away!'

She barely had the words out before he took her hands and clasped them firmly in his.

'It's an ambush,' he said. 'She shouldn't have done this. There was no reason.' His touch and his voice – although harsh – enveloped her in warmth and a calm settled over her.

'But she has done it and I must face it.'

'I'll come down with you,' he said.

'No, you stay with the boys. She's left the girls with Iris – getting her out of the way, no doubt. Afraid Iris might give them a piece of her mind.'

'Louisa, if they had wanted to take the children away, they would've done so without coming for a visit.'

She cocked her head and listened to his words again in her head. 'So, you think there's a chance? That I could convince them that Oxburrow Manor isn't a den of iniquity?'

She saw that spark in his eyes – flint striking steel. 'You aren't alone in this fight.'

Louisa took hold of the bronze handles on the double doors, paused for a moment and then stepped in quietly and without fanfare. There were three school governors – no, four – ignoring her as they examined their surroundings.

The late-morning light called attention to the room's defects – the gap near the ceiling where a chunk of plaster cornice had broken off a couple of years back and the cracked pane in the corner window. The drawing room had always retained an atmosphere of abandonment even when in use. It looked like a shrine to Victorian Gothic ornament – the massive walnut fireplace carved with elephants and tigers, the dark lampshades that selfishly hoarded their light. The entire room was trimmed in gilt.

The nearest man, white-haired and dressed in a dark suit, was bent over the lamp table peering at a miniature of a lady with her plaited hair in coils round her ears.

'Hello,' Louisa said to him.

He jerked upright when she spoke, as if he'd been caught pilfering.

'I'm Lady Brightford.'

'Oh,' he said, 'are you—'

His mouth remained open but no more words came out. Louisa wondered if he had stopped himself in the nick of time from saying, 'Oh, are you *still* Lady Brightford?'

'Lady Brightford,' he said at last. 'Yes, er... delighted to meet you. I... er... What a lovely... er... room.'

Was the entire interview to be carried out in fits and starts? Louisa closed the doors behind her.

'Thank you,' she said and waited for him to proceed. At the very least introduce himself. Across the room, two other men – one with a heavy moustache and the other in a worsted-flannel suit the colour of mulberries – looked away from a small, dark still-life painting of overripe pears. In no way did it disguise the much larger shadow on the wallpaper of the Gainsborough landscape that had been sold off years ago to keep Oxburrow afloat.

The other two men shifted uncomfortably. A woman stood in silhouette against the window. When no one spoke, Louisa realised they were embarrassed – chagrined to be faced with her at last and find she was not the ogress they had expected. This thought momentarily calmed her nerves.

'And so, you are the school governors for Hazel End?' she prompted them.

'Yes!' the man with the moustache exclaimed, and then, as if he'd startled himself, coughed. 'That is, we are four of the five.'

'Well, a good show nonetheless.' Louisa waited again.

The moustache man looked past her, and she realised they must be hoping for a rescue from Mrs Harrison. Caught on the back foot, were they? She saw no reason to make it easy for them.

'How lovely of you to take the time to call on us here at Oxburrow – and all the way out from London!' She smiled. 'Gosh, you must've left awfully early. And you didn't get lost? Well, you've done better than most. If you meant your visit to be a surprise then you have succeeded. You've even interrupted the children's lessons.'

'Oh dear,' said the man in the mulberry flannel. 'We didn't mean for that to happen.'

'But you came out at Mrs Harrison's... invitation, didn't you?' Louisa asked.

At that moment, the woman herself burst into the room, out of breath.

'I'm terribly sorry,' she said, 'I've been arranging the coffee as the cook was otherwise engaged, but she's seeing to it now.'

Turfed you out of her kitchen, that's what Iris did.

Louisa smiled at her. 'We've just been discussing what a surprise it is for me to meet the school governors, as I had no idea they were coming for a visit.'

Mrs Harrison's face turned the colour of the mulberry flannel suit. 'You see, my lady—'

'And such a journey out from London,' Louisa continued sweetly. She gestured to the white-haired man. 'Mr... Mr... Oh dear, I don't believe we've been introduced.' She gave him a confused smile.

The governor looked aghast. 'Please forgive me, Lady

Brightford – where are my manners? I am Thomas Hargreaves, and this is Edwin Ilkington' – moustache – 'and Oscar Merrick' – mulberry flannel. Louisa nodded to the men while Hargreaves continued. 'And this is Mrs Marian Perrymont.'

Louisa's head whipped round so fast that a hairpin went flying.

Mrs Perrymont stepped out of the window recess, slowly, as if she were a film star making an entrance. With the light no longer at her back Louisa could see her features. She had clear skin and her arched eyebrows were drawn on, but not in an exaggerated fashion. Her blond hair was swept back and curled round her ears in a perfect coiffure. She wore a suit so well made it had to be from Paris, and she had a small mouth that drew up in an economical smile at the corners.

So here she was at last – Marian Perrymont. Max's mistress.

Louisa lost all feeling in her limbs, and gripped the back of a wingback chair to steady herself. Marian Perrymont had been Max's mistress for the past two years – not that he'd ever mentioned her. It hadn't occurred to Louisa that she would ever lay eyes on the woman. In a carefully studied move, Louisa smiled not at any one person, but to the room.

'How lovely to meet you all,' she said, hoping the words didn't sound as if they were stuck in her craw, which they were. She needed out of the drawing room. She needed to breathe. 'Would you excuse me for a moment? I'll go and help with the coffee.'

Louisa turned to flee, but in that moment Iris entered with the coffee tray.

'Oh, thank you, Mrs Darnley,' Louisa said. Iris did a double-take and Louisa realised she must look as pale as she felt. 'This is Mrs Darnley, our housekeeper, cook and my dear friend.

These are the school governors come to see how well the children are doing – is that correct?'

Louisa raised her eyebrows at them and the men murmured what sounded like wary assents.

'Here is Mr Hargreaves,' Louisa said, 'and Mr Merrick and Mr Ilkington. And here is Mrs Marian Perrymont.'

She had waited until Iris had set the tray on the table or there might've been coffee and broken cups everywhere. As it was, Iris shot upright so fast Mr Hargreaves, nearest to her, jumped.

Iris recovered quickly, but her wiry frame became stiff with disapproval even as she poured the coffee.

'If you'll excuse me,' Louisa said, 'I won't be a moment. Please do enjoy Iris's currant cake, It's the very best.'

She strolled out and closed the doors slowly, then tore up the stairs to the boys' room, pausing just outside to catch her breath. She heard Jack say, 'Sydney, how do you spell "platypus"?'

The girls had joined the boys and when Louisa opened the door all were laughing, but they stopped and stared at her with wide eyes and open mouths. What did she look like? She tried a smile.

'Bring them down,' she said to Jack. 'Bring them all down and let the governors see for themselves how well the children are doing.'

Jack gave a nod and, without further ado, Louisa returned to the drawing room.

'Coffee?' Iris asked her when she walked in.

'Yes, thank you. Pour one for yourself, too, and sit down.'

If the school governors saw anything unusual about the cook sitting with guests in the drawing room, they didn't show it. Perhaps Mrs Harrison had warned them of the odd household.

Louisa had never gone in for dramatics at school, but had to commend herself on the calm and confident act she put on while they drank their coffee and ate their currant cake. Not that they appeared to be interested in grilling her on her marital status – not a word was said of personal matters. Instead, the discussion kept to the safest topics.

'Dry year?' asked Mr Ilkington.

'Quite flat in Suffolk, isn't it?' Mr Merrick asked.

'Are you near that warrior ship that was found – Sutton Hoo?' Mr Hargreaves enquired.

Throughout the innocuous conversation Louisa kept Mrs Perrymont in her peripheral vision, but, although the women attended, she asked no questions and made no comment. She sat perfectly poised and polite.

Mrs Harrison, too, kept herself to herself. Her colouring had returned to normal and her savoir faire allowed her to give nothing away. What was behind that façade of serenity? Did she want to shout about her victory at surprising Louisa? Was she confident that the governors would see the situation at Oxburrow as the teacher saw it?

It seemed to Louisa to take for ever, but it had been only a few minutes before there came the sound of shuffling from without. The double doors opened to frame the children as if they were on a stage, clustered together, with Jack standing at the rear.

They presented quite a picture. Johnno wore his netted pith helmet. Alf held a calm but alert Lulu in his arms. Athena had pulled on her mother's cloche, which Iris had done her best with, and Dolly held up an egg basket. So it went, each child with a bit of Oxburrow to show. Even Gracie clenched the copy of *The Tale of Tom Kitten*, as if she might read it aloud. Her eyes were glued to Louisa, whose heart was full.

'We thought you would like to see the children,' Jack said, 'and hear how they've been doing since arriving at Oxburrow on Friday.'

'What?' Mrs Harrison exclaimed, but then caught herself. 'Really, the school governors do not need to hear—'

'What a fine idea,' Mr Merrick said. 'It's Mr Barrie, isn't that right? Come in, children. Come in.'

The children filed in, girls first, then boys, jostling a bit in a good-natured fashion. *Look at them*, Louisa thought with pride. It had been only five days since their arrival and yet she would swear that already they appeared healthier and happier. Surely the governors could see that?

'Children,' Louisa said, taking command – this was, after all, her own house. 'Have you met the school governors before?'

There was emphatic head-shaking all round, accompanied by replies of 'No, Lady Bee.'

'I say' – Mr Hargreaves leaned forward in Louisa's direction – 'is it proper, the children addressing you that way?'

'It's their special name for me and I find it endearing,' Louisa said, the merest suggestion of a challenge in her voice. When none came, she made short work of the introductions and then looked at Jack.

'Johnno,' he said, 'you're the oldest. Would you like to start?'

Johnno threw out his chest. 'This hat and my coat are what I wear when I'm helping Mr Gedge keep the bees.' *Well done, Johnno*, Louisa thought. He would learn about botany, chemistry, entomology and the science of weather while tending bees, but, if all the school governors saw was a poor boy learning a trade, then so be it.

Alf talked about cooking and being responsible for Lulu, who had been his mother's dog, and on it went until only the youngest remained. Gracie.

'Gracie doesn't talk,' Athena informed the governors.

'Athena!' Mrs Harrison said in that same tone of chastisement Athena was so good at ignoring.

'Gracie likes to read,' Louisa said, 'and she's brought in one of her favourite books to show you.'

Gracie stared at Louisa, who nodded. Without losing her scowl, the girl raised the book and held it in front of her face, upside down.

'It's *The Tale of Tom Kitten*,' Louisa said. 'I'm not certain, but I think Gracie might be reading it to Mrs Moffatt, our cat here at Oxburrow.'

Gracie lowered the book only far enough for Louisa to see her eyes widen with surprise. Louisa winked at her.

As if on cue, Mrs Moffatt herself strolled into the drawing room, tail in the air and nose sniffing out the possibility of butter.

Lulu yipped, squirmed out of Alf's arms and hit the ground. Mrs Moffatt puffed up into a cat twice her normal size. Then they were off on a circuit of the drawing room, knocking into Mr Ilkington, who spilled coffee onto his tie, before they escaped out the door. The children broke out in peals of laughter and Louisa joined them, but her laughter dried up when she saw Mrs Harrison's steely look.

Iris came to Mr Ilkington's rescue with a cloth pulled from the pocket of her apron. She dabbed the spot and asked, 'Shall I rinse that out for you, sir?'

Mr Ilkington declined. Iris collected the dishes and left with the tray. With the entertainment moved off stage, the room dropped to a deadly quiet. The men looked none too happy, and Mrs Perrymont unreadable.

The children closed ranks as if they sensed the tension in the air. Louisa felt her ire rising. Couldn't the children be children?

'We went to church on Sunday,' Athena announced to the room. She ran over and put her arms around Louisa's neck. 'Lady Bee took us and it's called St Gregory's. We sat in the front row.'

Louisa took note of how canny the girl was. What better

way to show they were being given good instruction than church attendance?

'Reverend Hugo came to dinner and everything, didn't he, Lady Bee?' Athena added.

'He did. You're a good recorder of events, Athena,' Louisa said. 'Perhaps you should write everything down in a diary.'

Athena frowned. 'My writing isn't very good.'

'I'll help her,' Priss said.

'Well, there you are then,' Louisa said. 'You and Priss can write a story about how you lived at Oxburrow Manor during the war. Perhaps years from now people will read it.'

She glanced at the governors, whose gazes darted to each other and away.

Iris took the children off and the school governors stirred in their chairs.

'Before you leave,' Jack said, 'I'm sure you'll want a general report on the state of things, which I am happy to give you, if Mrs Harrison allows.'

Mrs Harrison folded her hands in her lap. 'Proceed, Mr Barrie.'

The governors settled back in their chairs.

Jack began by describing their warm welcome to Oxburrow even though they'd arrived a day early. He refrained from mentioning that Louisa had been mistaken for a scullery maid.

He explained that Lady Brightford had given the children clothes from the WVS to replace what they'd lost, that Mrs Darnley cooked wholesome and delicious meals and that the children's recovery was already evident.

'Wouldn't you say, Mrs Harrison?' he asked.

Mrs Harrison frowned. 'The children... yes, yes.'

He told about the care and sense of safety Lady Brightford

and Mrs Darnley offered to the children. He wrapped up the report by mentioning the school's lack of supplies.

At the end of it all, the only question the governors had was about the best route back to the London road and could Mr Barrie please explain that to their driver.

Louisa looked out of the window and saw that Iris had taken coffee and cake to the fellow who sat behind the wheel of a Rolls-Royce, and was chatting with him through the car window.

'Wouldn't you like to see how we've arranged the school?' Louisa asked.

The men mumbled apologies, citing the time and business in the city, but Mrs Perrymont suddenly found her voice.

'I'd like to see the schoolrooms,' she said.

Of course she would, Louisa thought. She was a mole, a spy, and would scurry back to Max and paint the situation in the direst of terms, agreeing with him that Oxburrow was fit for nothing and should be pulled down.

The tour didn't last long. In the schoolroom, the men gave a cursory glance at the times table pinned up and the Families of the Animal Kingdom list on the chalkboard. They made innocuous comments – 'Ah yes' and 'I see.' Mrs Perrymont said nothing. In the library, a large atlas lay open to the Caribbean and Jack explained the children were interested in where *Robinson Crusoe* was set.

At a thundering of footsteps on the stairs, he excused himself. The school governors returned to the drawing room for left-behind satchels. Louisa stayed in the library for a moment, quiet and alone.

Had the school governors seen that the children were on the mend? What was their charity for if not this?

She closed the door and returned to see the visitors off. As she approached the drawing room, the doors opened and the men emerged. They had their backs to her as they headed for the entrance hall.

'It was barely controlled chaos in there,' Hargreaves said to the other two. 'Whatever happened to normal school?'

'What are we expected to make of this?' Merrick asked.

'I don't see the point of coming all the way here without Richards,' Ilkington said.

'Well, Marian did insist,' Hargreaves said, 'although I don't know why. It's really Richards' business.'

Louisa reeled from this exchange, taking hold of the door handle to steady herself as she watched them go. The 'point' of their visit had been made, hadn't it? Mrs Harrison wanted the children moved and now they would be. Louisa saw children healing and the governors saw chaos.

At that moment Mrs Perrymont, lagging behind the men, came out of the drawing room, saw Louisa and stopped.

'One of the children,' she said as she pulled on her gloves, 'Gracie, is it? She never speaks?'

Louisa was at once on guard. 'Didn't Mrs Harrison tell you what happened to the children?'

'Yes, of course,' Mrs Perrymont said. 'We knew about the children's homes being destroyed and them losing their mothers. But I didn't realise there was such a dire case as this.'

'Gracie isn't a case, she's a little girl. She's had a terrible experience and needs time to recover. She needs love and care and patience – not to be packed up and toted around like an unwanted parcel.'

Louisa had poured her fear and anger into her words, knowing that it was too much, that she was most likely giving Marian Perrymont ammunition to use against her. Against Oxburrow, the children. Against Gracie.

Her outburst had not cleared the air, but at least it had been said. Practical matters overtaking her for once, she added, 'We could do a good deal more for the children if we had the fifty pounds promised us.' She cringed at the petulant tone in her own voice.

'You've not received any money?' Mrs Perrymont asked.

'We are not destitute,' Louisa said, lest Max get word of her complaints. 'We can do for ourselves very well in the country and the children all have their new clothes from our local WVS – it's only that there are other costs.'

A small frown wrinkled Mrs Perrymont's brow. 'Thank you for telling me that – I'll make note of it.'

With that, Louisa knew she'd well and truly put her foot in it.

Mr Hargreaves appeared.

'Marian? We're ready.'

Louisa brought up the rear as they walked out to the drive, where Mrs Harrison spoke to each of the school governors before they climbed into the Rolls. Louisa stood nearby, silent. Mrs Harrison watched the car motor away with an enigmatic expression – slightly furrowed brow, determined line to her mouth. Triumph? Frustrated that she and the children weren't in the Rolls with them? Mrs Harrison sighed as the car disappeared down the drive.

'The best-laid plans,' Louisa said to her and left to help Iris with dinner.

The moment Louisa walked into the kitchen, Iris whirled round and said, 'Bloody hell! What's her game?'

There was no need to clarify who Iris referred to – Marian Perrymont.

'Same as Max's, don't you think?' Louisa said as she took the pot of carrots and turned them into a serving bowl. The steam rose in her face, which was already hot. 'They've come to take the children away so that the army can have Oxburrow as Max had intended. That's all there is to it.'

'They can't do that to the wee things,' Iris said, pulling a meat and macaroni pie out of the oven and after that a sheet of haricot bean croquettes.

'Mrs Harrison will have them packed up and back on that charabanc as quick as a wink and what power do I have to stop them?' Louisa asked. 'None.'

'But then why allow the children to come in the first place?' Iris asked.

'William Lowrey made the arrangements,' Louisa said, whacking a wooden spoon on the edge of the table. 'I asked for the children from Hazel End after I'd read about the terrace being bombed. It all happened so quickly. Now they'll be gone just as fast.'

'Are you going to let them do that?' Iris asked in a sharp voice. 'Take the children?'

Steel suddenly coursed through Louisa's veins. 'I most certainly am not.'

But by dinner, she realised her brave words were shallow. She wielded no power here. Perhaps the school governors were kind and had good intentions, but were they strong enough to withstand Mrs Harrison's moral objections or the behind-the-scenes machinations of Max and Mrs Perrymont?

A black cloud hung over Louisa and she had no interest in banishing it.

She noticed others at the table noticing her silence. Jack, on her right at the end of the table, watched her with a slight frown. Gracie, on her left, scowled at her plate and kept her hands in her lap. Louisa made a show of taking up her own knife and fork. She caught Gracie's eye and wiggled the utensils in the air. 'I'm not going to let a single macaroni escape my plate!'

Athena giggled. Gracie opened her hands, took up her spoon and got to work.

'The children are going to paint this afternoon,' Louisa said to Mrs Harrison in a pleasant tone. 'Did Mr Barrie mention that?'

Mrs Harrison's fork paused halfway to her mouth. 'No, I had not heard,' she said, 'but an art lesson would be useful, I'm sure.'

Louisa, suspicious of Mrs Harrison's sudden obsequiousness, said, 'You must work closely with the school governors. They probably not only have a say in how the school was set up, but also oversee its moral standards. Tell me, how is it that you know Mrs Perrymont?'

'Mrs Perrymont's husband was a generous and charitable man when he lived,' Mrs Harrison said, 'and Mrs Perrymont is continuing his practices.'

That answer was sufficiently vague for Louisa to suspect that Mrs Harrison knew next to nothing about the woman. Would it help or hurt Louisa's cause if she did?

'It's unfortunate all five governors couldn't be here today,' Louisa said.

Mrs Harrison stabbed the last piece of carrot on her plate. 'Mr Richards was greatly missed.'

That told Louisa on which side of the fence the fifth school governor stood. That was two governors on Mrs Harrison's side, albeit for different reasons, and three wafflers – Merrick, Ilkington and Hargreaves.

As they tucked into their pudding – tinned apricot crumble – Louisa glanced up to see Jack still watching her. He deserved an explanation – about Marian Perrymont, about Max and her marriage – and Louisa found herself quite willing to give it. But for the moment, all she could offer was a quick smile.

.   .   .

They set up the art school on the terrace using several rickety easels dug out from the attic and several more decrepit chairs. At first, nothing seemed to stay upright. Once an easel had been set up, it would topple when the drawing pins were stuck in to hold the children's 'canvases', which were unused pages torn from an old estate ledger.

But eventually each child had an easel, a blank canvas, an assortment of coloured paint tiles, a brush and a bowl of water. Louisa gave them a quick lesson, dipping her brush into the water, swirling it on first one paint tile, then another, and applying colour to the paper. Then she held up her own painting to them.

'What is it?' Johnno asked.

'It's a bear!' Dolly said.

Louisa pulled a face and the children laughed. 'It's Lulu!' she said.

The dog had found them on the terrace and now sat at Alf's feet. The children's gazes went from dog to painting.

'Are you sure it's Lulu?' Athena asked.

'Oh yes!' Alf exclaimed. 'Look, there's her black nose.'

The children nodded and murmured assents.

'Right,' Louisa said. 'Off you go! Paint anything you like – something you see or something you remember.'

Mrs Harrison had discovered that she had a great deal of tidying to do in the schoolroom and did not come out, which left Jack and Louisa to oversee the activity. She helped Dolly find a blue tile for the sky and noticed Jack showing Sydney how to extend his arm and hold up his thumb to measure a distant object. Louisa glanced back to see Gracie hard at work.

At first she had only frowned at her canvas, but then, as if hit with sudden inspiration, she'd started in. She still frowned, but also worked diligently – dipping her brush in the water, grinding it into the tile in her hand, then applying it with fierce back-and-forth brushstrokes.

Louisa approached and, when she came round behind Gracie, the girl dropped the brush and looked down at her hand where the tile lay in a boggy mire of paint. Black paint.

Slashes of black covered the page and black water dripped off the edge of the paper. Surely Gracie had painted what she had seen and still must see in her mind's eye. The inky darkness under the rubble where she had lain for two days. All the while holding on to her dead mother's hand.

Louisa knelt down beside the girl, who scowled at her painting of darkness.

'Oh Gracie, love,' Louisa said, her heart breaking. She reached out her arms, but Gracie stiffened and, once again, Louisa retreated.

CHAPTER 13

Louisa and Jack took the children's paintings off their easels and pinned them up in the library, where they hung in front of a shelf of Greek plays.

They put Gracie's picture up, too. The girl looked at all the paintings, but paused to study her own. Louisa thought perhaps she saw a sliver of relief in the girl's face. It was as if taking the heaviness from her mind and heart and putting it on paper had its own healing power.

Mrs Harrison came into the library to view the children's work. She took her time perusing the paintings – Athena's orange chicken, Dolly's blue sky, Alf's depiction of Iris in the kitchen and George's large, lozenge-shaped object.

'Is it an aeroplane?' she asked.

'No, ma'am,' George said. 'It's the charabanc that brought us here.' Louisa's heart gave a lurch as she offered a prayer that the holiday coach wouldn't soon return and take them away again.

'Well done, children,' Mrs Harrison said. 'When your pictures have dried, we'll take them down and put them away.'

'No,' Louisa said, her face as crestfallen as the children's.

'I'd like them to stay up. It brightens up the library. We'll leave them. And the ones you paint next time, too.'

'*Next* time?' Mrs Harrison asked with a note of incredulity. She said no more, but turned to the children. 'Upstairs now, and wash your hands for tea.'

The children fell into line behind her and marched out like good soldiers.

'Was Mrs Harrison a Wren in the Great War?' Louisa asked Jack, but then remembered that Mrs Harrison was an enigma to them both. She switched to a more timely topic.

'Jack, this morning, I noticed that the school governors didn't know you.'

'The school governors don't know me from Adam,' he agreed, 'and that's fine with me.'

'How did you come to be a teacher at Hazel End with no interview for the post?'

'Mrs Harrison took me on – I suppose you could say I'm one of her charity cases.'

When he didn't continue, Louisa said, 'You don't think you're getting away with such a meagre explanation, do you? I remember you said you trained as a teacher, but after the war didn't return to it.' She softened her voice. Perhaps she shouldn't ask about his private memories. 'You don't need to tell me about it if you'd rather not.'

'I'm happy to tell you,' Jack said, 'but it's not the most exciting tale.'

Louisa leaned against the back of the chesterfield and waited.

'Right, then,' he said, and took the place next to her. 'Three years ago, I was working in a coal yard with Chuff. It was the best and steadiest work I'd had in a great while. I noticed that, every day after school, the boss's son came to do extra school-work in the yard's office. Ten years old and he couldn't read – the letters were a jumble to him. His father wanted a better life than the coal yard for his son, but it wasn't looking good. I asked if I could help the boy during my tea break. Six months later, I found myself a tutor to five boys. The father of one of the boys is a cousin of Mrs Harrison. He was starting up a charity school with her as head and needed a teacher... and well, Bob's your uncle.'

'Lucky for the governors and the school,' Louisa said. *Lucky for me.*

'About the school governors,' Jack said. 'What happened this morning? It wasn't only their arrival. Something knocked you for six.'

'Someone. Mrs Marian Perrymont. I'd never met her until today. She is Max's...' Louisa hesitated. She'd never said the word aloud except to Iris. It was William Lowrey who had told her about the woman, calling her Max's 'particular friend'.

'She is my former husband's mistress and has been for the past two years.' Louisa frowned. 'But perhaps she isn't a mistress now, because the marriage is dissolved. Will they marry, I wonder?'

'Would it bother you if they did?' Jack asked.

'Oh no, she's welcome to him,' Louisa said without rancour. 'Our marriage was finished in all but name years before they met.'

'Is that how we ended up here with the children?' Jack asked. 'Because of Mrs Perrymont?'

'Rather in spite of. I can't imagine she had anything to do with it. The Brightford solicitor arranged for you all to come to Oxburrow after I read about what happened in the newspaper. It just so happened that Marian Perrymont is a school governor. The house is mine, you see, but the land is still Max's, and if he persuaded the army to take Oxburrow for training it's quite likely the place would be burned to the ground or blown up or something and, at the end of the day, he would still have land he could sell out from under me.'

Jack frowned in concentration as if trying to follow the story.

'Marian Perrymont told Max about the school coming and now they both see a way to turf us out, by sending the children elsewhere and bringing the army in. There's a Captain Wentworth who rang, probably wanting to make arrangements. But William will put a stop to it.'

Louisa rather hoped the captain would go away on his own if she ignored him. But still she paused, as if at any moment the sound of the army's lorries on the drive might prove her wrong.

'So now I have a battle on two fronts – Max wanting to move the army in and Mrs Harrison—'

'Lady Brightford?'

Louisa nearly leapt out of her skin. Where had Mrs Harrison come from?

'Yes?'

'The children have gone down for their tea.'

That night, Louisa stayed dressed, preparing for the worst. When Gracie's nightmare came, she hurried up to the girls' dormitory, walked past Mrs Harrison and perched on the edge of the mattress. She spoke quietly as Gracie screamed and writhed, until the girl calmed. When Gracie, still asleep, squeezed Agnes the sock kitty under her chin, Louisa gently stroked the girl's cheek, and she did not pull away.

Louisa thought about her own mother, who had fallen ill and declined slowly until she'd needed a nurse for daily care, and then had died a quiet death when Louisa was nine. No bombs, no terrace falling on her. Louisa had been lost without her, and she could still feel the hole left when she remembered the kind woman who had loved her. She had tried to be that sort of mother to David. Given the chance, she would be that sort of mother to Gracie, too.

She rose. The best she could say was that Gracie's night-mare was no worse than the other nights. Had it been better? As usual, the other girls had barely stirred.

'Good night, Mrs Harrison,' Louisa said.

The teacher had remained at her post at the end of the bed. Now she followed Louisa out into the corridor.

'My lady,' she began.

Louisa stopped and waited.

'It was my duty to inform the school governors of our situa-tion,' she said. 'I meant no disrespect to you.'

Louisa took those words, ran them through her mind as if they were a secret code and came up with a translation. Mrs Harrison had been let down by Mr Richards, her ally, and now must regroup.

'I wish you would explain to me what terrible thing I have done that would seep into the children's hearts and minds and turn them into despicable people.'

'Really!' Mrs Harrison said in a harsh whisper and threw a glance over her shoulder as if afraid the girls would hear. 'This is a matter of principle. If we do not hold fast to our vows – our beliefs – what do we have?'

'And do you require the same high moral standard of every-one? Of the school governors, for example?'

Mrs Harrison's eyes widened, but she quickly recovered, and adjusted her dressing gown as she said, 'The school gover-nors' dedication to helping the poor is beyond reproach.'

Louisa was a second away from disagreeing with her, but stopped. What good would it do the children if Mrs Harrison got Marian Perrymont booted off the board of governors? They could still take away the children. Max would remain deter-mined to plant the army at Oxburrow. The children were in enough peril as it was.

Then a thought came to her and, before she knew it, she spoke it aloud.

'Perhaps this doesn't have to do with me at all. Perhaps it's about you and what's happened in your own life?'

Mrs Harrison sucked in her breath. 'I find what you imply to be offensive, Lady Brightford.'

Ah, the shoe is on the other foot.

Without another word, Louisa turned and left.

Jack had waited for her on the landing. Louisa took his hand and they continued to the library. She closed the door behind them, leaned against it and gave a heavy sigh.

'Painting today helped Gracie, don't you think?' she asked. 'But then, later, she picked up my own black mood. She was upset because I was – that's why she had the nightmare. It's my fault.'

'How can this be your fault?' Jack asked. 'You've allowed them to feel safe – including Gracie. You've given them a home. If the governors didn't want to improve the children's lives, then why start the school in the first place?'

Louisa handed him the whisky bottle and he poured their drinks while she switched the wireless on low and waited for her orchestra. When the strains of 'Moonlight Serenade' emerged, she and Jack sat on the chesterfield and turned toward each other with glasses in hand.

With the real possibility of losing the children weighing heavy on her mind, Louisa got a wild idea. 'How's this – when the school governors come to take the children, I'll hide in the attic with them. You can tell them we're making for Scotland and, when they give up searching for us, we'll rendezvous.'

'Where will we meet?' Jack asked, taking her hand in his.

'Inverness,' she said. 'At my dad's.'

Jack's eyebrows jumped. 'I thought you were from Sheffield.'

'Yes,' she said, 'but he lives in Scotland now.' She would've said more, but Jack had begun to stroke the palm of her hand with his thumb. She watched as the sensation moved to every part of her body, then looked up at him.

They met halfway and kissed gently, hesitantly, as if it were an experiment. Then again with decidedly more confidence on both sides. He tasted of whisky and apple dumpling – that evening's pudding – and there was about him a hint of Pears soap, which Louisa had left in both his and the boys' bathrooms. She wouldn't've guessed that could be such a heady mix.

A small voice in her mind said *What are you doing, Louisa? There's a war on, there's a crisis at Oxburrow – do you really have time for a dalliance?* Too late for that warning – this was no dalliance. She felt her heart and soul ready to take a chance.

They paused and considered each other. Louisa noticed a scar high on Jack's forehead running into his untamed hair. She rather liked his hair that way. They gazed at each other and, this close up, Louisa fancied she could see so deeply into his dark eyes that she saw his hopes and dreams.

She shook her head at such a silly thought and a lock of her hair came loose and collapsed on her shoulder. Jack picked it up and twisted it gently round his finger.

'I lost a hairpin in the drawing room this morning,' she said.

He touched his lips to hers and said, 'Shall we go and look for it?'

She laughed. 'No – tomorrow will do.' She kissed him – long and lingering – then sighed. 'I want to tell you how I came to Oxburrow – the whole rigmarole. If you're up for it.'

He let go of the lock of hair and took her hand. 'I am.'

She took a drink of her whisky. 'My mum died when I was nine years old.' She imagined his question and continued. 'Yes, I know that's going back a bit, but I need to start there for it all to make sense. If any life makes sense.'

'Carry on.'

'I missed her terribly and so did my father. Bless him, he did the best he could. I always felt loved, but he was a man of business – textiles – and that is what occupied his days and many evenings, too. He longed for a baronetcy, you see – the closest he'd ever get to the peerage. Apart from a housekeeper, I was pretty much left to my own devices. That might've contributed to my decision, when I was sixteen, to run off with an Italian tenor from a touring opera company.'

She pulled a face. Jack coughed, poorly disguising his laugh.

'You ran off to Italy?' he asked.

'Oh no, we barely got down the road to Wadsley Bridge. Two days later I came to my senses and saw the fellow for what he was—'

'A poor singer?'

'Not only that, he wasn't even Italian – he was from Scunthorpe!' Louisa giggled – the story had become infused with humour over the years – but then she sobered up. 'My poor dad. He blamed himself for ages and I felt terrible that I'd done that to him. A few years later, he got wind of Lord Brightford sniffing around the north for a rich wife. He put me forward – parties, dinners, that sort of thing. Max and I hit it off, and I knew me becoming Lady Brightford would be as close as my dad would ever get to a title. I felt I owed it to him. Max would get the fortune he so needed. I'd have Oxburrow – I fell in love with the place the moment I saw it – and we'd fill it with children. That was my dream – the curse of an only child, I suppose.'

'It sounds like a happy ending,' Jack said.

'Might have been, but my dad's latest scheme fell through. He'd invested nearly everything and he lost it all. Max never got his money, and decided he'd been hoodwinked. He blamed my dad, who really did have the best intentions of making the fortune he had promised, and he blamed me for being complicit, which I was not.'

'He didn't leave you when he found out?'

'No. It all came to light when we'd been married just over a year – the same time I found out I was going to have a baby. An heir to the title – life was too uncertain for Max to throw us both out. But by the time David was about ten, Max had started absenting himself from our lives, and for years now he's lived in London. He works in the War Office.'

'And he left you and David alone here in Suffolk?'

'We had a few servants to begin with, but they've drifted off over the years in search of greener pastures. Old Figg has stayed and Iris has always been with us. She and I have known each other since we were in our prams. When I married, she was at a loose end, and so came along. And there you have it – the life and times to date of Louisa Esmeralda Spreck, as was.'

Jack's face lit up. 'Esmeralda?'

Louisa held up her forefinger. 'And I give you that name in the strictest confidence, you understand.'

'Mmm,' he said. 'So, you were a dollar princess.'

'Meant to be,' Louisa said. 'I turned out to be more of the threepenny-piece variety. Can't do much with that.'

'I don't know – twenty years ago, I could've bought five ciga-rettes for tuppence.'

'Do you smoke?' Louisa asked, not having seen any signs of it before.

'No,' Jack said. 'It came to me that I'd rather spend my money on food than cigarettes. And what about your dad?'

'Gave up business altogether when he married again eight or nine years ago. They moved to Scotland where they run a bookshop. Makes one believe in real happy endings, doesn't it?'

The next morning, Louisa went to the drawing room to hunt for the hairpin, and spent a good ten minutes crawling round on the Axminster. She discovered the pin hiding behind a table leg.

'Gotcher!' she said and looked up to see Jack in the doorway.

'Good morning,' he said, offering her a hand.

She took it and rose, stepping close to him. 'Good morning,' she murmured. He kept hold of her hand and his other arm slid round her waist as they kissed, then stood close, their foreheads together.

They had parted the previous evening on the landing and Louisa had drifted off to sleep with pleasant, if slightly frustrating, dreams. Now, here in the drawing room, they seemed to be picking up where they'd left off – until three small figures appeared outside the door, each holding a small basket.

'Look,' Louisa said a bit too brightly. She stepped back, but kept hold of Jack's hand. 'George, Dolly and Gracie are coming along with me to collect eggs so that Mrs Darnley can cook something delicious for our dinner today.'

'I'll look forward to that,' Jack said. 'See you at breakfast.'

They left him, and had got as far as the stairs to the basement when Mrs Harrison caught up with them.

'Children, breakfast. Where do you think you're going?'

'We're helping Lady Bee,' Dolly said.

'These are egg baskets.' George held his up. 'We're going to collect eggs. It isn't dangerous.'

When Louisa had proposed it, all three children had looked apprehensive. George had asked, 'Isn't it stealing?'

'It's good for the children to know where their food comes from,' Louisa said to Mrs Harrison.

'Potatoes from the ground, eggs from hens,' George said.

'And honey from bees,' Dolly added.

'Sometimes we must eat one of the chickens,' George said, his voice full of regret. 'And so it has to be killed.'

'But Mrs Darnley takes care of that,' Dolly said. 'We're not to worry.'

Gracie held her basket in silence, but she had followed the

conversation with great interest, as if she were truly a part of it and wanted to comment. The words must be piling up inside her, Louisa thought.

'They're learning a lesson even before they have their porridge,' Louisa said to Mrs Harrison as she ushered the children past before an objection could be raised.

They walked down the slope, the children with their baskets and Louisa with an old biscuit tin.

'Do hens bite?' Dolly asked.

'They squawk,' Louisa said as she took the rope latch off the door of the chicken run. 'And they flap around a fair bit. But they aren't like geese. It's geese you have to watch yourself with. You'll be passing by and they seem to take no notice, and all at once they're after you, biting your heels.'

Gracie's eyes grew wide.

'Good thing we don't have geese,' Louisa said. 'Chickens mostly mind their own business. Today, they'll be interested in the treat we brought them.'

They stood in the run with the hens crowded into the opposite corner, clucking quietly and watching the children. One of the roosters loomed in the doorway of the hen house. When Louisa popped the lid off the biscuit tin, both hens and children came close.

'Corn flakes!' Dolly said.

'They love corn flakes,' Louisa said. 'Each of you take a handful and toss the flakes on the ground.'

The first tentative offering landed in three small piles at the children's feet. The hens rushed forward. Dolly and George squealed and Louisa could've sworn Gracie nearly laughed.

'Try again, but throw them in the air.'

Now, it rained corn flakes, but at least the chickens were kept busy. Louisa led the children to the back of the hen house and opened and propped up the wall to reveal rows of empty nests. She poked her hand into one and brought out an egg. The children gasped.

They had a dozen eggs to carry back all told, and not a one broke – although the children walked so carefully Louisa thought they might be late for breakfast or be soaked by the shower that began when they were ten feet away from the door.

The rain continued throughout the morning, which worried the children, because Mr Gedge had sent a note inviting the entire school down to the hives for a lesson with the bees that afternoon, which he and his apprentice, Johnno, would conduct. Johnno swelled with pride as Jack read those words.

It was the sort of day Louisa had envisioned when she had dreamed of taking in evacuees at Oxburrow. The children occupied with school and yet the countryside at their fingertips. Let the war rage – they would be all right. She thought about this during the morning, as she and Iris cooked up a vat of apple sauce and chatted about normal, everyday things, ignoring the unpleasant topics of school governors, Marian Perrymont and Max.

Iris had set a hotpot with mutton, onion and sliced potatoes into the oven to cook for a few hours before the midday dinner. It was a Lancashire recipe, one of the only mementos Iris had brought back from her brief sojourn in Morecambe. She had married at seventeen, moved away from Sheffield and then, widowed at nineteen, had returned home. It had been not long after that Louisa had married Max.

Louisa had been desperate to cheer her friend up, and also nervous about her own upcoming marriage and moving away from all she'd ever known. The solution had been to bring Iris with her to be the cook at Oxburrow. Max soon cottoned on to their scheme, and tried to explain to Louisa that Lady Bright-ford should not be dear friends with one of the servants.

'Well, of course she isn't a servant,' Louisa had said. 'Shall I call her my secretary?' For a while after that, every day after breakfast Louisa and Iris would hole up in the morning room to 'take care of correspondence', but really to drink coffee and talk about their new lives. It was early days, when Max looked on Louisa's behaviour as quirky but charming and so he had left them to it.

The Lancashire hotpot met with great acclaim, as did the fig charlotte made from only a bit of suet and breadcrumbs and as much custard as possible.

After the meal, Louisa went to tidy up in the library. She switched on the wireless in time for the *Music While You Work* programme and heard a lively brass band playing, 'When the Red, Red Robin'.

'That's my dad!' Athena said, running into the library. 'He plays the trumpet and that's him.'

'Is it?' Louisa asked. 'This music might be from London.'

Athena frowned. 'My dad lives in Paris. I wish he were here.'

Paris had fallen to the Germans in June. Mrs Harrison had already taken Louisa aside and asked her not to encourage Athena in her daydreams. But if dreams and wishes were all the girl had, why not let her keep them?

In the afternoon, the sky cleared and Oxburrow became deserted. Iris had gone to the shops and the children and teachers were down at the beehives with Mr Gedge. Louisa was crossing the entrance hall when she heard it. A bicycle bell being rung. The crunch of chippings on the drive.

At that moment, she knew.

She was living and breathing her worst nightmare. As if an automaton, she went to the door and opened it before the knock came.

There stood Colin – poor dear Colin, only sixteen, who did everything from delivering groceries in a horse and cart to delivering telegrams to families. He had seen boys barely older than he go off to war. Now he had been left behind to deliver the worst of all possible news.

The angel of death.

'Telegram for you, Lady Brightford,' he said, barely above a whisper, the nervous quaver in his voice all the more evident. His face was washed of colour and he looked as if he were about to be sick – or had just been.

Louisa looked down at his outstretched hand.

What if she didn't accept it? What if she refused to touch the telegram? Would that make its news go away?

'Thank you, Colin,' she said in a calm but distant voice as if she did not feel the dread pressing upon her.

'I'm sorry, my lady,' Colin added. He choked back a sob as she closed the door.

Louisa remained still, her mind empty. Then, she whirled round with a thought to escape – but there was no escape. She looked at her hand clutching the telegram. She would go somewhere quiet and be alone to read it. She looked about her at the empty entrance hall and shivered, realising she was already alone. Entirely alone. Without another thought, she tore open the telegram and read it.

THE AIR MINISTRY REGRETS TO ANNOUNCE THAT YOUR SON, FLIGHT OFFICER MAXIMILLIAN DAVID BRIGHTFORD, IS MISSING IN ACTION. LETTER TO FOLLOW.

An economy of words did not weaken the anguish they carried.

Louisa began to tremble and couldn't catch her breath. She read the telegram again and then released the bit of paper as if it had scorched her hand. She fled to the morning room.

There, she would be far enough away from the schoolroom and library that, when the children returned, she wouldn't disturb anyone. Closing the door, she glanced at her surroundings. This room had always been her refuge, but now it was a cold reminder that she had started a letter to David that morning and it was still on her desk. Should she finish it? Would leaving it half-written be the same as believing he would never come back?

Missing in action.

She made her way to the desk on wobbly legs, knocking into an occasional table and setting the lamp rocking. She would finish the letter. She would finish it and put it in the post. That way, he would be safe. Alive.

But instead, she reached for the photo of David from the desk, clasped it to her breast and dropped onto the chaise longue as a wail rose up from her depths. The brave faces of WVS mothers who had already lost sons filled her mind. How did they do it – pretend it would be all right when their world had been destroyed?

The wail became a howl. She pressed her eyes closed, but the tears flowed regardless. Her body convulsed and she hung her head and sobbed.

How long did she cry? Time had no meaning. It seemed like for ever and still fresh tears fell. Who knew she had this many tears in her?

At last, through the pain, Louisa felt a soft pat on her arm.

She looked up and there stood Gracie, sobbing, the tears streaming down her own cheeks.

Louisa didn't speak, but took the girl in her arms and pulled her up onto the chaise longue, where they clung to each other in their grief.

. . .

When she awoke, stretched out on the chaise longue, Louisa looked down at Gracie, who was asleep and snuggled up under a light blanket that covered them. She looked peaceful. Louisa glanced round the morning room. The thought came to her that it would make a good place for story times if they got a fire going. She'd ask Mrs Harrison and Jack about it.

She had an arm wrapped round Gracie and in her hand she still held the photo of David in his cricket whites.

It wasn't that she'd forgotten the telegram or its terrible news, but a strange calm had come over her. She knew she would have to continue with everyday life even if all the while her mind was on her son. Missing.

'Letter to follow,' the telegram had said. Where had she put the telegram?

Gracie stirred, opened her eyes and looked up at Louisa, who brushed the girl's cheek with her free hand. They sat up, dislodging Mrs Moffatt, who had settled atop the blanket at their feet. The cat jumped to the floor and stretched.

Louisa's hair fell to her shoulders, and she felt round in the tangles. 'Oh dear, what's become of my hairpins?'

Gracie slid off the chaise longue, bent down and straightened again, holding a hairpin between her thumb and forefinger.

'Here's one,' she said.

CHAPTER 14

Even though her voice was a bit raspy, Gracie spoke as a matter of fact – as if she'd been speaking all along. Louisa, filled with equal parts elation and sorrow, felt dizzy, but took Gracie's words as she had said them – to be nothing out of the ordinary.

'Thank you,' she said. She laid David's photo in her lap, took the pin and repaired her hair. Gracie picked up the photo and looked at it.

'Are you sad about David?' she asked.

Louisa's heart beat triple-time, but with effort her voice remained calm. 'David had to land his aeroplane somewhere far away and we aren't sure where he is.'

'Is he dead?'

Louisa swallowed hard. She didn't want the word 'dead' coming within a mile of David's name. But she couldn't say so to Gracie.

'He might be hurt, but he will try his best to come home.'

'Mama died.'

Gracie spoke calmly and Louisa's eyes filled with fresh tears.

'I'm so sorry your mother died,' she said and stroked the

girl's hair. She kissed Gracie's cheek. 'It's all right to be sad about it, you know.'

Mrs Moffatt jumped back up on the chaise longue and gave the two of them a pointed look. David may be missing, but Louisa knew she must carry on no matter how much of a struggle it was – for her son's sake, for Gracie's and the other children's. For Jack. For Iris. She took a resolute breath and checked her wristwatch.

'Oh my, the time,' she said. 'Do you want to go down for tea? We wouldn't want to miss our bread and butter. Would you rather have strawberry or damson jam?'

Gracie gazed at her for a moment, and then said, 'Strawberry, please.'

Louisa smiled. Gracie had a lisp. When she'd imagined what the girl's voice would sound like, she hadn't imagined a lisp. But it suited her. And she was only six.

'Well, then, let's tidy ourselves up.'

Gracie took Louisa's hand as they walked to the door. When Louisa opened it, Jack, who had been sitting in a chair in the corridor, leapt up. His face was wrinkled with concern, his eyes dull and dark. In his hand was the telegram, and Louisa remembered that she had dropped it in the corridor.

Beyond, somewhere else in the house, she heard the children's voices.

'Iris has been trying to keep them busy,' Jack said, nodding toward the sounds.

'How long have you been out here?' Louisa asked.

'About an hour. I've been gatekeeper.' he said. His gaze searched her face. 'I looked in and saw the two of you and we thought it best to leave you be for a while.'

'Gracie – time to wash our hands for tea!' Athena called from round the corner of the staircase. She glanced at Louisa nervously. 'Is that all right, Lady Bee?'

'Yes, it's fine.' Louisa let go of Gracie's hand and nodded her on.

'Where's Mrs Moffatt?' Gracie asked. 'Mrs Moffatt, it's time for tea!'

Jack's brows lifted. 'Well, well, Gracie,' he said gently. 'There you are.'

The cat sauntered up and Gracie looked up at Jack. 'I'm going to ask Mrs Harrison if Mrs Moffatt can come to tea.'

'You're talking,' Athena said in a matter-of-fact way.

'I'm having strawberry jam with my bread and butter,' Gracie told her as they headed off.

Louisa watched the girls disappear round the corner, and then turned to Jack.

'Isn't that the sweetest sound you've ever heard?' Her voice began lightly, but ended choked with tears. Jack pulled her close and she wrapped her arms around him and held on.

'Thank you for watching over us,' she said.

'You can send us all away if you like,' he said. 'For good. You've every right if it's too much.'

She tightened her grip. 'I would never send you away. Why would I want to do that? Just let Mrs Harrison try to take the children. Let Max try and send the army to pull Oxburrow out from under us. They'll be in for a fight and their efforts will come to nothing.'

Here was a battle she would win, a cause she could throw herself into to fill the minutes of the days that seemed to stretch into infinity. Then, her grand declaration gave way to the reality of the moment. Her salty tears had dried on her face and pulled at her skin, her eyes were swollen and her hair needed combing. She must look an awful fright.

Nevertheless, Jack cupped her face in his hands and kissed her cheeks, her eyelids and her forehead.

'Remember, he's "missing",' he said. 'There's nothing final about that.'

'You're right, there isn't. I've had my cry and that's that,' she said, feeling her strength return. 'I can't let David down by thinking the worst. I won't. At least, I will try not to.'

'Good.'

They wrapped their arms tightly round each other, and might've stayed that way the rest of the day if wild yipping and skittering on the flagstones hadn't heralded the arrival of Lulu. The little dog flew past them with Mrs Moffatt on her tail. The animals rounded Louisa and Jack as if the human legs were the farthest post in a race. Then they took off back the way they had come, meeting with cheers from the children out in the entrance hall.

Louisa looked up at Jack. 'Well then,' she said and kissed him. They got no further than that for a moment, then she smiled. 'I'll see you down at tea.'

Louisa neatened her appearance before going down to the basement, where Mrs Harrison waited for her at the bottom of the stairs.

'Lady Brightford, I'm so sorry to hear the news about your son. I am praying for his safe return and will continue to do so until he walks in the door.'

She said it in practical terms, but in such a heartfelt way that it caught Louisa by surprise and she had to blink rapidly. *No more tears.*

'Thank you, Mrs Harrison. David is a resourceful boy – man – and I know he is doing his best to come back to us.'

It came to Louisa that her own words were not hollow. In a recent letter of David's he'd recalled when he was seven years old and had packed up and set off all alone to a small lake about ten miles away. He hadn't told a soul. It was one of their favourite day trips, as well as suitable for a camp-out, if it was only one night. Lake Puddle-Duck, that was what David had christened it when he'd been only a wee thing. Louisa had continued to use the name through the years when David was of an age to cringe when he heard his mother say it. Then he'd come out the other end of that stage and seized the name with proprietary pleasure.

He had been gone for twelve hours on that lark, and everyone in the village as well as the local policeman had searched the nearby fields and wood, expanding the search as they went. Louisa, frantic, had just decided to get Max back from London when there came David, walking in the door, bedraggled and hungry. He had lost his way, eaten the two sandwiches he'd packed, but ended up making his own magnet using the needle in the first aid kit he'd had the forethought to take along. He'd made it back without any of the searchers noticing.

The vast difference between going on a day's tramp a few miles away and being dropped into a wilderness – behind enemy lines? – was not lost on Louisa, but she clung to the principle of the matter.

Gracie put her head out of the dining room door and said, 'Mrs Harrison, Mr Barrie says to ask you if we can practise our song before supper.'

Mrs Harrison appeared to melt on the spot, as if she were hearing Gracie's voice for the first time ever and not after an absence of a few weeks.

'Oh my,' she said, and repeated it twice more as she placed a hand over her heart. 'Oh Gracie. Oh my Gracie.'

Gracie waited and glanced at Louisa, who suspected Jack had sent the girl out with the question specifically for Mrs Harrison to hear her speak. Louisa winked at her.

'Yes,' Mrs Harrison said at last. 'You may practise the song before supper.' Gracie nipped back into the dining room and Mrs Harrison turned to Louisa. 'You have... I...'

Mrs Harrison's brows twitched, a frown appeared and

vanished. The firm line of mouth softened, then hardened again, as if a battle raged inside her.

'If I've been a comfort to Gracie,' Louisa said kindly, 'if I've helped her through her pain, then she will be as much or more for me.'

A clatter of cutlery from the dining room drew Mrs Harrison away – looking grateful for the excuse.

Louisa went into the kitchen, where Iris looked up from pouring glasses of milk. She set the bottle down and she and Louisa embraced.

'I remember the time the three of us were lost in London,' she said in a hoarse voice in Louisa's ear, 'and who was it found the way to Liverpool Street station? David, of course. Was he eleven at the time?'

'We bought chocolate bars for the journey home.' Louisa laughed, but it ended in a sob.

'He's a good scout. We're not to worry.'

Yes, David could find his way round, but what if he had been injured? What then?

Louisa gave a sharp sniff and took control of herself. 'Oh dear, what about Hugo?' she asked.

'He rang,' Iris said. 'The entire village knew about the telegram and thought the worst, so I had to correct him.'

Louisa gave Iris's arm a squeeze. 'Good, thank you. I'll see him after tea. Iris – Gracie is talking.'

'Yes, she certainly is,' Iris said and grinned. 'Sashayed in here and asked for strawberry jam, she did. And that's down to you.'

'Where are you going?' Gracie asked. She had followed Louisa to the boot room after tea.

'We are going to visit Reverend Hugo,' Louisa said. 'You and Mr Barrie and me. Go and fetch your coat.'

Gracie raced up the stairs – the breakthrough had even affected her activity level – and returned wearing Louisa's red boiled-wool jacket. She paused on the bottom step.

'May I wear this?' she asked.

'Yes, you may.'

Jack joined them and the three set off, their faces to the sun, low in the western sky. Another glorious Suffolk day – at least on the surface.

'Are there rabbits in the wood?' Gracie asked.

'There are some that live at the edge of the field over there,' Louisa said.

'Do they eat Mr Figg's carrots?'

'Mr Figg tries his best to keep that from happening.' Louisa hoped Gracie wouldn't press the point.

Gracie proceeded to chat about Peter Rabbit eating Farmer McGregor's carrots and the consequences thereof, although it was clear she sided with the rabbit.

'He must've been awfully hungry,' she said, then switched topics. 'Mr Barrie, you told us in class that there are birds in the wood. Can we see a robin?'

'We'll keep an eye out for robins and blackbirds and perhaps even a woodpecker.'

'Next time, I'll paint a robin,' Gracie said. 'Robin redbreast. Or Mrs Moffatt.'

They neared the church and, when Louisa led the way past the lychgate, Jack went along, but Gracie pulled up.

'You said we were going to visit Reverend Hugo,' she said.

'Yes, but he doesn't live in the church. He lives just there.'

Louisa pointed to the vicarage, which sat just the other side of the church. It was a humble cottage, but comfortable and warm. Everyone in the parish knew it to be a place where one could stop for a cup of tea and a blessing. Louisa knocked on the door, but got no answer.

'He may be out the back,' she said, and left Jack and

Gracie on the doorstep to go and look. There, she found Hugo wearing his cassock and digging in the ground at the edge of the veg garden, stabbing the fork into the soil again and again.

'Hugo?'

He whirled round. His eyes were red-rimmed, his fair skin blotched scarlet and streaked with dirt. He rubbed a cheek with the back of his hand, which only made matters worse.

'Bindweed,' Hugo said. 'Sneaks in and winds itself round whatever it can find. It's insidious.' He wiped his nose on his sleeve and dislodged his glasses.

Louisa held her arms out and they embraced over the dying leaves of the rhubarb.

'He'll do everything he can to get back to us,' Louisa said.

'I know he will,' Hugo said, his voice thick.

'And we won't let each other forget that, will we?' she asked.

Jack and Gracie appeared at the corner of the cottage. Hugo straightened up and threw his head back. He wiped his hand on his cassock and stuck it out to Jack. 'Jack, I'm glad you came, too.'

'We've brought Gracie with us,' Louisa said.

'Hello, Reverend Hugo,' Gracie said.

For a moment, Louisa thought that hearing Gracie's voice might do it for Hugo – that his barely controlled emotions would overcome him. His eyes filled, but he laughed the tears away and said, 'Well, Gracie, you are very welcome, too. Now, I have a tin of shortbread inside – a gift from Mrs Greet. Would you like some?'

'Yes, please,' Gracie lisped quickly, as if intent upon making up for treats lost to her mute phase.

Hugo led them to the sitting room, where Louisa and Gracie arranged themselves on a chintz sofa, sinking deep into the cushions. The men took the two wingback chairs, the adults with sherry and Gracie with orange squash.

'I keep it on hand for the confirmation class,' Hugo explained. The orange squash, he meant.

'There will be a letter coming,' Louisa said. 'It said so in the telegram. Will they tell me where it happened? And when?'

'Does Lord Brightford know?' Hugo asked, a tentative note in his voice.

'Oh, I didn't think,' Louisa said. Max worked for the War Office and it seemed logical that he would've been told even before the telegram had been sent out to her.

'I've heard nothing from him,' she said. 'If he knew right away, why didn't he tell me?'

'The telegram was from the Air Ministry,' Jack said. 'Perhaps they sent it to Oxburrow as a matter of course.'

Then it would be Louisa's fault for not telling David's father. That had not occurred to her.

'I'll ring when we get back.'

Gracie had finished two shortbread fingers and now asked, 'Reverend Hugo, may I look at your book about birds?'

She pointed to a row of Observer Guides on a shelf by the fireplace. Hugo took the one about birds and handed it to her.

'We had a sparrow at home,' Gracie said. 'Mama's sparrow.'

She turned the pages of the book, unaware of the furtive looks between the grown-ups. Louisa thought it best to let details of her mother come out naturally, although she was half afraid of what she might hear.

'Mr Barrie said he would show me a robin,' Gracie said, 'didn't you?'

'I did and will,' Jack said.

'And a blackbird and a woodpecker. Do you have blackbirds in your garden, Reverend Hugo? And robins? Do you know what they eat?'

'I know for certain that blackbirds like worms,' Hugo said, 'because they follow me about the garden waiting till I turn a few up.'

'Would blackbirds eat the bee-yor-ess worm?' Gracie asked, drawing the word out.

Hugo gasped. 'A blackbird can't eat a dragon!'

Gracie broke out in a fit of giggles.

'What a delight,' Hugo said quietly. Louisa could see the strain at the corners of his good-natured grin.

'You should've heard teatime,' Jack said.

The fastest racing car had nothing on Gracie – she had gone from zero words to a constant stream in a flash. At teatime, Mrs Harrison had smiled indulgently and said nothing about rules of the table as there had seemed to be ten different conversations going on at once. Or perhaps it had been one conversation divided into ten parts and every one of them involving Gracie. She had talked about Tom Kitten, asked questions about bees, wanted to know if hens sang, and expressed the wish that Mrs Moffatt could sleep with her at night.

'It was a bit of a riot,' Louisa said to Hugo, 'but lovely. I'm sure this evening's meal will be more sedate. Will you join us?'

'I'll be all right, Louisa,' Hugo said. 'And I have ARP duty tonight, so it won't be as if I'm not busy.'

Watching the skies, patrolling, listening for radio transmissions, waiting for something to happen – the job of the ARP warden in the country was lonely work. Louisa knew that, all through the night, Hugo's mind would be on David.

'If not this evening, you're welcome to join us any time,' Louisa said. 'Now, we'd best get back before Iris has our supper on the table.'

Hugo walked with them as far as the church, where they paused.

'How goes the singing for the harvest festival?' Hugo asked.

'As well as can be expected,' Jack said and looked at Gracie. 'And now we have another voice to add.'

'I know the words already,' Gracie said. 'Can we sing it now?'

The three of them sang as they walked back to Oxburrow –
Jack in a strong baritone and Louisa in a serviceable soprano.
Gracie, who didn't actually know all the words yet – or the tune
– sang with gusto.

The sun was at their backs as they reached the drive, casting
long shadows in front of them. Suddenly, the warmth seemed to
go out of the day for Louisa and a darkness surrounded her as if
she were in a small, airless room.

Since David had joined the RAF, she had pictured him in
his Spitfire, smiling, even giving her a wave. Now, in this murky
gloom, she could only see a dim image of his solemn face.

She shivered. Jack put an arm round her and the darkness
cleared. Then Gracie took her hand as she gave an account of
their arrival the Friday before.

'... and Lulu was hiding in Alf's rucksack and Johnno was
angry and you had a bucket of worms for the chickens and
jam on your face and Mrs Harrison thought you were the
maid!'

'She did, didn't she?' Louisa asked, warm again. She
wondered if they would be listening to a retelling of every
moment since Gracie's arrival at Oxburrow now that the girl
was talking.

Once they were in the door, Louisa said, 'You two go on.
Gracie, make sure you tell Mrs Harrison you've returned. I'll be
along soon.'

Gracie skipped off.

'I've got to ring Max,' Louisa said to Jack. 'If he already
knows, maybe he has details.'

He nodded and took her hand.

She held on to it and said, 'Your strength – yours and Iris's
and Gracie's' – her voice caught – 'you've no idea what it
means.'

'Then lean on us,' Jack said. 'Do whatever it takes until he's home.'

She nodded, but wondered how long she could go on filled with equal parts hope and fear.

Louisa went to the telephone room and sat down. She rarely rang Max at the War Office and could never remember the number – or didn't want to – and so she looked it up.

A woman answered in a dull but efficient tone. 'Undersecretary's office.'

'Lord Brightford, please.'

'Lord Brightford has left. Would you care to leave a message?'

'This is Lady Brightford.'

Silence. In the background, Louisa could hear the sounds of people talking and typewriters clacking.

'Lady Brightford,' the woman said with more emotion. 'I'm so terribly sorry. Truly I am.'

'Yes, thank you.'

'Shall I enquire where he's gone?'

'No, thank you. Just leave my name. Goodbye.'

She set the receiver on its cradle and sat quite still. Her thoughts floated through time, merging the present with the past. She could almost see David as a child running down to the garden with Alf and Dolly to help Figg dig carrots. When the telephone jangled, it sent a jolt through her.

Her heart pounding, she answered, 'Oxburrow Manor.'

'Did Iris tell you I rang?'

Louisa reminded herself that, this time, Max had a reason for his bad-tempered tone.

'No, I was out and just returned. I rang the office only a moment ago and you'd gone.'

'Out where?'

'I went to see Hugo.'

It was as if she could hear Max squeeze the telephone receiver to try to control his anger. He knew about David and Hugo and he didn't like it one bit. He was convinced that he could talk his son out of being homosexual, as if it were a choice of having coffee or tea, boiled or scrambled, chipped or mash.

'Do you know anything more?' Louisa asked. 'The telegram said there would be a letter.'

'He went down somewhere north of Rouen. Countryside. Two of them had chased a group of bombers that far. The other pilot was being chased back and said he saw David go down. But there was no... no burst of smoke or fire as there would be on a hard impact.'

No crash. 'So, he really could be alive?' Louisa asked, her hopes soaring and then plummeting just as quickly. 'Will he be captured?'

'We'll hear if he's captured, but it will take time. Everything takes too much damned time.'

Louisa would be wandering in this limbo, this no man's land for ever.

'Do you want me to come down?' Max asked in a quieter voice.

There he was at last. Despite their differences and many arguments, Louisa knew he wasn't a bad person. Why was he always so intent on acting so?

'No, it's all right. Look, Max, you've probably already heard about the children.'

'That was a legitimate assignment, the army,' he said, sounding annoyed once more.

'Don't try that on with me, I know what you want. If it hadn't been for William you would've got it, too.'

'William? What's that old— What do you want?' Max turned away to speak to someone else. There was a muffled exchange and then he said to Louisa, 'I've got to go,' and rang off.

By supper, as far as Mrs Harrison was concerned the bloom had worn off the rose of Gracie rediscovering her voice. Once they were seated and the teacher had blessed the meal, she reminded the children that, although everyone was delighted Gracie was herself again, there would be no talking at the table 'out of respect for Lady Brightford'.

Louisa bristled at David being used as an excuse to keep the children quiet and countered with, 'I would rather hear the children than silence, Mrs Harrison. If you don't mind.'

'Oh, well, if you prefer. Boys and girls, please do remember your table manners.'

'Children,' Louisa said, half-hoping she hadn't annoyed Mrs Harrison and half-hoping she had, 'you've been here nearly a week now. If you were to write a letter to a friend, what's the first thing you'd tell them about Oxburrow?'

They went round the table. 'I'd tell them about the bees,' Johnno said. 'In the library, you have an atlas of the entire world,' George said. 'Chickens eat corn flakes,' Dolly said. And so it went until it was Gracie's turn.

'I would say Oxburrow is my home.'

Louisa went to the girls' dormitory and said good night to each of them as Mrs Harrison stood by the lamp, ready to extinguish the light.

Louisa had saved Gracie for last. She tucked her up with Agnes the stuffed cat.

'Sweet dreams.'

Gracie crooked a finger and Louisa drew close.

'When we said our prayers,' Gracie said, her lisp standing out in her whisper, 'I said a prayer for David.'

Louisa kissed her cheek. 'Bless you,' she whispered back.

At first, Louisa went to her own room. She picked up a book, then put it down again. She switched off the light and opened the blackout curtains to look out. The clouds covered the starlight.

Louisa was fairly certain Gracie was past her nightmares now. She went to the library and sat on a low stool in front of the wireless listening to her orchestra play. Now, she waited not for Gracie, but for Jack.

He opened the door and looked in just as 'In the Mood' began.

'There you are,' Louisa said. 'I thought I might have to come up and knock on your bedroom door.'

From all the way across the room, she could see the spark in his eyes.

'I have to admit,' he said, 'I wouldn't mind if you did.'

Louisa switched off the wireless and stood. 'No, I don't think that's a good idea.' She held out her hand. 'We'll go to my bedroom.'

The next morning, Louisa oversaw the burbling pot of porridge. She had just shifted it off the fire and turned to find Jack standing in the doorway watching her. Her face went hot – and not because of the steam from the porridge, but because she remembered the night before and his hands on her bare skin and the warmth of his body. She brushed a lank tress out of her eyes.

He came into the kitchen only as far as the table. They smiled at each other – that secret smile. Neither spoke. Neither needed to.

'Good morning,' Mrs Harrison said.

Both Louisa and Jack spun round. With her hands clasped at her waist and elbows stuck out like wings, Mrs Harrison filled the doorway. She glanced at one of them and then the other.

How did she do that? Had Mrs Harrison been a spy in the last war – is that where she'd learned to walk so quietly?

Louisa saw an accusatory look in the woman's eyes, and bristled. She hadn't caught them in a compromising situation – there had been a table between her and Jack.

'Good morning, Mrs Harrison,' she replied pleasantly. 'Breakfast is nearly ready.'

Gracie slipped into the kitchen, ducking under one of Mrs Harrison's elbows.

'Good morning,' Louisa said to the girl.

'Don't be late for breakfast, Gracie,' Mrs Harrison said. She turned to go, adding, 'Nor you, Mr Barrie.'

Louisa rolled her eyes at Jack. He grinned and followed Mrs Harrison out.

Gracie watched them go. Priss and Athena walked by to breakfast, too.

'What is it?' Louisa asked, bending down.

Gracie came round the table and in a low, conspiratorial voice said, 'Today is Gloria's birthday.'

Louisa's head shot up and she saw Gloria walk by the kitchen. Her chin stuck out and so did her bottom lip – her face was a combination of bravery and misery.

'Is it?' Louisa asked quietly. 'We should have a party.'

'Mrs Harrison told her we shouldn't have a party,' Gracie said, 'and that Gloria should be brave.'

'Why shouldn't we have a party?'

'Because of David.'

That vice-grip squeezed Louisa's heart.

'Of course we'll celebrate,' she said, hoping her enthusiasm would override the pain in her chest. 'We mustn't not celebrate. David loves birthday parties. You should've seen the cake Iris made last year. I'm sure she can do something today.' She looked down at Gracie. 'How did you find out?'

'I was the only one left in the room,' Gracie said, 'and Mrs Harrison was talking to Gloria and Dolly by the fireplace. Gloria was crying. Mrs Harrison made them promise they wouldn't say anything.'

'Did she not realise you were there?'

'I was doing my corners,' Gracie said. 'I didn't hide. It's only that... I was being quiet.'

Quiet, as she had been for weeks, making her nearly invisible at times.

Louisa gave her a hug. They had barely begun to chip away at Gracie's trauma. It would be an arduous task for the girl, but perhaps coming out in small broken pieces would make it easier.

Morning lessons had begun, the breakfast dishes had been washed up and Iris had already collected the morning post.

'There's a past due from the builders from Ipswich. They patched that corner of the roof that had been leaking – through the attic, a bedroom and into the library.'

'That was in April,' Louisa replied, drying and putting porridge bowls back into the Welsh dresser.

'And you'd not believe the cost of mutton,' Iris said. 'When it's there. You can't ration what doesn't exist. We might have to live off tinned pilchards – at least fish isn't on ration.'

'I've left William a message about the money from the War Office' – in rather vague terms, as she recalled, but he would understand – 'there's no sense in badgering him. He can do only so much.'

'Well, at least we've paid our quarterly sixpence in the pig club,' Iris said, brightening. 'We'll need a great deal of pork to go with all that apple sauce.'

'That's the war spirit, Iris Darnley,' Louisa said with a grin. 'I'm going into the village this morning – I'll see about the pilchards.'

'I can do that,' Iris said with a frown of concern.

'No, I have to face them,' Louisa said, laying her tea towel over the back of a chair. 'The people, not the fish. Steel myself for everyone's sympathy. It's better to get it over with.'

'Wait, Louisa.'

'What is it?' Louisa asked.

Iris dried her already dry hands on her apron. 'There... there was a letter from David in the post, too.'

'But he—' Louisa began but couldn't go on, the words catching in her throat. When pain had passed, she said, 'Posted it before he flew out, I suppose.'

'Do you want me to go in with you to read it?' Iris asked.

Louisa reached out and took her friend's hand. 'No, but thank you.'

The letter lay waiting for her on the desk in the morning room, just as if it was any of the dozens David had sent since he went off to war. Louisa settled in her chair and ran a hand over the envelope as if she could feel her son's hand doing the same. After a moment, she opened the letter and read.

My dear old mum,

Dark days, I'm afraid. We've lost three good men in one sortie overnight. It's such an odd feeling – there's grief, yes, but the thing is, you're sat across from a fellow every morning at break-fast and then comes a morning when his place is empty and you can't quite understand where he's gone.

Louisa's hands trembled so violently she could read no further. She dropped the letter and told herself aloud, 'Stop it. He is not speaking of himself. It is not some premonition of... of...'

She slapped her hand on the desk and the sting of impact shook her mind free.

'You come home, David. Listen to me. Come home.'

. . .

A few minutes later she closed the morning room door behind her, determined to carry on. She had learned that through experience – how to carry on when you think the world is falling down on you. Hadn't she done so after the many arguments she and Max had had, and when she'd realised their marriage had ended? They had done all right, she and Iris and David. They'd done more than all right. And now, Louisa had Gracie, too. And Jack. She would keep her mind set on the good.

Jack had been doing his best to teach the children 'We Gather Together' a cappella, but it was clear that some sort of musical support was needed. Iris had remembered that there was an old concertina in the attic that had belonged to an uncle of Max's. Jack said he'd played the concertina a bit long ago and was willing to give it a go, and so Louisa had gone up to the attic before breakfast. She'd rummaged around in boxes and had come down – her head adorned with cobwebs – and handed the dusty thing over to him.

Now, she opened the library door just in time to see the children clustered round his chair as if he were Father Christmas about to hand out gifts. He unsnapped the latch that kept the concertina tightly closed and it expanded with a sigh.

He stuck his thumbs in the leather loops on either side of the instrument and pressed a button or two as he pushed and pulled at the bellow. Squeaks, creaks, gasps and what sounded rather like a train whistle emerged and the children squealed and laughed and covered their ears. Mrs Moffatt launched herself off Gracie's lap and skittered out the door past Louisa.

But after a moment or two, out of the cacophony emerged a single note and then another, and before long the children quietened as the tune of the hymn came through.

Louisa gave Jack a smile and left them to it.

· · ·

She put a brave face on and set out to visit the shops in the village. They would all be so kind, she was certain of it, and would tell her not to worry – as if that were possible. As she neared the shops her feet dragged, but they weren't dragging as slowly as the War Office's. She hadn't bothered to ask Max about the money – he could be using it to twist her arm, to exchange the children for the army. She would starve first.

Not one shopkeeper said a word about overdue accounts, but everyone expressed encouragement at the news about David. Several of them had their own stories to tell, including Mrs Nethergate.

'He's bound to be fine and home before you know it,' the woman said as she polished the tins of pilchards she'd set on the counter. 'He was always such an enterprising boy. I remember when you would bring him along with you. And the time he came in on his own wanting to buy a penny chocolate bar with a farthing.' She clucked her tongue, but smiled. 'I told him how much it would cost and he asked if he could work for it. The little tyke – imagine!'

'I remember after that he regularly swept the floor for you. You provided him with a steady supply of chocolate.'

'And you taught him how the post office account works. It's not many who would think such practical matters would be of use for the heir to a title.' Mrs Nethergate reddened. 'I mean no offence by that.'

'And none was taken,' Louisa said, but reddened herself at the mention of their savings.

They both sighed, then Mrs Nethergate tapped each of the tins and muttered, 'One, two, three, four times nine pence each – that's three shillings. I'll just put it on account, shall I?'

She said it in a businesslike manner, and Louisa was grateful. The woman reached under the counter for the ledger, but then her hands flew into the air.

'Oh no!' she said. 'No, that won't do at all.'

Mortified, Louisa began to make excuses. 'Yes, I realise that we haven't been able to keep up with—'

'No, my lady, it isn't that,' Mrs Netherfield said. 'It had gone clean out of my head with the news of your son. It's your fifty pounds – it's arrived!'

If she could've marched into Bates, Lowrey and Lowrey in Cambridge, Louisa would've thrown her arms around William. He had come through – dear man, he always came through for her in a pinch. Louisa practically danced back to Oxburrow, went to the telephone room and rang his office. She was put through immediately.

'William, how can I thank you—'

'Oh, Lady Brightford, I am so sorry to hear the news. But missing is better than it might be, don't you think?'

David. Where are you, my son?

'Thank you,' Louisa replied. 'Yes, all we can do is wait, which is its own hell. Max said he went down north of Rouen. We have all the hope in the world he'll make it back to us.'

'Indeed,' William said. 'David is not only spirited, but also remarkably good at getting out of a pickle. I recall the time he found himself in trouble with that fellow who owned the garage there in Debden Ash. David had repaired a bicycle left on the rubbish pile and the fellow accused him of theft. So the boy offered to attach a sign for the garage to the bicycle as an advertisement and no more was said about it.'

Louisa laughed. 'I had forgotten that. He's not a bad negotiator, is he?' She sighed. 'I don't know what details they have at the Air Ministry but, when we hear something, I'll give you a ring. Now, about the children from Hazel End Charity School.'

Louisa had to raise her voice as she heard the children themselves talking and laughing in the entrance hall.

'Still with you, are they?' William asked, raising his voice, too. 'Lord Brightford had second thoughts about the army after all?'

'You must've been very persuasive,' Louisa said. 'And getting us the payment from the War Office, too. It's just come through.'

There was a moment of total silence in the entrance hall, and in that moment William said, 'What? Oh yes. Good of—'

Then the choir burst into song with the chords of the concertina soaring above, and William's goodbye was drowned out.

'Cheers, William,' Louisa called into the receiver. 'Bye!'

Gloria's birthday was not forgotten. That afternoon, when lessons were finished and the children sat down for their tea, the table was bare. Puzzled looks were exchanged until, with pomp and circumstance and a flourish from the concertina, Iris paraded in with a cake decorated with a drizzle of raspberry sauce for icing. It held a single burning candle to represent nine years, and came accompanied by a paper crown leftover from Christmas for the girl to wear. Gloria's eyes widened with amazement.

Louisa had managed to find a copy of the *Schoolgirls' Adventure Book* at the newsagent and had wrapped it in tissue paper and tied it with a hair ribbon. Such a small thing to spark so much joy.

'May I read from it at story time, Mr Barrie?' Gloria asked. 'May I?'

'You may indeed,' Jack said.

Iris's cake was large enough to be filling, yet small enough that nothing was left of it. As the children went off for a game in the yard, Louisa, holding a stack of plates, stopped at Mrs Harrison's place.

'Do you have a list of all the children's birthdays?'

Mrs Harrison, who had been quiet during the party, looked up at Louisa as if she'd forgotten where she was. 'Oh,' she said at last. 'Yes, I do. I hadn't mentioned this because I wasn't sure it was proper to celebrate, considering the circumstances.'

'Every child deserves a party, no matter what.'

'I want to do it,' Gracie said, shaking her head and squirming out of Louisa's reach just as she'd got one of the girl's plaits in order.

Gracie had not only found her voice from being mute a mere three days earlier, she had also recovered an obstinate streak that, Jack confessed to Louisa, 'might've shown itself occasionally in the past.'

It was Saturday morning and, just after breakfast, Gracie had announced she wanted her hair in plaits, even though it was barely long enough. They all needed to be off to the harvest festival, but instead Louisa stood behind her now at the dressing table mirror in the girls' dormitory.

'We can't be late,' Louisa reminded her. 'And I must help Iris pack up the cups and saucers for the tea table.'

'You can go on,' Gracie said, as if encouraging Louisa in a race. 'I'll do the other one and I'll come down and show you. Please, may I?'

'All right,' Louisa said, putting her hands behind her back.

Louisa had never had a little girl of her own to fuss over and Gracie had been through so much, she saw no reason not to indulge her.

'But remember, separate your hair into three and—'

'I will,' Gracie said in a cheerful but dismissive way.

With a reluctant smile, Louisa left the room.

.   .   .

'Iris, how did you ever have enough sugar to make fairy cakes?'
Louisa asked as Colin toted cartons of food and dishes out to his
cart in the yard, trying to keep his feet out of the way of Lulu,
who had apparently assigned herself as escort.

'A couple of the ladies at the WVS were good enough to
share their rations – in fact, Mrs Greet's maid, Pauline, sent
over a packet.'

'Mrs Greet?' Louisa echoed. She had thought the woman
shared Mrs Harrison's sympathies as regards Louisa's lack of
moral capability to care for the children. Had she got that
wrong?

'Also,' Iris continued, 'I've kept back a bit here and there.'
She counted the little iced cakes and then closed up the box.
'The harvest festival is about abundance and I refuse to skimp
until I absolutely have to.'

Iris went ahead with Colin, and the rest of them gathered
on the drive to walk down to church.

'Where's Gracie?' Mrs Harrison asked.

Louisa had been watching and waiting for the girl, and had
taken one step toward the house when Gracie burst out and ran
to them.

'See,' she said to Louisa, 'I did it!'

A plait on either side of her head. The one Louisa had done
hung straight down, not quite touching the girl's shoulder. The
other stuck out horizontally, looking as if it had been caught in
its own personal wind storm.

'Well done, you,' Louisa said.

Gracie beamed.

Mrs Harrison raised her eyebrows but said nothing.

'Well, Mr Barrie,' Louisa said, 'I don't suppose you know a
marching tune you can play for us as we walk down to church?'

. . .

Autumn sunlight – that golden glow – shone down on them and the scent of damp leaves rose up as they scuffled their way through the wood. Growing up in Sheffield with no front or back garden to speak of, Louisa had had little experience of the natural world. Trees and such lived in the park, which was a fair walk away. When she'd moved to Suffolk as a new bride, she'd been amazed at the enormous beeches with their smooth grey bark, and the spreading oaks that seemed as at home in a thick wood as they did standing alone in the middle of a field.

'For our next art lesson,' Louisa said to no one in particular – although glancing at Mrs Harrison out the corner of her eye – 'why don't we paint trees?'

Before anyone could answer, she hurried through the lych-gate and pulled open the door of the church.

Everyone walked in, looked toward the front of the church and stopped.

'Children,' Mrs Harrison said, 'keep away from the altar. And don't touch anything.'

Her warning was practical rather than sacramental. The church altar had become a veritable cornucopia. It held a mountain of cabbages with wide, green-leaf collars; long, straight, white parsnips; bristly-looking artichokes; globes of purple beets and brown Spanish onions; carrots; potatoes; apples from red to russet; pears with fat bottoms and sprays of chrysanthemums tucked in here and there.

People were coming and going in the sanctuary, making ready for the harvest festival. Most everyone gave the altar a wide berth, but if someone walked too close to it, an apple would dislodge itself from the arrangement, roll to the very edge and stop, as if daring the other fruit and veg to join in the escape. Before that could happen, it would be captured and put back in place.

Minns's grandad, Mr Grainger, stood before the altar studying the bounty. Next to him was Uncle in his wheelchair.

In his lap he held a round, orange orb about the size of a foot-ball. Mr Grainger leaned over and gave the thing a *thump*.

'We'll set this on the floor if that's all right with you, Reverend,' he said.

'Fine, Mr Grainger,' Hugo said. He looked around himself in a harried fashion. 'Now, what is it I'm doing? Ah, yes!' He turned and saw Louisa and company still at the back of the church. 'Good morning, Oxburrow! If anyone is looking for me, tell them I've gone up to Mrs Nethergate's cottage to carry her tray of dahlias.'

As Hugo left, Johnno crept up the aisle. 'What is that thing?' he asked Uncle. At Mrs Harrison's throat-clearing he added, 'sir. What is that thing, sir?'

'It's a pumpkin!' Mr Grainger exclaimed. 'A prize-winning pumpkin it'll be, too. Have you never seen a pumpkin before?'

'No one around here has seen a pumpkin before, Grandad,' Minns said from the window where she was fussing with a vase of flowers. 'You and Uncle are the only ones to ever grow one, and so you've no competition.'

'Our competition was Dame Nature,' Uncle replied. 'And we bested her.'

Mr Grainger rested his walking stick against the altar and bent over to take the pumpkin in both hands.

'Let me take that for you, sir,' Jack said and rescued the pumpkin as it was slipping out of the man's grip and about to land hard back in Uncle's lap. He placed it on the floor at the corner of the altar. 'About here?'

'There,' Mr Grainger said, taking his walking stick and tapping the floor precisely in the centre. 'Front and centre, that'll do. Minns – you'll take it through when it's time for the judging?'

'I will indeed.'

'Good, good,' Mr Grainger said. 'Uncle and I will go home now and come back when Mrs Darnley serves the tea.'

Mr Grainger handed his walking stick to Uncle and pushed the wheelchair out the door.

'What's that?' Gracie asked Louisa as she pointed up to the altar.

'What's what?' Louisa asked. 'Here, let's get a better look. It's all right, Mrs Harrison, we won't get close enough to touch. Will we?'

The children clustered around Louisa and they all shuffled their way up the aisle until they stood a few feet away.

'Now, Gracie, what were you looking at?'

Gracie pointed and said, 'It looks scary.'

'It's an artichoke,' Louisa said. 'They are tasty, but you don't actually eat very much of it.' She felt sure that the Ministry of Food would look askance at the water, soil and effort of growing a vegetable that was mostly waste. 'Now, what do the rest of you see?'

When they'd exhausted the fruit and veg identification, Mrs Harrison carefully backed the children away. Good thing, too. Louisa knew all too well how little it took to upset the arrangement. Five-year-old David had taken the opportunity to poke a quince that, it turned out, had been the keystone in that year's display of abundance and... Well, in the end – and much later – they'd laughed about it. There were still light purple marks on the stones where an errant blackberry or two had been squashed underfoot, and the church mice hadn't minded the stray crab-apples that had rolled behind a tapestry. She felt as if David were beside her now, laughing about it, and she smiled.

She slipped out of the sanctuary to the church hall to help Iris. The hall wasn't terribly large – more of an anteroom, actually – but could accommodate most events. At one end, tables had been set in front of the kitchen and cups and saucers lined up. Along both walls were more tables for the display of fruit and veg entered into competition.

'Here you are,' Iris said, pushing a cup of tea towards her.

'Exactly what I needed.'

'I noticed the girl when you arrived,' Iris said. 'That's some new Hollywood hairstyle, is it?'

Louisa giggled. 'She insisted, and who am I to stand in the way of creativity?'

The strains of the concertina drifted in from the sanctuary.

'She gets something in her head and that's it,' Iris said. 'I wonder, who does that sound like?'

Louisa didn't reply, but couldn't help but be secretly pleased. Let Gracie try things, why not?

Cup of tea in hand, she took a brief tour of the entries into the harvest festival competition – a twining stem of late-blooming honeysuckle, a dark red apple called Bloody Plough-man, rusty-pink rosehip jam and jars of Mr Gedge's honey were just a few of many. Figg had come down early to arrange his three perfect beetroots, brushed free of dirt and with their red-veined leaves still attached, along with a tray of five straight-as-an-arrow French beans.

Louisa had nothing to do with the judging and was very glad of it, but, every year since her arrival at Oxburrow Manor, she had presented Best in Show ribbons. At the end of the day, the entries would be auctioned off and the proceeds would go to the Red Cross parcels.

Louisa wondered, if David had been captured, would he end up in a prisoner-of-war camp and receive one of the parcels. Dried milk, tea, Marmite, a tin of biscuits. Chocolate if they were lucky. The blackness crept around her, but then the children began to sing. She sniffed and got hold of herself.

We gather together to ask the Lord's blessing

'They sound good, don't they?' she asked Iris. 'I mean, at least they're in tune.'

He chastens and hastens His will to make known

'They've a good choirmaster,' Iris said.

Louisa smiled behind her teacup. 'Yes,' she said, suddenly teary, 'He's a man of many talents.'

The wicked oppressing, now cease from distressing

Iris laughed and said, 'Oh, do tell!'

Sing praises to his name, He forgets not his own.

The last strains of the children's voices seem to go on longer than necessary, but then Louisa heard the sound for what it was – a waxing and waning tone that surrounded them.

It was the air-raid siren.

CHAPTER 16

For a moment, Louisa and Iris stared at each other, and then there came a shout from the sanctuary.

'Let's go!'

Without a thought, they ran into the church, and met with a confusion of villagers who were pushing their way out.

Jack and Mrs Harrison, near the choir screen, were busy counting the children.

'Mrs Greet's house,' Louisa called to them. 'It's the old rectory. Her cellar is the village shelter – it's closer than Oxburrow.'

Jack lifted his chin in acknowledgement.

Directions were unnecessary, because everyone who had left the church was heading the same way, toward the village.

'Priss!' Mrs Harrison called as the girl raced ahead.

'Stay together,' Jack said, catching George by the collar.

They were last out of the lychgate, and hurried along without actually breaking into a run. Louisa kept looking at the sky. Were they about to be bombed? Had it been only a test? Where was Hugo? He was the warden and should be the one to sound the alarm.

At that moment, Colin came rushing up from the lane that led to the ARP hut, formerly a bird hide. That was where the hand-cranked siren resided. Hugo had been instrumental in getting it – not all villages had a siren. It had given them a sense of security.

'They rang from Woolpit,' Colin said as they hurried along. 'A single plane. They think the pilot parachuted out. They tried the reverend but there was no answer and so they rang the shop. Unmanned plane, they said, but best get to the shelter.'

He joined them as they rushed up the hill. The village seemed deserted as they reached the shops, but up ahead they could see the tail end of the crowd trotting along to the old rectory. When they had crested the hill, they disappeared down the other side.

Then, from a distance, Louisa heard the roar of approaching aircraft.

The sound grew and grew as if when it came in sight the sky might be filled with planes. The children reacted by scattering in different directions. Jack called to Johnno to grab Sydney, Mrs Harrison caught hold of Athena and Gloria and Gloria held Dolly. Louisa took Gracie and Priss. Iris held on to George and Alf.

'Go on,' Louisa said. 'I'll make sure Hugo is out – I don't know what's happened to him. I'll catch up. Go on, Gracie – go on with Mr Barrie.'

Jack and Mrs Harrison herded the children forward, but Gracie dug in her feet.

'No, no, no!' she cried.

Mrs Harrison came back and reached for her, but Gracie slapped at her, her voice rising in pitch and volume until it matched the roar of the aircraft.

'I don't want to go,' she sobbed, 'no, no, no, Mama, no, please Mama!'

She threw her arms around Louisa's hips.

Suddenly, there it was – only one plane, with its nose pointed down and smoke shooting from its tail as it dropped from the sky, coming for them. The children and grown-ups froze.

'Messerschmitt!' Johnno yelled.

A second later the plane disappeared behind the hill and there was a crash and the earth shook beneath their feet. A cloud of black smoke rose up in the air.

Gracie shrieked, nearly pulling Louisa over as she sank to the ground in a real-life nightmare.

'Gracie, look at me.' Louisa wrenched free from the girl's grip, but kept hold of her arms as she knelt down. Gracie didn't speak, but looked up at Louisa with the same dark, lifeless eyes and dark scowl that she'd had when she'd arrived at Oxburrow.

Shouts and screams carried from the other side of the hill.

'Louisa!' Jack called out from the front of their group.

'Go on,' Louisa shouted to him. 'It's all right.'

It was obviously not all right. He frowned but, when the other children took off at a run, he followed them, with Mrs Harrison on his heels. Gracie watched them go and trembled, her hands closing into fists. Louisa took the girl in her arms and held on.

'Is it Oxburrow?' Gracie asked, her voice small and remote.

'No,' Louisa said, 'it isn't Oxburrow at all. Oxburrow is back there.' She pointed in the opposite direction from the smoke.

Gracie spun round and looked at the trees that blocked Oxburrow from a distant view.

'Did Mrs Moffatt run away?' Gracie asked.

'Not a bit of it,' Louisa said, wiping tears off the girl's cheeks. 'Mrs Moffatt and Lulu are back at Oxburrow, and I'm sure they will be waiting for their supper when we return. Do you want to go back to the church?' she asked, although she was desperate to find out what had happened.

Gracie shook her head. 'I want to look.'

'Come on, then,' Louisa said. 'We'll go and find the others.'

Gracie stood and took Louisa's hand, and they set off.

They crested the hill where the road turned, and dipped, before rising again on the other side of Mrs Greet's house. Across the road from the old rectory had stood a row of four tiny old flax workers' cottages.

Now, two of them were gone, obliterated by the Nazi plane that itself was a wreckage of twisted metal, fire and smoke.

Louisa looked down at Gracie. 'All right?'

Gracie stared at the desolation and breathed hard. Louisa squeezed her hand. She prayed Gracie wouldn't retreat again into that dark place, but didn't know how to stop her other than holding on for dear life.

The rest of the children were just ahead.

'Alf!' Gracie shouted and the boy turned.

'Lulu is all right,' she said. 'Lulu and Mrs Moffatt are at Oxburrow.'

Alf nodded to her.

Louisa felt light-headed with relief, but it didn't last long as she looked closer at the destruction.

Through the smoke and dust rising into the dry air, she could see that an exposed fireplace still burned at the far end of the row of cottages. On the near end – which was untouched – Mr Gedge and Johnno were helping two old ladies sit down on the low brick wall. Several men, including Jack, picked their way around what was left of the plane, looking into the smashed cockpit.

In Louisa's mind, the Messerschmitt changed to a Spitfire, and she saw David in the burning wreck.

Shouts brought her back to the moment.

It was Minns. She ran toward the wreckage – the last cottage in the row had been hers, where she lived with her grandad and Uncle. Now that end of the row had been reduced to a pile of rubble.

Jack caught Minns, taking hold of her wrists, but she struggled to break free, shouting, 'They were coming home! Grandad said they were coming home!'

'Minns!' Louisa shouted. She looked down at Gracie. 'Will you stay here?'

Gracie held on to Louisa's hand even tighter.

'Gracie!' Athena called. 'Mrs Harrison says can we serve tea.'

Mrs Greet's maid had brought out a tray of steaming cups.

'Will you do that?' Louisa asked Gracie. 'Will you be a helper?'

Gracie's attention shifted from the destruction to Athena and Priss, who each carried a cup and saucer.

'C'mon!' Athena said and off Gracie went. Louisa threw a grateful look at Mrs Harrison, then ran down to where Minns still fought to escape Jack's grip.

'I should've come back with them,' she cried. 'Mrs Nethergate, too, and her dahlias.'

'Hugo!' Louisa exclaimed. 'Hugo had come to help Mrs Nethergate. Where is he?'

Mrs Nethergate lived in the cottage next to Minns's and half of it had collapsed.

'Where is Mrs Nethergate?' a woman called out.

The first real sign of panic set in as those in the crowd looked round at the destruction. Then, Minns shrieked.

'Grandad!'

She pointed up the road to the silhouettes of recognisable figures at the top of the rise – Mr Grainger leaning on his walking stick, Uncle in his wheelchair, being pushed by Hugo, and Mrs Nethergate beside them.

Both Minns and Louisa ran up to meet them as they came down.

'We were over at the allotments,' Uncle explained, taking in the scene with wide eyes.

'They were helping me choose my dahlias.' Mrs Nethergate nodded to a tray of puffed-up magenta flowers with white tips in Uncle's lap.

'When we heard the warning,' Mr Grainger said, 'we went inside the shed and watched the plane come down.' He shook his head at the sight before them. 'Ah, but did he have to land on our cottages?'

'Is everyone all right?' Hugo asked.

'Yes,' Louisa said, 'apparently so. All accounted for.'

Hugo spread his arms as if he were in the pulpit. 'And are we yet alive?' he sang in a booming voice.

Jack laughed, but others looked puzzled.

'Charles Wesley,' Hugo said. 'Yes, I know he was a Methodist, but he wrote some cracking hymns. Now, what about the pilot? And where is Colin?'

'Here, sir.' The boy stepped out of the crowd. 'The ARP from Woolpit rang the shop when they couldn't reach you. Cambridge bombing and this one escort lagged behind, they said. The pilot parachuted out on the way back. They've gone out to look.'

'You did well,' Hugo said. 'You can give me the details later, but for now – do you want to sound the all-clear?'

'Will do, Reverend.' And off he galloped.

Louisa surveyed the scene from the edge of the rise. A calm had settled on the place as everyone tended to practical matters. Athena, Priss and Gracie carefully carried cups of tea to those villagers milling about. Men and women started on the cleanup.

Louisa could see even from a distance that Gracie's hands shook a bit as she made the journey of five feet from the tray to Mrs Nethergate, and it was possible that a bit of the tea sloshed out into the saucer, but Mrs Nethergate received the cup with a smile and said a few words to Gracie, who smiled in return and dashed back for another cup.

Dolly and Gloria sat next to the old ladies resting on the low wall. George was counting steps from the road back to the old rectory's cellar stairs as a few more people emerged. When Mrs Greet had offered her cellars as the shelter for the village, the space had been kitted out with camp beds and tinned food and books and magazines. No one had thought it would ever be needed.

Mrs Greet herself brought out her first aid kit, and she and Mrs Harrison saw to small injuries – cuts and fresh bruises mostly, acquired in the rush to the shelter. They worked in a businesslike manner, but with a touch of care that Louisa hadn't noticed before. Mrs Greet and Mrs Harrison may be conspiring against her, but this reminded Louisa that few people are all one thing or another.

Iris chatted with a few of the women from the village, but conversations were constantly broken off as mothers kept their children from the siren's call of the wreckage.

'Minns,' Louisa said, 'you come to stay with us until things can be sorted. And you two' – she turned to Mr Grainger and Uncle – 'can have the old chauffeur's cottage next to Figg. It's all on the level and easy to get round and the path up to the house is solid.'

'Oh Louisa, thank you,' Minns said, her eyes sparkling. 'You two would love to be near Mr Figg, wouldn't you?'

'At last I'll be able to see what magic old Figg uses on those sprouts of his,' Mr Grainger said. 'Thank you, my lady.'

'Are you sure we wouldn't be in the way, what with the children and all?' Minns asked.

'The children will love to have you there and so will I.'

'What about the harvest festival?' Uncle asked in a voice loud enough for almost everyone to hear.

'Don't we have Mrs Darnley's cakes waiting for us in the church hall?' the man who ran the garage asked.

'We're not forgetting the competition, I hope,' Mr Grainger said.

'And the children are to sing,' Iris added as she picked up a village toddler who had been heading for a sharp piece of the plane that had landed near the road.

'Aye!' came a voice and then another and there were nods all round.

They stood quiet for a moment, contemplating the pile of rubble that had been cottages, then Minns said, 'I'll collect the children.'

On the way back to church, Louisa noticed Gracie talking with a girl about her age from the village, tugging on her plaits, both of which now stuck straight out sideways. Perhaps she was giving her instructions.

She may look chipper now, but the girl's terror had been real and Louisa knew Gracie wasn't out of the woods yet.

Next to her, Hugo said, 'It's odd. Now that we here in Debden Ash have been attacked, even though some may say we got off easy, it feels as if we can at least hold our heads up when we hear of others' misfortunes. As if we've joined some sort of club.'

Those first in the door of the church stopped abruptly and the ones behind bumped into them and grumbled – until they caught sight of what lay ahead.

It looked as if a cue ball had been shot straight into the middle of the mountain of abundance on the altar and had sent the apples, pears, potatoes and beets skittering off into the nether regions of the apse, leaving carrots and parsnips with their green tops dangling over one edge, while a sizeable marrow teetered dangerously at the opposite corner.

'What about the pumpkin?' Uncle called from the back.

Mr Grainger peered over the shoulder in front of him. 'Looks all right from here!'

'Thank you, Lord, for your bounty,' Hugo said with a sigh. 'Now, we'd best find it all before the mice do.'

Hugo and Colin went off to the vestry to confer, because Hugo would need to write up the report and account of damages. Compensation may or may not be forthcoming. No one could remember who actually owned the row of cottages – they had once belonged to the old rectory, but Mrs Greet said she hadn't acquired them. Regardless, everyone hoped the occupants might get a shilling or two.

Figg arrived at the church hall, saying he'd heard the warning and had gone to the basement of the house, as was the plan at Oxburrow. He'd felt what he thought was a bomb, but was actually the plane hitting the ground, and waited for the all-clear to sound before he left. He listened to several accounts from different points of view. Fairly quickly, the talk segued into comparisons to the Great War. Debden Ash had not been attacked then, but older folk remembered with clarity – as if they'd seen it themselves – that in 1917 a Zeppelin had crashed in Suffolk, over nearer to the coast.

Iris made tea and the judges carried out their duties. Hugo gave a blessing to the proceedings, the hands that prepared and grew the food and flowers as well as the courage and forbearance of everyone in the village.

His voice caught slightly as he asked for God's protection over the British men and women who were at that moment in the thick of things, whether fighting or captured or missing.

The children from Oxburrow sang 'We Gather Together' accompanied by concertina and the children from the village sang 'Come, Ye Thankful People, Come' with Hugo on harmonium. Everyone joined in to sing 'God Save the King', after which ribbons were awarded and tea and cake consumed. It was a bit of a rush, but nothing was overlooked.

'I'm growing one of them pumpkins next year,' one old fellow called to Mr Grainger from across the hall. 'Then we'll see who wins the ribbon.'

'I accept that challenge!' Minns's grandad replied, and was seconded by Uncle.

The auction of the fruit, veg, jam and honey brought the highest ever total, of forty-six pounds, twelve shillings and sixpence – ten shillings for the pumpkin alone.

Despite everyone's devil-may-care attitude toward the Nazi plane and the devastation of the cottages, the day had taken its toll. After the auction ended, people began to look about them with glassy eyes.

'Come to supper,' Louisa said to Hugo as they packed up and swept the floor.

'Thank you,' Hugo said. 'Jack and I will help Minns with the move. You're very good to take them all in.'

'I welcome the distraction,' Louisa said.

At Oxburrow, the older children were put to work helping Iris while Mrs Harrison took the younger ones into the library, but not before Gracie had rushed off toward the morning room and returned holding Mrs Moffatt by wrapping both her arms under the cat's forelegs, which stuck straight out while her hind legs stretched so far as to almost brush the floor. The cat looked at Louisa placidly.

'I'll read to her,' Gracie told Louisa as girl and cat followed the others into the library.

Louisa, relieved to see Gracie's high spirits had returned, said, 'She'll enjoy that, I'm sure.'

Iris scoured the pantry for enough food to feed the burgeoning numbers. Alf, newly appointed kitchen assistant, with Lulu at his feet, peeled potatoes and scraped carrots.

In the waning light of late afternoon, Jack and Hugo arrived and took two of the remaining servants' beds down to the chauffeur's cottage. Louisa and Iris beat the mattresses out in the yard while Johnno and Athena moved the left-over oddments out of the cottage and into the garage, which hadn't held a car in ten years.

The children took to the work without complaint, but also without their usual good humour. Louisa caught Athena as she wheeled David's old bicycle – how did it get into the chauffeur's cottage? – into the garage.

'All right there?' she asked.

Athena glanced past Louisa into the cottage. Priss was dusting, but stopped to wipe her nose on her sleeve.

'Priss's mum had a bicycle,' Athena said. 'It had a basket on it and she would do the shopping for my mum, too. Priss wanted to look for it after the bomb, but all the men found was the basket.'

Louisa gave Athena a hug and then went to Priss and gave her a cuddle, too. Painful memories didn't just vanish into thin air, she reminded herself as Priss sobbed into her shoulder.

Colin appeared on the cart, and Minns, Mr Grainger and Uncle sat in the back with their legs dangling over the side. With many hands helping, they disembarked, and, when Uncle was settled once again in his wheelchair, everyone went inside and sat down to supper.

On Sunday morning, Minns borrowed a dress from Mrs Harrison for church, and Iris and Louisa worked up to the last minute to raise the hem and sort out the snug waist by leaving one button undone and covering it with a belt. While they worked, Louisa noticed Gracie peering round the doorpost while, beyond, the children could be heard racing up and down the stairs, with the old men in the entrance hall egging them on.

'Are you all ready?' Louisa asked her.

Gracie nodded. 'May I have plaits like Minns?'

Minns's plaits went over the top of her head from ear to ear and were pinned down neatly, her black hair shining.

'I can show you how to do it,' Minns said, 'but we'll need to wait for your hair to grow a bit longer. Is that all right?'

'Is that all right?' Gracie asked Louisa.

'Of course it's all right, Gracie,' Louisa said and, noticing Mrs Harrison standing at the door, added, 'We've got all the time in the world for your hair to grow.'

Despite the chaos, they arrived at church before the bells finished ringing, their clothes and hair decorated with tiny jewel-like droplets of mist. The rest of Sunday passed in a subdued manner, as if the events of the day before had only just taken effect. No one complained when, fully an hour early, Mrs Harrison sent the children to bed.

When the house had quieted, Louisa went to the library and, keeping the lights off, parted the blackout curtains, opened the French windows and stepped out onto the terrace. In the starlight, she could see in the distance a mist hugging the ground like a thin strip of grey silk.

Jack came up behind her and wrapped his arms around her waist. Louisa covered his hands with hers and leaned back, resting her head against his chest.

'I don't know how you did it,' she said. 'In London. Destruction all round and you had to carry on. We've had one plane drop out of the sky and our very souls are frayed. At least we still have the countryside to look at.'

'You get through it because you have to, and by holding on to what's important,' Jack said, and gave her a squeeze. 'That's how you do it.'

How remarkable that war had brought them together. Louisa had never thought she'd have this in her life – even the possibility of it had seemed foreign to her. Might they make a life together – would there even be time to find out?

She could only live each day now – under threat of bad news about David or Gracie and the other children being taken away. Would Jack go with them?

CHAPTER 17

Louisa awoke the next morning with resolve, but alone. Jack had left her bed in the early hours to go back to his own room in case one of the boys called out. She smoothed the bedsheet on his side, pulled the pillow he'd used close and took a deep breath, letting it out with a slow sigh. Over the years she might've imagined what it would be like to have another man in her life after Max, but she could never see it working out. Now, in the moments her mind wasn't clouded with darkness, she had an overwhelming sense of possibility about the world around her – that world being Oxburrow. David, Gracie, the rest of the children. Perhaps it would all work out and Jack would be a part of it. What a remarkable medicine making love was, she thought, and giggled.

Still, they would need to do something about their arrangements – she'd never cared for skulking and she saw no reason to hide.

It wasn't until after breakfast that she caught both Jack and Mrs Harrison, at the bottom of the stairs in the entrance hall.

'I'm going to invite the school governors for a coffee morning,' Louisa said. 'I want to talk with them about their plans for the school. It's only fair, don't you think? I will start by ringing Mrs Perrymont.'

The idea had come to her out of the blue. If she had the school governors all there at Oxburrow, she could learn what their intentions were. At the same time, she would find out if Marian Perrymont was in league with Max to turf out the children and move in the army.

Mrs Harrison looked at Louisa as if she'd just said she would fly to the moon.

'Mrs Perrymont? I don't see what she has to do with—' Mrs Harrison stopped abruptly. 'Thank you, Lady Brightford, but that won't be necessary.'

'A clear plan can only help the children,' Jack said, although he'd known nothing about her announcement. 'Surely you can't object to that?'

Mrs Harrison raised an eyebrow. 'If I were you, Mr Barrie, I would remember which side your bread is buttered on. Now, it's time for morning lessons.'

Louisa stared after the woman as she walked off. 'Is she threatening you with dismissal?'

Jack frowned at Mrs Harrison, but didn't answer.

'Jack?' Louisa asked.

'You're right to focus on the school governors,' he said, which wasn't an answer. 'She wants them all to herself – in her own pocket. But she doesn't seem to know much about Mrs Perrymont.' He turned to Louisa. 'You aren't actually going to telephone her?'

'I believe I will,' Louisa said loftily. 'That'll put the wind up Mrs Harrison. How do I get hold of her?'

'You could ask Max,' Jack said, and Louisa sniggered.

It was tempting, but in the end Louisa didn't have to ask Max. Mrs Nethergate had a London directory and Mrs Marian Perrymont was listed. Louisa wrote down the number, tucked it into her pocket and went off to help Iris with yet another batch of chutney.

Despite the events of the weekend and the scene at the other side of the village, routine was the rule of the day at Oxburrow. The children were at their lessons, Minns ironed upstairs and the older men were with Figg down in the glasshouse. While they peeled and chopped apples, Louisa told Iris of her plans concerning the school governors.

'You'll use my currant cake to wheedle their intentions out of them?' Iris asked.

'It will be our secret weapon,' Louisa said.

They'd put up twelve jars of chutney and, as Louisa washed the pot, she asked, 'Is that it for the apples?'

'Not by a long chalk,' Iris replied as she plunged the mop into a bucket of clean soapy water. She rested the handle against the table so that she could shoo Lulu and Mrs Moffatt off their respective beds.

'Mopping the floor,' she said to the animals, 'means mopping the whole floor. Go and find yourselves something to do.' They both rose, stretched and sauntered off, the dog keeping a wary eye on the cat.

Louisa dried her hands, stuck them in her pockets and drew out the paper with Mrs Perrymont's telephone number on it. She stared at it without moving.

'Well, are you going to ring her or not?' Iris asked.

'Yes,' Louisa said peevishly and stuffed the paper back into her pocket. 'Yes of course I am. I'm going right now.'

Still she didn't move until Iris came towards her, mop in hand, then she took off and up the stairs to the telephone room. She sat down at the desk to compose herself.

In her mind she rehearsed what she would say. The reason she was ringing was to thank the school governors for sending the children from Hazel End Charity School to Oxburrow Manor. She would ask if any progress had been made in searching for any living relatives for the children – hadn't Mrs Harrison said something about that? The question would make it sound as if Louisa were a part of the general administration of the school.

That was when she would slip it in – in a by-the-by sort of way: Were the school governors considering moving the school away from Oxburrow? If so, what reason did they have for disrupting the children, whose fates had already been cast to the wind? And oh yes, please come for coffee.

Once she had her thoughts in order, she rang the number.

'Mayfair 6486,' said a woman's voice.

'Hello, I'd like to speak to Mrs Perrymont.'

'I'm sorry, Mrs Perrymont isn't at home. Is there a message?'

Oh, there was a message all right. There were several messages.

'Please tell her... that the children from Hazel End school are doing well at Oxburrow Manor.'

'Is that all?' the woman asked.

'Yes,' Louisa said. She placed the receiver gently on its cradle and sat quietly for a moment, then stood and caught sight of her reflection in the window.

'Coward,' she said.

Louisa hadn't abandoned her intentions entirely. She went to the morning room and sat down to write an invitation to Mrs Perrymont to visit Oxburrow on an agreed-upon day. She would be calm and circumspect in her invitation. Should it be addressed only to Mrs Perrymont? No, she would write to the others, too – Mr Hargreaves, Mr Merrick, Mr Ilkington and the phantom Mr Richards.

Her fountain pen hovered over the stationery, its nib nearly touching the paper, when the door creaked open and Gracie peered in.

'Mrs Darnley says where are you, because it's almost time for dinner.' As she spoke, Mrs Moffatt slipped in behind her, the cat's tail curling round Gracie's legs. The girl giggled.

Louisa knew exactly what Iris was doing – making sure Louisa didn't lose herself in thoughts of hopelessness.

'Come in while I tidy up and we'll go down together,' she said, screwing the top of the pen back on.

Gracie went to the desk and began helping – moving the fountain pen from one side to the other, switching the lamp off and then on again and opening drawers. Then she pointed to the stack of letters Louisa had left by David's photo.

'Did David write you all those?' she asked.

'He did,' Louisa said. 'I like reading them over and over.' And how long would it be before a fresh letter arrived? She picked one out from only the week before the children arrived. 'Here, let's see what he said.'

My darling mum,

I'm becoming what they call a night owl – we're just back from a little jaunt chasing Nazis and it's time for breakfast. Here now, before I forget – can you ask William if he's in need of a clerk?

Louisa paused. She'd replied asking if David was now interested in the law, but he hadn't answered the question and she'd forgotten to mention it to William.

Gracie had wandered off and was looking at a watercolour high up in the corner. Not a Turner or a Constable – a light and simple depiction by a homegrown artist.

'David painted that,' Louisa told her. She went over, took it off the wall and set it on a low table so Gracie could get a better look. 'It's Lake Puddle-Duck.'

Gracie's jaw dropped. 'That's Jemima's name!'

'David loved her story,' Louisa said, 'and he made up the name. It's a lake we like to go to for picnics and camp-outs.'

'Can we go? Can we go to Lake Puddle-Duck?'

'Well,' Louisa said, 'I don't see why not. We'll go for a picnic.'

Gracie frowned. 'We should wait for David.'

For a moment, Louisa couldn't speak. She kissed the top of Gracie's head, recovered and said, 'That's very kind of you, but we can go now and then we'll go again after David comes home.'

Louisa returned to her desk, but Gracie's optimism had triggered something in her – shaken loose a bit of her own optimism. This would be no visit for the school governors to carry out an inspection. No, this time Oxburrow would be in charge.

She leapt up again.

'Where is Mr Barrie?'

'Eating his dinner?' Gracie said.

'Yes, right, dinner. Let's go.'

When they walked past the library, Jack came out.

'Dinner, Mr Barrie!' Gracie said.

'Righto, Gracie.' But Jack was watching Louisa.

'We'll be just behind you,' Louisa said to Gracie and the girl skipped off. Louisa turned to Jack. He caught her round the waist and she stretched her arms round his neck. For a moment they did nothing but gaze into each other's eyes.

'How was your morning?' Jack asked.

'Full of chutney,' Louisa replied.

'Did chutney put that gleam in your eye?'

'You put that gleam in my eye,' Louisa said and kissed him. 'But also, I have an idea to get the upper hand with the school governors, and not with a mere cup of coffee. We go on the offensive. We'll arrange a school fete for them. A day where there's such a variety of games and displays that each child has a chance to shine. George could recite the counties in England and Athena write a story. That sort of thing. Hugo would come and give the day a blessing and that would put the weight of the Church behind us. What do you think?'

'It's a brilliant idea. Did you invite Mrs Perrymont?'

'I rang, but Mrs Perrymont was not at home,' Louisa said. 'I lost my nerve and left a vague message. We'll do it properly – each school governor will receive a written invitation, but' – she put up a forefinger – 'I won't be the one to write to them. C'mon – we need to chat with Mrs Harrison.'

'This'll be interesting,' Jack said.

It wasn't until after the midday meal that Louisa cornered Mrs Harrison. After the children had left the table, she explained the idea as nearly completely arranged with only a few details to be pinned down. The woman's eyes grew wide with alarm.

'It will be rather like a parents' day, but with school governors,' Louisa said and, throwing caution to the wind, added, 'I deserve this chance.'

'Lady Brightford—' Mrs Harrison began.

'I know you want to take the children away. I know you are seeking support from the school governors.' Louisa could do nothing else but lay her cards on the table. 'But I want them to see that Oxburrow isn't just a replacement for a schoolhouse, it's a place for them to heal. I want to convince them. And you.'

'It isn't just Oxburrow,' Jack said. 'Lady Brightford is the reason the children are recovering.'

'Thank you, Mr Barrie,' Louisa whispered, all the sound she could produce.

'It's a...' Mrs Harrison said, but slowly, as if giving herself time to find the loophole. 'Of course, we have no idea if the school governors would be available for such a day out.'

'We'll hold it two weeks from Saturday,' Louisa said. 'That's more than a fortnight away – plenty of time for them to get it into their diaries.'

'Think of the lessons the children will miss getting ready,' Mrs Harrison said.

'Getting ready for the day will be as good as lessons,' Jack countered.

'It would be a terrible amount of work for you and Mrs Darnley.'

The woman was grasping at straws. Louisa broke into a wide smile. 'Iris will be thrilled about it. Well, Mrs Harrison, what do you say?'

Louisa could not read anything in the woman's face – not because it was vacant, but rather because there was too much there. Raised brows were followed by a frown of either disapproval or hard thinking. Pursed lips might mean she was sticking to her guns or that the chutney at dinner was causing wind.

Mrs Harrison made a last-ditch effort. 'It's too late for an invitation in the post.'

'Nonsense,' Louisa said. 'They'll go out in the last post today. Plenty of time after tea for you to write them.'

'What?'

Louisa nearly laughed.

'That's a fine idea,' Jack said. 'It will be official, coming from you. That is, if you're willing to give Lady Brightford the chance.'

'Well...' Mrs Harrison's voice petered out.

'I'm sure your invitation will be written in an objective manner,' Jack said.

'Say whatever you like,' Louisa said. 'Tell them it's Lady Brightford's last stand.'

CHAPTER 18

It had been a gamble, but it had paid off.

'How on God's green earth did you manage it?' Iris asked, pulling a loaf out of the oven and then fanning herself with her apron.

'She needs to face facts,' Louisa said. 'The children are thriving. This fete is as much to make her realise that as it is to convince the school governors. I said it straight out. I asked her to give me a chance. I don't know, Iris. Is it really such a moral outrage that I'm divorced? Is that what stops her from embracing Oxburrow as their home? I'd like to think her resolve is weakening – Oxburrow working its magic.'

'It's you being relentless,' Iris said. 'Good on you. But doesn't she have Mrs Perrymont on her side?'

'And this Mr Richards. But she agreed and has written the invitations, so the difficult part is over.'

'It is, is it?' Iris said, 'Now all you and Mr Barrie need to do is put the show on. That's going to take a great deal of late-night planning, I'm sure.' She wiggled her eyebrows at Louisa.

'I think we'll manage it,' Louisa said and wiggled hers back. Then, without warning, the dread crept up on her. 'It'll keep me busy and, when I'm busy, my thoughts about David are positive. It's when I'm still and unoccupied that—'

A squeal and burst of laughter and applause came from upstairs, but, as there was no ensuing crash, Louisa ignored it. Then a giggling Gracie appeared at the kitchen door.

'Alf and Sydney are taking turns to see who can throw Mr Barrie's hat over the upstairs railing and on the statue man. Sydney is ahead by three. Come and watch!' Gracie held out her hand and Louisa took it.

'There you are,' Iris said as they left, 'you've got your opening number for the fete.'

Oxburrow's residents came and went, but Iris managed with remarkable accuracy to know who would be at which meal. On Monday evening, Minns and family were added in while Johnno and Jack were taken away – they'd been invited to supper with the Gedges. At breakfast the next morning, Louisa asked the boy about their visit.

'They're Quaker,' Johnno explained to the other children. 'That's a kind of church.' To Louisa he added, 'Mrs Gedge says she's sorry about David and hopes he's home soon.' Johnno glanced at Jack as if asking if he'd done the right thing. Jack nodded his approval.

Louisa knew that the Gedges' son, a conscientious objector, was driving an ambulance in London – and facing his own dangers.

'That's very kind of her,' Louisa said. She had nothing against the Gedges, or Quakers, and found their non-violent beliefs admirable. But she could not reconcile those beliefs with what then could be done about Hitler, who was bent on violence and destruction and overtaking the world with hate.

Louisa thought she heard a note of wonder in Johnno's voice when he spoke of the Gedges, as if he'd not encountered many quiet, kind and hard-working folk before. Johnno was of an age that he would look up to David rather like a younger brother would. She glanced at Gracie, who had her mouth full of porridge but smiled regardless. *You already have a little sister waiting for you, my son.*

As the children gathered for morning lessons, Louisa pulled Jack aside and asked for his view of the visit.

'Johnno has had a rough life,' he said, 'but Mr Gedge sees something in the boy.'

'Look what he's done for Johnno already,' Louisa said. 'He's showing him a life without anger. What will Johnno go back to if the school governors insist the children return to London? Where will he live? Where will *you* live?' For a moment they were silent, Louisa all the while wanting very much to ask him to stay.

'And where will Gracie live?' Jack asked. 'We can't all camp out on pallets in the schoolhouse. Hasn't Mrs Harrison thought of that?'

Louisa asked special permission from Mrs Harrison to allow Gracie to miss her late-morning lessons. The woman gave it, but in a distracted way. Louisa thought that the impending fete was occupying her mind and that made it easier to catch her off guard. It made Louisa feel a bit freer as she and Gracie strode through the wood.

'Is Reverend Hugo at church?' Gracie asked as they both scuffed through the leaves.

'Let's find out.'

When they came near to St Gregory's, they heard a voice coming out of an open window. When Louisa pulled the door open, they found Hugo practising his message for Sunday.

Louisa gave him a wave and whispered to Gracie, 'We'll come back later,' but Gracie let go of her hand, walked down the aisle and sat in the Brightford pew. Louisa followed, raising her brows at Hugo.

'You're very welcome,' he said, 'as long as you don't mind me stumbling over my words occasionally.'

'Carry on.' Louisa put her arm round Gracie and they snuggled together in the chill church air. Hugo looked down at his notes and then continued.

'Oh, well, I...' He shifted the papers in front of him, then looked up. 'I am reminded of the hymn about the sparrow.' He smiled at Gracie. 'It's about God's care for us. "Why should I feel discouraged?" it says.' Hugo paused and swallowed hard. '"For his eye is on the sparrow, and I know he watches..."'

He stopped and took a ragged breath. Louisa's chin quivered. She looked down, to see that Gracie was unperturbed. The girl had that faraway look in her eyes as she listened – just as she'd had during the Sunday services.

Hugo turned the pages over. 'Well, enough of that.' He drew his handkerchief out of the pocket of his cassock and blew his nose. 'I say, Gracie, would you like to see the harmonium?'

He showed Gracie the foot pedals, but her legs weren't long enough, so he worked the pedals and pulled the stops while she pressed the keys – hesitantly at first, and then with more conviction and a great deal more noise.

'You've quite an ear for music, don't you?' Hugo asked.

'I can sing, too,' Gracie said.

'Gracie and David share that quality,' Louisa said, and Hugo grinned. David was notoriously tone-deaf.

'We are told to make a joyful noise,' Hugo said. 'The Lord didn't mention being in tune.'

At the end of the lesson, Louisa kissed Hugo on the cheek and she and Gracie took their leave. As they passed through the lychgate, Louisa asked, 'You enjoy visiting Reverend Hugo, don't you?'

Gracie nodded. 'He looks like Brother Michael,' she said.

'Brother Michael?' Louisa repeated – a stall for time as she thought about this. 'Does Brother Michael wear a cassock – a black robe like Reverend Hugo's?'

Gracie nodded again, but the topic didn't hold her interest any further.

'Does Mr Barrie know the sparrow song?' she asked. 'Will he teach it to us?'

They paused outside the post office shop for a moment as Gracie studied a poster in the window admonishing children to *Drink Milk!* and another with a drawing of a swede – leaves, roots and all – *Plan and Plant for Winter!* Mrs Nethergate proudly displayed anything the Ministry of Information sent her.

'Look who I've brought along,' Louisa said when they went inside.

'Good morning, Mrs Nethergate,' Gracie said.

'Lovely to see you, Gracie,' the woman said, clasping her hands. 'I enjoyed your singing at the harvest festival.'

'Thank you.'

As Gracie wandered the shop, looking at its treasures, Louisa asked, 'How are you settling in? Were you able to salvage any of your things?'

The other of the two cottages destroyed by the plane was Mrs Nethergate's, and Mrs Greet had offered her lodging in the old rectory.

'I found very little,' Mrs Nethergate said, shaking her head. 'But I'm not wanting for anything, thanks to Mrs Greet.'

Louisa noticed that Gracie had stopped to gaze at the jars of boiled sweets. 'I tell you what, Mrs Nethergate, we'll take a quarter of mixed sweets.'

When they'd left the shop, Gracie eyed the bag Louisa held and, her voice full of awe, said, 'That's a lot of sweets.'

'There are nine of you,' Louisa said.

'There are grown-ups, too,' Gracie said. 'You, Mrs Darnley, Mrs Harrison, Mr Barrie, Minns, Minns's grandad, Uncle and Mr Figg. That's... more than nine.'

'Let's see if we can do the sums and find out how many altogether,' Louisa said. That way, she'd be able to report back to Mrs Harrison that they'd had a maths lesson on their outing.

They stopped adding when they reached the bend, where the road dipped down. They looked at where the cottages had been, where now a few men were still sorting out bricks and sticks of furniture. Gracie drew close and leaned against Louisa.

'It was a scary thing when the aeroplane fell,' Louisa said. 'Did it remind you of what happened before?'

Gracie stayed silent for so long, Louisa feared that she was retreating once again inside herself. But at last the girl spoke.

'The siren started and Mama said to run. "Run, Gracie! Go on!"' Her voice trembled. 'But I didn't want to. "No, Mama, I don't want to go." And then' – a sob caught in her throat – 'I woke up and I couldn't move. Mama was holding my hand. But she wouldn't wake up.' The tears fell and Gracie shuddered as she cried. 'She died. She died because I didn't run away.'

'Oh Gracie, love.' Louisa knelt down as her own eyes welled. 'Your mama died because the bomb fell. It was never your fault. Please, please remember that.'

Fresh tears fell as Gracie looked deep into Louisa's eyes. Then, she threw her arms round Louisa's neck and held tight.

'Is Mrs Greet at home, Pauline?' Louisa asked the maid who answered the door at the old rectory.

'She is, my lady, come in and I'll tell her you're here.'

Louisa bent over and combed her fingers through Gracie's fringe. They'd both recovered their emotions, but it was difficult to disguise the aftermath of tears.

In the silence, Gracie said, 'I hear birds.'

'Do you?' Louisa tried to listen, but Pauline returned and said, 'She's just in the morning room. Let me take your coats.'

The door to the room stood open and Mrs Greet rose from her desk.

'Lady Brightford and Gracie, you're very welcome.'

The coolness had gone from Mrs Greet's manner and Louisa chalked it up to the crash of the Nazi plane. Such things can bring a community together. It was the only good thing one could say about it.

'Good morning,' Louisa said, and Gracie echoed the greeting. 'We've come to thank you for adding to Iris's sugar supply so she could make the little cakes for the harvest festival.'

Also, Louisa wondered if Mrs Greet might know something about Mrs Harrison wanting to take the children away.

'You and Iris do enough work for the village – I was pleased to make a small contribution. Please sit down. Pauline will bring us tea.'

Conversation kept to lighter topics over tea and biscuits and, after the biscuits were gone and Gracie began to squirm, Mrs Greet said, 'Gracie, would you like to see the parakeets?'

'Yes, ma'am.'

'Pauline will show you them.'

Gracie drank the last of her milk and followed the maid out. Louisa's tea was gone and she had nothing to occupy herself.

For a few minutes, they chatted about the WVS and the destroyed cottages and the shelter in the basement below. Then, in a pause, Louisa plunged in.

'I noticed you and Mrs Harrison chatting,' she said. 'It's been difficult for the children, but for the teachers, too, to be taken away from their normal lives.'

Mrs Harrison's normal life was, of course, an enigma. But at that moment Louisa realised she knew nothing of what had filled Jack's time either. Pub in the evening? British Museum's reading room on Saturdays?

'Mrs Harrison and I have found common ground,' Mrs Greet said. 'In one way. And you and I have it in another. In regards to marriage.'

'You're divorced?'

'Yes.' The single word sounded like a brave declaration. 'As soon as the law passed I applied for divorce through desertion. He had scarpered eight years before, and good riddance to him. Mrs Harrison hasn't been so lucky.'

Louisa gasped. 'Mrs Harrison isn't a widow?'

At that moment, Gracie ran in.

'I saw five parakeets!' she announced. 'Two blue ones and three green ones. They live in a cage as big as the wall.' She held her arms as wide as she could to indicate its vastness.

Mrs Greet rose and Louisa took this to mean she would hear no more about Mrs Harrison.

'Gracie,' Mrs Greet said, 'you may come any time and visit the birds.'

'Thank you!' Gracie said. She turned to Louisa. 'May I come tomorrow?'

'You have a busy few days ahead of you, so perhaps we'll wait on the next visit,' Louisa said. 'Thank you so much for tea.' Gracie skipped on ahead to the front door, but Louisa paused.

'Mrs Harrison complained to the school governors the moment she learned Max and I were divorced. She believes Oxburrow isn't a wholesome place. If she's divorced, why is she pointing the finger at me?'

'She isn't divorced,' Mrs Greet said quietly. 'And that's part of the problem. But it started before that. It's what she gave up to marry that rankles. But more than that she will have to tell you herself.'

Gracie went ahead of Louisa down the walk to the gate,

where she stopped and waved at Colin coming up the road with his horse and cart.

'Are you on your way back to Oxburrow?' he asked, giving a tug to the reins and stopping. 'If so, hop on. I've a delivery and I'll carry you there.'

'Will the horse bite?' Gracie said, eyeing the big brown beast.

'Queenie wouldn't hurt a fly,' Colin said. He jumped down, dug in his jacket pocket and came up with a knobby piece of carrot. 'Come here now, and you can feed her.'

Gracie drew closer to the horse, but stayed behind Colin. He showed her how to hold her hand flat and placed the carrot on it. 'Now, see if she'll take it.'

Colin had the good sense to not only guide Gracie's hand, but also keep hold of her arm, holding it still as Queenie took up the carrot – nuzzling the girl's palm and causing a burst of excited breathing.

Gracie examined her empty hand and then held it up to Louisa.

'Did you like that?' Louisa asked.

'It tickled!' Gracie said.

'You'll have to start carrying a few carrots in your pocket,' Colin said. 'That's what Mr David does.'

Colin froze and stared at Louisa as if afraid he'd spoken out of turn.

'He certainly does,' Louisa said and smiled at him. 'Thank you for remembering that, Colin.' She worried that people might stop talking about David in front of her out of some misplaced concern for her feelings. She wouldn't stand for that.

They climbed up onto the cart and sat behind Colin alongside the groceries, and the entire trip back Gracie talked first about parakeets and how she would like to have one or two and then about Queenie and how perhaps she could have a horse.

'A horse instead of the parakeet?' Louisa asked.

'A horse *and* a parakeet,' Gracie said. 'They could be friends.'

That evening over drinks in the library, Louisa told Jack about visiting Hugo.

'Gracie said he reminded her of Brother Michael,' she said. 'Is he a monk, do you think? Or could her mother have been chapel?'

Jack's brows drew together. 'I can't imagine Irene being involved with a community of priests. Chapel would be more likely – the Methodists, perhaps, although I don't recall them attending.'

'I know very little of any of your lives in London,' Louisa said. 'What did you do with yourself when you weren't in the schoolroom?'

'I felt myself on probation,' Jack said, 'having come out of the coal yard into the schoolroom. So I kept my head down and worked so I didn't upset Mrs Harrison's apple cart. Walked the Embankment. Planned lessons. I was in the same building as all the children, and so I became a sort of jack-of-all-trades for the mothers. I was often called in to clear the drains.'

'Oh dear.'

'On Saturdays I'd go to the reading room in the museum.'

Louisa was inordinately pleased she had got that right.

'And your favourite pub?'

'A little place along the docks – I hope it's still there. It's called the Lighter. Attracts a good sort of crowd, including a Russian princess – or so she says.'

'Fancied her, did you?' Louisa asked.

'Like mad,' Jack said. 'But as she was eighty-four on her last birthday, we knew it would never work.'

Louisa laughed.

Jack took her hand. 'Will you come to London with me after the war and I'll show you round?'

'Yes, I will. Will you come to Inverness and meet my dad?' she asked.

'Certainly, although won't he mind I'm not a peer of the realm?'

'Dad went right off titles after Max accused him of fraud,' Louisa said. 'Called Max an upstart crow because the Brightford title's been around only since George the Fourth.'

'Good, then I'm in with a chance,' Jack said. 'What will you say to David?'

Louisa kissed him for that. 'He isn't the sort of son who wants his mother all to himself,' she said. 'I look forward to introducing the two of you. I think you'll get on.'

She swirled the last of her whisky and drank it down. She fought to be brave and cheerful about David, but at the same time, didn't want to make any danger he may be in seem inconsequential. In war, danger and destruction were the order of the day.

'This morning, Gracie talked about when the bomb hit the terrace,' she said. 'We walked down to see Mrs Greet, and you can't help but look at where the cottages stood.'

'What does she remember?' Jack asked.

'Bits,' Louisa said. 'It seems that, when the air-raid warning sounded, her mum tried to get Gracie to run – to the shelter? To school? She didn't say. But Gracie didn't want to go. And now she thinks her mother died because she disobeyed.'

'God,' Jack said. 'What we blame ourselves for.'

'She cried,' Louisa said. 'She didn't scream and fight as she did before – she cried the way she cried with me about David.'

CHAPTER 19

Louisa filled her days until the fete with as much work as she could cram in. It helped keep the dark thoughts away, but even so, that became harder and harder. As time grew shorter before the fete, it grew longer since David had been reported missing. With every passing day, hope for his survival faded.

And so, she threw herself into any task she could. She listened several times a day while Gracie practised reading *The Tale of Tom Kitten*. Between readings, she advised Athena on writing her story and helped Priss stitch and restitch a blouse the girl had designed from an old shirt of Max's. She acted as George's assistant in making a 'footstep map' of Oxburrow Manor.

She embarked on a campaign of repairs around Oxburrow, replastering cracks and reweaving bare spots in the Axminster. All the while, Louisa kept up her work with the WVS and looked in on Hugo regularly. Often, the two of them sat in silence.

Another idea came to her, but she consulted with Jack before springing it on Mrs Harrison.

'I have a book request for reading time at the end of the

school day,' she said. '*Swallows and Amazons.*' It sounded a random choice, and so she confessed, 'David has always loved those books.' In some strange way, she felt as though the familiar words might travel over the miles to wherever he was and he would hear them again.

'The three of us could read in turns,' Jack said.

'No, you and Mrs Harrison ought to do it,' Louisa said. She didn't want to be seen usurping a schoolroom activity.

As it happened, Mrs Harrison declined to read, but didn't voice an objection about Louisa doing so.

On the first afternoon, the children came in from ten minutes racing around the lawn and scattered themselves about the library – on sofas and chairs, or on the floor with their heads resting on pillows. Louisa began, but when she reached the end of the first chapter the children wanted more, and so she handed the book to Jack, who read until Iris marched up the stairs and told them she would be eating all the bread and butter and jam herself if they didn't hop to it.

There remained six days to go before the fete when Jack walked into the library to find her on the ladder dusting the highest bookshelf.

'Lousia,' he said, 'come down.'

She sneezed.

'You can finish tomorrow,' he told her. 'I'll finish it tomorrow.'

'You've done far too much,' Louisa said as she stepped carefully on her way down. He'd had a hand in making repairs, too. That morning he'd been up on the roof filling a gap in the tiles and stopping one of the many leaky spots that had gone unpatched for far too many years.

Now, when she reached the bottom step, Jack slid his arms

around her waist. With him as support, she could pause and breathe.

'All right?' he murmured.

'Yes,' she replied. *For the moment.*

In the morning Louisa walked into the kitchen, and Minns and Iris stopped talking.

'Right, what's this about?' Louisa asked them.

'I was at the shops first thing this morning,' Minns said. 'It's Mrs Waite. She's had word about her son, Albert.'

'He was in North Africa,' Louisa said, going cold as a sense of dread crept over her.

'Reported missing a month ago,' Minns said. Her gaze darted to Iris.

'And now she's had the news that he was killed,' Iris said. She shook her head, her brows knitted. 'He was such a good lad. He wanted to be a racing car driver.'

'And he loved the football,' Minns added.

That was the progression, wasn't it? – first missing, then dead – as if being ambiguous to begin with would soften the blow.

It was no wonder Iris and Minns had thought to keep the news from Louisa.

Louisa leapt into action before the blackness could come over her. 'Is she alone?' she asked, going into the pantry to look for an empty basket so that they wouldn't see her shaking hands. 'We'll pack a hamper of jam and eggs and bread and take it to her.'

Iris followed her and put a hand on Louisa's arm. 'We will, but there's no hurry,' she said. 'The one daughter in the ATS in Cambridge has come. The other one who lives in Peterborough with the two little girls is on the way.'

'Good, good,' Louisa said, but in a distracted way. What was she to do now? Her thoughts wouldn't settle – or maybe she didn't want them to settle.

She turned and left and went directly to the telephone room, where she rang Max at the War Office. She was put through without waiting.

'Louisa, what is it?'

His voice held anxious concern and it so unnerved her that her throat constricted. She forced out the words. 'Has there been any news of David?'

Max exhaled and it sounded as if a gust of wind had blown by. Was he relieved? Had he thought she had heard something first?

'No,' he said. 'There's been nothing.'

'How long is it before David is no longer considered missing?'

Silence at first, then he said, 'Four weeks.'

It had been nearly three since she'd received the telegram.

Louisa rang off and went to the morning room. She sat down at the desk, took out a sheet of stationery and picked up her fountain pen, and wrote a letter to David. She wrote and wrote, barely paying attention to the words. At last she paused, put the pen down and picked up David's photo.

'Where are you, my son?'

The door creaked open and Gracie looked in.

'Mrs Darnley said to come and see you.'

Louisa smiled. 'Did she now? How wise of her. Come round here.'

Gracie went to Louisa's side and rested her forearm on the desk.

'Were you talking to David?' she asked, pointing to the photo.

Louisa smiled back at her son's crooked smile. 'Yes, I might've been.'

'Are you writing a letter to him?' she asked.

'I am,' Louisa said. 'There's so much news to tell him. This is what I've written so far. I know it's joined-up writing, but can you read any of those words?'

Gracie put her finger on the paper. 'That's my name!'

'Well spotted. Do you want to write your own letter to David?'

'Yes. I'll tell him Mrs Moffatt misses him and we'll be happy when he comes home.'

'That's a splendid idea,' Louisa said, the words barely escaping before the tears took over.

The next morning, heavy dark clouds gathered on the horizon as if they were looking for trouble. A hard rain in Suffolk – a deluge – was not unheard of and could change the landscape in an instant, creating rivulets and streams in the ridges of dry ground and turning low spots in the drive into chalky pools. Louisa eyed the clouds from her bedroom window, wishing to make a bargain – rain all you like today, just leave us a decent day for the fete.

'Johnno would like a run-through today, if you don't mind,' Jack said at breakfast.

Johnno had brought his beekeeping gear into the dining room with him and it now sat waiting by the cold fireplace.

'Of course you may,' Louisa said. 'That is, it's fine with me. Mrs Harrison – could Johnno have perhaps an hour of school time later? We'll all go down to the hives and he can give us his talk.'

Mrs Harrison looked up from the porridge she'd hardly touched.

'Yes, yes.'

.   .   .

The children were finishing their first lessons of the morning and Louisa, her hair tied back with an old tea towel, had been sweeping the doorstep when she heard a car on the drive and looked out of the window to see a Rolls-Royce pull up and stop on the forecourt.

Louisa's heart began to race. The letter promised by the Air Ministry with further information about David had not yet arrived. If someone had come out in person, it could only be bad news.

But she could see no occupants other than the driver, who was not wearing a uniform. So, neither the Air Ministry, nor the school governors arriving days early. Her heart slowed to its normal pace again. She rested the broom in the crook of her arm and watched as the man put down the window and leaned out.

'Is this Oxburrow Manor?' he asked.

'It is,' Louisa replied.

'How can a place be so hidden in plain sight?' he complained, getting out. He retrieved a thick brown envelope tied with twine from the car seat.

'We're easy to find when you know where we are,' Louisa said.

The man started to speak and then stopped, frowning, as if trying to sort out whether she was having him on.

'Lady Brightford,' he said, his face clearing up. 'Is she at home?'

'I am she,' Louisa said.

The frown returned. 'You aren't,' he said.

'I am,' she replied in a commanding voice. 'Do you need proof?'

'No,' the man said, looking bewildered. 'I'm very sorry, my lady. I only thought – well, I suppose it's the war, isn't it? This is for you.'

She took the packet and saw that it was addressed to her in an elegant hand.

'Who sent this?' she asked.

The driver looked surprised. 'Mrs Perrymont, my lady. She said you were expecting it.'

'Did she?' Louisa muttered to herself. A packet of papers driven out from London – think of the petrol! She smiled at the driver. 'Thank you. Would you care for a cup of... ginger beer?'

Louisa and Iris had been bemoaning their inadequate supply of tea, which was on ration, and for two days had gone without in order to have enough to serve to the school governors. She wasn't about to squander any now.

'Thank you, my lady,' he said. 'It's very kind of you and I'd really prefer to say yes, but must say no, because I'm expected back.'

Either he was genuinely expected back or he thought he might try a country pub and have better luck at a drink.

'Yes, all right then. Thanks.'

Louisa left her broom on the doorstep and went to the morning room, where she stood at her desk staring at the packet. What had Marian Perrymont sent to her – floor plans for when the army moved in? Did Louisa really want to see this now? She picked up the letter opener, but at that moment heard a voice from the entrance hall calling out, ''ello, 'ello, 'ello!!'

She shoved the packet into a desk drawer and went off.

Chuff stood in the entrance hall, and the moment he saw Louisa he swept his worn flat cap off his head and bowed.

'Good morning, my lady,' he said.

'It's Mr Chuff!' Gracie called out as the children poured out of their schoolrooms.

''Ello, children! Jack, 'ow are you?' He spotted Mrs Harrison and bobbed his head. 'Mrs 'arrison.' He gave a sweeping gesture out to the forecourt where his lorry sat. 'Look what I've brought you. It's the four other desks, repaired, clean and ready for the children.'

The children peered out the open door, as Chuff spotted Iris coming up from the basement. His eyes lit up. 'Oh now, Mrs Darnley, it's lovely to see you again.'

'Passing through, are you?' Iris asked, her hands in her apron pockets.

'Well, I do have a return journey organised,' Chuff said. 'I'm to collect three trunks of goods and carry them back to this nice lady in Bermondsey. All above board – petrol coupons and all.'

'Of course, the desks,' Louisa said. 'Just think, children, now each one of you will have your own desk.'

The children called out, 'Thank you, Mr Chuff.' Louisa glanced at Mrs Harrison, who furrowed her brow and worried her hands, but then got hold of herself.

'Yes, yes, the desks,' she said. 'Well, Mr Chuffleigh, although I've no doubt you started out from London with clean desks, I would rather they have a rag run over them before they come indoors.'

Chuff pulled his yellowed handkerchief from his breast pocket and gave it a snap.

'Not that one,' Mrs Harrison said.

'Minns can help,' Iris said, smiling as if she were enjoying the show. 'I'll go and fetch her. After that, Mr Chuff, will you stay for a cup of tea?' She threw Louisa a look.

'Yes, Chuff,' Louisa said with a grin at Iris. 'Plenty of tea for you.'

Chuff stayed not only for tea, but also for Johnno's practice talk about the bees. Everyone trooped out, up the rise, then down to the hives on the other side of the walled garden. Even Mr Grainger, Uncle and Figg joined the group.

Johnno wore his beekeeper's kit and held up what looked

like a watering can, but one that spouted smoke. As he began his talk, Louisa listened but kept an eye on the clouds that had mushroomed.

They were dark purple-blue, like a fresh bruise and they seemed to grow even as she watched. Then, she heard a rumble. Thunder. She couldn't smell the rain yet and would hate to interrupt Johnno, but perhaps they should move to cover. She glanced around at the grown-ups and children.

'Athena,' she said quietly, 'where is Gracie?'

'She stayed back to practise reading *Tom Kitten* to Mrs Moffatt,' Athena whispered.

The rumble grew louder. Then the aeroplane broke out of the clouds.

She could see the iron cross on its underside. Dark and lumbering, it seemed to move slowly, like a dying bluebottle.

'Get to the other side of the wall,' Jack called. 'We won't be seen there.'

Louisa broke out in a run towards the house.

'Louisa!' Jack shouted.

'It's Gracie,' Athena said. 'She's inside. She'll be scared.'

Louisa ran through the garden, in one gate and out the other, and headed up the rise toward the terrace.

She came to the top of the rise, where she was within sight of Oxburrow. The library French windows were open and there stood Gracie at the bottom of the terrace stairs, on the path, but unmoving as she gaped at the aeroplane.

Then she saw Louisa.

'Mama!' she shrieked. 'Mama!' and started for her.

'No, Gracie,' Louisa shouted. 'Run! Run away!'

A whistling pierced the air. Louisa looked up, saw a large cylinder shape falling through the sky and knew she was too late. In what seemed like the same instant, the bomb hit, the earth shook and soil flew up into the air like a fountain – and Gracie disappeared.

CHAPTER 20

As the earth shuddered and a fountain of dirt and rocks flew into the air, Louisa screamed and took off, but Jack caught her arm. She struggled to get free as he shouted, 'Louisa!'

'It's Gracie!' she cried. 'She was there.'

They both looked toward Oxburrow, standing as it ever had. But the dust had begun to settle and they could see between where they stood and the terrace an enormous hole in the ground.

'Stay with the others,' he said. 'I'll go.'

'No, I won't stay.' She pulled away and he grabbed her again.

'Louisa, look at me.'

She tried to bring her eyes to focus on his face, but couldn't. She couldn't see that spark of flint striking steel. She could only see Gracie's face.

'Jack, I have to go to her.'

'Louisa, the bomb didn't explode.'

That brought her up short. Was this a warning? To her, it was hope.

'I'll find her,' she said. 'I have to find her.'

'Yes, but we'll have to go carefully.'

They ran the rest of the way, but slowed as they neared the crater, which looked ten feet across. Louisa called out, 'Gracie! Gracie!'

She heard dirt sliding down the insides of the crater a few feet away.

'Gracie!'

'Mama!'

The cry was near and came from inside the crater.

Jack took Louisa's hand. 'Slowly,' he said and they crept forward as Louisa called to her.

'Gracie, love, I'm here. Are you all right? Gracie?'

At the rim of the crater, they peered over, and there she was, out of reach and buried up to her chest in soil, only her arms free and flailing.

Her face was pale, her eyes wide and her mouth open in terror. She had a cut on her cheek and she coughed and sputtered and cried as soil and rocks sifted down into her hair.

'Gracie love,' Louisa whispered. 'Jack, where is the bomb?'

'Buried itself – it could be ten or twenty feet or more below. But that doesn't make it safe. Gracie,' he called down, 'be still. Don't move and we'll come for you.'

Gracie's sobs decreased into ragged breaths and quiet moans of 'Mama' as if she were losing strength. Louisa leaned over the rim of the crater, holding out her hand, but there was no reaching Gracie if she stayed up top.

A shower of rocks and soil tumbled down the other side of the crater. Louisa held her breath, but it stopped, and so she wriggled on her belly, nearly upside down and breathing in dust that caught in her throat. Somewhere below lay the bomb that could go off at any second, but that seemed an abstract concept next to Gracie reaching out, her tears forming dirty streams down her cheeks.

'Ah!' Louisa cried out as she slid too quickly, and she felt

Jack grab her ankles to stop her. She was close enough to take hold of Gracie's outstretched hands. 'Hold tight,' she said. Whether she meant it for Gracie or Jack, it didn't matter, because both of them tightened their grips.

But as hard as she pulled, Louisa couldn't pull Gracie out of the soil that surrounded her.

'Jack, let go.'

'I won't,' he said.

'Let go. I have to dig her out.'

He released her slowly and Louisa slid down, righted herself, and, with her knees dug in, began scooping the soil away from Gracie. The girl did what she could, pushing dirt away.

Was time of the essence? Had the bomb below their feet continued to tick away the seconds until it detonated? Or would a random movement – Louisa's foot pushing into the soil to gain purchase – trigger it? She knew nothing about bombs and so cleared her mind and focused on the matter at hand. She spoke softly to Gracie as she scrabbled in the soil until her fingernails were thick with dirt and her hands pricked and smeared with spots of blood.

Seconds seemed like hours, but at last Louisa had cleared the soil as far down as Gracie's waist. Her legs were still buried.

'Jack!' Louisa called.

He eased down the side of the crater on his stomach, wiggling and digging himself in to keep from sliding down too far. 'Gracie,' he said, 'reach up and take my hand.'

The girl stretched her arms up and he caught hold of one by her wrist. Louisa wrapped her arms around Gracie's chest and, inch by inch, they pulled her up. Her legs came free and she kicked wildly, spraying Louisa with dirt and fine sharp stones.

When she was free and above ground, Jack dragged her away and told the girl, 'Stay back.'

Next, he took hold of Louisa and she gripped his forearms.

She was of little help to him, because the soil fell away when she tried to get a foothold. But at last, she clambered up and crawled out. Gracie, who had stayed back, now lunged at Louisa with a cry.

They sat wrapped in each other's arms. Louisa rocked Gracie gently and could feel the girl's sobs ease.

'Here we are,' Louisa said, her voice coming out in a squeak as she kissed Gracie's hair. 'Here we are. We're all right.'

Jack put his arms around the two of them. 'We need to get away. Let's go quickly – but carefully.'

Then came a call from across the lawn at the top of the rise. 'Louisa!'

It was Iris. Louisa had only enough time to look up and register that fact before Iris pointed toward the drive where the others were headed and yelled, 'Move your bloody arse!'

'Right you are,' Louisa muttered.

They moved, but they weren't quick about it. Instead, they trudged up to the drive – Jack with Gracie in his arms and holding Louisa's hand. The girl had tucked her head under his chin.

At the crest, Louisa looked across the forecourt to where Mrs Harrison was standing at the edge of the wood.

She turned to Jack. 'Can we stop?' She was out of breath, a bit wobbly, and there was a stone in her shoe.

He held up and then nodded across the drive to the edge of the beech and oak wood. Louisa followed his gaze and saw Mrs Harrison leaving and Iris rushing toward them.

Louisa ran to her and the two women embraced.

'You're meant to run away from a bomb,' Iris said, 'not towards it.'

'It didn't explode.'

'Not yet it hasn't, you mean,' Iris said. Her anger covered both her fear and her relief. Louisa knew that and didn't mind her tone a bit. 'What were you doing down there?'

'Gracie fell in the bomb's crater and we had to get her out.'

At the sound of her name, Gracie stirred. Her face was streaked with dirt, blood and muddy tear tracks. She squirmed herself to the ground, saying, 'I can walk.' Then she looked up at Jack and patted his chest.

'The poor wee thing,' Iris said.

Gracie took a few steps and stopped. 'My feet hurt.'

'Here now,' Louisa said. 'Sit down and let's take off your shoes.' She touched Jack's cheek, then knelt down in front of the girl, untied her shoes and slipped them off.

If Louisa had had one stone in her shoe, Gracie must've had a shovelful.

She emptied them, peeled off the girl's socks and gave them a good shake.

Hugo burst onto the forecourt, coming not from the wood but from the other side of the drive and dressed in his ARP warden's uniform.

'Here you are,' he said, panting. 'We had no warning, but I was in the warden's hut and had my field-glasses. I saw the plane open its doors and the bomb fall, but there was no explosion, so I rang the bomb disposal squad up at Uxbridge. They're on their way.'

'I sent the others to the church,' Iris said.

'Well done, Iris,' Hugo said. He took a closer look at Gracie, Louisa and Jack. 'Are you all right?'

'Yes, it's only that—' Louisa started.

'Tell me about it when we get to the church,' Hugo said. 'The bomb squad said to keep at least a quarter of a mile away.'

'Hang on,' Louisa said. She put a hand on Jack's shoulder and shook out her shoe, then nearly lost her balance trying to get it back on.

'Here,' Jack said. He took the shoe and knelt in front of her. She put a hand on his shoulder to steady herself as he slipped the shoe onto her foot.

Gracie pointed at Louisa. 'You're Cinderella!'

In that odd moment when fear had all but drained away, Louisa giggled and Iris snorted.

'There's no time for this,' Hugo said. 'Hop it – all of you!'

They came out of the beech and oak wood and stopped at the lychgate.

'You two go on to my cottage,' Hugo told Louisa and Gracie. 'First aid kit in the bathroom. Stay in and rest if you like, or come over when you're ready.'

The others went into the church and Louisa and Gracie continued. Stopping on the doorstep of the vicarage, she brushed as much dirt out of Gracie's hair as possible, and they both dusted themselves off. Then in the bathroom, she washed the girl's face gently, filled the sink with water and told Gracie to put her face in it to rinse. Gracie put her face in and blew bubbles, and came up with her eyes scrunched tight and a smile on her face.

'All right, you,' Louisa said, and returned her smile.

Once the cut on Gracie's cheek had been tended to and her hair combed, Louisa said, 'That'll have to do for now.'

She examined herself in the mirror.

'Hmmm,' she said. She combed her fingers through her hair and bits of grass and soil dropped into the sink. There was a hole in the shoulder of her cardigan and something inside her dress that shouldn't be there. She bent over, took hold and shook. A woodlouse fell to the floor, righted itself and trundled away.

Gracie gave a little girl's gleeful squeal. 'That's funny.'

Louisa would shake all the woodlice in Suffolk out of her dress to hear that sound. It was as if Gracie hadn't just nearly been buried by an unexploded bomb that could've gone off at any second. Louisa felt pretty giddy herself.

'I'm going to put my hair in plaits,' Gracie announced. 'I'll do both sides myself.'

It was an ambitious statement that never saw the light of day, because at that moment Athena could be heard in the front room of the cottage.

'Gracie! Gracie! Reverend Hugo says he'll teach us a new song. C'mon!'

Gracie dashed off. Louisa washed her face and arms and did her best with Hugo's nail brush. She would buy him a new one – if she could find one to buy. There was a war on, she reminded herself yet again – were nail brushes in short supply?

Then she stood at the mirror contemplating her dishevelled state. She gathered her hair, twisted it round and then held it on top of her head. It didn't help, but neither did it matter, because in the mirror she saw Jack standing in the open door of the bathroom.

'I'll never get tired of watching you pin your hair up,' he said.

She let go and her hair fell to her shoulders as she turned to him. 'Do you think the bomb disposal squad will find them for me – my hairpins?'

'No harm in asking,' he said.

Louisa laughed. 'It could've gone so wrong,' she said, her voice choked with sudden tears. 'I thought she'd been hit, that she was—'

'But she wasn't,' Jack said. 'You pulled her out.'

'We pulled her out,' Louisa said. She stepped close and considered switching on Hugo's wireless to see if her orchestra were playing.

Jack kissed her, and again, and after that Louisa didn't care if the orchestra played or not, but she did wish they were in her bedroom at Oxburrow with the door closed.

Somehow, although his lips were on hers, Jack managed to

say, 'There's a crowd in the church and I'm sorry to say they'll be wondering where we are.'

The Oxburrow contingent – children, Mrs Harrison, Chuff, along with Minns's grandad, Uncle and Figg – had settled themselves in the sanctuary while in the church hall Louisa found not only Iris and Minns, but also Mrs Byers and a few other members of the WVS.

Some in the village had seen the aeroplane, some hadn't. After Hugo had rung for the bomb squad, he'd told Colin, and the boy had told others as much as he knew, and so the news had spread – and the women responded.

'We were that afraid for you,' Chuff told Louisa as they stood in the doorway between the hall and sanctuary. 'Everyone was worried about the little one. And you, of course, and Jack and the reverend.'

'And Iris,' Louisa reminded him.

'I'd never forget Mrs Darnley,' Chuff said, holding his tattered flat cap over his heart. 'Couldn't possibly. She told us to get a move on.'

'Mr Chuffleigh,' Minns called from the kitchen. 'Could you shift this crate of milk bottles for us?'

'At your service, ladies,' Chuff said, and ambled away.

For a moment, Louisa stood amid the industry of the women in the hall, grateful for every one of them. They knew almost instinctively what was needed and, whatever happened, they were there to make sandwiches and tea.

In the rear of the sanctuary, near the baptismal font, Alf was demonstrating to a few of the children the trick he'd taught Lulu – walking on her back legs. Johnno – still wearing the netted pith helmet – sat in the first pew talking animatedly with Mr Gedge and Jack.

Mrs Greet came in with a bottle of brandy.

'I went back to get it,' she told Louisa, a bit breathless. 'I don't care if it isn't even midday. I thought you might need something. I'll let you pour.'

Louisa carried a tray out to the sanctuary and said, 'Children, sandwiches and orange squash for you in the hall.'

She stepped out of the way of the sudden rush, then took brandy to the men and, with two glasses left, approached Mrs Harrison warily. The woman sat nearly slumped in a back pew as if all the stuffing had gone out of her. Next to her was Mrs Greet, who rose and smiled at Louisa.

'I'll go and see what I can do,' she said and left.

'Well, Mrs Harrison,' Louisa said. 'Brandy? It's medicinal.'

Mrs Harrison took the glass and had a sip. 'That was a very brave thing to do,' she said, her voice sounding ragged.

'I didn't think it was brave,' Louisa said. 'I only thought of Gracie.'

'The three of you,' Mrs Harrison said. She sniffed and took another drink. 'The three of you coming up to the drive, safe. The three of you together.'

Gracie came rushing up and wrapped her arms around Louisa's legs.

'Hello, love,' Louisa said and saw a frown on Gracie's face. 'What is it?'

'Did Mrs Moffatt run away?' Gracie asked.

'No, Mrs Moffatt wouldn't run away,' Louisa said. *Please don't prove me wrong, cat.* 'She's probably hiding under the Italian credenza in the morning room.'

'The what?' Gracie asked.

'The high table in the corner. We'll find her when we go back.'

CHAPTER 21

'It didn't explode!' George exclaimed.

'Lady Bee saved Gracie!' Athena declared.

The church was abuzz as the story was told and retold among its participants. This lasted until, full of sandwiches, orange squash and possibly every biscuit left in the village, the children and grown-ups quieted down.

'When can we go home?' Gracie asked.

'Not yet,' was the only answer Louisa had.

Hugo came and went as the afternoon wore on. He reported that the Royal Engineers had arrived at Oxburrow. He offered up a prayer for their safety and thanks for the well-being of Lady Brightford, Mr Barrie and little Gracie.

'We've had a great deal of action here at Debden Ash and Oxburrow,' Uncle observed. 'What do the Nazis have against us?'

There was a bit of laughter at that.

'We just happen to be on their way home,' Hugo said. 'They've bombed Manchester or even Cambridge and are heading for the coast. This one probably had a left-over bomb and saw the chance for more destruction.'

'Our boys usually chase them off,' Chuff said.

As David did, Louisa thought. All the way to France. And then what? Did he find a local church for sanctuary? Suddenly, she felt old and tired.

Finally, hours after they'd arrived, the bomb squad appeared at church and had a word with Hugo.

'It's finished,' Hugo announced when they'd gone. 'The bomb's been defused and they're taking it away – far away – to be detonated.'

The grown-ups cheered and the children – most of whom had fallen asleep in the pews – awoke to the news.

'Shame we couldn't watch them,' Sydney said. 'How did they do it?'

'They separated the timer from the bomb, you see,' Hugo explained. 'But first they had to dig down to uncover the thing and hope and pray it didn't start ticking.'

In that instant, Louisa was back in the hole, smelling the earth around them, praying the same prayer. She glanced at Gracie, whose eyes had a faraway look.

'Perhaps we could save the details until later,' she said. 'Now, let's clean up here and then we can go back to Oxburrow.'

But the WVS waved off their offer of help. 'Go home and rest,' the women told them.

Everyone stood, stretched, and filed out of the door, blinking in bright sunshine. Was it still day? Louisa looked at her wristwatch and found that it was not even four o'clock. The day seemed longer than a lifetime.

They came to a stop when they'd reached the drive.

'Indoors, children,' Mrs Harrison announced.

'Can't we see the bomb?' Alf asked.

'The bomb is gone,' Priss said.

'We could look at the hole, couldn't we?' George asked. He looked at Jack. 'Mr Barrie?'

'Just a quick look,' Jack said and led them round the side of the house. All except for Gracie, who ran indoors.

'Hang on,' Louisa said, 'wait for me.' It could be that the French windows had been blown open and shattered upon the bomb's impact. There might be books and broken glass and all manner of things strewn across the floor. Louisa wouldn't believe that danger had passed until she saw for herself.

But Gracie was quicker. Louisa had made it as far as the entrance hall when the girl came out from the morning room.

'I found her.' She held Mrs Moffatt, whose forelegs stuck out and hind legs hung down as if she were made of rubber. 'She was hiding under the cathensa table. We're going to the library.'

'I'll go first,' Louisa said and hurried past them. 'Wait until I tell you.'

Apart from a few books that had been dislodged and a lamp table that had fallen over, the library was remarkably untouched. The French windows stood open and the only damage Louisa could find was a twisted hinge on one. Tears of relief threatened, but she tamped them down with an offhanded thought – *lucky that*.

'All clear,' Louisa said and turned, to find Gracie and Mrs Moffatt already settled on the sofa.

'Mrs Moffatt wanted to read *Benjamin Bunny*,' Gracie said.

'Mrs Moffatt is quite fond of bunnies,' Louisa said as she jiggled the door and then stepped out.

The bomb pit lay not far from the terrace. At the bomb's impact, the soil had erupted as if a giant mole had been excavating below. This had pushed the stone steps up and they sat askew at odd angles.

The pit itself had been partly filled in and now Jack, Chuff, Mr Grainger and Uncle, along with the children, gathered around it much as mourners gather round for a graveside service. Louisa shuddered at what might have been.

. . .

Dinner now became supper – ham, potato and carrot casserole and pilchard rissoles – but the day had taken its toll and, although the food was eaten, it wasn't with the enthusiasm it deserved.

The children nearly fell asleep over their plates. The strain showed on every grown-up face with freshly minted lines of care and hollow looks in their eyes. Mrs Harrison, with heavy eyelids and a pinched mouth, looked fretful, as if in the throes of an internal argument. She avoided Louisa's gaze.

Once again, the war had come entirely too close and had stirred Mr Grainger and Uncle's memories of the last one.

Louisa remembered, too. There had been a Zeppelin raid on Sheffield in 1916 – she and Iris had been full of both fear and awe. But Jack had been in the thick of that war.

She watched him at his end of the table encouraging Sydney to finish his rhubarb and apple tart. What horrors had he not only seen, but experienced?

Considering how late in the day it was, Chuff was invited to stay – having abandoned the idea of collecting trunks meant for Bermondsey. He bunked with Figg. The gardener had lived alone for years and yet didn't seem to mind.

As Louisa and Iris started on the dishes, Mrs Harrison appeared in the kitchen.

'Lady Brightford,' she said.

'Yes?'

Mrs Harrison looked as if a heated conversation was going on in her mind, her mouth twitching with words fighting to get out.

'I... am... sorry...' After three words, she fell silent.

'Mrs Harrison,' Louisa said, 'would you like to sit down? Why don't we go to the library?'

Mrs Harrison started as if she'd been stuck with a hatpin.

'No,' she said firmly. 'No, that is... good night to you both.'

She fled up the stairs. Had she been about to capitulate? For no reason at all, tears welled up and Louisa sank into a chair at the worktable.

'What's this about?' Iris said and sat down across from her.

'I've no idea, but it can't be good,' Louisa said, blowing her nose on a tea towel and then shoving it into her pocket. She put a hand to her forehead. Was she coming down with something? They had escaped a great tragedy that day, and yet the dark thoughts seemed to close in on her.

'It's the end, Iris. What else could it be? Why would the school governors leave the children here just because it's what I want? Why would David be safe just because I want him to be? What good have I done?'

That night, the house lay quiet from a rather early hour. The children hadn't complained about baths and everyone was tucked up. Louisa had a bath too, and when she was wrapped in her wool dressing gown she went down to the library.

Jack already had the wireless on and Louisa could hear 'Kiss Me Goodnight, Sergeant Major' being played. He'd poured them drinks and left them on the table and, when she came to him, he took her in a fierce embrace.

'You nearly scared the life out of me today,' he murmured into her hair, and the catch in his voice made her hold on to him that much tighter.

'I had to go to her,' Louisa whispered.

He leaned his head back to look at her without letting go. 'I know that, and I'm not saying you shouldn't've, it's only that...' He frowned.

'This was nothing new for you – bombs dropping. I don't mean now, but in the last war. What was it like for you?' she asked. 'What did you see?'

For a moment, he didn't speak but looked at her, with an intensity that bored a hole through her.

'I saw unspeakable things,' he said. 'And sometimes I see them still. I see the fellow next to me have his head blown clean off when, only the moment before, he had a grin on his face. I see the bodies piled up in the trenches as if they were sandbags. I see the soldier who stepped on a mine and all we could find of him the next day was bits.' He shook his head as if to fling the images away. 'I'm sorry, I shouldn't—'

'You should and you'd better,' Louisa said. 'You can't hold those things inside, Jack. Not if we're to—' She saw the spark in his eyes – flint striking steel – and felt the earlier darkness pass.

'If we're to what?' he asked.

She laughed. 'That's the question, isn't it?'

But they needn't answer it just yet. Louisa picked up her drink, keeping one arm round him. The orchestra had moved on to a more danceable number and they stayed in each other's arms and swayed to the music.

CHAPTER 22

My darling mum,

We had an early start this morning – too early. Still, I woke before I needed to, and in the darkness I saw a vision of birch trees across the water and the smell of burning bacon over a campfire. A dream, a memory, a hope for more to come.

Louisa's moods seemed to swing like a pendulum, and the morning brought back a sense of hopelessness. Jack had arisen early and gone back to the boys' dormitory, but she lay abed, not even bothering to open the blackout curtains. When Iris arrived, she gave a single knock and walked in before Louisa could even sit up.

'What's this then?' she demanded, strode across the room and, with one hand, flung open the curtains.

Louisa shielded her eyes from the sunlight streaming in.

'Here,' Iris said and held out a cup of tea.

She sat up and took it. Iris perched on the edge of the bed.

'Why aren't you up?'

'I couldn't quite see the point,' Louisa said and cringed at the self-pity in her voice.

'The fete on Saturday isn't enough of a point?' Iris asked.

'What will we accomplish?'

'You'll convince them that they should leave Gracie and the others here,' Iris said.

'Will we? I don't see them being swayed by a few recitations.'

'What about Jack?' Iris said. 'Will he go if they go or have you discussed it at all?'

'Jack has a vocation, Iris – work he's wanted to do his entire life. If they move the school, how can I ask him to give that up?'

'You don't think Mrs Harrison has come to her senses?'

'I don't think her befuddled act is an indication that she's giving up,' Louisa said. She took hold of the blanket's edge and worried it. 'I dreamed about David, but now I can't remember anything about it. Is that a bad sign? It's nearly a month since he went missing. Four weeks. That's what Max said they would wait before he's declared—'

'I'm making a Dundee cake today,' Iris cut in.

Louisa stared at her and felt a stirring. 'Are you?'

'I found a packet of sultanas in the back of the pantry that I'd forgotten all about. And so, I'm making a Dundee cake, and then I'm putting it away and won't bring it out until he's home.'

'Oh Iris,' Louisa said and threw one arm round her as she held a jiggling teacup in the other.

'Now you get yourself dressed and downstairs.'

'Will do,' Louisa said. 'Are there potatoes to peel?'

'There are always potatoes to peel,' Iris replied and headed for the door. 'But Chuff's on kitchen duty today.'

'Is he now?' Louisa asked in a suggestive tone.

Iris walked out, but then put her head back in. 'I'll have none of that.'

· · ·

Once downstairs, Louisa went directly to the telephone room and rang William Lowrey to give him the latest news on the school.

'I won't give up without a fight,' she said. 'It's just that I wanted to find out if you've heard anything from the army.'

'Not a word. Well, apart from someone named Captain Wentworth who rang but didn't leave a message. Perhaps it's about a different matter.'

Captain Wentworth? Would he not let them alone? What did he want? Was Max trying to sneak the army in through the back door?

'No word of David yet?'

William's question brought Louisa back to the moment.

'No,' she replied. 'Not yet. I will let you know as soon as we hear. You've been such a friend to me through the years. And rather a father-figure to David. Not that Max doesn't love his son, but you have more understanding about some things.'

They rang off just as she heard a car on the drive come to an abrupt stop and a door slam. By the time she'd leapt up and peered through the window, she could catch only the shadow of a figure heading round the terrace side of the house. She marvelled at how even his shadow could look pompous.

She went out the front and followed him round.

Max stood at the rim of the pit, with the broken steps up to the terrace behind him and hands on his hips.

He'd always made a striking figure, with his tall, wraithlike build and thin face. He wore his hair as he always had – slicked straight back, which now accentuated his receding hairline. He looked up at Louisa with that piercing gaze that she had at first fancied, then had for a while thought intimidating, but had come to understand was only a thin veneer of arrogance.

'Why wasn't I told about this?' he snapped at her.

'Well, obviously you were told,' Louisa said, 'otherwise you wouldn't be here. Unless it's about David.'

Max shook his head and lost a bit of stuffiness. 'No, there's been nothing.'

The French windows to the library rattled as they were opened. Until the damaged hinge could be repaired, Chuff had sorted out a rope closure that looped round the handles and kept the doors from flying open at the lightest breeze.

George, Sydney and Dolly came dashing out, each one taking the three-foot leap off the terrace as if they would go airborne, all of them calling out, 'Hello, Lady Bee!'

'We're building a wall,' George said. 'Mr Chuff has found us some flat stones.' And off they ran, up the hill.

Jack came out after them and called, 'Remember, George, Hadrian didn't build his wall in a day.' He looked down at Louisa and Max and said, 'Sorry.'

'Jack,' Louisa said, nodding him over. He hopped down off the terrace and went to her. 'This is Max. Max, Jack Barrie. Jack is one of the schoolteachers.'

'Lord Brightford,' Jack said. 'Pleased to meet you.' He managed to be respectful while at the same time giving off an air of defiance.

'Mr Barrie.' After a moment, Max extended his hand, and the two men shook briefly, but continued to eye each other.

'There's no news about David,' Louisa said, ending the competition. 'Max only wanted to see where the bomb dropped. There was no damage to the house.'

She waited for Max to say, 'More's the pity' but instead he muttered a comment about how the rope ties had 'turned the French windows into a farmyard gate'.

Louisa ignored him as Gracie, Priss and Athena came out, with Gracie in the middle of a story.

'... and then Mrs Moffatt hopped up on the shelf and pretended to be a statue' – Gracie stopped and held up her hands like cat paws frozen in the air – 'and Lulu couldn't find her!' She broke out in peals of laughter and the other two joined her.

'Hello, girls,' Louisa said.

'We're playing hopscotch on the terrace today,' Athena said. 'Mrs Harrison said it was all right.'

'Do you have chalk?' Louisa asked. Priss held up a piece. 'Good. Carry on.'

'Chalk?' Max asked as Priss began to draw out the squares.

'Yes,' Louisa said, 'chalk.'

'Mama,' Gracie called, 'Mrs Moffatt chased Lulu round the kitchen three times after breakfast.'

Louisa ignored the look Max sent her way. *Mama.*

'They make a good game of it, don't they,' Louisa said.

'Mr Barrie' – Athena practised a few hops – 'can you play the Siegfried Line song on the concertina and we'll sing it at church?'

'We'll need to practise a bit first,' Jack said and, when he saw the aghast expression on Max's face, added, 'And we may not want to sing it during the service.'

Louisa snickered, but her attention turned when Priss called out, 'Mr Chuff! Would you like a new pocket on your shirt? Minns is teaching me how to sew them.'

Chuff came up from the direction of the kitchen yard, wearing his ragged flat cap pulled down so far that his ears stuck out.

'A man can never have too many pockets,' he said. 'Though, I'm too modest to remove my shirt at this particular moment.'

That brought giggles from the girls.

'Jack,' Chuff said, 'thought I'd pop into the village and see if I can't scare up a hinge to replace the one that twisted off.' He smiled at Max.

'Max, this is Mr Chuffleigh. Chuff, Lord Brightford,' Louisa said.

Chuff dragged his cap off and squeezed it in both hands.

'Lord Brightford,' he said and nodded. 'It's an honour to meet you, sir.'

'Mr Chuffleigh,' Max said and nodded. He looked to Louisa.

'Chuff brought a few school desks out,' Louisa said, 'and so he was here when the bomb fell.'

Iris came out onto the terrace, caught sight of Max and said, 'Oh my, would you look at that.'

'Iris,' Max said with a weary note in his voice. 'How are you?'

'Not too bad, thank you,' she said and looked him up and down. 'I'd say you could do with coffee and a slice of cake.'

Max lifted his eyebrows and his spirits seemed to go with them. 'Yes, well, if it's convenient.'

'I was just going to do some for Mr Grainger and Uncle. Figg is coming up, too. The library all right, Mr Barrie? Lessons finished for the morning?'

'Yes, go ahead.'

The girls abandoned their game of hopscotch and ran off to the front of the house. Alf looked out through the French windows and said, 'Mr Barrie, Mrs Harrison is asking for you.' Jack nodded at Max, gave Louisa a smile and followed the others indoors, leaving Louisa and Max standing near the rim.

'Are all these people living here?' Max asked.

'You mean apart from the nine children and two teachers?' Louisa asked. 'Well, Chuff is staying for the moment, and he's bunked in with Figg, but I'm sure it's only temporarily.' She was sure of nothing of the sort. 'When the plane crashed into the cottages in the village, Minns moved into the house, and her grandad and Uncle are down in the chauffeur's cottage.'

'Is that all?' Max asked.

'At the moment.'

'So, you're taking in paying guests now? Have you sunk that low?'

'Have you taken a look at the household budget you allow us?' Louisa snapped. She let go of her annoyance with a sniff. 'No one is paying. They're guests of Oxburrow Manor.'

'Keep this up and you won't need the army,' Max said, 'you'll run the place into the ground all on your own. Dear God, it's like a circus. How do you stand it?'

'I wouldn't have it any other way,' Louisa said. 'The place is alive, as it hasn't been for ages.'

Max clicked his tongue, but didn't argue further. 'Louisa, about that girl.'

'They have names, Max. Her name is Gracie.'

'I know they have names,' he said. 'I also know you go on the attack when you're frightened. For her? Are you worried that she's mistaken you for her mother?'

'I'm not frightened for Gracie,' Louisa said. 'She under-stands what happened to her mother. But she's had a terrible time of it.'

'Is she the one who doesn't talk?' Max asked.

So, Mrs Perrymont had given him an account of the school governors' visit.

'She's talking now, as you can see. Calling me "Mama" is probably a phase in her recovery. But I am frightened – for David. Time is passing, Max. Where is he? Will we ever know?'

He didn't reply, but stood looking to the south, as if he could see all the way to France.

The grown-ups gathered in the library for coffee, and the children had been given the assignment to sit at their desks in the schoolroom and work quietly. As there had been no unto-ward crashes, that seemed to be going well.

Mr Grainger and Uncle brought Lord Brightford up on

local events and Max responded with polite comments. Figg – a fish out of water when he was indoors and even more so now – stood behind Uncle's wheelchair as if for protection.

When the cake had been eaten and the cups were empty, Louisa stood and began to collect dishes. Minns popped up to help her and everyone else rose.

'Excellent cake, Iris, as always,' Max said. He glanced round at the others and, ever the diplomat when times called for it, added, 'It was a pleasure to meet you all.'

Mrs Harrison rose. Chuff darted over to hold the chair for her and she flinched.

'I'd best see to the children,' she said. 'No, Mr Barrie – you stay.'

The others began moving toward the door, but Louisa leaned against the back of the chesterfield next to Jack.

'You wouldn't play them out on your concertina, would you?' she asked quietly.

'I'd be happy to. What shall it be? "I'm in a Dancing Mood"?'

Louisa leaned into him and sniggered, but then she heard Max say to Iris, 'I'm after some papers that are in my study.'

'Oh dear. I'd better see to this.' She squeezed Jack's hand and hurried off. 'Max! Wait, please. I forgot to mention that we—'

Too late. Max had opened the study door to what could've been a cupboard behind the scenes at the British Museum. Porcelain vases standing in the dark like stately sentinels, portraits, landscapes and still-lifes stuck between broken chairs, gaudy yet rickety candelabra and the now extraneous spindly tables.

'What the devil?' Max asked.

'We needed to move a few things out of the formal dining room,' Louisa explained, 'to make it into a schoolroom.' She left out the part where she'd been using his study as a lumber room long before that.

Max reached over to where an old estate ledger with a large portion of its pages missing lay atop an upturned chair.

'What's happened here?' he asked.

'The children have been painting, but we didn't have any paper,' Louisa said.

'And you ripped apart the accounts for' – he flipped to the front – '1898?'

'We used only the blank pages,' Louisa said. 'Now, what is it you need to find?'

She left him to rummage through the study on his own. Although invited, he didn't stay for dinner.

Louisa's spirits went up and down as the day progressed – optimistic one moment, sunk in the mire of despair the next. In the afternoon, she was sitting at her desk in the morning room staring off into space when Jack tapped at the door and looked in.

'Oh,' she said. 'Is it reading time?' She would be very glad to read a story about good and bad things happening to people far away from her.

'Er, yes,' Jack said. 'But there's something to discuss first.'

Had he sounded ominous on purpose? Louisa rose from her desk and reached the door as Gracie raced past him.

'Mama, we're going on a picnic!' she said. 'We're going to Lake Puddle-Duck!'

Jack gave a chagrined smile. 'Surprise,' he said.

'Are we?' was all she could reply as they led her to the library where the children, Mrs Harrison, Iris and everyone housed at Oxburrow had gathered. It was explained to her by Jack, with the children generously sprinkling in comments, that they'd been inspired by *Swallows and Amazons* and decided they could all do with a day off before the school governors arrived.

'But we have to prepare for the fete,' Louisa said. 'We could wait and go after.'

'There isn't a thing left to do for the fete,' Iris said. 'And you know it.'

'Please,' Gracie said. 'Please may we?'

'Did you tell them about Lake Puddle-Duck?' she asked Gracie.

'Yes,' Gracie said. 'And Mrs Darnley did, too. And we told Mr Barrie.'

'A conspiracy, was it?' Louisa asked, suddenly longing to see the little lake again. 'When will we go?'

'Tomorrow.'

There would be no boats à la *Swallows and Amazons*. David had once had a small sailing dinghy, but Figg had located it down in the stables and reported it unlikely to be seaworthy.

Still, the idea of an outing had caught fire, and Louisa couldn't help but be swept up in everyone's enthusiasm. Preparations lasted the rest of the day, and she joined in. When she went to the linen chest to retrieve the old plaid blanket they'd always taken to the lake, she held it close. Her eyes filled with tears, as much for the memories of David as a boy as with gratitude to the others for wanting to cheer her up.

Chuff swore he had enough petrol in his lorry to get them the ten miles there and back again, but confessed he wouldn't then have enough to get back to London any time soon. No one was surprised.

The next day, Oxburrow shut up shop and piled onto the lorry. Mrs Harrison waved away her privilege to ride in the cab and so

Mr Grainger and Uncle rode with Chuff and Lulu. The dog sat at attention on Uncle's lap the entire trip, as if she knew the way.

'A bit of fresh air never hurts, does it?' Minns asked Mrs Harrison as they got settled on the lorry bed. 'Here, let me tuck in your headscarf.'

'Not only is it swept out, Mrs 'arrison, ma'am,' Chuff called up to her, 'but washed off last evening and now spread with dry straw. My lorry's the cleanest place to set your good self down as ever you'd find.'

'I can't believe she's game for it,' Louisa told Jack as they waited to climb up last.

Gracie came up and took Louisa's hand. 'When David went to Lake Puddle-Duck, did he go in Mr Chuff's lorry?'

'No,' Louisa said, 'we had a car then and rode in it.'

'I think a lorry is the best,' Gracie said as Jack lifted her up on the back. 'David would like it, wouldn't he? Next time, he can sit with me.'

Louisa nodded, struggling to find her voice. 'He will like that,' she said at last.

They set off. Chuff took the rutted sheep track that led to the lake with care, while also engaging in a loud and lively conversation with Mr Grainger and Uncle on the matter of the recent barley harvest. In the back, grown-ups held on to children and children held on to hampers carrying precious cargo.

As they rattled along Sydney began singing 'We're Going to Hang Out the Washing on the Siegfried Line'. Soon everyone had joined in and the song rang out in the wood as they trundled along.

Lake Puddle-Duck had everything anyone needed – a swimming end and a reedy end with a dry, shallow bank spread along the near side. On the far side, a stand of birches now turned autumnal gold.

'Birch trees are called the "lady of the wood",' Louisa explained to the children as they climbed down off the lorry and stood straightening their clothes.

Sydney squinted across the water. 'They don't look like ladies.'

'Birch trees are graceful and bending,' Louisa said.

'They're graceful like Gracie!' Athena said.

Gracie raised her arms above her head and twirled. 'I'm a lady of the wood!'

They played games of duck, duck, goose and blind man's buff, interspersed with splashing in the shallows, during which everyone ended up dripping but no one cared because the sun was warm and the air still.

Alf, Priss and Athena all declared they would live by the lake for the rest of their lives if they could. George let go of his need to keep things in order and didn't bother with counting steps from the lakeside to the lorry, and Minns taught Gracie, Dolly and Gloria how to make little people out of braided reeds.

There were bottles of lemonade and ginger beer to quench their thirst – Louisa suspected Iris had been hoarding the stuff since before the war. They feasted on boiled eggs, sandwiches and raw carrots, which were looked at askance until Louisa reminded the children what a treat they were to Peter Rabbit. A mountain of small, sweet russeted apples finished off the meal.

In the afternoon, Iris boiled water for tea in a kettle that she set right down into the fire. Its bottom was blackened from years of use and it sported a sizeable dent on one side.

'One year,' she said as she brought out the cakes, 'David didn't see it when he stomped on the fire to put it out.'

'Can we stomp on the fire?' Johnno asked eagerly.

· · ·

By the time they climbed back onboard Chuff's lorry in the late afternoon, the children's eyes were heavy. They snuggled under the blankets and, as the lake disappeared from sight behind a copse of birch, George waved it goodbye.

Daylight was truly fading as they climbed the drive at Oxburrow. Louisa opened one eye to see Iris yawning. Lulu had ridden in Alf's arms on the return journey and now dog and boy – and most of the children – were sleeping peacefully. Mrs Harrison had several of them gathered round her like chicks and with her headscarf askew she looked comfy, rather like an indulgent aunt. Gracie and Sydney had their heads in Louisa's lap, and she herself had dropped off leaning against Jack. When Chuff shut off the engine, it backfired, and everyone jumped.

They stretched, blinked and climbed down. Then began the dreary business of unloading, and the best they could say about the task was that the hampers were a fair bit lighter than when they'd started out that morning.

Lastly, Louisa brought a crate of empty ginger beer bottles into the kitchen, where Iris stood, hands on hips, surveying the scene.

'We couldn't just leave it, could we?' Louisa asked. 'And come back down early in the morning?'

'Another hour and they'll be wondering where their supper is,' Iris said. 'We've beef bone broth and I'll see what I can throw in it now. We'll have a stew.'

'I don't see how you can think of anything useful at all,' Louisa said. 'I need a cup of tea.'

'I'll give you a cup of tea if you'll take it and yourself to a bath,' Iris said. 'You've quite a scent about you.'

Louisa pulled at her skirt, trying to see the back. 'It was the mucky bit in the shallows where I lost my footing,' she said, picking off a bit of straw that had stuck to her. 'Right, tea and a bath. If I'm not down in an hour, come and wake me.' She went to the door, then paused. 'You knew just what I needed, Iris – this day to get me back on the right track.'

'I'd claim responsibility if I could,' Iris said, 'but it all started with little Gracie going to Jack, because she wanted to see David's lake.'

Louisa climbed the stairs. She could hear Mrs Harrison up on the second floor chivvying the girls into the bath.

'I don't care if it isn't bath night, in you go,' she said. 'Put on your nightdresses or pyjamas after. Mrs Darnley will have something tasty for supper and you wouldn't want to miss it.'

Up the stairs on the other side of the landing, it sounded as if Jack and the boys were having the same sort of discussion, but with a bit more whinging. Louisa continued to her own bath.

She came down in a clean dress and carrying her muddy skirt and empty teacup to find children dashing about the entrance hall, wearing their nightclothes under dressing gowns or cardigans. Gracie had on Louisa's red boiled-wool jacket. The exceptional circumstances seemed to have given them an extra burst of energy.

'Aren't you the smart ones to be ready for bed,' Louisa told them. 'Perhaps I should go up and put my pyjamas on, too.'

Mrs Harrison came down with an armload of the children's clothes in need of a wash.

'I'll take those from you,' Louisa said. Mrs Harrison protested only mildly. She looked done in herself. 'Where is Mr Barrie?'

'Mr Barrie has gone out to Mr Chuff's lorry,' Athena reported. 'George lost his notebook in the straw.'

The blackout curtains had already been drawn. 'I don't know how they'll find it now in the dark,' Louisa said as she continued to the basement.

Iris had the kitchen in reasonable nick, and was slicing

bread for their supper, so Louisa walked straight through to the washroom and left the heap of clothes for the morning.

'How is it you look so clean?' she asked, eyeing Iris in her starched apron.

'Some of us don't relish mucking about, and we keep out of the reeds,' Iris replied.

'Some of you – that is, you and Chuff – wandered off into the wood on your own while others were drinking their tea,' Louisa said. When she saw Iris blush, she knew she'd hit the mark.

'Never you mind about Chuff,' Iris said.

A great uproar of voices came from above, but then they fell silent.

'So,' Louisa said, 'what do you need doing?'

'We need a new jar of chutney opened,' Iris said.

'I'll get it.' Louisa went back to the pantry, and returned as Jack called down the stairs.

'Louisa!'

She looked at Iris, who glanced out the kitchen door and back, her eyes troubled.

Louisa set the chutney on the worktable and walked out of the kitchen. Jack stood halfway down the stairs.

'Louisa,' he said, 'come upstairs.'

A cold sweat broke over her and she couldn't swallow. Had there been the sound of a bicycle on the drive? The ring of its bell?

'No,' she said. 'I won't.'

'Yes,' Jack said firmly. 'You must.' He held out his hand to her. His face gave nothing away. He was being brave for her.

She did not take his hand, because she needed both of hers on the railing to pull herself up, step by step.

Why didn't he just say it – the telegram had arrived. Get it over with. She would know the worst and then move on. No, she would never be able to move on.

At the top of the stairs, Jack took her hand and led her out to the entrance hall. It was empty apart from a figure in the centre. Even though he stood in silhouette against the lamp in the far corner, she could see he wore a uniform, but what drew her attention was the light that created a golden halo round his head.

She felt the anguish rise up in her – he was dead and this angel apparition was all that was left. She felt her body give up, but, as she began to sink to the floor, Jack took hold of her shoulders and kept her upright.

Then, the angel spoke.

'Hello, Mum. I'm home.'

CHAPTER 23

David rushed toward her, limping, and only then did Louisa notice he carried a walking stick. Jack let go of her and she threw her arms around her son as a dry sob escaped her throat.

He felt real, solid – he felt like David, although too thin. She didn't want to let go, but after a moment she pulled away and looked at him to make sure he was truly there. There was something about his eyes – he looked older, wiser, sadder. But then he grinned at her and she cupped his face in her hands and stroked his cheek with a thumb.

'What are all these marks on your face?' she said, fussing. 'And what's happened to your leg?' Then she looked round the empty entrance hall as a sudden panic took hold. Perhaps she'd been right to begin with – he was an apparition, a ghost. 'Where did you come from?' she asked. 'How did you get here?'

'Dad drove me,' David replied, and then winced as if anticipating his mother's response.

Louisa's emotions swung from panic to righteous anger in an instant.

'He knew you were alive and safe,' she said hotly, 'and he didn't bother to tell me?'

'Yes, but he—'

'Look, Mrs Moffatt,' Gracie said from behind Louisa.

She turned, and there stood the girl – nightdress sticking out below the red boiled-wool jacket – holding Mrs Moffatt as usual, with the cat's forelegs stuck straight out and hind legs nearly dragging on the floor.

'See,' Gracie said to the cat, 'David is home.'

Louisa laughed and cried and gave up, for the moment, trying to understand. Instead, she rushed off to the top of the basement stairs calling, 'Iris! Iris!' until Iris hurried up and then stopped dead.

'Here's the boy,' she said, her voice thick with tears, and held out her arms, 'and not before time.'

'Ah, Iris.'

They embraced. Iris gave him a good squeeze and finished off with a few energetic pats on the back.

The rest of the children came charging out of the library, followed by Mrs Harrison.

'We were quiet, Lady Bee,' Athena said. 'Mr Barrie said it was a surprise and could we hide in the library and be very *quiet*' – she mouthed the word with no sound – 'and we were, weren't we?'

'You were indeed,' Louisa said. 'Well done.'

'Now, children,' Mrs Harrison said, 'Supper!' She gave Louisa a warm smile as they left.

Iris followed, muttering about setting more places at the table, but Gracie stayed behind and handed Mrs Moffatt off to David.

David cradled the cat, giving her a scratch behind the ears. 'I've missed that rumbling purr against my chest.' He bowed his head and Mrs Moffatt rubbed her face against his chin, then he reached down and stroked Gracie's hair. 'Gracie tells me she's been reading to Mrs Moffatt.'

'Have you met them all?' Louisa asked.

'Briefly, before they went to hide,' David said. 'Thank you for clearing the decks for my big moment, Mr Barrie.'

'It's Jack,' he replied. 'Good thing the suspense didn't last too long. Your mother has been on edge. She knew that when the four-week mark came it would be bad news.'

Louisa took Jack's hand. 'But instead it was the best news. Right, you,' she said to her son, 'I want to hear every detail, but first, supper. Since the children arrived, we've been eating in the servants' dining room, but we could bring a tray up so you don't have to take the stairs.'

'Mum,' he said in that cajoling tone of his, 'I've walked across half of France with this ankle, so I'll be fine on the stairs.'

'All right, all right.' Louisa smiled and kissed his cheek. 'Before we go down, could you tell me just the last part first. When did you arrive?'

'About two hours ago. There was no one about. Dad had tried to ring earlier and there was no answer. He thought that odd – he said the place had been filled with people when he last visited.'

'He said it was a circus,' Louisa said. 'I'm sure he told you the same.'

David's eyebrows jumped as an answer. 'So, we tracked old Figg down – gave him a good surprise, I can tell you – and he said you'd gone off on a picnic. I told Dad to leave and drive back to London before it got dark. There've been far too many car crashes now that headlamps are hooded.'

'Have you been down in Figg's cottage all this time?' Louisa asked.

'No,' David said. 'I got Dad to leave me at the church.'

'Did you?' Louisa asked, astonished. 'What did he have to say about that?'

'Not a single snide remark,' David said. 'He was quite polite – in a strained fashion.'

'Well, that's one for the books. I'm so glad you've seen

Hugo. We've tried to keep each other from being too despon-
dent. But then you walked back here in the dark alone? You
could've injured yourself. Further.'

'Not alone,' Hugo said. Louisa whirled round to see him
standing in the library door wearing his ARP warden's uniform
and a large grin.

'Hugo!' She embraced him, too.

'I'd just got in from my warden rounds,' Hugo said, 'and was
sat in the chair by the fire and drifting off to sleep. I thought he
was an apparition.' He beamed at David. 'I insisted on walking
back up with him. Didn't trust him out of my sight.'

'And I met the two of them,' Jack said, 'when I went out to
look for George's notebook.'

Athena came dashing up the stairs from the basement.

'C'mon Gracie – Mrs Darnley is frying potatoes! And
there's cake.'

'Dundee cake!' Iris shouted from below.

Supper was riotous as David seemed to shed the years he had
on the children and become one again himself. He sat
between Gracie and Athena and across from Johnno, who
seemed a bit starstruck. The children peppered him with
questions about flying and the war. He answered with funny
anecdotes about French cows and gooey cheese, but, in his
voice and the dark look in his eyes before they flashed with
quick wit, Louisa could tell that there was another version of
each story.

After the meal, Mrs Harrison led the children out and Iris
followed. Louisa hung back, as did Jack, and, as they gathered
the serving pieces, Gracie reappeared.

'Hello, love,' Louisa said and sat in a chair to be eye level
with her. 'Come to say good night?'

Gracie stood in front of her and leaned against Louisa's

knees. She glanced across the table to David and Jack. 'Is David my brother now?' she asked in a loud whisper.

Louisa wondered how to temper her emotions and answer with the facts, but she didn't need to.

David leaned across the table and said, 'I, for one, have always wanted a little sister.' Then he deftly changed the subject. 'When did you begin school, Gracie?'

Gracie wrinkled her nose in concentration. 'A long time ago.'

'It was spring of last year,' Jack said. 'You were five when you came to us, Gracie.'

Gracie broke out in a grin. 'I remember! When I started school, Mr Barrie sang a song!'

'Did he, now,' Louisa said with a glance at Jack. 'And what was this song about?'

'It was about flowers and trees,' she said. 'We got to be trees in the song and wave our branches around.' She waved her arms. 'Then Mrs Harrison came in and we started our sums.'

A fresh bottle of whisky was opened as the grown-ups gathered in the library after the children had gone to bed. Mr Grainger and Uncle had not been at supper, but didn't want to miss hearing David's story, so Minns brought them up. Furniture was shifted around so that the chesterfield and the sofa from the corner faced each other, and extra chairs were brought over. David sat in a wingback chair at one end and Hugo at the other end, facing him. The rest filled in. Everyone had a glass except for Mrs Harrison and Minns, who kept to Ovaltine.

After a few minutes of idle chit-chat, David began.

'We'd chased three Stukas across the Channel and past Rouen and decided to turn round as fuel was low. Ned gave me the signal, but as we turned this Messerschmitt came out of nowhere.'

'It was a Messerschmitt we had crash here in the village,' Uncle said.

David nodded. 'It's about the only fighter they have. He fired at me head-on and shattered the windscreen. I was wearing my goggles, which was out of the ordinary, and so the glass splinters hit the rest of my face, but didn't go in my eyes. Those are the little scars you can see, Mum. I was lucky.'

He frowned for a moment. Louisa's hand tightened round Jack's. She was there in the cockpit with her son. 'He's here,' Jack whispered to her. 'He's safe.' Louisa eased her grip.

'I got a good shot at him,' David continued, 'but he went after Ned, probably thinking I'd be going down fast. My engine cut out and so I glided. It was a bit of a challenge to see round the broken glass, but I hit the ground... fairly softly. It would've been fine except at the end of the field was a wood and both wings were sheared off. My only real injury apart from cuts and bruises was that I twisted my ankle and then had to walk on it.'

'The plane landed in good cover?' Jack asked.

David nodded. 'My Spitfire had the sense to tuck herself away and out of sight.'

'Right, you're down on the ground,' Louisa said. 'Then what?'

He thought for a moment as if piecing the story together. 'Well, then I had to get home.' He stretched a leg out and stuck a hand in his pocket. 'So, I opened my compass.'

He held out his hand to show a button – a brass button from a uniform. Then he popped the cover off it and passed it round.

'Well would you look at that,' Mr Grainger said, holding the button at arm's length.

Louisa peered at it when it came her way. There was indeed a tiny compass inside.

'They gave us a few trinkets that would be useful for evasion or escape,' David said. 'In addition to that, I had help along the way. Sometimes you just have to trust you'll find the right people. So, a message was sent ahead about me and I was directed to a fishing village along the coast, where I caught a boat.'

Louisa noticed how vague his story had become. Would he ever be allowed to tell her more?

'When I arrived in Southampton, I was sent to an airfield and I rang Dad.'

Again, Louisa noted a discrepancy. Why would he ring Max first? Because Max was his father or because of Max's work in the War Office?

'He told me to stay put until he got there. This was last night. He drove down with a fresh uniform – he must've left London before dawn. He said we would go directly back to London, but I told him the only place I wanted to go was home to Oxburrow. I told him he could ask me anything he wanted on the journey, but if he wouldn't bring me here he could leave me by the side of the road and I'd walk.'

Louisa shook her head. 'And so, your father drove to Southampton, drove here to Oxburrow and then drove back to London?'

'He did,' David said. 'So you see, Mum, I did come directly home.'

The talk continued until Louisa could see fatigue catching up with her son.

'Right, you,' she said, 'off to bed.'

There was a great deal of hand-shaking and hugging all round, then the party broke up. Hugo pushed Uncle's wheelchair and Minns went down to the cottages to keep an eye on her grandad.

With only Louisa, David and Jack left in the library, she asked her son, 'How did you spend so much time in an enclosed space with your father and not have a raging row?'

David laughed. 'More of a miracle than my landing, don't you think? I don't know, Dad seems... maybe not more understanding, but softer, somehow.'

'You've worked a miracle then,' Louisa said. 'He's been trying to take Oxburrow for army training. I still have some Captain Wentworth nosing around.'

'Fitz?' David said. 'Fitz Wentworth?'

'Fitz?' Louisa echoed. 'You know him?'

'The army is right down the road from us and I met him at the pub,' David said. 'He's very much interested in the law and when this is all over wants to get on with a firm as a clerk. I thought you could mention it to William.'

'Oh!' For a moment it was all Louisa could say, then she added, 'That's who you meant in your letter. I had the wrong end of that stick, didn't I?' But Captain Fitz Wentworth aside, she thought, the army remained a problem.

Hugo appeared at the door again.

'I just thought I'd say good night,' he said to the three of them.

Louisa nodded to her son. 'Go on.'

The next morning, David didn't show himself until nearly midday. Louisa had taken him a cup of tea first thing, ordered him to rest and left him to it. Later she'd taken up a breakfast tray and they'd had a long talk. Relief at his safety loosened her tongue, and she told him how the children had arrived and that moment when she'd first seen Gracie.

'I only received the one letter where you mentioned her,' David said, 'and already I could see a connection.'

'She was angry and hurt and scared,' Louisa said. 'But I knew from that moment that she belonged with us.'

'Good thing you got over your first impression of Jack,' David said with that crooked grin.

Louisa blushed. 'Life is full of surprises, isn't it?'

'I like him, Mum,' David said. 'And you deserve to be happy.'

'But we don't know what will happen, really. There's a problem with the school governors wanting to take the children away. Take Gracie away.' The room seemed to darken. 'If the school goes, Jack may go, too. I can't ask him to stay.' But hadn't she done just that? 'I realise it's been very quick.'

'There's a war on, Mum,' David said. 'What are you waiting for?'

She ruffled his hair. 'All right, you. That's enough talk for now. You stay in bed all day if you like.' She leaned over and kissed his forehead now marked with an array of tiny scars from the windscreen of his plane.

'Well,' David said, putting his hands behind his head, 'at least until dinner. I wouldn't want to miss that.'

Louisa left him, went downstairs and rang Max at the War Office. He was in a meeting and so she left a brief message – 'Thank you' – then rang William, who was 'over the moon' at the news. After that, she walked into the village, but she was too late – Hugo had got there ahead of her and everyone knew about David. She didn't mind one bit.

The morning had flown and it was nearly dinnertime when Louisa returned to Oxburrow. She found David and Gracie – along with Mrs Moffatt – on the sofa in the corner of the library as Gracie read *The Tale of Tom Kitten*.

'I'm practising,' Gracie told her. 'For tomorrow.'

It struck Louisa like a jolt – the fete was the next day. The school governors would arrive by twelve, and she had sworn she would persuade both them and Mrs Harrison that the children should stay at Oxburrow. She needed to ready the displays and the food and— She made a beeline for the kitchen.

Chuff sat at the worktable with tea and a plate with a few

crumbs on it. He stood when Louisa entered, but she waved him down.

'Iris, the fete is tomorrow.'

'Do tell,' Iris said. With a flourish, she threw a tea towel over five plum tarts, one of them with a piece missing.

'How was it, Chuff?' Louisa asked.

'I ate that as a favour to Mrs Darnley,' Chuff said, putting his hand on his heart. 'It was a scientific experiment, if you please.'

'Very noble of you, I'm sure,' Iris said, drying her hands on her apron. 'We were running out of sugar and I didn't know if the plums were sweet enough. I watched as he ate it to see his reaction.'

'Not a pucker,' Chuff reported.

'Another miracle by Iris,' Louisa said.

'I am the saint of sweetness,' Iris replied, batting her eyes.

'And so,' Louisa said, 'everything is in order? There's nothing for me to do this afternoon? You know how important this is—'

Chuff leapt up from the table. 'Were you looking for me, Mrs 'arrison?'

Louisa whirled round and there she was, having crept up silently once again.

'My lady,' Mrs Harrison said, 'I hope your son is enjoying a day of rest.'

'He is, yes,' Louisa said.

An awkward pause made the kitchen feel stuffy. Louisa wondered if she should excuse herself, and then decided that she didn't feel like being turfed out of her own kitchen. Let the woman say what she wanted.

'Mr Chuffleigh, may I have a word?'

Louisa hadn't expected her to say that. She and Iris exchanged looks.

'Yes, ma'am,' he said with dignity. 'I am at your service.'

Mrs Harrison led the way down the corridor and Louisa put her head out the kitchen door to watch. She turned back to Iris and said, 'They've gone out into the yard. What is she up to?'

After the midday dinner, Louisa was crossing the hall when she heard Mrs Harrison's muffled voice coming from the telephone room. The door was closed and no words were audible, but Louisa didn't need to hear details, not after that private word the woman had had with Chuff. Mrs Harrison was planning a getaway.

Louisa crept closer to hear what was being said, but all she heard was Mrs Harrison ringing off. She dived into the boot room and hid behind the mackintoshes hanging from a row of hooks so as not to be seen eavesdropping. Mrs Harrison walked by none the wiser and after a moment, Louisa heard the school-room door close and she crept out of her hiding place.

There was trouble, no doubt about that. Louisa stood gazing out of the side window panel by the door. Mrs Harrison was scheming to steal the children. She had made arrangements so that they would pile onto Chuff's lorry and be off. A fanciful image arose in Louisa's mind of Chuff reversing his lorry on the forecourt and the children being tossed round in the back and Lulu flying through the air, and suddenly it was Mrs Harrison in disguise, wearing Chuff's flat cap pulled down over her severe bun, making her head look like a wooden post.

'Louisa?'

'Ah!' Louisa cried and grabbed Jack's hands to steady herself. He'd come up from behind when her mind was off in some cloud cuckoo land.

'What is it?' he asked.

'Something is up,' she whispered. 'And I don't like it.'

'There you are, Jack,' David said, coming downstairs carefully, one step at a time. He'd donned everyday clothes and, when he reached the ground floor, he said, 'I'm nearly ready. I'll just go and have a word with Iris.'

Louisa looked from one to the other. 'Where are you going?'

'Pub,' David called as he walked back to the stairs leading to the basement. 'I thought it best that Jack and I have a little chat, don't you think?'

David called down to Iris, who came upstairs, and the two of them went off to the library. Louisa turned to Jack, who, she noticed, was wearing his good jacket and had taken a comb to his unruly hair.

'You've smartened up for the pub, haven't you?' she asked. 'Are lessons finished?'

'No,' he said, 'but David had a word with Mrs Harrison on my behalf. She's got all the children in the schoolroom.'

Louisa looked toward the schoolroom and frowned. 'Really?'

'Yes, it's odd. She seems a bit distracted,' Jack replied. 'I'm not sure she knew what she was agreeing to.'

'I can imagine she is distracted. She's got something up her sleeve and I don't like it. Before we know it, the school governors will have moved all of you to some respectable country manor in Kent.'

His brow furrowed but he didn't answer, and Louisa's heart sank. She'd said it in a flippant way, but the fear was real. If she couldn't persuade Mrs Harrison and the school governors to let the children stay, how would she fight it? She would ring William Lowrey, of course, but what then? She had no power to threaten court action and couldn't imagine on what grounds. These thoughts roiled inside her and she balled up her hands into fists.

Jack led her out onto the portico, where an autumn breeze nipped at her ankles. He took one of her hands, gently opened it and raised it to his lips.

'Teaching has brought me back to myself,' he said. 'It had

been buried for so long that it surprised me that I could find my vocation again. Being a teacher gives me hope.'

'It shows,' Louisa said, letting go of her own fear. 'It shows in how you are with the children and how they are with you.'

Jack's eyes sparked. 'But as surprised as I am to be teaching, I'm nearly overwhelmed with my love for you.'

Louisa smiled so wide she thought her face would split.

She kissed him and said, 'And I love you.'

But how bittersweet – she had regained her son only to lose Jack and Gracie.

'If they move the school,' Jack said, 'no matter where it is, I could come back for the holidays.'

He frowned as he said it. Louisa joined him. She heard the commitment he was making – that they would be together no matter what. Was she too selfish to want more?

'But you're a part of Oxburrow,' she said.

He acknowledged that with a wry grin. 'I haven't had a home for a very long time – not a real sort of home. Until now. But it isn't Oxburrow, it's you. Or perhaps you and Oxburrow are one.'

David popped out the door. 'Ready for that pint, Jack?'

David and Jack returned in time for supper, with Hugo in tow. With the addition of Chuff and the men up from the cottages, it was a raucous table and no one, apart from Louisa, seemed to notice that Mrs Harrison neither participated in any of the multitude of conversations nor objected to them.

As dishes were cleared, Mrs Harrison said, 'Now, children, say good night.'

When the wishes had been exchanged and they had gone on their way, Chuff stood with a stack of plates and said, 'Good night to you, Mrs 'arrison. See you first thing.'

Mrs Harrison coloured at this remark, but nodded.

Later, when the dishes had been washed and the floor mopped, Louisa said good night to Iris and climbed the stairs up to the ground floor, where Mrs Harrison appeared to be loitering by the Chinese palm.

'My lady,' she said. 'I wonder if I could have a word – as soon as I've turned the girls' light out.'

Ah, so this was it, Louisa thought. Well, at least she wasn't trying to take the children off in the dead of night.

'Of course,' she said. 'I'll be in the morning room.'

Louisa thought she might've caught sight of Jack on the landing, and hoped he'd heard and understood that she could very well need a shoulder to cry on after this 'word'.

Two mugs of Ovaltine were sitting on the small table between the wingback chairs in front of the cold fireplace when Mrs Harrison announced her arrival with a small knock.

'The girls all tucked up?' Louisa asked.

'One can only hope,' Mrs Harrison said, taking her chair. She contemplated the Ovaltine for a moment before reaching for it. 'Thank you so much for your hospitality.'

'You're welcome,' Louisa said. Despite the perils that may lie ahead, she was calm in herself and felt no need to hurry the woman.

Mrs Harrison, on the other hand, shifted in her chair, set her mug down and then took it up again. She opened her mouth as if about to speak, but then closed it. She tried again and failed, but the third time was the charm.

'Long-held beliefs can be difficult to let go of,' she said, as if beginning a lecture on the subject.

'You mean "the world is flat" – that sort of thing?'

Mrs Harrison made a sound like a gasp of breath or a cough or... a laugh? But she got hold of herself in a flash and continued.

'It's only recently I've come to understand that, instead of me holding a belief, the belief has had hold of me.' She shook her head. 'I have done you a great disservice, Lady Brightford. I have made assumptions that are false. I have proclaimed to be protecting the children when in fact I was more concerned with what others may think of me. As if I have never made a mistake! My own inadequacies and my past have been my downfall.'

It was a heartfelt confession – Louisa was certain of that – but too convoluted to follow. She kept quiet, hoping for more, and at last it came.

'I believe Mrs Greet told you about Mr Harrison.'

Did neither of the Harrisons have a Christian name?

'She made mention of him,' Louisa said cautiously. 'He abandoned you many years ago.'

'Nineteen years in November,' Mrs Harrison said. 'And not a word from him since the day he walked out.'

'That's dreadful, Mrs Harrison,' Louisa said. 'You don't deserve such treatment. But now, you can do something about it. You can apply for a divorce because of desertion.'

Mrs Harrison reddened and shook her head. 'I have come to understand that recent changes to the law make divorce the best way forward for you and perhaps for others, but it cannot help me. It would do nothing to allow me to return to my... my...'

'Return to your family, you mean?' Louisa said.

Mrs Harrison raised her brows as if she'd never considered that.

'No, not my family,' she said. 'That is, yes – my chosen family. Before I married, you see, I was in holy orders.'

Louisa's jaw dropped. That hadn't occurred to her but, really, was it totally unexpected? She recalled the square corners on the beds and the discipline of standing in line and not talking at the table. And that silent way of walking. A nun – yes, she could quite see it now.

'It was an Anglican teaching order,' Mrs Harrison added with a wistful note.

Louisa could perfectly picture her as a nun. 'What was your name?'

Mrs Harrison looked surprised at the question, but also a bit pleased.

'Sister Luke,' she said.

'Sister Luke,' Louisa said. 'Of course. All those teaching parables – it makes great sense.' They were quiet for a moment, then something occurred to her. 'So, if you were divorced, you couldn't return to the order – but what if your husband has died?'

'If he's dead—' Mrs Harrison's mouth snapped shut, leaving Louisa to imagine the next words would've been *then the devil take him.*

'I don't know how I would ever find out,' Mrs Harrison said.

'There are ways. There are people to help. Just think how knowing would put your mind at ease one way or the other.'

Mrs Harrison made a small noncommittal sound into her mug, then gave a heavy sigh. 'How does one's life get off track?' she asked. 'Even from my girlhood, I had hoped to do good in the world – a rather vague, pie-in-the-sky aspiration, I suppose.'

'But you have done good – look around you!' Louisa exclaimed with a wide-ranging gesture that nearly knocked her mug of Ovaltine off the table. 'Look at the children you've saved, the care you've given them.'

'The stumbling blocks I put in your way.'

'Well,' Louisa said, not sure if she were willing to overlook that. 'Do the school governors know about your past?'

'My concern now is not for what the school governors know or don't know – it's for the dog's breakfast I made out of this entire affair by being so high and mighty!'

Louisa was stunned into silence and Mrs Harrison continued.

'Mr Richards, you see, is a cousin of sorts. He is enthusiastic and generous in doing good works, but he sees the world in black and white and I'm afraid he's rather dug in his heels about this. At my instigation, I admit. The other school governors give their money, but leave the running of the charity to him.'

'Even Mrs Perrymont?' Louisa asked.

Mrs Harrison shrugged. 'I assume so. It was Mrs Perrymont's late husband who was an associate of Mr Richards. He seemed surprised that she wanted to be so involved.'

Louisa didn't like all these threads of connection – Max and the army, Max and Mrs Perrymont, Mrs Perrymont and the school governors.

Mrs Harrison threw back her shoulders. 'Tomorrow, I will do what I can.'

'When they arrive for the fete?' Louisa asked.

'No. I am going to London first thing in the morning,' she said. 'Mr Chuffleigh will take me to the station and then I will return in the car with the school governors. They will listen to me then – they'll have no other choice. I will put forward the case that Hazel End school must stay at Oxburrow. I will do everything I can.'

'Oh, Mrs Harrison,' Louisa said, and quickly picked up her mug of Ovaltine before she lost all control and threw her arms around the woman.

They parted in the entrance hall, and Mrs Harrison climbed the stairs with what seemed to Louisa to be a lighter step.

Louisa went directly to the library, and found Jack with the wireless on low. He rose.

'Whisky, please,' she said. 'I've had enough Ovaltine.'

He poured and handed her the drink. She took a sip and put her arms around his neck.

'Mrs Harrison's past,' she said, 'is an enigma no more.'

. . .

Chuff and Mrs Harrison were gone before breakfast, and the meal took on an odd fits-and-starts quality as no one was quite sure whether talking was allowed or not. The children, excited and nervous about the fete, were fidgety.

'Are they nice people?' Gracie asked after she'd scraped clean her porridge bowl.

'I'm sure they try their best,' Louisa said, who was sure of nothing of the sort.

'Mrs Harrison said not to get dirty,' Alf said. 'What are we going to do until they arrive?'

'Reverend Hugo is coming to take you to church,' David said as he reached for another piece of toast. 'Mr Barrie and I are going, too. It's a special Saturday morning lesson on birds as well as a competition – the person who can name the most birds at the end of the morning wins a bar of chocolate. We'll be leaving soon.'

The children leapt up from the table and made for the stairs. Louisa could hear Gracie saying, 'I know a robin and a blackbird and a sparrow. I know parakeets, but they live with Mrs Greet.'

David turned to his mother. 'Mrs Harrison wants them clean and Iris wants them out from underfoot. It's the best we could think of apart from reading Bible stories for three hours.'

Louisa patted his cheek. 'It's perfect.'

When she came up from finishing the breakfast dishes, Gracie and Dolly were watching Priss as she tossed Jack's hat at the bust of Aristotle. No one else was about.

There came the sound of a vehicle coming up the drive, and Louisa stepped out to see. It couldn't be Chuff – he'd returned from taking Mrs Harrison to the station just after breakfast. Also, this was no rough-running engine prone to backfires.

Her answer came as the nose of a car showed itself at the

top of the drive and then, reaching the even ground of the forecourt, levelled out to reveal that it was a Rolls-Royce.

Louisa's blood ran cold – had the school governors arrived early? Was Mrs Harrison with them or had they left her behind? Frozen to the spot under the portico, she waited until the car stopped, the driver climbed out and went round to open the passenger's door.

Out stepped Marian Perrymont.

CHAPTER 24

'Lady Brightford, I'm sorry to surprise you with my early arrival.'

Marian Perrymont was as perfectly dressed and coiffed as she had been on her first visit to Oxburrow, but now as she approached the portico, Louisa could see anxious lines around the woman's eyes and a hesitancy in her voice.

'It's only that I thought I might hear from you before today – after your read through the papers I sent out.'

'I am sorry,' Louisa said, already on the back foot. Was this how the day would go? 'I have to confess I forgot all about them – so much happened that day. A bomb fell' – she flung her arm out in the direction of the pit – 'and... but you have heard that already, haven't you?'

'Yes, I have,' Mrs Perrymont said. 'And that David is home. Although, I didn't hear that news until yesterday.'

'Please, do come in,' Louisa said, at sea as to what to do next. Was this a showdown? 'Would you like coffee?'

'If you wouldn't mind, I'd very much like you to read the papers. I'm happy to wait elsewhere while you do—'

'No, come with me.'

Louisa led her into the entrance hall and saw Minns on the landing with the carpet sweeper.

'Minns, would you ask Iris to bring coffee to the morning room. And see to the driver, too.' But Louisa had not gone two steps before she stopped. 'No, instead, would you please show Mrs Perrymont to the morning room. I'll go and ask Iris for coffee.'

Gracie left the game to Dolly and Priss and followed Louisa to the top of the basement stairs.

'You don't need to come down with me,' Louisa said. 'Why don't you and Dolly get your books and pictures ready to show everyone?'

She didn't wait for an answer, but left the girl there and hurried down. She stopped outside the kitchen to calm her nerves, then walked in.

Iris looked up from chopping cabbage, and when she saw Louisa her face went white.

'What is it?'

'Marian Perrymont has arrived on her own before the others,' Louisa said.

'She what?' Iris could barely choke out the words.

'This is it, Iris – I know it is. We may have Mrs Harrison on our side now and she will try her hardest to sway the men, but it will come to nothing. All along, Max and Mrs Perrymont have had the army in their back pocket. That'll be it – the children will leave as quickly as they came. Look out for the charabanc, because it's probably on its way.'

'Now hang on a minute,' Iris said.

Louisa was nearly in tears. 'Iris, they'll take Gracie away. What will I do?'

'You let me have a word with the woman,' Iris said.

'I don't know what good it would do,' Louisa said and sniffed. 'I suppose I'll have to hear her out. Give me twenty minutes, then bring up coffee.' She stepped out of the kitchen and heard footsteps on the stairs ahead, but whoever it was had already disappeared.

Jack? David? No, the steps were lighter. Probably Alf looking for Lulu.

Louisa walked into the morning room and stopped. Marian Perrymont was at the window, looking out at the lawn and the countryside beyond. *Perhaps she's sizing up the place for when Oxburrow is razed*, Louisa thought glumly. Then, behind her, the door opened and there was Gracie, holding her latest watercolour.

'May I show the lady my painting?' she asked.

'It isn't quite time for the fete to begin,' Louisa explained. 'You should go and join the others, all right?'

But Gracie didn't move, and when Marian Perrymont turned from the window the girl said to her, 'May I show you my painting?'

'I'd love to see your painting,' Mrs Perrymont said. 'You're Gracie, aren't you?'

Gracie marched over, holding her watercolour out in front of her like a banner. It had been painted on another blank page from an ancient Oxburrow ledger. Louisa followed and the two women peered over the girl's shoulders.

It was a painting of a cat. The cat's head was nearly as big as the entire paper, its whiskers abnormally long and its green eyes the size of shillings. Its body – small and crowded into a corner as if an afterthought – was cinched into a blue sweater. The proportions were a bit askew, but the truth of the matter was that anything was better than Gracie's first attempt – an entirely black painting – because it meant she was healing.

'And who is this?' Mrs Perrymont asked.

'Sometimes it's Tom Kitten,' Gracie said, 'and sometimes it's Agnes and sometimes it's Mrs Moffatt.'

'Mrs Moffatt is our cat here at Oxburrow,' Louisa explained.

'Agnes was my cat before, but she ran away,' Gracie said and the shadow of a scowl crossed her face. 'Now I live here. Mrs Moffatt belongs to David, but we can share.'

Tears pricked Louisa's eyes and when Gracie looked up at her she tried to blink them away, but they fell regardless. She kissed Gracie on the top of her head.

'And is this part of your painting?' Mrs Perrymont pointed to an orange blob of paint in another corner.

'That's a robin. Mr Barrie showed one to me in the wood. And I know Reverend Hugo at the church and Mrs Nethergate in the shop.'

Athena appeared at the door. 'Gracie!' she said and then added, 'Begging your pardon, Lady Bee. Gracie, we're ready to go to the church. C'mon!'

Gracie looked from Mrs Perrymont to Louisa. 'I don't want to go.'

'Just for a bit,' Louisa said. 'We won't be long.'

The door closed and Louisa set Gracie's painting at one corner of the desk without comment.

'She's done well,' Mrs Perrymont said. 'You've done well with her.'

Louisa refused to talk about Gracie with the woman.

Instead, in a businesslike tone, she said, 'Well now, to the papers.' She retrieved the packet from the drawer, cut the string and drew out a stack of papers. On top of the stack there was a separate letter in a fine white linen envelope, addressed to her. This, she set aside and began with the note on the uppermost page.

Lady Brightford, Mrs Harrison and Mr Barrie,

As requested, the governors did our best to search out any existing relatives of the children who might possibly be able to take them in. The enclosed details are for you to do with as you will. We have no intention of giving up on Hazel End Charity School wherever it may be housed, but we also understand there are extenuating circumstances.

Yours respectfully,

Marian Perrymont (Mrs)

'It's about the children,' Louisa said. 'Why did you give this to me and not Mrs Harrison?'

'Because I thought you had a right to know,' Mrs Perrymont said, 'and I wasn't entirely sure you would see it otherwise.'

Louisa looked at her sharply. 'The school governors want to move the children away.'

'Mr Richards wants to move the children. The other three men follow him, but I don't believe they care which way the wind blows.'

'And does Mr Richards listen to you?' Louisa asked.

'Mr Richards listened to my husband,' Mrs Perrymont said, 'and, at first, preferred to assume that I would say the same. Lately, I have become a thorn in Mr Richards' side and he has become rather twitchy every time I open my mouth.'

Louisa saw doors opening in her mind, but she slammed them shut again.

'You and Max want the army to move into Oxburrow.'

'I do *not* want the army at Oxburrow, I want the children here,' Mrs Perrymont said, 'and I made that quite clear to Max. He has given up on the idea now, but I assure you it wasn't anything I said. You've put up quite the fight. Also, I believe David had a word with him about it.'

The bathtub of worry Louisa had been sloshing round in began to drain. No army!

'Did you want to stay married to Max?' Mrs Perrymont asked.

The question caught Louisa by such surprise that all she could do was laugh, but she cut it off quickly.

'No,' she said, 'the divorce made it official, but our marriage had dissolved years before. You are certainly not responsible.' It was the first time Louisa had admitted that – a pity Iris wasn't in the room to hear. 'But,' she added, 'just because we both agreed to the divorce doesn't mean I want to be turned out of my own house. Thank you for telling me about the army – there's no knowing how long it would be before Max got round to it. You realise that I didn't know you were a school governor when I wrote to William Lowrey and asked for the children.'

She nodded. 'Mr Lowrey wrote a letter to the school governors, but I'm the only one who pays any attention to correspondence. When I read it, I thought it was a smashing idea.' Mrs Perrymont smiled and her eyes twinkled. Louisa smiled back.

'Will you and Max marry?'

'No,' Mrs Perrymont said firmly. 'Although I prefer to have a gentleman in my life, I no longer need those legal details that can only make a tangled mess of things later.'

Louisa was warming to the woman more by the second.

'Well, Marian – may I call you Marian and you'll call me Louisa? – let me say thank you from the bottom of my heart for sending the children here.'

'The children and the teachers, Louisa,' Marian said. 'I can see that you're thankful for at least one of them.'

A strong knock at the door was followed by a glowering Iris carrying a tray.

'Come in, Iris, come in,' Louisa said with all good cheer. 'It's all right. Everything's all right. You'll need to stay. I hope you've brought three cups.'

'Indeed I have.'

'Good,' Louisa said, 'then let me introduce you to Marian Perrymont. Marian, this is Iris Darnley.'

Marian rose. 'I'm pleased to meet you, Iris.'

Iris's gaze went from Marian to Louisa, who said, 'It turns out Marian is an ally, Iris, not an enemy. Come and sit down.'

Iris sat and poured out the coffee. There was cake, too.

'Madeira cake,' Marian said. 'However did you find a lemon these days?'

'It isn't black market,' Iris said. 'It was well and truly above board – an accidental shipment that just happened to make it all the way through.'

'You wouldn't have caught me saying anything either way,' Marian replied.

That was good enough for Iris.

'Marian is on the children's side in this business,' Louisa pointed out.

'But if Mrs Harrison doesn't persuade the others,' Iris said, 'you're still in the minority and the men could insist on moving the children.'

'They can do nothing of the sort, actually,' Marian said. 'They've no legal right, although they do like to presume to be in possession of power. Those children who have family could go to them and those who don't—'

'Those who don't will stay here,' Louisa said. She patted the stack of papers. 'Marian has searched for the children's families. Shall we see what she's found?'

There were both promising and heartbreaking details.

Marian had written to every relative, however distant, that the school governors knew about.

'You did this all yourself,' Louisa said to Marian.

She shrugged. 'I didn't mind. Sometimes, it was like following a trail of breadcrumbs.'

First off, Dolly and Gloria's grandmother had lived in Pickering with her sister. The granny had died, but their great-aunt was still alive.

Sydney had an uncle in Chester. Alf's mother had a cousin in Whitby.

'Those were the easy ones,' Marian said. 'Their mothers had given us next of kin when the school started. But for the others, if it hadn't been for the local post office, I don't know where we'd be.'

She told them how the postal workers now sifted through bomb sites in London looking for letters that could be saved for those who survived. When post came in for those street numbers that no longer existed, the letters were kept on hand.

'Look,' Louisa exclaimed, 'here's a letter from Athena's father. He fled Paris when it fell to the Nazis and he's in Southampton.'

'George's mother died in the terrace bombing thinking her husband had gone down with his merchant navy ship in the spring – the Battles of Narvik.' Marian held out an envelope. 'But here's a letter from George's father saying he survived and has signed onto another ship.'

There was a letter from someone named Dodie to Priss's mum. It carried a cryptic message:

He died last week – his lungs got him at last. Why don't you come home? Bring the girl, too – you'll be welcome.

And so it went on. Marian had written to each possible connection and every one had written back offering their young relative a home.

'There's been nothing about Johnno, I'm afraid,' Marian said.

'From what Jack has said, that sounds about right,' Louisa told her. 'But there's a local family that might want to take him in. I'll find out.' She eyed the envelope addressed to her. 'Is that about Gracie?'

'Yes,' Marian said. 'The post office received a letter to Gracie's mother, Irene Standing. I wrote back and this is the reply.'

Louisa's fingers danced on the top of the envelope, unable to hold still. Iris put her hand over Louisa's for a moment and then said, 'Go on.'

'Right.' She took up the letter opener, slit the envelope and pulled out the one-page letter, which was written in small, scratchy writing. She read it through quickly, then again more slowly.

'Oh my,' she said. 'Iris, do you remember I told you Gracie mentioned a Brother Michael? Well, it seems that he is one of the Little Brothers of St Anthony near Norwich – and he's also Gracie's actual brother.'

'How do you work that out?' Iris asked. Louisa handed her the letter and Iris scanned it, then read it aloud.

'Dear Mrs Perrymont,

Thank you for your letter and the sad news about my mother. She left me with the Brothers when I was an infant twenty-three years ago, but has visited four times since then. The last time was in the spring a year ago and that is when I met my sister, Gracie. A lovely little girl. As you can imagine, I am unable to care for Gracie as my days are taken up with prayer and tending the reed beds for the baskets we make, but there is an orphanage associated with our order. Now that Mother is dead and there is no one else, I will make ready a place for my sister there.

May God bless you in your work as He has blessed me.

In our Father's Name,

Brother Michael'

Iris handed the letter back to Louisa, who set it down carefully, as if it were an adder about to strike.

'It's kind of him to offer Gracie a place to live,' Louisa said thickly. 'But an orphanage is not a home. This – Oxburrow – is her home. We are a family now. Gracie and Jack and I are like a family. And Iris.'

'And why wouldn't her brother want that for her?' Marian asked gently. 'You must explain it to him.'

But even as she said the words, Louisa still felt both Gracie and Jack slipping away from her.

There came a sharp knock at the door.

CHAPTER 25

Jack opened the door of the morning room as he knocked. His gaze darted from Marian to Iris to Louisa.

'Good morning, Mrs Perrymont,' he said. 'Mrs Harrison and the rest of the school governors are arriving.'

Iris popped out of her chair. 'Good Lord, the coffee.'

Louisa popped out of hers. 'I'll go and meet them.'

Jack lifted a finger. 'Could I have a word first?'

Marian rose. 'You stay here, Louisa. I'll go and meet the governors and Mrs Harrison.'

Jack stepped into the room and, when Marian had gone, he closed the door and went to Louisa.

She took his hands. 'I've been such a fool,' she said. 'I've jumped to conclusions and made assumptions and nearly made a mess of things. Marian doesn't want the children to leave. That is, she does, but only because she's found relatives who want them. The school governors can't stop that. And Max has given up on the army – that's down to David, I'm sure.'

'What about Gracie?'

Louisa looked down at the letter from Brother Michael.

'Gracie is another matter, but I'll explain later.' She exhaled in a huff, then noticed the gleam in Jack's eye. 'Now, what is this?'

'Did you know one of the teachers at the village school is leaving?' he asked.

'Old Mr Peterson – is he ill?'

'No, young Miss Kerry. She's getting married and moving to King's Lynn.'

'Is she?' Louisa asked, then gasped. 'That means there's a teaching vacancy here.'

'Not any longer,' Jack said. 'With Hugo's help – he is, after all, on the local council – I've just taken the post.'

For the briefest of moments, Louisa was too stunned to speak. Then she squealed and threw her arms around him. That was all the celebration time allowed, because from the entrance hall came a cacophony of excited children's voices and Lulu yipping to beat the band. Louisa threw open the door and they went out. Messrs Hargreaves, Merrick, Ilkington and one other, who wore a slim grey suit and had a thin moustache – Richards – had closed ranks while Lulu and Mrs Moffatt rang rings round them. Mrs Harrison stood to one side, aghast – although Louisa detected a smirk – while Marian stood on the other with the children, laughing.

Louisa clapped her hands sharply and said, 'Shoo, the both of you!' And off the cat and dog went. 'Hello and welcome back to Oxburrow,' Louisa said to the governors. 'Mr Barrie, should the children man their displays?'

'Grand idea,' Jack said and led the troop in.

Iris and Chuff appeared with trays of coffee and cake. For the occasion, Louisa and Minns had dragged a heavy round oak pedestal table out to the entrance hall. The table was showing its age – and not in a good way – but they had covered it with a lace cloth and set a vase of asters in the middle. It had a slight wobble to it but, as long as the coffee cups were distributed evenly, Louisa thought they were safe.

They were joined by the other Oxburrow residents and, as everyone tucked in, Louisa sidled over to Mrs Harrison, who had taken refuge by Aristotle. The woman seemed to have lost all her starch and there was a greyish cast to her face. She needn't look so forlorn – Louisa needed to set her straight about a few things.

'Did you have a miserable journey?' she asked, full of sympathy.

'I'm afraid my plan did not go well, my lady,' Mrs Harrison said. 'Mr Richards will not budge.'

'Well, Mrs Harrison, you'll be relieved to know that it doesn't matter a whit what Mr Richards thinks.'

Mrs Harrison's brows shot up and colour returned to her face. 'What do you mean?'

'You were missing Mrs Perrymont on the journey.'

'She came separately,' Mrs Harrison said, 'due to a previously arranged... something. I can't recall what excuse Mr Richards gave.'

'She came out with news about the children's families. She did all the digging herself. Listen to this.' Louisa filled her in while keeping an eye on the others – the coffee and cake was disappearing quickly. When she had finished, Mrs Harrison remained perplexed.

'But then, is today's fete for naught? I thought it was to convince the school governors.'

'Whatever it was meant to be,' Louisa said, 'it is now a day to celebrate the children's hard work and how well they are doing.'

Still, a frown lingered on Mrs Harrison's brow. 'I wonder if they would even want me back as a teacher now – if they begin again with Hazel End Charity School in London.'

'I can't imagine they could find anyone better,' Louisa said. 'Although, it turns out that Mrs Perrymont is something of a detective. Why not put her on the trail of Mr Harrison? You deserve to know.'

Louisa handed Mrs Harrison coffee and cake and engaged in idle chit-chat with Chuff about his business of moving goods from one place to another. 'Bricks and the like,' Chuff said. 'They don't have legs, do they? London is where the work is, but I have to say it would be nice to be out of it.'

When their cups were empty, Louisa led the school governors into the library. Trailing behind came Mr Grainger, Uncle, Hugo, David and Iris. The children were stationed next to the displays they'd created and the watercolours they had painted and the books they had read.

George started them off. The school governors and others gathered round as the boy told about Hadrian and his wall and showed them *Our Island Story*, the book he'd read. Sydney had marked Debden Ash on a map of England and talked about its vital statistics.

The program was taking a bit longer than Louisa realised it would, but the children were doing marvellous jobs – there were even a few questions from the grown-ups. It wasn't until during Priss's report about clothing styles and how collars had changed – this courtesy of Minns who was teaching the girl fine needlework – that Louisa looked to see who was next.

'Athena,' Louisa said, 'where is Gracie?'

'When we got back, she went upstairs to get Agnes the sock kitty and then she wanted to find Mrs Moffatt to stand by her picture.'

Louisa would give her a few more minutes and then go and see about her. Gracie had recovered from her trauma, but that didn't necessarily mean she enjoyed being on display.

When Priss had finished, Dolly began her piece by holding up one of Figg's seed catalogues. 'Peas grow in pods,' she told

Mr Hargreaves. 'And you can eat them while you're standing in the garden if you like. Although, not too many or there wouldn't be enough for dinner.'

After a while, Iris left and returned with a platter of sandwiches she set on the map table. She nodded to Louisa, who followed her out of the door.

'I've half a platter of sandwiches missing, and a currant cake I hadn't cut yet.'

'Oh dear. Did Lulu get them?' Louisa thought that, if so, they would have a very sick little dog on their hands.

'Lulu is in there with Alf,' Iris said, nodding into the library.

'It wasn't Chuff, was it?' Louisa asked.

'He already knows better than to incur my wrath,' Iris said.

'Lady Bee,' Athena said, sticking her head out of the door of the library, 'we're going to sing the church song. Where is Gracie?'

'Gracie? You told me she'd gone upstairs.'

'Oh,' Athena said, 'that's right. I'll go and get her.'

An uneasy feeling crept over Louisa as she watched Athena bound up the stairs. In no time at all, the girl returned to the ground floor. Out of breath, she said, 'She's not there.'

And with that, panic set in.

Louisa couldn't remember how long it had been since she'd laid eyes on the girl – thirty minutes? An hour? More?

Where was Mrs Moffatt? Where the cat was, Gracie would be. Louisa had to see for herself – she ran upstairs to the girls' dormitory and stood in the doorway, scanning the room, looking for movement. The room was empty.

She returned to the ground floor and stopped, swaying slightly but telling herself to stay calm. She didn't need to keep her eyes on Gracie every minute of the day – let her be a little girl.

At that moment, David and Hugo came out of the library with the children.

Louisa gripped her son's arm. 'Have you seen Gracie? Or the cat?'

'No,' he said and frowned. 'Not since earlier.'

'Is Gracie lost?' Athena asked.

Jack appeared next to her. 'It's Gracie,' Louisa said, a lump in her throat making it difficult to talk. 'I don't know where she is.'

'Morning room?'

'Morning room.' Off she ran, and the others followed suit, going in every direction to find the girl – the basement dining room, the schoolroom, the boys' dormitory, the bomb pit. Marian joined in, but the other school governors stood off to the side of the hall. At least they kept out of the way, Louisa thought.

Gracie was nowhere to be found. If she wasn't at Oxburrow, where was she?

'The church?' Hugo said. 'Or my cottage. I'll go and look, and ring you.'

'Has she done this before,' David asked. 'Gone off on her own?'

'Yes,' Louisa said. 'When she was looking for me. But I'm here.'

'Why else would she leave?' Marian asked. 'And where would she think it safe to go?'

Louisa stared off into space, and the answer to *Why* came to her. It had been Gracie Louisa had heard on the basement stairs when she had commiserated with Iris about Marian's arrival. Louisa had voiced her fear that Gracie would be taken away. That was why the girl had wanted to show Marian her painting – she wanted Mrs Perrymont to know that she belonged at Oxburrow.

So, before she could be taken away, she had run off on her own. The answer to the second question came to Louisa in a flash. She ran to the morning room, and to the corner where she'd taken David's watercolour off the wall and set it down so Gracie could see it better. The painting was gone.

She returned to the entrance hall and told the waiting crowd.

'I think she's gone to Lake Puddle-Duck.'

'A lake?' Marian asked. 'How far is it? My driver can take us.'

'I've my lorry, too,' Chuff said. We'll take as many as necessary and spread out when we get there.'

There was a chaotic moment while too many voices were trying to be heard. Louisa dragged herself back up to the landing, held on to the newel and sank down on a step, wishing she could think, just think.

'Quiet!'

In the silence, everyone looked up at Jack, who had gone halfway up to the landing to Louisa. 'Thank you, Mrs Perrymont and all of you,' he said. 'We'll take the car and your lorry, Chuff. David and Hugo, see if she's gone to the church and check the wood, too. Perhaps it's best if we wrap up the afternoon.' He looked at the school governors. 'Thank you for coming. Goodbye.'

'Well, if this is the sort of thing that happens here,' Mr Richards said, 'then it's just as well that we take them away.'

The other men voiced agreement until Mrs Harrison's commanding voice cut through.

'That decision is out of your hands,' she declared. 'I will write and explain, but for now you should be on your way so that we can find Gracie and bring her home.'

Iris chivvied the four blustering men out of the door, handing them their coats and hats on the way.

Jack divided up searchers and went out onto the forecourt with them while Mrs Harrison took the children – who were huddled together looking pale and worried – back to the library.

'We'll have a quiet story,' she told them, 'and a rest. You aren't to worry – Lady Bee and Mr Barrie will find Gracie.'

The entrance hall had emptied of people – Mr Grainger and Uncle had returned to their cottage, but said they would look in the garden on their way. Minns and Iris had each given Louisa a hug, and now went out to join the search party. 'She's taken those provisions,' Iris said, 'so she'll be well fed.'

Jack returned and went up to the landing, where Louisa had remained as if glued to the spot. He knelt in front of her and took her hands.

'You stay here in case she comes back. If she's gone off to the lake, we'll find her. You know that?'

Louisa knew Jack worried that she would remember the many perils of the lake and lose hope, but she was more confused than scared.

'She wouldn't leave me, Jack,' she said. 'Even if she were scared of being taken away, she wouldn't leave *me*.'

'I'll go over to the church before we leave to check with David and Hugo. She could be hiding in the churchyard.'

Louisa shook her head. 'It doesn't make sense.'

They stayed that way – hands clasped and without speaking. Outside the open front door, everyone waited for Jack to come out or for word to begin.

Louisa listened to the silence of Oxburrow and it was as if, in the distance, she could hear the swell of music. It sounded like... a waltz.

She gasped and leapt up, nearly knocking Jack over, and falling on top of him. She steadied herself, turned and flew up the stairs and then up the next set and down to the end of the corridor, where the door to the attic stood open.

Drifting down to her came the scratchy strains of *Swan Lake*.

· · ·

A dim light spilled out from the open door at the top of the winding stairs to the attic. Louisa reached the top step and paused to catch her breath and take in the scene. The single bulb hanging from the rafters shone down on Gracie, who sat against a steamer trunk with her knees drawn up under her chin, looking up at Louisa with small dark eyes. A tea towel lay open. On it lay a few sandwiches and an entire currant cake that looked as if it had been nibbled at the corner by a mouse. Next to Gracie, Mrs Moffatt, guard cat, perched on the rim of a rush-bottom chair missing most of its rush. Nearby, the gramophone played on.

Behind Louisa, Jack had crept halfway up the stairs and then stopped. She smiled and gave him a nod. He reached out his hand and she took it for a moment, then he retreated. Louisa leaned against the doorpost – her legs had gone weak with relief. She turned her attention back to Gracie, who watched and waited.

'I forgot and left the gramophone open, didn't I?' Louisa asked. It had been the morning the school governors had arrived without warning. She kept her manner calm so as not to alarm girl or cat. She lifted her eyebrows. 'So.'

'I didn't run away,' Gracie said, presenting her defence without question. 'You said not to run away and I didn't.'

'Although, it was a bit like running away,' Louisa said, 'because we didn't know where you were.'

'Mrs Moffatt knew.'

'Were you going to send her down with a message?'

'And I played the music so you would know.'

She's got me there. 'Budge up a bit,' Louisa said and squeezed herself in beside Gracie. The record slowed, making the waltz sound as if the swans were moving through treacle. Then it stopped altogether. They sat for a moment in silence. How peaceful it was.

'Mrs Perryman wants to take me away,' Gracie said.

'That was a misunderstanding that is entirely my fault. Mrs Perrymont doesn't want to take you away. She wants you to stay here at Oxburrow where you belong.'

Gracie looked up at Louisa with eyes shining.

'I can stay? And you're my mother now. Aren't you?'

'Yes, I suppose I am. And I like it an awful lot. Do you remember telling me about Brother Michael? Did you know that he is your real brother?'

Gracie nodded, unconcerned. Louisa would write and explain that a place at the orphanage would not be necessary.

'What about Athena and Priss and... everybody?' Gracie asked.

'Anyone who wants to stay here is welcome but, do you know, I believe Mrs Perrymont has found families for some of the others, and so they will have their own homes.'

'Oxburrow is my home,' Gracie said. 'With you and Mr Barrie and David. And Mrs Darnley and Mrs Moffatt. And Mr Figg.'

Louisa took the girl in her arms and said, 'Yes. Anyone else you'd like to add?'

'A parakeet?'

What is home? Louisa thought about this as she and Gracie made their way down the stairs with the cat following. A welcoming place. A safe place. A place to be with someone you love. A place to be a child. Not everyone got that, but why shouldn't she fight for it for as many children as she could?

There was great promise for the other children, but if arrangements fell through they would be welcomed back to Oxburrow. And there could be other children who needed at least a temporary home, a refuge. They would be welcome, too.

But for Gracie, this would be her home for ever.

EPILOGUE

A month later, there was a great gathering on the forecourt at Oxburrow, come to see the children off. In addition to the entire household – which still included Minns, Mr Grainger, Uncle and Chuff – Marian Perrymont was there as a representative of the school governors. At least, that was what Mrs Harrison had told them. Marian had been the one to find the children's families and had paid their train fare to come to Oxburrow, and Louisa had insisted she be a part of the morning.

A row of ragtag suitcases stood in a line awaiting their journey, in much better nick than when they'd arrived. That was thanks to Chuff, who had sorted out broken latches and given them all a good spit and polish.

Colin and his cart pulled by Queenie had arrived. He would take the children to the station, and the grown-ups would travel in more prosaic fashion in two cars. But before that could happen, the children were having one last lesson.

'Hold your hand like this,' Gracie told them, demonstrating a flat palm with fingers together. She placed a piece of knobby carrot on her hand and held it up to Queenie.

The horse reached out and nuzzled Gracie's palm as she picked up the treat, and then gave a snort.

'That means she likes it,' Gracie told the other children. 'Here, Dolly, you try it.'

Gracie took another bit of knobby carrot from the pocket of her coat – formerly Louisa's red boiled-wool jacket – and handed it over.

'She'll make a good teacher, won't she?' Louisa asked David. They stood under the portico watching the proceedings. 'She's learning that from Jack.'

'Daddy!' Gracie called and Jack broke away from talking with Chuff and Hugo.

'Yes?' he said.

'Could I have a horse?'

Jack's eyebrows shot up. Gracie giggled, but Louisa burst out laughing.

'We'll see,' he replied.

Gracie turned to Athena. 'I knew he would say that.'

Louisa looked from Gracie to her son and over to Jack. Her emotions had been hovering too close to the surface all morning. The children were leaving and she would miss them terribly, but at the same time she felt a wave of relief to know they would be well cared for.

In the end, there had been someone for each of them in one way or another. But not all were leaving Oxburrow.

Athena's father – a black American jazz musician – had found work in London. And George's father, the merchant navy seaman, wasn't expected back on dry land any time soon. So, in the meantime, both children would stay at Oxburrow. Johnno would be nearby, living with the Gedges.

Gracie had been a different matter. Louisa had wasted no time in writing to Brother Michael, offering a solution other than Gracie living in the Little Brothers of St Anthony orphanage. He had accepted.

'Offered a solution?' Iris had repeated, scoffing, when Louisa had told her. 'I'd say you laid down the law.'

'Perhaps I was firm,' Louisa had said loftily, 'but kind. He understood.'

Louisa and Jack had gone together to William Lowrey to discuss legally adopting Gracie. Louisa had worried about what those in power would think of her, an unmarried – divorced! – woman.

'I doubt there will be any difficulty,' William had said. 'There's a war on and the number of orphans is growing at a shocking rate. I heard tell of a widow with only a daughter who went up to an orphanage in London and asked if she could adopt a boy to help out around the place. They brought out nine boys and told her to take her pick. She took them all and there were no complaints.'

Louisa thought of the empty beds at Oxburrow. 'You'll let us know if you hear of anyone in particular, won't you?'

'Of course,' William said.

'Will it be possible to put us both down as Gracie's parents?' Jack had asked.

'Why not?' William said. 'I hardly think anyone will notice. Although, if someone did, it might help if you were married.'

Jack cut his eyes at Louisa and smiled. 'It's under discussion.'

'We can't marry in the church,' Louisa said, 'because of the divorce. Hugo offered to marry us at Oxburrow.' For a moment, she imagined the scene – the sun pouring in the morning room windows, surrounded by the people she loved in the place she loved, marrying the man she loved – but shook off the daydream. 'But Hugo wouldn't be allowed to perform the ceremony. He says it wouldn't matter to him one whit if he's allowed or not, but I don't want to get him in trouble. The registry office seems a dull last resort.' She looked at Jack. 'We'll sort something out.'

'We will,' he said.

Married or not, Gracie knew who her parents were. Still, Louisa had a talk with her about it.

'It's rather like me being your mum now even though you had a mum to begin with.'

Gracie nodded – she had grasped this idea from the start. 'Mama died, and now you're Mama. But I didn't ever have a dad and so Mr Barrie is my only one.'

'Hugo?' Louisa called across the forecourt. 'We're ready.'

Hugo spread his arms and children and grown-ups gathered round him. 'Let us pray.'

All heads were bowed, except Louisa, who looked around through vision blurred by tears as Hugo offered a blessing for those travelling and those staying behind.

Louisa embraced each child.

'You are all very welcome back to Oxburrow any time,' she said in a quavering voice. 'Your families, too. And I hope you'll write or at least send a picture now and then.'

Louisa had ordered new watercolour sets and pads of paper from the newsagent, and had presented them to the children at breakfast that morning.

Everyone turned toward cars and cart, but then a low rumble caught their attention. They gazed up at the sky and waited as the sound grew.

Three planes appeared over the canopy of trees and David said, 'Johnno – what are they?'

Johnno peered at the planes for a moment and then shouted, 'Lancaster!'

Everyone nodded in agreement – especially when the roundels on the wings were spotted. Lancasters, indeed.

'Alf!' Johnno shouted.

'Coming from the north-east!' Alf reported.

Louisa took Mrs Harrison's hands. They'd said their goodbyes earlier and Louisa had reminded her that Marian was already digging for information about Mr Harrison.

'We'll see you again soon,' Louisa told her.

As the cars pulled out and Colin followed, the song arose, from not only the children, but also the grown-ups.

'We're going to hang out the washing on the Siegfried Line...'

The vehicles disappeared from sight, but those remaining at Oxburrow continued to sing until the end.

They were silent for a moment, the only sounds the complaints from the jackdaws high in the old ash tree down by the church.

Louisa turned to David. 'You aren't going into London today, are you?'

David's foot continued to give him trouble and there was little chance he'd go back to flying, but Max had found work for him in the War Office. It had something to do with the compass that had been hidden in his button. *Evade and escape*, he told his mother, and tapped his finger beside his nose. Whatever the work, Louisa was happy that it kept him on the ground.

'No,' David said. 'I wouldn't have missed seeing them off.'

'I'd say we could all do with a cup of tea,' Louisa said. 'We'll go downstairs.' The basement dining room had become quite homely.

Most of the household ambled down and in the direction of the kitchen yard, leaving Louisa and Jack, Iris and Chuff and Gracie.

'I'll go and slice the bread,' Iris said. But she didn't move, instead stayed staring out towards the drive even after the cars and the cart had disappeared. 'I'm going to miss that boy.'

'Alf will be a famous chef at the Ritz some day,' Louisa said, 'and he'll attribute his success to you.' She put her arm around Iris's shoulders and gave her a squeeze.

'Now, now,' Chuff said, 'you haven't lost everyone. You've still got this boy.'

'God help me, so I do,' Iris said.

'I'll slice the bread for you,' Chuff offered.

As they turned to go, Iris said, 'You'll wash your hands first.'

Before Louisa turned to follow them, she saw Mrs Greet coming up the drive. She carried a small box with holes in it and tied with twine.

'You're very welcome,' Louisa said. 'Would you like tea?'

'Thank you,' Mrs Greet said. 'Perhaps I will stay for a cup. I saw them leaving and managed to give a wave as they passed. Everyone looked happy.'

'We are happy and sad at the same time,' Gracie said. 'That's what Mama says.'

Mrs Greet nodded. 'It's a perplexing feeling. Gracie, I've brought you something.' She held up the box. 'Your mummy and daddy said it was all right.'

Gracie looked up to Louisa and Jack with wide eyes. 'A present? What is it?'

'It could be a very small horse,' Jack said.

Gracie laughed. 'That's silly!'

The box made a noise – *Chirrup! Chirrup!* Gracie crept forward and peered in one of the holes and gasped.

'Parakeets!'

A LETTER FROM MARTY

Dear reader,

I want to say a huge thank you for choosing to read *The House for Lost Children*. If you did enjoy it, and want to keep up to date with all my latest releases, just sign up at the following link. Your email address will never be shared and you can unsubscribe at any time.

www.bookouture.com/marty-wingate

The House for Lost Children opens a year after the Second World War began, when London is under attack. Children at a small charity school suddenly become orphans and are evacuated to Suffolk. The story is inspired by the very real experiences of those who lived through the war. I've chosen to set this tale of love and loss in one of my favourite places and hope that, as you followed Louisa's efforts to help, you were transported not only to 1940, but also to the beautiful east of England.

I hope you loved *The House for Lost Children* and, if you did, I would be very grateful if you could write a review. I'd love to hear what you think, and it makes such a difference helping new readers to discover one of my books for the first time.

I love hearing from my readers – you can get in touch on my Facebook page, Goodreads or my website.

Thanks,

Marty Wingate

www.martywingate.com

facebook.com/martywingateauthor

ACKNOWLEDGEMENTS

The House for Lost Children would never have seen the light of day without these talented and generous folk:

My agent, Christina Hogrebe, and Casey Conniff of the Jane Rotrosen Agency.

My editor Rhianna Louise and everyone at Bookouture who have created a clear and easy-to-navigate publishing process.

My weekly writing group – Kara Pomeroy, Joan Shott, Louise Creighton, Sarah Niebuhr Rubin and Meghana Padakandla.

My husband, Leighton Wingate, who has never seen a plural possessive he didn't like.

Continued thanks to these family members, fellow authors and dear friends who never mind listening to the latest results of my research or taste-testing my latest recipe find from the Second World War: Carolyn Lockhart, Ed Polk, Katherine Manning Wingate, Susy Wingate, Lilly Wingate, Alice K. Boatwright, Hannah Dennison, Dana Spencer, Jane Tobin, Mary Helbach, and Victoria Summerley. With loving thoughts for my dear friend Mary Kate Parker, after forty years of tea and chat – I miss you.

Cheers!

PUBLISHING TEAM

Turning a manuscript into a book requires the efforts of many people. The publishing team at Bookouture would like to acknowledge everyone who contributed to this publication.

Audio
Alba Proko
Melissa Tran
Sinead O'Connor

Commercial
Lauren Morrissette
Hannah Richmond
Imogen Allport

Cover design
Eileen Carey

Data and analysis
Mark Alder
Mohamed Bussuri

Editorial
Rhianna Louise
Ria Clare

Copyeditor
Jacqui Lewis

Proofreader
Anne O'Brien

Marketing
Alex Crow
Melanie Price
Occy Carr
Cíara Rosney
Martyna Młynarska

Operations and distribution
Marina Valles
Stephanie Straub
Joe Morris

Production
Hannah Snetsinger
Mandy Kullar
Nadia Michael
Charlotte Hegley

Publicity
Kim Nash
Noelle Holten
Jess Readett
Sarah Hardy

Rights and contracts
Peta Nightingale
Richard King
Saidah Graham

Dear Reader,

We'd love your attention for one more page to tell you about the crisis in children's reading, and what we can all do.

Studies have shown that reading for fun is the **single biggest predictor of a child's future life chances** – more than family circumstance, parents' educational background or income. It improves academic results, mental health, wealth, communication skills, ambition and happiness.

The number of children reading for fun is in rapid decline. Young people have a lot of competition for their time, and a worryingly high number do not have a single book at home.

Hachette works extensively with schools, libraries and literacy charities, but here are some ways we can all raise more readers:

- Reading to children for just 10 minutes a day makes a difference
- Don't give up if children aren't regular readers – there will be books for them!

- Visit bookshops and libraries to get recommendations
- Encourage them to listen to audiobooks
- Support school libraries
- Give books as gifts

There's a lot more information about how to encourage children to read on our websites: **www.RaisingReaders.co.uk** and **www.JoinRaisingReaders.com**.

Thank you for reading.